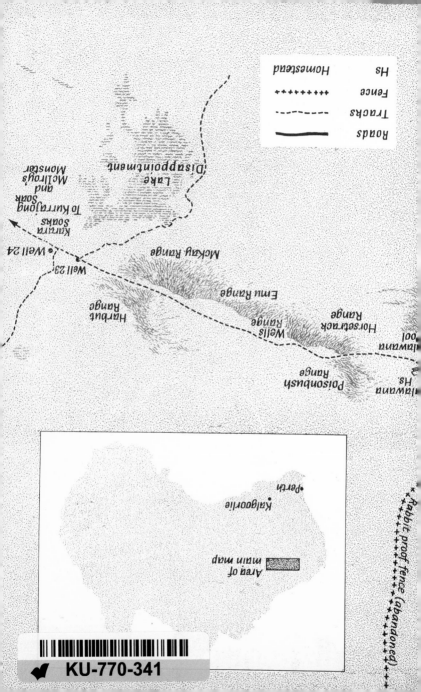

Roads

Tracks

Fence ++++++++++

Hs Homestead

Lake Disappointment

To Kurrajong Soak
and McIlroy's Monster

Karara Soaks

Well 24

Well 23

McKay Range

Emu Range

Harbut Range

Wells Range

Horsetrack Range

Poisonbush Range

Illawann Hs

Illawann Pool

Rabbit proof fence (abandoned)

Area of main map

Perth

Kalgoorlie

KU-770-341

GOLDEN SOAK

'Golden Soak' is an old abandoned mine in the iron
cauldron of the Pilbara, and the heat can literally be felt
burning through the pages of this story of the outback of
Australia at the height of the mineral boom. What had
once been a pastoral empire of a million and a half acres,
ruled by Big Bill Garrety, is now reduced to drought-
starved tracts of land where Janet, his young grand-
daughter, rides her camel day after day, mustering the
stock and fearful of losing all she holds dear; while her
father, Ed Garrety, obsessed with Golden Soak, guards
its secrets and allows nobody near the mine. Alec Falls,
who has left England and come to Australia in pursuit of
Janet and the wealth he believes she will inherit, finds
that the Australian dream of riches beneath the ground is
not enough to satisfy him in his quest for personal
fulfilment. Only on an appalling journey into the vast
emptiness of the Gibson Desert does he find himself
again, and satisfy the need of something from life over
and beyond material riches.

GOLDEN SOAK

*

HAMMOND INNES

THE
COMPANION BOOK CLUB
LONDON AND SYDNEY

This edition, published in 1974 by
The Hamlyn Publishing Group Ltd,
is issued by arrangement with
William Collins, Sons & Co. Ltd

THE COMPANION BOOK CLUB

The Club is not a library; all books are the property of members. There is no entrance fee or any payment beyond the low Club price of each book. Details of membership will gladly be sent on request.

Write to:

The Companion Book Club,
Odhams Books, Rushden, Northants.

Or, in Australia, write to:

The Companion Book Club,
C/- Hamlyn House Books, P.O. Box 252,
Dee Why, N. S. W. 2099

---

*Made and printed in Great Britain
for the Companion Book Club
by Odhams (Watford) Ltd*
600871738
4.74/273

To
TASS and MAISIE
In appreciation of his view
of Australia on canvas

Author's Note

I HAVE TAKEN certain liberties with that area of the Pilbara dominated by the mountains of the Governor, Padtherung and Coondewanna. There is no Golden Soak, no tribal area known as the Pukara, nor any sheep or cattle station called Jarra Jarra. The characters are, of course, equally fictitious. I mention this because to those few who know this locality well, I feel some explanation is due for changes in the topography which I have made for purposes of the story. And for those very few who have leaseholds in the area, my apologies for what may seem to them an invasion of their privacy. Though I have travelled the backtrack through the Ophthalmia Range from Mt Newman to Mt Robinson, I have not actually climbed the gap between Padtherung and Coondewanna, so that there may be some inaccuracy in the description, which is based on a gully slightly further to the east.

My choice of the Pilbara as the setting for this story of the Australian outback and the mineral boom of 1969–70 was made after very extensive travelling. That my wife and I were able to see so much of this vast, underpopulated country before making my final choice was due to the encouragement and assistance I was given by Sir Reginald Ansett, through his Ansett Airline, and of course by Qantas, and in the mining world by Sir Val Duncan, Sir Maurice Mawby and Sir James Vernon. More personally, because they gave of their time, energy and knowledge, I would particularly like to thank John Davidson, Colin Smith, Jock Ritchie, Arthur Peck, Colin Sampey, Jim Edwards, John Tozer, Administrator at Pt Hedland, Mike Oliver, Mark de Graaf, Mike Napier; and there were a host of others—mine managers, geologists, bush pilots, station owners, prospectors and survey team workers. To all of these my sincere and grateful thanks, and my hope that this book conveys something of the unique quality of the country they took so much trouble to reveal to me.

Kersey, April 1972

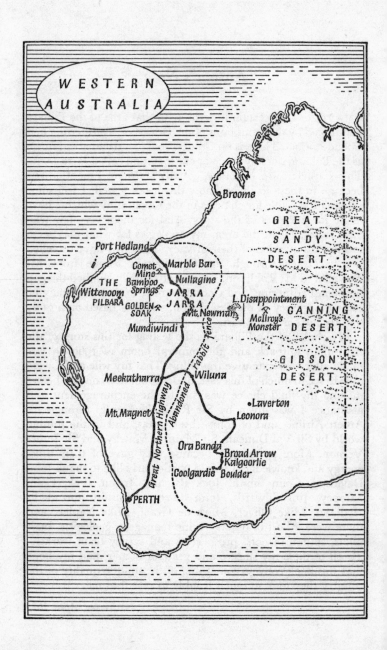

WESTERN
AUSTRALIA

Broome

GREAT

SANDY

DESERT

Port Hedland

Comet Mine   Marble Bar
Bamboo   Nullagine
Springs
THE   JARRA
Wittenoom   JARRA
PILBARA
GOLDEN   L. Disappointment
SOAK   Mt. Newman   McIlroy's   CANNING
                                        Monster
Mundiwindi

                                                       DESERT

                                                       GIBSON

Meekatharra   Wiluna   DESERT

                                        Laverton
Mt. Magnet   Leonora

                    Ora Banda
                         Broad Arrow
                         Kalgoorlie
                    Coolgardie Boulder

Great Northern Highway

Abandoned rabbit fence

PERTH

ONE

Drym

THE STONE SKELETON of the old Wheal Garth engine housing came at me out of the dark, its chimney pointing a gaunt finger at the night. It was there for an instant, glimpsed in the headlights, and then it was gone and there was nothing but the road and the moor and the slanting rain. That derelict mine building stayed etched on the sodden retina of my mind, a symbol—my world in ruins, and all because of that stupid, bloody meeting. I was driving too fast, feeling vicious after all the solitary drinking I had done since I'd walked out on them that morning. Trevenick shouldn't have said it. He shouldn't have called me a crooked thieving bastard. What had he ever contributed to the company, jumping on my band-wagon just because his father had left him a fortune? I sucked at my knuckles where the skin was broken. Too bad my temper had got the better of me again. A bunch of landowners, all of them, who wouldn't recognize a mother lode if they saw one. And before that, facing me with the mine foreman, as if I didn't know we'd run into granite over six months ago.

'Australia! You won't get me going to Australia.'

I could hear her voice, remote and hostile above the noise of the engine, the splash of the wheels as they ploughed through water. But what else—what was the alternative?

'You should have thought of that before.'

I could see her face, white in the rods of driving rain, her beautiful, soft-lipped, childish face. My wife, my darling bitch of a wife, sitting there at the breakfast table in her dressing gown, accusing me of deceiving her. 'All your big talk—I never realized . . .' But she'd known. She'd known all along.

My foot was hard down on the accelerator, the moors and the rain streaming by and the swish-swish of the windscreen wipers, my mind recalling every word. Maybe I had talked big.

But Rosa liked it that way. A big house, a big car, clothes, parties, jaunts to London, with the sense always of riding the crest of a wave; but when it came to the pinch, when the tin gave out and we'd nothing to live on but hope, that was different. She wouldn't even write to that cousin of hers who owned a mine and 200,000 acres in Western Australia. Oh no, the Garretys weren't her sort of people—not smart enough. And she didn't care a damn about Golden Soak, or any other Australian mining prospect for that matter.

The Standing Stone rushed past, a druidical milestone on the way home, and I was thinking of our honeymoon, how I'd made love to her in the dry adit of Balavedra, where my grandfather had worked as a miner, and then gone on alone to discover that damned vein of mother tin staring at me in the torchlight beyond a recent fall of rock. Two years we'd had, the world at our feet, until that wild wet day, with the wind blowing in gale force gusts off the sea, when the mine foreman had broken the news to me in his broad Cornish. After that nothing had gone right. We were into solid granite, no vestige of tin or any other mineral. And then Trevenick smelling a rat and calling a board meeting.

I needed a new start, a new country, and Australia was the obvious choice for a man with my qualifications. And when I told her I'd written to Kadek almost a fortnight ago, she'd rounded on me—'If you can't keep me without turning crook, there are other men who can.' She was scared, of course, but that didn't make it sound any nicer.

I told her to go to hell, stalking out to the car and driving straight to that meeting in the stuffy little office we rented in St Just. If I hadn't left then I'd have belted her.

I was off the moors now, on the long dip down to Drym, the first bend coming up fast. I braked, remembering how I'd walked out of the meeting, promising to pay them back by the end of the month. I'd braked too hard, I knew that, still seeing their faces, the three older ones hostile and Trevenick sitting on the floor looking dazed. The skid started as I recalled Captain Bentall's words, my hands correcting automatically, the shriek of tyres on wet tarmac—'We'll give you till the end of the month, Falls. Now get out'—his voice sounding as though he were giving orders to a naval rating, and then the headlights spinning and the car crashing sideways through old fencing, rolling gently to rest against a bank of heather.

I wasn't far from home, but still far enough in the rain to get soaked and chilled, reaction setting in. I was shaken, nothing more, only now the crash had started a new train of thought.

They said afterwards that I looked like death, alone there at the bar—that they weren't a bit surprised. It was all in the papers, the landlord's comments, an interview with Rosa. But they didn't understand. I hadn't been drinking because it was the end of the road. I'd been drinking because I didn't know what the hell to do about my wife. And though I'd got it all worked out, every step, so that it would look spontaneous and quite natural, I still didn't know how I was going to cope with her.

But the house, when I reached it, was in darkness. Stumbling up the drive in the rain, it looked much as it had done that first time we'd seen it, in the dark, walking hand-in-hand between the laurels and laughing excitedly because she'd found a house to match the fortune I'd discovered underground. It nestled deep in a hollow, surrounded by the dark of cedars and the blue of *Abies nobilis*, its nice Georgian front ruined by a Victorian brick addition of extreme ugliness. But that was what had kept it on the market, and it had looked a lot better when we'd torn down the rusting iron verandah and the rotten conservatory at the end, painted the bricks a warm shade of pink and rooted out the laurel shrubberies. It still had a slightly dilapidated air, but it was home—the only home I'd known since my parents died in a plane crash when I was studying at the Royal School of Mines in London.

I fumbled the key into the lock, sober now, but my hands still trembling with shock. I called to her as I switched on the light. 'Rosalind!' No answer. The house silent and watchful, hostile even. 'Rosa. Where are you?' Did the old walls know what I planned to do? 'Rosalind?' Still no reply, the stillness all about me, communicating the emptiness. I switched on more lights and climbed the stairs to our room, wearily and with a feeling of loneliness. I knew she had gone.

The room was empty, but with a special emptiness, a sort

of desecration as though a burglar had been there, the dressing table bare, the drawers still open where she had rootled for clothes and costume jewellery, the personal things that added up to our two years of marriage. And the suitcase gone that she used for London.

I went back down the stairs, slowly and in a daze, searching the drawing room first, the study, then the dining room. I ended up in the hall, staring at the oak chest which had been her latest success in a local sale. No note, nothing conventional like that. Not that I expected it—she wasn't that sort of person. I went into the study, to the big court cupboard we used as a bar, and poured myself a Scotch, not bothering about water. I took it to the desk, drinking it slowly, slumped in the red leather chair she had given me on our first anniversary when everything was rosy, with tin high, the mine a bomb, our future assured. The keys were in the drawer where I had been hoarding cash against the day when we'd have to get out. It was a long time before I nerved myself to open it.

But it was all right. The money was still there—four hundred and thirty-six pounds. I counted it carefully, my hands trembling. No question of an assisted passage now. It would have to be Naples or the Piraeus, and though an emigrant ship, I'd have to pay my passage. The money was my lifeline and if she'd taken it. . . . But she hadn't, though she'd taken her passport. And no note to say she was sorry. Yet she'd still put the afternoon's post neatly on the desk and there was a vase of late roses that hadn't been there the night before.

Automatically I reached for the paper knife, its moss agate handle smooth to the touch. A Christmas present from one of our richer friends. But I knew he wouldn't be a friend any more. I hadn't any friends. Not any real friends. Only acquaintances, men who liked my style, who provided me with an audience. I picked up the letters; two bills, an invitation to dinner, a list of foreign cars on offer, but no airmail—nothing from Australia. I sat back then, feeling chilled.

Was he away? Had he moved from Perth? My letter hadn't only been about Golden Soak. I'd been fishing for a job as well. Why the hell hadn't he answered? At least he could have told me what the prospects were. But then why should he? I'd only met him once and that was nearly four years ago. We had spent a long evening together drinking on the terrace of an hotel overlooking the Costa del Sol, the night air warm, the sound of dance music and the moon making a silver path across a calm sea. I'd been working for Trevis, Parkes & Pierce then, a firm of mining consultants in the City, and it was Kadek who had first put it into my head to form a company of my own. It was about the time Western Mining's Kambalda prospect was providing the first whiff of the Australian nickel boom to come and he was busy flogging the shares of an unknown Australian company to rich English exiles with tax-free money to burn.

I glanced at my watch. It was past eight already. Soon I would have to make up my mind. I poured myself another Scotch, adding soda this time, and settled back in the chair again, thinking of the only other person I knew in Australia. I had come back from Balavedra on a Friday night to find her in the drawing room with Rosa, sitting silent and very tense. I'd given her a large dry Martini, and after that she'd relaxed and all through dinner she was telling me about the North West— the Pilbara, she called it—the sunshine and the red rock, its wild beauty. And about Jarra Jarra. Particularly about Jarra Jarra. How it was thirty-one miles from one end to the other and they ran three thousand head of cattle and owned an old abandoned gold mine.

Golden Soak. It was just a name, and yet somehow it had stayed in my mind—an idea, a prospect, something to go for if things didn't improve.

I remembered the freckles and the snub nose and the odd way she'd talked, like somebody out of an old-fashioned magazine. And her eyes, her slightly prominent grey-blue eyes, the bubbling vitality of her. She was just twenty-one, the absolute antithesis of my darling wife, and driving her to the station in the morning she had invited me to visit them at Jarra Jarra, suggesting laughingly that I might have a shot at opening up their mine again the way I'd opened up Balavedra.

I finished my drink. Thinking about Janet Garrety, I was almost glad Kadek hadn't answered my letter. Clever. That was the word that best described him. And interested only in money. I was sick of men like that—sick of mining, too. An

13

outback cattle station was just what I needed. A chance to sort myself out. I'd write to her on the boat.

I got to my feet then, my mind suddenly made up. The Scotch had warmed me, relaxed my nerves. I went upstairs and changed into dry clothes, a sweater and an old pair of flannels, and then I had a look in the kitchen to see if Rosa had left me anything to eat. There was wind at the back of the house, rain lashing at the scullery window and seeping in under the back door as it always did with a storm off the sea. It would be a wet ride. But that didn't matter. That was physical. It was the mental beating that had shattered me, the feeling that an unkind fate had stripped me of all I'd worked for these past two years, and in that mood the idea that had leapt into my mind as I stumbled home through the rain after the crash seemed less wild, a logical progression, an escape into anonymity.

Cold chicken, tomatoes, cheese, a bottle of beer. I put it all on the kitchen table. A man on his own, in a state of shock, would hardly bother to take it through into the dining room. Even charred embers contain evidence for those who know what to look for. Everything had to support what I wanted them to think. Sitting there, alone, I had time to go over it all again in my mind. I ate slowly, unconscious of time, working it out step by step, logically and carefully.

It was almost nine by the time I had finished and the only doubt then left in my mind was the motor bike. I had used it to get to and from the mine before the Company had been able to provide me with a car. Since then it had been under an old tarpaulin in the pump house next to the garage. I had checked it over quite recently, knowing that the Company car, and probably our own as well, would have to go. It worried me that somebody might remember its existence, but that was a chance I would have to take.

The garage was in the old stables, separate from the house. I wheeled the bike inside and topped up the tank from a jerrican of petrol kept there for the lawnmower. It started first kick and I left it to warm up while I folded the tarpaulin and tucked it away behind some deck chairs.

Back in the kitchen, I cut myself some sandwiches, wrapped

14

them in greaseproof paper and put them in a suitcase. Into this went the clothes I'd need and everything of value that I thought would not be noticed—a small diamond brooch that had belonged to my mother, my father's signet ring and an old gold hunter that had been left me by an uncle. I also took the cuff links from my evening dress shirt. And after that I started on the electrics.

I began on the flex of the bedside lamp, roughing it up with a nail file until the copper gleam of the wires stood bare. Then out to the fuse box on the landing to replace the 2-amp wire with a piece of ordinary wire. Finally back to the scullery, where the mains fuse was supplemented by one of those sensitive trip switches. A small piece of grit jammed it successfully. Candles I knew we had and I stuck one on to the plastic top of a jam jar, cut two grooves in it near the base and took it up to the bedroom. There I set it on the floor beside the bed, slipped the bared wires of the flex over it, slotting them into the grooves on either side, and jammed a heavy spring clip over the top.

Now it remained only to set the scene. From the study I brought up the half empty bottle of Scotch, with the soda syphon and a glass on a brass tray, and put it down beside the bed. I had also put a full bottle in my pocket and this I emptied on to the carpet and over the bedclothes. I pulled the whisky-sodden eiderdown on to the floor so that the corner of it over-laid the flex just clear of the candle. Then I took off my wrist-watch and put it under my pillow. Finally, I switched on the bedside light and stood looking round the room, checking that everything was as it should be. My pyjamas, of course. It was always possible that a button might survive, and the glass on its side, on the floor, as though it had fallen from my nerveless hands.

I felt strung up then, my nerves taut—memories of the house and of our life together, and that big double bed mocking me. The room reeked of whisky, and the house, solid to the wind, silent, waiting for the end. I shivered, feeling chilled again, depressed by the thought of two centuries of occupation, all those others who had lived there. I bent down quickly, the box of matches in my hand, and lit the candle.

I stopped a moment to see it burning, a golden flame. So small and innocent a thing, hardly bigger than a child's nightlight. I shook myself, knowing the moments precious. An hour at the most it gave me, no more. An hour to be gone from Cornwall into a new life. I turned and hurried down the stairs, leaving the bedroom door open behind me. I had helmet and oilskins ready, the suitcase strapped to the back of the bike. It took only a moment to get myself dressed for the road, and I was just going out by the back door when something, some instinct, made me pause.

I stood there for a moment, holding the door open with my hand, desperately searching my memory. And then suddenly it came to me. Christ! My passport. I had nearly forgotten my passport. It was in the slim black expensive briefcase my fellow directors had given me to mark the Company's first year of operation. With it was my birth certificate, all the papers I'd thought I might need.

I hurried through to the study, shocked to find my keys still in the right-hand drawer. They should have been in the pocket of the suit I had left discarded on a chair in the bedroom. But perhaps it was natural that they should be in the desk. I found the one I wanted, my fingers trembling as I unlocked the centre drawer. The briefcase was still there. I checked the contents, and then went out into the rain, round the house to the garage.

The last I saw of Drym was a dark ivy-clad shadow crouched behind the shaft of light pouring out from the uncurtained study window. Then I was round the sweep of the drive, my back towards it, riding out through the gates, up by side roads on to the moors, two years of my life expunged, an episode. Now I had nothing but what was with me and I sang as I rode, yelling an old marching song into the wind and the rain, feeling free—gloriously, magnificently free.

It was not a mood that lasted long. Beyond Camborne, headed for Truro, I was wet and cold. The hour would be just about up and I was wondering about the candle and those frayed wires and whether it would work. The mood of elation had drained away; ahead lay the cold hard slog through the night.

I refuelled at Exeter and again near Wimborne. The rain

had ceased about an hour ago and I ate my sandwiches there, cold and wet and tired, waiting for the garage to open. Later I stopped in the New Forest to consider what I should do about the bike. I had no road licence for it and I didn't dare take it into Southampton. Still thinking about it, I lay down on a bank of heather and went to sleep, too tired to care. The sun was up and it was almost warm.

In the end I rode the bike into a dense thicket and dumped it there. I had removed the number plates and these I buried about half a mile away. Then I went back to the road and hitched a ride on a lorry I found parked in a lay-by.

It was almost dusk by the time I finally reached Southampton. I found my way to the docks, and after booking a cabin on the night ferry to Le Havre, I went into the Skyways Hotel, where I had a shave and then drank three whiskies straight off in the bar. I was very near the point of exhaustion, my mind going over and over the events of the last twenty-four hours. In that state you don't think logically. All I knew was that I was scared. Scared at the finality of what I had done. Scared of what it might lead to, of the future—of just about everything. I'd no relatives. No friends now. I was alone and bloody lonely, feeling sorry for myself, utterly depressed. And then a boy came in with the evening papers, and there it was—in the *Standard*. *MINE DIRECTOR DIES IN BLAZE.* And an interview with Rosa: *I had no idea Alec was in difficulties. He was always gay, always full of life. How was I to know the Company was bankrupt? If I'd known, if he'd confided in me, of course I wouldn't have gone off to visit my family like that. After all, he was my husband.* As if she didn't know! She knew damn well we were living on borrowed time. *Mrs Rosalind Falls*—there was a picture of her inset against the burned out remains of the house, another of the mine. But no picture of me, which was all I cared about at the moment.

I lit a cigarette, my hand trembling, my eyes searching the bar over the flame. But only one other person had bought a paper and he was reading the sports page. It was just another item of news, so why should he, or anybody else, care a damn? I finished my drink and went into the dining room, going over the story again quietly with my meal. There was a statement from Trevenick denying there had been any disagreement among the directors. 'The high grade ore was mined out— that's all.' Another from the landlord of the pub at Sennen Cove: 'I wouldn't say he was drunk, but he had been drinking heavily. He seemed upset about something.'

But my eyes kept going back to that picture, the gutted shell with the slates all gone and the roof beams blackened by fire. The finality of it took a long time to sink in, the fact that I was dead, burnt to a cinder in the ruins of our house. Alive and eating roast duckling it was difficult to realize that officially I no longer existed. I felt slightly sickened at the enormity of what I had done.

At the ferry terminal the immigration official barely glanced at my passport. The relief at being on board, no questions asked. . . . I didn't wait to see the boat sail, but went straight to my cabin feeling utterly drained. I heard the engines start, the thump of the screws as we began to move. The dock lights swung across the deck beams above my head, then darkness and I knew England had slipped away, my own country, all my life gone—and Australia a 14,000 mile journey. But it wasn't of the future I was thinking as I lay sleepless in my bunk. I was thinking of Rosa, the lusty, passionate vitality of her, the small firm breasts and the golden skin. All gone now, the world we'd shared in embers.

TWO

Jarra Jarra

I

I WOKE TO A LONG-DRAWN HOWL, quite close. It was dark and very still, and I thought the truck had come to a stop. I moved stiffly, conscious of the hard surface under me, the yielding coarseness on which my head was pillowed. Then I remembered that the truck had gone. I pulled the gold hunter out of my pocket and flicked my lighter. The time was three-forty, no moon, but the stars brilliant in the night sky. The sound that had woken me was gone now, but far away I heard the echo of it, an answering call.

I was tired, exhausted by the long rattling journey north in the appalling heat. Vaguely I remembered where I was, how I had seen the bulk of Mt Whaleback black against the moon as I stood watching the tail lights of the truck disappear in a cloud of dust down the dirt road. The howl came again, long drawn out, throbbing in the darkness. Something crawled across my hand, a feather touch of small legs moving. I shook it off. An ant probably. And faint in the distance came the answering howl. The weirdness of the sound, the loneliness of it, and myself alone, lying on a stony gravel bed.

I remembered Emilio arguing with me, trying to persuade me to go on with him to Nullagine. 'The Conglomerate—issa no very good, but you getta meal there, some beer. Is better than living bush, yes?' But the telegram I had sent her had said I'd be waiting at the turn-off by the old airfield, and in the end he had agreed to make the detour. He knew where it was, for he sometimes made deliveries to the motel at Mt Newman.

I stared up at the stars, wondering what the day would bring and whether she'd come, what I was going to tell her if she did. The dingoes were silent now, the night hot and still, not a breath of wind. I could see the Southern Cross, and lying there alone I was overwhelmed by the strangeness of it all, even the night sky entirely different, no sign of the Bear.

I closed my eyes again, but sleep eluded me now, my fears taking over and chasing each other through my heat-stunned brain. I hadn't worried on the voyage out; it had been like a dream, a sort of hiatus, myself in limbo and all sense of reality suspended. But now it was different. Now reality stared me in the face and there was no escape. What the hell did I tell the girl? That I didn't exist? That I was almost penniless? She'd want to know about Rosa, about Drym—she'd want to know what the hell I was doing in Australia. Come in the spring, she had said—not in summer. And here I was in summer and the luck she had envied clean run out.

I was thinking back now, tired and trying to convince myself it would be all right. It had seemed all right at the time, a way out. There'd even been a sort of inevitability about it. And at 14,000 miles' remove Jarra Jarra had appeared a sort of oasis, a place where I could find myself again, a springboard from the security of which I could make the plunge into a new life. But now that it was only 60 miles away the prospect of it was quite different. It wasn't only Janet who would be full of questions. There was her father, too. What would Ed Garrety think of a stranger arrived out of the blue, almost penniless and wanting a job? She had talked of drought and an iron ore company moving in on them, but with all that acreage and 3,000 head of cattle they were still rich enough to scare me.

I reached into my hip pocket, to the slender wad of notes, counting them by starlight. But I knew the score—one hundred and twenty-seven dollars. That's all I had, all that was left after I had got myself to Naples, paid my passage out and all the incidentals. And naturally they had been expecting me to arrive by car. The letter I had found waiting for me when I got off the boat at Fremantle made that clear, and she'd given me detailed instructions—where to turn off the Great Northern Highway, how to find the start of the backtrack leading to the station. But instead of a car I'd wired her to meet me. How was I going to explain that? And no job, nothing to go back to?

The dingoes sounded again, but very far away. I dozed, my head fallen forward, and when I woke again it was to a different sound, a soft-toned bellow and the rumble of an ore train going north. The stars were paling now, the leaves of the eucalyptus tree under which I lay visible against the growing light of the sky. Something moved behind the patch of scrub to my right, a tall grey shadow. I watched, suddenly wide awake, my nerves tense. It was bending down, screened from my view, and then, with three quick leaps, it was within yards of me, standing erect and balanced by its tail, its short front legs hanging limp, its head lifted, alert and listening, the muzzle twitching like a rabbit's.

In the half light the kangaroo looked big as a man. Instinctively I scrambled to my feet. Its head turned in a flash. I had a glimpse of soft eyes, and then it was bounding away at a gallop. And all around me grey shadows were moving at speed, heads thrust forward to balance the powerful strokes of the back legs as they covered the ground in great leaps. One moment they were there, the whole bush around me erupting in lolloping forms, then they were gone. No sound. It was like a dream.

I sat down again and lit a cigarette, my back against the gum, watching the sky pale to eggshell green, the dawn coming fast. And as the light increased, the shapes of trees and scrub emerged from shadow to become hard outlines. All gums. Nothing I knew or recognized, the earth red like dried blood, everything cruel and harsh, baked in the oven of yesterday's heat. I tried to recall the sound of her voice, familiarly English, yet oddly different—not harsh, not metallic like the men on the boat, but different all the same: 'Come in the spring,' she had said, driving to the station that morning. 'It's lovely then with the wild flowers out.' And she'd gone on to talk about the country, speaking of it as something beautiful, something to be loved as well as feared.

There'd been Australians on the boat. But like the man from Batemans Bay I'd shared a cabin with, most of them were bound for Sydney. They didn't know the West. Only Wade, who'd boarded the ship at Capetown, had ever been in the Pilbara. He'd worked with a construction gang on the iron ore railway, and the way he'd described it up here, he and the girl might have been talking about two different countries. I could hear the sound of his voice grating, see the fringe of gingery hair above the long face, the pile of beer cans in the cabin basin. He'd hated it.

That had been the night before we'd docked, the Italian immigrants lining the rails, staring out across the heat-still sea, the moon's path like spilled milk. I had stood there with them for a time, all of us staring towards the future that lay veiled in the hot moon-haze. And when finally I had gone below, I had found the cabin packed with drunks, half awash with beer, and Wade perched on my bunk, his long legs dangling, sweat gleaming on his face, his hands trembling as he sucked at a cigarette. 'You're there, brother. Back in good old Aussie land. The Big Country.' His cackling laugh, that grating voice— 'So you're headed for the Never Never, up into the Pilbara— the Iron Cauldron. Christ! You'll fry. You'll wish you'd never seen the blasted country.' His drunken words merging with her clear, vibrant voice. 'Come in the spring. It's lovely with the wild flowers out.' And Kadek, long ago on that terrace in Spain, talking of the Golden Mile, envying me my degree: 'If I'd had your education, I'd have been a millionaire by now.' Dozing, I chased a wisp of molten gold through miles of desert blooms in a flat red waste, the only sound the rattle of the truck and Wade's cackling laugh, his hatred of the Never Never.

I woke with a jerk, the fallen cigarette burning a hole in my old khaki trousers. I stubbed it out and got to my feet, moving down towards the track. Would she have set out in darkness for the sake of a cooler ride? There was no sound, just the stillness, and the light increasing all the time.

Feeling stiff and in need of exercise, I walked down to the junction with the dirt road. The sky was already flaring in the east, the shape of Mt Whaleback showing black on the horizon. It did look rather like a whale, and above it hung a haze as though it had just vented. But it wasn't moisture; it was iron ore dust, and as I stood there it began to redden with the rising sun. Something moved to my left and I turned my head. But it was already gone, a shadow, insubstantial.

The sun came up and I retired to the shade, a prey to the fear that something might have been discovered in the long weeks I had been travelling out here. The police might accept the evidence of their eyes, but the insurance assessors would almost certainly probe deeper before they agreed to payment, and they'd find no body, no trace of human remains. All through the voyage I had been able to push this thought to the back of my mind. But now that I was thrusting myself on people who knew who I was, I could no longer ignore it.

Everything I had done that night was clear in my mind, fixed there indelibly by knowledge of the risk I was taking. In spite of all I had had to drink, I could remember every detail, and going over it again step by step, remembering the emptiness of the house, my own numbness, the appalling sense of finality as I had lit that candle, I was sure I hadn't slipped up. It had all been so carefully planned—everything except the sudden decision to involve myself in the destruction of the house. Again and again my mind came back to that, and to the absence of human remains. Not even the fact that I had been allowed to enter Australia without any questions asked could dispel the nagging fear that in time they would catch up with me. Flies crawled with the sun, the smooth bark of the gum I was propped against hard under my shoulders.

About eight o'clock two vehicles passed along the dirt road, but from where I was sitting all I saw of them was a cloud of dust. After that nothing stirred as the heat built up and the sky turned from blue to a blinding white. I was trying to visualize Jarra Jarra, recalling vaguely the girl's young face, the things she had told me. But it was all blurred by time and nothing she had said had prepared me for the wild red desolation of this country, the sense of geological age I had felt on the long oven-lid drive north from Perth. If I hadn't written to her I could have lost myself in the immensity of it, changed my name. There was Kadek, too. He'd been away, in Kalgoorlie they said, when I had visited his office in Perth, and I had left a note for him, giving Jarra Jarra as my address. If Rosa talked and they started making inquiries in Australia. . . . I closed my eyes against the blinding glare, hoping to God they wouldn't think of that.

I was dozing again, my hand brushing automatically at the flies, when I heard the murmur of a truck's engine, an insect drone in the bush behind me. I was on my feet in an instant, listening tensely to the sound of it coming steadily nearer. Then I caught a glimpse of it through the gum trees, an elderly Land-Rover driven at speed. By the time it was round the last bend I was out on the track, waiting. It slowed at the sight of me, a bare arm waving to me out of the driver's window, and then it had stopped and Janet Garrety climbed out.

'Sorry—we should have been here two hours ago, but we've no spare and we had a puncture.'

She was smiling, coming towards me, a stocky, practical girl in a faded blue shirt and khaki slacks. The shirt clung to her, dark patches of sweat under the armpits and in the vee of her trousers, her face caked with dust, streaked with runnels of perspiration. But the smile of her greeting had the youthful, exuberant freshness I remembered. 'Have you been waiting long?' She shook my hand, a hard, dusty handshake that still managed to convey a sense of excitement. 'I couldn't believe it when we got your message. What are you doing in Australia?' She laughed, a flash of white teeth, freckles showing through the dust. 'I suppose you're out here looking for a new Poseidon.' Laughter bubbled in her eyes, the whites brilliant in the hard sunlight. 'I'm full of questions, but we can talk as we drive.'

A shadow moved behind her and she turned, 'Oh, Tom—come and meet Mr Falls.'

He was an aborigine. I had seen pictures of them, of course, but I hadn't expected anything quite so black, so primitive looking—the face broad-nosed with a low brow and ridges of heavy bone above the eyes. 'Tom is as much a part of Jarra Jarra as we are.' He came forward and shook my hand, a soft, limp touching of the palms, his thick lips spread in a yellow-toothed grin. The eyes were dark brown, the whites yellow against the wrinkled black of his skin. He was short and broad, and the only part of him that wasn't black was his hair; his woolly hair, that sat like a skull cap over the low brow, was grizzled, almost white. The thick lips moved below the broad spread of the nose, soft words, guttural in a strange tongue.

'He's bidding you welcome,' she said. Her quick eyes had found the tree where I had sat waiting. 'Is that all your gear?' She nodded to the aborigine and he went to get my suitcase. 'Gosh! This is marvellous—to see you here. When that message

24

came through—the news that you were in Perth and coming up to see us—you've no idea—it's what I dreamed, that some day you'd come out here.' It came out in a rush of words and then she added, 'You're the only mining man I ever met I'd trust a yard.' She was laughing, bubbling over with excitement, as though my arrival was some great event in her life. 'How did you come out? Did you fly?'

'No, I came by ship.'

'Yes, of course. You wrote me from Capetown. I thought perhaps you'd been having a look at the South African gold mines. But I suppose it's the nickel boom. Was it the *Botany Bay* you came on?'

I remembered then that she'd got herself to England working her passage as stewardess on a passenger ship out of Fremantle. 'No, it was an Italian boat,' I said.

'And you hitched a ride up from Perth. You certainly believe in doing things the hard way. That's real Australian.' She turned back to the Land-Rover. 'Come on. It's hot enough now, but if we stand here talking you'll be fried before I get you home. You can tell me all about it as we drive.'

My gear was already in the back with Tom. I climbed into the cab beside her and she drove down the dirt road, turned at the junction and headed back up the track, talking all the time as she twisted between the gums, her foot hard down. The track wasn't really a track at all, it was just a way through the bush that followed in the treadmarks of the first vehicle that had passed that way. It wandered in and out of the scrub, twisting endlessly in a flat plain with glimpses of Mt Newman. I wasn't really listening to what she was saying. She seemed oddly nervous, talking for the sake of talking—about the dry being worse than usual, a drought and cattle dying. It was as though she were trying to prepare me for something. 'For near on a month now we've been mustering, driving them in bunches through the Robinson Gap, down into the Water-snake.' She changed down for a stretch of dust. 'Coming to pick you up is a real break. Tom and the other two boys have hardly been out of the saddle for weeks.'

'And you?'

'Me? I'm sore.' She grinned, wriggling her bottom on the

seat. 'Riding Cleo every day—I must have ridden that damned camel a thousand miles this last month. Feels like it anyway. And Daddy out in the Land-Rover every day. We're just about all in, both of us.'

The country was more broken now. We were climbing imperceptibly, Mt Newman close and lower hills to our left, a gap opening up ahead. 'The Ophthalmia Range,' she said. 'It's all iron country here. Dry as a desert.' And then, abruptly —'I'm sorry, I haven't asked after Rosalind. How is she?'

'All right.'

'You haven't brought her with you?'

'No.'

She didn't pursue that line. She hadn't exactly hit it off with Rosa. 'So it's a business trip.'

'An exploratory look at Australia, shall we say?'

'And that includes Jarra Jarra.' She laughed, a trace of bitterness in her voice. 'The only thing we have to show you is an old abandoned mine. Not much for you there, I'm afraid.' And then she looked at me, a quick, searching glance. 'What really brought you out here? Or shouldn't I ask?'

This was the moment. I should tell her now if I was going to tell her at all. And I would have done if she'd still been staring at me with those perceptive, rather prominent eyes. But her gaze was back on the track as it snaked through an area of larger gums. 'Rosa,' I said. 'We've separated.'

'I'm sorry.' She didn't sound it and there was no surprise in her voice. 'So you've come out here—to forget her?'

It made sense, and that way I didn't have to tell her anything more. Not yet, anyway. 'I suppose so,' I said.

'And what about Balavedra?' she asked.

'Oh, I expect it'll get along all right without me.' I glanced at her, my mouth dry, wondering whether she'd guessed I was telling her only half the truth. My damned pride, of course, but what else could I say? What the hell else? If I told her the mine was bankrupt, that I was in debt and that was why Rosa had left me, then I'd have to tell her the rest. And I couldn't do that. Not now, before I'd even seen Jarra Jarra or met her father.

But all she said was, 'I remember that morning—you

26

showed me where it was, the engine house standing above the cliffs and the Atlantic beyond. You've chosen a damn silly time to exchange Cornwall for the Pilbara. Oh, well . . .' She laughed. 'Hitching a ride up the Great Northern at the beginning of summer sure is one way of getting it out of your system. What was it you rode up in—one of the iron ore company cars?'

'No, a refrigerated truck—a cousin of one of the Italians I met on the boat fixed it for me.'

She didn't say much after that. The going had become more difficult and she had to concentrate. Here, between the Ophthalmia Range and Parmelia Hill, we were into a narrow strip of flattish country, the track winding. Later it straightened out and our speed increased again. The air was oven-hot, the scrub thinner, and in the distance I could see a hill, brown like a sugar loaf, rising out of the flat plain.

'Mount Robinson.' There was sweat on her face, flies crawling and dark shadows under her eyes. 'The Gap is just to the left; that's where we've been sweating our guts out this past month.'

I asked her whether she'd like me to give her a spell, but she shook her head. 'I'm not tired. Not really. And in about twenty miles we begin to hit dry watercourses. You need to know the track then. This poor old Landy's over six years old. You have to nurse it.'

Half an hour later we turned a bend and dropped into a gully. I saw her point then. We were into an area of small hillocks, the track winding through them and the surface rough. No sign of Mt Robinson now, though we were within a few miles of it. More gullies and the white boles of ghost gums among the boulders.

We had been driving steadily west, but now the track turned north. We came to an old fence line, the gate sagging on its hinges, the wire rusted and broken, the posts leaning. 'Welcome to Jarra Jarra.' She said it with a wry smile, sitting tight-faced and very still as she waited for Tom to close the gate behind us. And shortly after that we passed a heap of bones bleached by the sun, the flies hanging in a cloud over the remains of the hide.

27

She glanced at the carcase, then at me. 'You'll see plenty of them around the station. About the only things that thrive at the moment are the carrion-eaters—we've enough wedge-tails here now to start an eagle reserve.' She said it angrily and with bitterness, staring ahead of her, her face clouded. 'All the years I've been growing up here,' she said, 'it's been one long struggle.' Her voice was barely audible above the noise of the engine, the rattle of the aged vehicle. 'And now this. If we don't get rain soon . . .' She gave a little shrug.

'Haven't you got any water on the place at all?' I asked, appalled at the implication, beginning to wish I hadn't come.

'Oh yes, we've got water all right—if we could afford to drill deep enough.'

'But at the house I mean. Surely you could bring the cattle——'

'Don't be bloody silly.' Her eyes flashed angrily and for a long minute after that she was withdrawn inside herself, her jaw set and that upturned nose of hers lifted as though in rebuke at my stupidity. Then impulsively she reached out, smiling, and touched my arm. 'I'm sorry. I've lived here all my life, y'see. I'm apt to forget there's any other world.' She took the hill ahead in a rush, her foot hard down. 'The home bore's still working. Of course it is. My grandfather knew this country better than I shall ever know it—driving his cattle up to the gold camps at Nullagine, opening up new territory, prospect-ing, mining, fishing. Before the crash came his leases ran to almost a million and a half acres. I'll show you his Journal some time. It's an incredible story—overlanding cattle from Queensland to the Ord, then down across the edge of the Great Sandy to settle in the Pilbara. That was in 1899. He was twenty-one years old and eight years ahead of Canning in opening up that section of the great Stock Route. All through the North West he was known as Big Bill Garrety.' She looked at me, the track easier now, and her eyes alight with a sort of hero-worship. 'Last year, after I'd fallen off my camel and broken a leg trying to race a motor bike cross-country, I learned to type, copying the whole thing out—four hundred and twenty-seven pages of it. I know that Journal almost by heart. There's a wonderful description, very sparse, very factual, of how this country was when he first saw it. And the site he chose for his homestead . . . of course there's water there, always.' She gave a little shrug. 'But cattle need food as well as water and there isn't much for them to feed on in the gullies of the Windbreak Hills.'

She shifted into four-wheel drive as the track followed the dry bed of a stream. Away to our left a black cloud of smoke billowed skyward. 'One of the boys signalling. Maybe he's found another bunch.' And she explained, 'When we want to call to each other in the bush, that's how we do it—set light to the spinifex. The turpentine in it gives off that oily black smoke.'

'Isn't it dangerous?' I asked, thinking of bush fires and the brittle dryness of the vegetation.

She laughed. 'In this country? There's nothing here to sustain a fire. In the old days, yes. They'd burn off whole tracts. It got the young green going in the spring. But it also burned up the seeds in the ground. In the end they destroyed all the grasses. That's what happened here, sheep tearing the young grass out by the roots and no seed to replace it.' And she added, a note of bitterness in her voice, 'If we'd known it was going to be taken from us, we'd never have concentrated all our efforts on the Watersnake. But twenty thousand acres was a manageable size, about all we could afford to keep fenced against the neighbours' sheep. We sowed new grasses, improved the waterholes, even got a bulldozer in and had them construct a reservoir.' Again that little helpless shrug. 'But it's progress, I suppose, and they were offering employment, roads, a railway line to connect with Tom Price, all the infra-structure the politicians down in Perth are so keen on.'

We were getting near now, for she went on, 'Meeting Daddy, you must remember what it has meant to him—make allowances. He had to rebuild Jarra Jarra virtually from scratch, everything against him, money owing, the land dead and nothing that worked, all the machinery, the bores, the vehicles, the generators, the shearing equipment, everything rusted with neglect. Grandfather . . .' She hesitated. 'He was an alcoholic. He was also mad—quite mad at the end.' She laughed, a brittle, bitter little sound. 'I think maybe I take after him. I'm a little mad myself sometimes.' She gave me a quick, sideways glance. 'Poor Daddy's had a lot to contend with, y'see.'

A flock of parrots burst in red-green brilliance from a tree beside the track. 'What about Golden Soak?' I asked, remembering the bright enthusiasm in her voice as she had talked of my coming out and opening up the mine again.

'I don't know,' she said. 'There was a time when all Daddy's hopes were centred on it. But then . . .' She gave a little shrug. 'Sometimes I think the only thing right about that mine is its name. It soaked up all the money Jarra Jarra produced when wool was booming.' And she added, 'Daddy's taken the ute up to the Lynn Peak homestead to get our stores and mail today. He may not be back yet. But when you meet him . . .' She glanced at me, something pleading in her eyes. 'Just make allowances, that's all.'

And after that she didn't say anything until we breasted a rise and caught a glimpse of hills ahead. 'The Windbreaks,' she said and ten minutes later we were into a flat area at their foot and there was the homestead, a huddle of tin-roofed buildings backed on to the hills, ghost gums white in the gullies either side and the skeletal metal shape of a wind pump lifeless in the torrid heat. We passed through a gap in a fence line, wheels drumming on a cattle grid made of rusted sections of old piping. 'I wish you were seeing it in the spring,' she said, her eyes creased against the glare and her voice wistful. 'Not all burned up like this. It was one of the first things Daddy did, sowing the home paddock with special grasses. A sort of pilot operation to see what the station could be like. I've walked through here after the wet with the grasses knee-high and the whole paddock a riot of flowers.' And she added, the wistfulness deepening into sadness, 'You've no idea—this place can be so beautiful.'

I had a momentary picture of her walking bare-legged through lush green grass picking wild flowers, but then it was gone, killed by the ugly reality of what my eyes saw. The track was dusty, the grass sered brown, the hills shimmered in the burning sun. And the buildings all dilapidated, the woodwork starved and flaking paint. It was almost a settlement, but as we drove into it I could see that most of the buildings were empty and unused. Horses stood among the ghost gums away to the left, nose to tail, brushing at the flies, and two dogs, one an Alsatian bitch, the other looking like a dingo cross, ran towards us barking. A cloud of grey and pink birds rose screaming from the branches of three great trees. We stopped in their shade, the leaves hanging listless and a camel couched by the furthest bole, a lather of froth on its rubbery lips.

She took me over and introduced me. 'Her name's Cleo. Suits her, don't you think? 'She was laughing, her hand in the animal's mouth, between its huge yellowing teeth. 'She loves having the roof of her mouth tickled.' The long neck stretched, the strange reptilian head lifted in ecstasy. 'Beaut, isn't she?'

'Where did you get her?' I asked.

'Why here—on the station.' She was bending down, brushing the flies away from its eyes. 'We've got at least five or six hundred roaming the place. Wild—like the brumbies. But she isn't wild. I've had her since she was a baby. We've grown up together, haven't we, Cleo?' The supercilious head turned, the pale amber eyes staring distantly as though searching some dimly remembered desert horizon. There was a deep rumbling, the noise exploding in a belch that blew a bubble of foam from its lips. 'She hasn't moved since we left this morning. I wish I could stay motionless like that for hours on end.' She straightened up, her sweat-stained shirt moulded to the swelling line of her breasts, and wiped her hand on her trousers. 'Come on in where it's cooler and I'll get you a drink. What would you like?'

'Tea,' I said, 'if there is any?'

'Yes, tea of course. It's what we mostly drink anyway.'

She led me through between two buildings, past an old hand-operated petrol pump and a wooden barn containing an elderly Morris Oxford tourer and the remains of a model-T. And at the side of the house itself there was a sort of patio of quartz slabs half-buried in red dust. There was a sundial in the centre of it, the bronze plaque set on a great block of stone, the white of the quartz shot through with reddish ochre, so that it looked like marble. Around the edges of the patio were the pitiful vestiges of a flower border. A deck chair stood forlornly, the canvas hanging bleached and rotted from the starved wood frame.

The house was a single-storey building with a verandah facing south across what had once been a lawn. It was built partly of reddish stone, partly of wood, and was separate from the kitchen and domestic quarters. She swept a beaded curtain aside and we were in the gap between the two buildings. It was walled off like a tent, with ragged hessian stretched over a double layer of wire mesh that was packed with fibrous vegetation. It was roughly furnished with cane chairs and a scrubbed wooden table. 'Come on in. We practically live here during the summer.'

'Ingenious,' I said, and she nodded.

'Yes, it is, isn't it. It's a design based on the Coolgardie safe in which the old-timers of the gold rush kept their food. The outback station owners adapted it for their own purposes and called it the Bough Shed—I suppose because it was a pretty rough job in the early days, rather like the humpies the aborigines build for shelter. Up here in the Pilbara we call it the cool house.' She smiled at me. 'I guess it's a bit hotter here, that's why. Cool sounds nice. I'm sorry the sprinklers aren't working, and there's no breeze today. Phew!' She made a face. 'Expect you'd like a wash. I know I would.'

Tom brought my suitcase in and she told me where to go, along a dim passage—'The second door on the left, and your room's at the end.' It was a single room, the shutters closed over the french windows and an air of spartan masculinity. The bathroom was almost as big. It was panelled in patterned zinc sheets painted green, the bath rust-stained, the enamel peeling, and the wood of the lavatory seat bare of varnish, the glued sections beginning to pull apart. The bathroom was a museum piece, the product of Golden Soak in its heyday, I thought, as I stripped off with a trickle of water running brown and tepid. Refreshed, I had a shave, put on a clean shirt and went back to the cool house. It was empty except for the Alsatian bitch, who stared at me, hackles raised, but made no move as I seated myself in one of the cane chairs.

I could see the glare outside through the hessian and the wire mesh and furze walls, the room itself dim and relatively

32

cool, the slightest current of air funnelling through the gap between the buildings. An aboriginal girl came in with a tray of tea, silent on bare feet, her cotton dress hanging like a shift. Her big brown eyes darted at me, shy as a wild thing, and then she was gone.

I poured myself some tea and drank it scalding hot, feeling relaxed and at ease, savouring the atmosphere of the place, the sense of continuity. There was a bookcase against the wall to my right. I lit a cigarette and sat staring at the titles. Old editions of Kipling, Galsworthy, Shaw, Forrester's *African Queen*, Shute's *A Town Like Alice*, Henry Handel Richardson, George Johnston's *My Brother Jack*, a battered Shakespeare, Poe, an anthology of Coleridge's poems, Morris West. It was a window into the personalities of three generations of Garretys. And in a lower shelf there was a row of books on mining.

The Alsatian got up from her guard post by the entrance, her ears pricked. Then she was gone and I heard the sound of an engine, outside in the glare. I poured myself another cup of tea. Hoover's *Principles of Mining*. It was an old book. Presumably it had belonged to the first Garrety, purchased when he began to operate the mine. Truscott's *Mine Economics* was more recent. The Alsatian's barking ceased abruptly and the silence of the bush crept into the room again. Chambers's Encyclopaedia and the Oxford Dictionary filled the bottom shelf. I pulled out the battered, much-thumbed Shakespeare, glanced at the flyleaf—*For Bill: This is the best companion I ever had. Take it with you—and my blessing too*. It was signed: *Your loving father*, and underneath, in the same careful faded hand, was written: *Emerald Downs, 9th March, 1897*.

I sat back, the book open on my lap, smoking and thinking of the man who had settled here seventy years ago, who had discovered the mine and built this house. And all the time this Shakespeare with him, a gift from his father. It surprised me to discover that Big Bill Garrety must have been an educated man. And he had passed his love of good books on to his son, and he presumably to his children. Had Janet any brothers, I wondered? I couldn't remember her mentioning a brother.

I was still thinking about this when I became uneasily aware of a presence in the room. I turned slowly and looked over my shoulder. A figure stood framed in the rectangle of the entrance, dark against the glare from the patio. He didn't say anything, just stood there, motionless, staring at me. His stillness was very strange. I put the book down on the table and got to my feet. 'Mr Garrety?'

For a moment I thought he hadn't heard. But then his head moved, a slight inclination. 'You're Alec Falls, are you?' He had a slow, very deliberate way of speaking. 'I thought for a moment . . .' He pushed his hand up through his iron-grey hair and then came slowly towards me. He was a big man with bushy eyebrows, the eyes themselves a startling, slightly prominent. 'The way you were sitting—and that book. . . . My father's Shakespeare, isn't it? Henry was very fond of that book.' He shook my hand and waved me back to my seat. 'Is that tea you've got there? Goodo.'

He poured himself a cup, added three spoonfuls of sugar and stirred it vigorously. 'I would have stayed to welcome you, of course, but the month's supplies came up from Perth yesterday. We have an arrangement with some people on the Highway. Aah! That's better.' And then, as though at a loss for conversation, he added, 'Hot today. Very hot. No wind, y'know.' Like his daughter, he had a strangely old-fashioned way of speaking.

He sat himself down and for the first time I saw his face clearly. It was dark like old leather, the skin dried and creased by the sun, but a bloodless, almost sick look, with lines of care etched deep and the lips a thin, compressed line. It was a stern, uncompromising face, yet somehow touched by sadness as though the outback hardness was a veneer concealing an inner sensitivity. Perhaps it was because the eyes were hooded now, the eyelids drooped in the dark sockets, but I had a strange impression of vulnerability.

'Jan tells me you're a mining expert. Tin, I think she said.' He drained his cup. 'Well, there's no tin here, young man. Up north of Nullagine, yes. But not here. The Hamersleys, right on down to the Ophthalmia, it's all iron country.'

'I appreciate that.'

'There's some copper, but none of it workable. Our mine down by Coondewanna is the only worthwhile discovery ever

34

made in this area, apart from the iron.' His voice sounded tired. 'Times have changed. All anybody wants now, it seems, is iron ore for Japan. They're no longer interested in gold.' He put his cup down, staring at me. His blue eyes had an extraordinarily penetrating quality. 'What brought you here?'

'Your daughter invited me.'

'I know that.'

He seemed to be waiting for some more definite statement and I said, 'I think she hoped I'd be able to find some way of re-opening the mine.'

'The mine's finished.' He said it abruptly and with unusual emphasis. 'It was abandoned years ago. Didn't she tell you?'

'Yes.'

'So why did you come?'

I didn't know how to answer that, the directness of the question disconcerting.

'You're a married man, I believe.' The blue eyes under the bushy brows were watchful. 'Where's your wife?'

'In England.'

'England's a long way away.'

I was conscious of hostility in his voice. 'We've separated,' I murmured.

'I see.'

He didn't like it and I realized then how dependent he must be on his daughter's company, the threat of loneliness tangible in every visiting male. I wondered what had happened to his wife as I sat there at a loss for words, the silence growing. Finally I sought refuge in the book I had been looking at. 'Your father must have had this with him when he settled here.'

He nodded. 'I should have had it re-bound.' He said it without conviction. 'That book's had a hard life—all across the north of Australia and on down here. He had it in his swag.' He leaned forward, peering at the inscription. 'Emerald Downs. That was my grandfather's place in Queensland.'

'An unusual book to give a youngster starting out on a long trek.'

'No, not really. The old boy had been a Shakespearean actor, y'see.' His eyes were friendlier now, the ice breaking a little as he explained why his grandfather had come to Australia.

35

'In those days it wasn't considered quite the thing to be an actor. Not in his family. They were Army people. I don't think he was a very good actor—though he claimed to have played in the same company as Irving. Then he got mixed up with an actress. There was a court case and the family got shot of him —shipped him out as a remittance man and he settled in Queensland.' He was smiling now, a dreamy look and his eyes no longer staring at me, but far away. 'We've all inherited that odd acting streak. I used to know those plays pretty well off by heart. Henry was the same. He could spout whole speeches.' And he added, still smiling quietly to himself, 'We read a lot. The same old books, but it helps to keep us sane. Isolated as we are, out here on the edge of nowhere.'

A door banged and Janet came in, bringing a welcome freshness into the room. She had changed into sandals and a gay tent frock and she had some make-up on. 'Oh, good, you two have met.' She tossed a bundle of newspapers on to the table and turned to her father. 'They forgot to include any rice, so no curries this month. They always seem to forget something.'

He was looking up at her, smiling fondly. But the smile faded as he took in the make-up and the dress. 'You look as though you're headed for some motel swimming pool.' There was an undercurrent of censure in his voice.

'I wish I were.' And then she pirouetted gaily, the tent skirt swirling. 'Anyway, I'm on holiday today.' Her eyes were dancing and she looked very young.

'Have you had tea?' he asked her.

'Yes, I had some while I was checking the invoice.' She was looking at him, and beneath the make-up and the gaiety, I saw her tiredness, the skin white below the eyes. 'Anything in the box for us?'

'Just the usual.' He produced a few letters from his hip pocket. 'And one for you,' he added, handing it to me. The address was typewritten, the postmark Kalgoorlie.'

She had taken the envelopes from him, and after glancing at them cursorily, she placed them with a pile of others under a piece of polished stone on top of the bookcase.

'We'll have to do something about them soon,' he said awkwardly.

'I told you, today I'm on holiday. I'm not even going to think about them today.' She laughed, a flash of even white teeth. But I could see it was an effort. 'And we have a guest. We haven't had a guest here for—oh, ages.' She smiled at me. But then she was looking at her father again and the smile vanished. 'Anything else?'

I could see him avoiding her eyes.

'It's Andie, I suppose.'

He didn't say anything and she turned to me. 'We're broke. Gloriously and absolutely broke.' She was trying very hard to make a joke of it. 'You may as well know the sort of company you're keeping.'

'Don't be silly, Jan. It's just a cash problem.'

'Then why don't you go and see Joe Davis? That's what banks are for, isn't it?'

'I've never run an overdraft or a mortgage in my life, not since I paid off all the debts here.'

Her eyes went to the pile of envelopes. 'Andie's got drought problems same as we have.' But then she saw the shut, obsti⌐ate look on his face. 'Well,' she said resignedly, 'the pump's full and we've got stores for a month anyway.'

'You must excuse us,' he said to me. 'We only have one bank, and that's our cattle. When we get some rain . . .'

'When!' she cried. 'When, when, when. . . . One of the boys just came in, told Tom they'd found a dozen head up in Red Rock George. He'll take the ute down this evening with water and try to shift them through the Gap.' She was gripping the table, her knuckles suddenly white, her face turned to the glare from the patio. 'A Cock-eyed Bob, a cyclone, anything, I don't care—but God give us some rain.' It came from the heart, a cry of despair almost.

Her father leaned forward and put his hand over hers. His hand was long and thin with bony fingers, the skin marked with the brown blotches of sun cancer; hers was small, short-fingered, the palm, as she turned it up to answer his touch, hard and calloused.

'It'll rain,' he said.

'But when?'

'In God's good time.'

'Damn God! I want it now.'

I could see him framing the words to reprimand her. But instead he said quietly, 'It always has, y'know—sooner or later.'

'But it's never been as bad as this.' She saw he was about to contradict her and added, 'Well, not in my lifetime anyway.' She turned her freckled face to me, her eyes a little wild. 'The trouble is, when it does come, it's so violent.' And she added wistfully, 'I remember that night at Drym, the softness of the rain. It's never like that here.'

'Perhaps not.' He leaned back, frowning at the tin roof. '*Rumble thy bellyful* . . . how does it go? Lear, y'know.' He closed his eyes. '*Spit, fire! Spout, rain! Nor rain, wind, thunder, fire are my daughters. I tax not you, you elements, with unkindness.*'

'But I do,' she cried. 'Our elements are unkind.'

'It's a hard country,' he admitted.

'Then why not sell the mine?' She turned to me. 'Golden Soak must be worth something surely? It's got mine buildings, machinery, gold—it wasn't worked out, you know. And this mineral boom——'

'It's nickel they're after,' he said gently.

'I know it's nickel.' Her voice sounded edgy. 'I read the papers, same as you do. I know about Poseidon and Western Mining. But with all these companies being floated, they're after anything they can get, and if we could sell Golden Soak——'

'No,' He said it flatly. 'We've been over all this before, Jan.'

'Well, it's time we went over it again,' she said tartly. 'Alec hasn't come all this way for nothing. At least he can tell us whether it's worth anything at all.'

'I think I am the best judge of what it is worth,' he said stonily.

'This letter may be of some help,' I told him. 'It's from a company promoter who specializes in West Australian shares. I asked him to make some inquiries about your mine.' And I slit the envelope.

'You'd no right to do that.'

I looked up, the letter open in my hand. He was leaning forward, staring at me, the long leathery face hard and a muscle twitching, anger glazing in those blue eyes—anger, and something else, something I couldn't place.

'The mine's closed,' he said, speaking very slowly, very emphatically. 'If it's ever opened again, it will be opened by me. Is that understood?'

'But he's only trying to help,' Janet cried. 'And if it's worth anything at all . . .'

'Daughter, please.' The sharpness of his voice, the edge in it —it was as though he'd slapped her in the face.

'Oh well, to hell with it then,' she said brightly, and began to talk of other things while her father sat there brooding in silence and I read Kadek's letter, my hopes dashed in the first paragraph. No offer of a job, only the vague outline of a proposition that left me with a feeling of helplessness. And then I was reading the last paragraph, scanning it quickly, absorbing the information with a sudden sense of excitement, wondering what it meant. I read it through again, slowly this time, and as I read I heard Ed Garrety's voice saying, 'Only this morning there was a Toyota through Lynn Peak with two men in it asking about Golden Soak.' And he added, 'It's bad enough having a mine that's marked on every map, but if we put it up for sale we'd have half the prospectors in the State tramping over the property, driving their trucks through our fences.' And Janet saying, 'Well, it wouldn't make much difference—our fences are in pretty bad shape anyway.'

There was a sudden silence and I looked up to find her staring at me. 'Well, what does your friend say?' she asked with frank curiosity.

'He's not interested in Golden Soak.'

I saw the light fade from her eyes and I turned to her father. 'Do you know where Lake Disappointment is?'

He didn't say anything for a moment, a stillness settling on the room, his eyes watching me. 'Go on,' he said. 'What else does he want to know?' The bleakness of his voice was chilling.

I hesitated. But his reaction, my own curiosity—I felt impelled to ask him. 'Does McIlroy's Monster mean anything to you?'

The silence deepened, his face frozen. It was as though I'd dropped a bomb in the room.

'McIlroy was your father's partner, wasn't he? Does his Monster exist, or is this talk of copper just a prospector's dream?'

He shook his head, frowning, a puzzled look in his eyes. 'I don't know,' he said slowly.

'Is it true he was searching for it when he disappeared?'

The stillness was absolute then, a silence so complete that I could hear the sibilant sound of the Alsatian breathing in her sleep as she lay sprawled by the entrance.

'But that's ages ago,' Janet said.

'Before the war—in 1939.' His voice was controlled now, very quiet. 'McIlroy was lost on an expedition into the interior.' He leaned a little forward. 'What's the name of your correspondent?'

'Kadek.'

'Why does he want to know about McIlroy?'

'It's just bar talk,' I said. 'A rumour he's picked up.' I folded the letter and put it away in my pocket. 'I imagine Kalgoorlie is full of rumours right now.'

He nodded slowly. 'It was all in the papers at the time. A lot of speculation—most of it nonsense.' And he added, 'All our troubles here stem from that man McIlroy. His expedition was a desperate, harebrained attempt to make good all the money he'd lost.'

'Gambling?' I asked.

'He was playing the stock market—our money, and a lot of other people's, too.' And he added, coldly and with an intensity that was almost violent, 'Pat McIlroy was a crook. He destroyed this station and he destroyed my father.'

'You never told me that,' Janet said.

He shrugged and got to his feet. 'No point. As you say, it all happened a long time ago now.' He looked down at me, still frowning, his eyes bleak—'Lake Disappointment is just below the Canning Stock Route, between the Great Sandy and the Gibson. They found his truck abandoned there, and east of Disappointment there's nothing, only desert.'

He went out then, leaving me with questions still unanswered and the feeling that there was more to it than that. Janet also disappeared, and shortly afterwards we had lunch. It was a cold lunch—cold beef, salad and cheese. The bread was home-made. 'Lucky your visit coincided with the monthly supply,' Janet said. 'We try to be as self-sufficient as we can, but things like cheese and flour, salad dressing—oh, lots of things . . .'

'And beer.' Her father paused in his carving. 'Jan drinks a lot of beer, and we don't brew that.'

'I don't drink much.' She was opening a can, and she passed it to me with a glass. 'Help yourself. Anyway,' she added, reaching behind her for another beer, 'I need it to keep my strength up.'

He smiled at her. 'You realize it's making you fat?'

'How could it, riding that camel day after day? Just because you don't . . .' She stopped there. 'Besides, it's good for me. Gives me a fine healthy sweat.'

It was a quick meal, none of us talking very much, and after-wards she took me over the house. Her father had gone off in the Land-Rover to have a look for cattle, over by Deadman Hill he said.

The rooms were larger than I had expected and there was actually a drawing room, not pretentious, but nevertheless a surprisingly stately room with two portraits in oils over the open fireplace and a cut glass chandelier hanging from the centre of the ceiling. The portraits were of a man and a woman. The man was bearded, a heavy, formidable face, the blue eyes large and compelling. The woman wore a high-necked dress, her hair long and piled on her small neat head. But it was the snub nose and the freckles that caught my eye and I turned to Janet. 'Your grandmother?'

She nodded, smiling. 'We still have some of her dresses, including that one. I tried it on once.' She giggled. 'We're as like as two peas.'

The furniture, shrouded in dust sheets, appeared to be of good solid mahogany and the walls were panelled from floor to ceiling with that same patterned zinc. It was painted a pale shade of green and the flower pattern was so delicate that it looked like wallpaper.

The bedrooms all led off that same dark passage and had french windows opening on to the verandah. 'We often sleep out here,' she said. 'It's wonderful when it's cooler. Daddy

41

won't have a dogger on the place, so we've plenty of dingoes. Sometimes, out here, I'll lie awake listening to their calls. I've counted as many as a dozen calling at one time, all round the house and quite close.'

'Doesn't your Alsatian see them off?'

'Yla? No, of course not—she likes them around. But we have to lock her up when she's on heat. She got away once and you can see the result, that dingo cross, Butch. We don't worry much about him. He spends most of his time roaming the Windbreaks, and when he does come back he's worn out, just skin and bone, and serve him right. He's a womanizer.' She laughed, glancing up at me as we moved back into the dimness of the passage, where she opened the door opposite and took me into a room facing north, which was part study, part office. 'My father's den,' she called it. Bookcases crammed with books and magazines, a rack of guns, and everywhere rock samples, most of them tabbed with a map reference to indicate where they had been picked up. There was a big mahogany desk, bare wood showing through the worn leather top, and a black upholstered swivel chair with the stuffing visible in patches. The desk was littered with papers held down with pieces of rock and on the floor beside it was a large steel canister, dome-topped and painted cream. It caught my eye because I hadn't expected to find such a modern instrument in a house that didn't seem to have changed in fifty years.

'That's Daddy's microscope.' She took the dome cover off so that I could see. 'It's Swiss.'

I nodded. 'A Wild Heerbrugg.' I was puzzled because it was stereoscopic, the sort geologists use for examing core samples. 'Does he know much about mineralogy?'

'Only what he's read.' And she added, 'D'you know how much it cost?—over eight hundred dollars. Enough to keep this place going for a couple of months the way we're living at the moment. And it was only a passing craze,' she added, the heat giving an edge to her voice. 'He was down at the mine every day for almost a month, collecting samples, examining them; and then suddenly he abandoned the whole thing.'

She replaced the dome.

'When was this?'

'Oh, about a year ago. It was just after the iron ore company took over the Watersnake lease. They had to pay compensation, of course, and he saw an advertisement for this microscope in a copy of the *Sydney Morning Herald* somebody'd left at Andie's place.' She got out her handkerchief and touched her brow, mopping at the beads of perspiration. 'He had this wild idea that if he spent some of the Watersnake money prospecting around Golden Soak he'd make our fortune. For a time he was like a child with a new toy, full of excitement, staying up till all hours poring over the results. He went down into the mine, too, which scared me stiff—the entrance has been boarded up for years. He was quite convinced the Watersnake people would bring him luck.' She looked at me, smiling a little sadly. 'It's sacred land, y'see—sacred to the Pukara, the Watersnake people. Grandfather was initiated into the tribe. There's a lot about them in his Journal—their rites, their way of life, how they survived in near-desert country.' She nodded to some paddles of dark brown wood hung on the wall above an old R/T set. 'Those are from the Watersnake. They're message sticks given him by the Pukara.' There were more in a pile on one of the bookcases, all intricately patterned. She said they had been found in a cave in a little rock gorge below The Governor. Then she took me over to a large scale map stuck flat on the wall opposite the window, an aeronautical chart that covered most of the Pilbara. The boundaries of Jarra Jarra were inked in red. 'Like a billy goat, isn't it?' She laughed and I saw that she was right. Jarra Jarra formed the body, stretching away to the east, and the head was represented by the Watersnake, the two leases connected by the narrow neck of the Robinson Gap. The goat image was completed by a beard, a vee of land extending in a south-easterly direction and embracing the peaks of Padtherung and Coondewanna. Near the tip of it was a small hieroglyphic of crossed pick and hammer and the name Golden Soak Mine printed against it.

'The iron ore people needed the Watersnake for the new township they're planning over towards Perry's Camp. The first thing they did, of course, was to close the Gap, and about five weeks ago, when Daddy found a mob of cattle pressed up against their brand new fence, he had Tom cut the wire. That

43

was when we started driving.' She turned towards the door. 'Well, it's done now, all except the odd bunch. I just hope nobody finds out till we've had some rain.'

'I'd like to have a look at your grandfather's Journal some time,' I said.

'Of course.'

She was out in the passage now, the door held open for me, and I stood there, looking around at the clutter of things in that extraordinary den, the radio, the paddles of patterned wood, the rock samples—I was thinking of the long hours he must have spent here, worrying about the future. And that incongruous microscope, the sudden burst of enthusiasm. 'What made him abandon Golden Soak as the solution to your difficulties?'

She shook her head, her eyes staring at me, luminous in the dimly lit passage. 'I don't know. I think he just came to the conclusion there wasn't any point.'

'Suddenly?'

'Yes. Suddenly. You do, sometimes. You have a period of wild optimism, working like crazy, then, suddenly, you run out of steam. Haven't you ever experienced that?'

I nodded slowly, thinking of Balavedra. But then I'd only abandoned hope when things had got beyond my control, and I'd found a solution—of a sort. I followed her out of the room and she shut the door. 'I'm going to have a rest now,' she said. 'I advise you to do the same.'

I spent the afternoon on the bed in my room, stripped to my underpants. It was stiflingly hot, but at least I could sweat in comfort, and I needed time to think, to sort out my impressions and make up my mind what the hell I was going to do. There was nothing for me here and not much hope that Kadek would assist me financially if I did hitch a ride down to Kalgoorlie. I retrieved the letter from the pocket of my trousers and read it through again:

Dear Alec:
    You missed me in Perth by two days. I got here Christmas Day. Hell of a place to spend Christmas, but I'm in on a mining deal near here at Ora Banda and my partner needed

44

me on the spot. I got your letters and I'm sorry to hear you ran out of ore. I think I told you my philosophy—if you do strike lucky, let others in on the gravy before you're scraping the bottom of the bowl. You should have floated your mine on the market while you were still into high grade ore.

I've nothing for you myself. I hire consultants when I need them. Few companies in Australia are big enough to employ experts on the staff, and those that are usually find them within the organization. I suggest you set yourself up as a mining consultant in Perth. There is still a shortage of qualified men out here, particularly those who can produce geological reports for the smaller companies that match the expectations of their shareholders. I can certainly introduce you to some useful people. I shall be here about a week, then back in Perth. Come and see me when you are next there. I have just started a mining newsletter and the services of a man of your qualifications and experience would give added weight to my recommendations. I am sure you realize how mutually profitable this could be.

I lay back, staring up at the ceiling and thinking about Kadek. I had no illusions about the sort of man he was. But though self-seeking, entirely egotistic, he had still made a deep impression on me. Partly it was his enormous vitality. But I think it was also because of his background. He was of middle European extraction, part Slav, with dark, rather saturnine features, black hair, cold, calculating eyes and a mouth like a steel trap. 'Nobody but a fool works underground.' There had been a suggestion of arrogance in his voice as he had said that. And then going on to tell me how his father had come out from Serbia between the wars and had ended up as a miner in Kalgoorlie, coughing his lungs out in a tin shack within sight of the Golden Mile. And Kadek had watched him die, with no sense of loss or sadness, no compunction even, only a feeling of contempt for the man who had given him life and then failed to provide him with an education to match his wits.

I picked up the letter again, relieved that he didn't know my real circumstances. . . .

*   *   *

Finally, you ask about the Golden Soak Mine. Work stopped there in 1937 and it was offered for sale. It was later withdrawn, no buyers. It's gold, of course, and if it were uneconomic then, it would be doubly so now. Since you're staying with the Garretys you'll have discovered all this for yourself by the time you get my letter. But while you're up there you might care to make inquiries about rumours of a copper deposit somewhere to the east of Lake Disappointment. Big Bill Garrety's partner was a gambler named Pat McIlroy and when they came unstuck financially McIlroy took off into the interior and was never heard of again. How he knew of the deposit and whether he ever found it I've no idea, but it's still talked about as McIlroy's Monster and there's an abo up at Nullagine claims his father was on the expedition. Chris Culpin, who is in on the Ora Banda deal with me, picked this up in the Palace bar here from a youngster who had just done a survey in the Nullagine area. The abo's name is Wally and you'll find him at the Conglomerate Hotel. It's a rum story, and even rummer that it should crop up again after all these years. See what you can find out. If there is any truth in it, I can tell you this—right now it would be every bit as good as Lasseter's Golden Reef. By which I mean it would fire the imagination of punters throughout Australia. Good luck to you!

Ferdie Kadek.

McIlroy's Monster! I savoured the sound of it, speaking it aloud, my eyes closed against the slatted glare from the shutters. The word Monster conjured visions of a gigantic deposit, a mountain of ore. I remembered Mt Whaleback, huge in the dawn, sprawled dark against the sunrise, and this was copper, not iron. McIlroy was an Irishman presumably. A gambler, Kadek had said. A crook, Ed Garrety had called him. And dead for over thirty years. Yet his Monster still lived, the subject of bar talk in Nullagine. Had he invented the whole thing?

I was thinking then about the country between the Great Sandy and the Gibson deserts, the miles of emptiness, the blinding red heat of it. Christ! it was hot enough here in this

46

darkened room. Nobody in his senses, however desperate, would go out into that, chasing a will o' the wisp of his own invention.

So the Monster was real. At least to him. Real enough for him to risk his life to find it, and he had died in the attempt. A fly crawled at the corner of my nostrils. I flicked it off, pulling the sheet up over my head, and then I was dozing, picturing that Irishman dying of thirst by the edge of a salt lake and babbling to himself of a mountain of copper somewhere to the east. It sounded incredible. Incredible that it could remain unexplored all these years. But anything was possible . . . anything at all in this extraordinary country.

2

I woke shortly after six to the sound of horses. It was cooler now, a slight breeze reaching me from the shutters. And my mind was made up. Somehow I had to get myself to Nullagine. The decision was a subconscious one, made while I slept.

I got up, had a quick wash, and when I was dressed, I went out through the french windows to find Tom and two blacks unsaddling their mounts, the camel watching them and the galahs flocked in the trees above. The horses were thin and very tired, their heads drooped, their bodies covered in sweat and dust. They were turned loose and I followed them as they moved dejectedly to join the others up among the ghost gums.

From this higher ground I looked down on Jarra Jarra, the house and the outbuildings golden in the slanting rays of the evening sun, and sitting there among the white boles of the gum trees, with the horses browsing near on the hard, dry vegetation, I realized how much effort had gone into the building of this settlement deep in the bush. Now the eagles kept voracious watch; I could see three of them circling slowly on stiff-spread wings, and everywhere I looked, from the hills behind me, to the long brown plain with the track winding through it, it was an arid, burned-up, waterless brown.

I sat there for a long time, nothing moving, only the wedge-tailed eagles in the sky and no sound except the horses behind me. The sense of solitude was immense. It was difficult to picture it in the old days with the bunkhouses full and the distant boundaries of the property a week's ride away. The sun set, the sky flared, a flame of fire slowly darkening to the colour of blood, and the land reflecting the sky's violence. A shiver ran through me. I was gazing eastward, the endless vista of the dried-up land turning to purple, the purple and the red divided by a hard line where land met sky. I was thinking of McIlroy again. A gambler. I was a gambler, too—both of us desperate. Somewhere out there, beyond the sharp line of the horizon, his bones lay white in the emptiness of the desert. And beyond his bones, still deeper into the emptiness. . . . I was thinking of the Monster, seeing in my mind's eye the curved back of a hill shimmering on the edge of visibility.

I got suddenly to my feet. I must be mad even to think of it. I was a stranger in a strange land, alone, with no money and nobody to help me. The Monster was just a dream.

I went quickly down the slope, back to the house, knowing it was crazy, yet still under the spell of its fascination. Mt Isa, the biggest copper mine in Australia, way over on the other side of the country—somebody must have discovered it. And if there was a mountain of copper in the trackless wastes of northern Queensland, why shouldn't there be one in the empty quarter between the Great Sandy and the Gibson?

Janet met me, her pale frock glimmering in the dusk as I came between the sheds to the little patio. 'I was getting worried about you. Tom said you'd gone up on to the Windbreaks.'

'I went up to see the sunset.'

'I suppose you thought it beautiful.' Her voice sounded flat and weary. 'But you'll get used to it. It's like that night after night here in the dry. In the end you'll feel as I do—you'll hate it.' She turned and went inside. 'Would you like a beer while we're waiting for Daddy? He's listening in on the radio. Port Hedland. It's the evening schedule. Soon as he's finished we'll have dinner.'

The cool house was cosy now, the light on and a generator humming in the distance. There was a white damask cloth on the table, silver candlesticks and wine glasses of cut crystal. 'Do you always dine like this?' I asked.

She laughed. 'No, of course not. We're usually going to bed about now. Saves running the generator, and anyway this last month we've all been away by first light.'

'You shouldn't have altered your routine for me.'

'Why not?' Her eyes were bright, a glow of excitement. 'Besides, it's New Year's Eve. I do believe you had forgotten.' She gave a little sigh. 'We might have forgotten it, too. We haven't much to celebrate, have we? But you've given us an excuse. And we've earned it. Oh, my goodness we have.'

Sitting there, drinking ice-cold beer and seeing that girl, so young and gay—it was hard to realize that they and the station, the whole world her grandfather had created was on the brink of final disaster. 'What exactly did McIlroy do?' I asked.

But she didn't seem to know. 'I could never get Daddy to talk about that. Y'see the world he grew up in was so different to the world he inherited after the war. Before the crash, Jarra Jarra was the centre of the social life of the Pilbara—they had race days here and balls, a way of life that is quite unbelievable now.'

'And you don't know anything about McIlroy's Monster?'

She shook her head. 'I'd never even heard of it until you mentioned it today.' She was staring at me, her eyes wide in the harsh glare of the naked light bulb. 'Why? You're not taking it seriously, are you?'

I slid away from that, asking her instead about the Journal. But apparently the Journal she had typed didn't refer to it. 'It doesn't mention McIlroy either. There's a reference to closing the mine, but only because it was running at a loss. The mine was closed long before the crash, about a year I think. And there's no mention of financial difficulties. It stops before then, y'see.'

'So it's not complete?'

'Oh no. It goes up to October 1938. Then it stops. The last entry is about a trip he made out of Port Hedland in a pearling lugger. He was very interested in pearling and the coastal fisheries and owned a number of boats operating out of Port Hedland and Broome. The last words are: *Picked up the news about Munich on the wireless as we were coming into Port Hedland—*

49

and that's all. It just ends there, abruptly.' She bent to light the candles and I was suddenly conscious of her femininity. 'I'll show you after dinner. A lot of it isn't really interesting at all, not to you at any rate—about the family and the people round, life generally. But it does give a picture of what it was like living here on one of the biggest stations in Australia, and there are bits that are really quite graphic, particularly the early pages. How he discovered Golden Soak, for instance. I thought at one time of sending it to a publisher. But that'd mean Sydney, and though he was a great figure here in the Pilbara, I doubt whether anybody's ever heard of Big Bill Garrety over in the East.'

Her father came in then with a bottle of wine, holding it carefully. 'I don't know whether it's still drinkable,' he said. 'It's been here a long time now—one of the few bottles left after the old man died. It's from the Barossa Valley in South Australia.' It was a red wine and I looked at the label as he poured it—St Emilion 1942. 'A lot of our wines have been given French names—silly, when they're quite different.'

Janet had cooked the meal herself, steaks with salad and chips. 'Quite like old times,' her father said. He was smiling his face younger and less careworn in the candlelight. 'Well, here's to you and the success of your visit to Australia.' He raised his glass and I saw it was less than half full.

Janet nodded and she too raised her glass. 'I have a feeling . . .' She hesitated, smiling at me over the wine—'I've a feeling now you're here things will change. Here's luck—to us all.' And she drank, quickly.

A shadow moved in the patio entrance behind her and in the darkness outside I saw Tom standing, squat and black. Ed Garrety had seen him, too, and he rose and went outside. He stood talking there for a moment, then he came back and sat down again, his face sombre as he started in on his steak.

'What is it?' Janet asked. 'Couldn't they shift that bunch out of the gully?'

'They shifted them all right. Got them through the Gap.'

'Then what is it?'

'A vehicle of some sort. Down by the old shearing shed. They saw the lights when they were on the Robinson slope.'

'Heading for the mine?'

He nodded. 'That Toyota I wouldn't wonder.' The twitch was back at the side of his mouth. I'll go down there after dinner and rout them out. Those damned prospectors think they own the country.' And he added, his face darkened with anger, his voice trembling, 'That's the curse of this mineral boom. Having a mine that's marked on every map—you might just as well put a notice up on the Highway saying "Prospectors Welcome." They don't realize it isn't a lease. We own Golden Soak and the flat land to the east of it, the mineral rights as well. That was one thing my father did get out of the government.'

We ate in silence after that, the mood changed, all the pleasure gone out of the meal. It made me realize how isolated they were, how vulnerable to intruders.

Later, when we had finished and were sitting over our coffee, Ed Garrety began to talk about the old days when he was a boy and there were over a dozen men working at the mine and some twenty blacks with their families living around the homestead, anything up to a hundred thousand sheep roaming the station. I think he was just talking to put the thought of intruders out of his mind, and he went on to describe what it had been like when he took over, after he had come back from Java at the end of the war. That was when I learned about his son. It was his room I was occupying and he had been killed in Vietnam. 'Perhaps it's as well,' he murmured. 'Henry loved this place and I wouldn't have wanted him to see it as it is now.'

'D'you think I like it?' Janet snapped.

'No. No, of course I don't. But it's different for a girl.'

I saw two spots of colour flare in her cheeks and I said quickly, 'He was in the Australian forces then?'

'That's right. Infantry. He was a real fighting boy. At eighteen this place wasn't big enough to hold him. He wanted to see the world, wanted action. Then we got ourselves involved in Vietnam. He was one of the first casualties.' He drained his glass, but didn't refill it, only ours. And then he got to his feet without a word and went through into the passage. He came out a moment later with a rifle in his hand. 'Be back in time to see the New Year in with you,' he said to his daughter. And

51

then to me, 'We listen in to it on the wireless, y'know. Makes us feel we still belong to the world outside.' He nodded. 'Back inside of a couple of hours.'

'Would you like me to come with you?' I asked. But he shook his head. 'They'll go as soon as they know we own the mineral rights. The entrance to the mine is boarded up anyway. It's unsafe, y'see.' He went out then, calling to Yla, and a moment later we heard the Land-Rover drive off.

'I'm glad you didn't press him,' Janet said, adding with an impish gleam, 'I know you'd rather be driving down to the mine than sitting here with me.'

'I'm sorry if my disappointment showed.'

'Oh, don't worry.' She was grinning, a flash of white teeth. 'I'm used to men who think mines are more important than women.' And then, suddenly serious again. 'Daddy's quite hopelessly possessive about that bloody mine. Won't let anybody go near it.' She got up. 'I'll get you the Journal. Then at least you can read about it—how it all started.' She came back a few minutes later with an old box file full of typed pages. She opened it and placed it on the table in front of me. 'You'll learn more from this than you would from Daddy. Sometimes I think he's scared of Golden Soak.'

'Because it's unsafe?'

'No, it's more complicated than that—a love-hate feeling he has.' She was turning the pages of typescript. 'I can't explain. I don't really understand it myself. But when he was a young man, think how exciting it must have been for him. Going down there, working with the miners—it made a change from riding fences and working sheep in the heat and the dust. And the miners themselves, he always says they were a different breed. He got a great kick out of the fact that we had a mine on the station.' Her fingers smoothed a page. 'There you are. December 22nd, 1905, and a drought every bit as bad as we've got now. Start reading from there.'

'But why should he hate the mine?'

'I think you'll understand when you read some of the later passages.' Her hand was on my shoulder, her breath on my cheek, and I heard her sigh. 'He won't talk about it. But I know he does hate it.' She straightened up. 'You've got to remember what a drain Golden Soak has been. It never made money, not after the first few years. And yet, owning a mine like we do, there's always the hope at the back of our minds—that one day it'll turn out beaut and make our fortunes and we'll be rich and live happily ever after.' She was laughing, a note of wistfulness. 'You read that while I clear the things away. Then you'll understand how my grandfather must have felt, why we all have this stupid, quite illogical feeling that we're sitting on a fortune, a sort of Pandora's box, if only we knew how to open the lid.'

'The official price of gold hasn't changed in thirty years,' I said gently.

'I know that. But it doesn't make any difference. I still dream dreams that one day. . . .' She shrugged, turning quickly away and beginning to clear the table. 'Maybe after a few days if you can spare the time, Daddy'll get used to you being here and I'll be able to persuade him to take you down. Actually, I've never been down myself. The ladders are gone and the winch gear broken. He always said it was too dangerous.' She went out then and by the light from the single bulb and the flickering candles I began to read Big Bill Garrety's account of driving cattle from the Turee Creek area to the goldfields at Nullagine:

22nd Dec: *Two more soaks gone and the last bore run dry. Buried a dozen carcases and started driving the live beasts at sundown. About 60 head. Maurie told me two days back they're short of meat at the goldfields now and the miners paying high prices. But these poor beasts are skin and bone and I doubt I'll get more than a score of them through. Camped at dawn where some eucs gave a little shade for us and the cattle. Made only 9 miles during the dark and still another 12 to Pukara. If that waterhole is dry, then there's nothing between here and the Fortescue, unless I take them into the gullies below Coondewanna and up through the homestead. But Pukara should be all right—it's one of the blackman's sacred waterholes inhabited by the ghosts of two Watersnake men of the Dreamtime. They sprinkle penis blood there. I've seen them do it. But not my two jackaroos—they're from down around the Kunderong.*

23rd Dec: *Left 7 dead, starting again at sundown. The sky a*

53

dying furnace, the sun a monstrous flaming ball. Could almost pray for a cyclone. But no cloud. Just burnished sky, and the cattle so weak they're sinking in their tracks. Thank God we're riding camels, not horses. Have called a brief halt having pushed the animals hard and made 8 miles. Good flat going, but too much spinifex, too little pasture. I'll have to complete the change-over to sheep. I'm about the only station up here that still runs cattle. But I hate sheep—they eat out everything, ring bark the trees in a drought. Another twenty years and I reckon the Sandy will have moved into this country. . . .

Hurrah! We made it and there's water—not much and brackish, but it's water. Trust the blackmen—the sacred soaks never seem to run dry. Reckon that's why they're sacred. You don't make a gash in your John Thomas and scatter blood around for nothing! But looks like we'll have to go the long way round by Coondewanna.

24 Dec: *Below Coondewanna now and just before sundown took a stroll up a gorge between Coondewanna and Padtherung to see whether the blackmen have made any of their funny drawings here like on the rocks behind the homestead. Found several, very faint, in a little ravine. Red country this, red like it is all to the west of JJ, but only a thin layer of iron rock. Where storms have eroded it I can see quartz, or maybe it's jasperite like at Marble Bar—it's coloured a sort of dirty grey and right under the overhang, where they've painted a rather odd-shaped roo, there's patches of it that glitter faintly. And at the bottom of the gully, there's another soak, carefully shielded by a slab of thin quartz stuff. The ground very moist underneath it and the dirt around it marked by roos urgent for water. Odd country this—very wild. I broke off a bit of the quartz and stuffed it in my pocket, more for curiosity than anything else. I think it's iron pyrites, or maybe a form of mica, but even now in the firelight, waiting for the billy to boil, I can see the specks glittering.*

This was the beginning of Golden Soak and all my troubles.

(Note: This last sentence was obviously added much later. Instead of an indelible pencil, it is written in ink with a fountain pen, probably in 1944. J.G.)

'That was the year my Grandmother Eliza died.' I hadn't even noticed she'd come back into the room. 'He was alone then. Daddy was the only son and still a prisoner of the Japs. I suppose the old boy had nothing better to do but relive his life through his Journal.' She was leaning over my shoulder again, her voice gentle. 'The handwriting is very shaky, so I imagine he had already taken to the bottle. There are quite a few comments like that, all added about two years before he died, including four or five pages on the mining techniques and problems peculiar to Golden Soak. They might interest you.' She refilled my coffee cup and began turning the pages. 'You'll probably have difficulty in following the sequence. I certainly did.' She found what she was looking for. 'There. I'll leave you to browse through it. I've got to go and see to the chickens.'

It was towards the end of the typescript, a semi-technical account that constantly referred to the high cost of treatment due to the presence of antimony and the inconsistencies of the reef. Faulting had apparently been a major problem. On page 324 he gave the date of closure—November 21, 1937. But on the following page he referred to *the final blow*—a cave-in and the mine flooded at the lower level. No indication of when this had happened. The writing here was very vague, mostly an angry diatribe against the absence of any increase in the price of gold and the collapse of the Australian gold share market. It concluded abruptly with these words: *The end of all my hopes —the effort of half a lifetime wasted. I wish I had never discovered that Soak.* And then, without a pause, he went on to deal with the problems of maintaining the wool clip in country that was deteriorating year by year. This, too, seemed to have been written at a later date, but it was much less vague, probably because he knew more about the land than he did about mining, had in fact a strange affection for it; and unlike other graziers around him he realized what the effect of overstocking must be:

I remember when I first came to JJ. It was so beautiful at times it took your breath away—saltbush, bluebush, a whole world of native shrubs and grasses, all tough enough to exist in the harsh arid heat of this outback country, and the mallee and the ghost gums shimmering their leaves in the wind, shading the ground from the sun. But now— my God! when I look at what I've done to keep that bloody mine going and those blasted miners in booze and women. The land is desert. It's shagged out. Maurie and Pete, they both say I should burn off like they do to encourage new growth in the spring. They don't see that that's the last straw in this poor unhappy land. I've tried it, seen the young growth come, and then there are more lambs, more hungry sheep-jaws champing, and before you can say knife the green that should have grown lush and big in the wet, the seedlings that might have been trees—they're all gone. It never has a chance to seed. And you burn again and it burns the seeds in the ground. Pete's mentally retarded, a grown child, not caring. But Maurie ought to be able to see it. Betty does, I know, but he's a pig-headed bastard. Eighteen years I've been running sheep here, more and more every year. Quantity to offset the steady decline in quality, and now I look at the place and I can't recognize it. Even the mulgas are dying with no vegetation to shade their roots in the heat, and this year in the dry those damned sheep were stripping the bark they were so famished for food. And Ed—what will Ed make of it when he comes home? Thank God he'll never know what this country was like when I first came to it. There's nothing left to show him by comparison what I grabbed and what he'll inherit. But my heart bleeds for him. One thing he must do is get rid of the blasted sheep, get back to cattle—a small herd, and give the land a rest, a chance to recover if it can.

I turned back to the early part, reading entries here and there, oblivious for the moment of anything but the world Big Bill Garrety had lived in. There was a lot about Golden Soak in the entries for 1905 and 1906—the first tentative shaft, the establishment of a mining camp, and then the adit driven into the side of Mt Coondewanna, the sinking of the main shaft to 200 feet, the difficulties of getting machinery to the site, the problem of supplies. The first cross-cut from the shaft into the quartz completed on April 4, 1907, and on April 6: *This day we brought up the first bucketful of ore from the 200-foot level—the booze-up went on all night, the men singing by the damp fires, four sheep roasted whole and the camels scared to death.* There was a lot about the camels after that—camel trains took the ore to Nullagine, coming back with the crushing machinery, all in pieces, and sleds for the heavier parts. Money pouring in, and all of it ploughed back into the development of the mine. And then, suddenly the entries became shorter, more widely spaced— Perth, a troopship, Gallipoli, finally the trenches and the mud of Passchendaele, all told with stark simplicity, just the facts, nothing more. Even the period in hospital, when he'd lost an eye after a sniper's bullet had grazed his head, only rated three short entries—the last dated June 9, 1918: *Invalided home. Arrived Fremantle feeling quite fit after voyage though ship very crowded. Can't wait to get back to JJ.*

'You've let your coffee get cold.'

I looked up, startled, to find Janet standing across the table from me and my coffee cup still full.

'Sorry, I hadn't noticed.' I was still in the past, thinking of his wound and how he'd died an alcoholic.

'Shall I heat it for you?'

'No, it's all right.'

'I had a little argument with a goanna—that's why I've been so long. Didn't you hear me shoot it?'

I shook my head. I couldn't remember hearing a shot.

'One of those big lizards—they're always trying to get into the chicken run.' She came round the table. 'You're back on the early part now.'

'You didn't tell me he'd been wounded.'

'He only mentions it that once. He doesn't refer to it again—not once in the whole Journal.'

'And you say he went mad in the end. Was that the cause of it?'

'Maybe. I don't know. I never knew him, y'see. And Daddy'd never discuss it with me.'

'Then how d'you know he went mad?'

'It's what I've heard, that's all. The older people, those who knew him, they don't talk about it in front of me, but I've heard it all the same.' And she added, 'He must have been a most extraordinary man. It wasn't only that he was tough physically. It was his personality. D'you know, even those who lost their money because of him—they still speak of him with a sort of hero-worship as though he were a man quite beyond the usual run of men. Did you read that bit where he described what he'd done to the land to keep those blasted miners in booze and women?'

'Yes,' I said. 'I read that.'

'To think that he knew. . . . I was so appalled when I was typing it that I burst into tears. He knew what he'd done—the problems Daddy would have to face.'

I turned to the last page, to that abrupt ending with its reference to Munich. 'It's strange,' I said, 'that he kept this Journal all those years and then ended it here.' I looked up at her. 'Are you sure there isn't some more of it?'

She shook her head. 'I've searched the house—everywhere. The same thought occurred to me.'

'Then why did he stop at this point? Was he afraid of another war—that your father would have to repeat his own experience?'

'No, I don't think it was that. Though it's what happened, of course.' She was silent a moment, her brows wrinkled, gazing into the candles. Then she said, 'I think myself he came ashore from that pearling boat, went up to the bank and was suddenly faced with the news that the company was broke and owed money all over the North West. It must have been a terrible shock. I think if I were keeping a Journal I'd stop there myself. All the rest was disaster—the sheep and the leases being sold off, the fishing boats, the bank building, and the mine a sort of golden elephant that nobody wanted. It was the end of an era, everything he'd worked for. . . .' Again she shook her head. 'No, I don't think I'd want to continue my Journal after that.'

It seemed reasonable enough. 'Could I see the original?' I was thinking that the handwriting might give some indication.

'I'll get it if you like. D'you want to see it now?'

'No, it doesn't matter.' I was running backwards through the pages, searching for some reference to his partner. But I couldn't see anything about McIlroy or his Monster, and when I commented on this she said, 'They were business partners, nothing else. And he was nearing sixty, his mind harking back to the old days.' She had moved to the patio entrance. 'All that last part of his Journal is about the social life here and the old-timers round about. I don't know much about McIlroy—only that he was a much younger man and that he was brought in, from Kalgoorlie I think, to run the bank.' Her hand was holding the bead curtain back and she half turned to me so that the shape of her body was clear against the patio light, her face with the upturned nose in silhouette. 'I thought we might walk down as far as the paddock grid and meet Daddy coming back. The heat's gone off now.' She came back, smiling, and blew the candles out. 'Come on. Do you good. It's lovely at this time of the evening and I could do with some air.'

I got up and we went out into the starlight together, the air hot and dry, but the day's heat done and a breeze stirring, the buildings a black complex of substance and shadow. She didn't talk and there was nobody about as we started down the dusty track through the paddock. It was very quiet, the old moon riding low so that I could just see our shadows like twins stretched out ahead of us. She took my arm and at her touch a spark leapt between us.

I didn't dare look at her—not then, not until I had myself firmly under control. And when I did it was to see her eyes gazing up at me, the whites bright in the tanned darkness of her face, an urgent excitement in the gleam of teeth between parted lips. The spark was stronger then, electric in the dryness of the atmosphere, and I looked away, quickly, to the black hump of the Windbreaks rising high to our right. 'No dingoes tonight,' I murmured, and I wondered whether she would detect the tremor in my voice.

She didn't answer, only the pressure of her hand on my arm conveying the message of her need and my blood throbbing in response. It was the heat. Man and woman alone in the quiet cruel beauty of the land's emptiness. Christ! I thought. Don't be a bloody fool. She was just a kid and I was remembering Rosalind, how urgent she had been, her long slender body soft beneath me. I bent down, pretending to take a stone out of my shoe, and after that we walked on, the contact between us broken.

'D'you miss her?' she asked, a tenseness in her voice.

'No,' I said. But I think she knew it was a lie.

'I never told you why I came to England.' And she went on to explain that she'd come over in the hope of raising a loan—the 'wind' she called it—from the Mann-Garrety branch of the family. 'It was a waste of time and Daddy would be furious if he knew.'

'You saw Rosalind's father then?'

She nodded. 'He didn't want to know he had Australian cousins with a cattle station in the outback. Rosalind was the

59

same. I can remember that night you came back from the mine —you must have known something was wrong between us. We were like two cats with our fur up. And you were so nice to me, I could have hugged you.'

'You didn't ask me for a loan.'

'No. I sensed you had troubles of your own.' And she added, 'I'm glad you've separated. There was something about Rosalind . . .'

'You didn't like her.'

'No.' And she added almost in a whisper, 'She was a bitch. Oh, she was beautiful!—all the things I'm not and would like to be—but underneath that lovely velvet exterior . . .' She looked up at me. 'I'm sorry,' she said. 'I shouldn't talk like that. But you're too nice, too real a person.'

I didn't say anything, knowing what I'd done, the lie I was living. The sooner I got away from here . . . I was hoping to God she wouldn't take my arm again—touch me here in the hot night with the track and our shadows running away into emptiness. She had been riding for a month, fit and full of energy and no men around other than her father and the blacks. I recognized her need and it matched my own. 'You're very different from Rosalind,' I said, thinking again of the golden skin, the soft dark hair falling to the shoulders.

'Yes, I realize that.' There was a note of resignation in her voice, a touch of sadness.

It was a cruel thing to have said, but it had the desired effect. After that she talked of other things and in a little while we came to the cattle grid at the end of the paddock. We waited there for almost half an hour, watching the track, but no lights showed and she became increasingly restless. In the end she turned suddenly and started back. 'I'm going to get the ute and drive down there.'

That drive in the starlight was beautiful. And with a girl— even a stocky, snub-nosed kid like Janet—it could have been idyllic. But the spark was gone now. She was only concerned about her father and she drove with hard concentration, the tinny vehicle bumping and slithering on the loose surface. In less than half an hour we were under the shadow of Mt Robinson, with The Governor to the west of us, and looming up ahead the twin shapes of Padtherung and Coondewanna. Golden Soak was at the foot of these two, in rough hillocked country with the stony beds of dry watercourses and nothing much growing there but mallee and spinifex. We came to it over a rise, round a big outcrop of red rock, a single tall chimney sprouting from a huddle of tin roofs and a gully that ran back up into the gap between the two mountains.

That was how I saw it first, at night, with Janet beside me, taut-faced and anxious, both of us staring urgently through the fly-specked windscreen. No sign of lights, the place deserted and the corrugated iron hanging in rusted sheets. She drew up beside the main building and we got out, standing there undertain what to do. 'Perhaps he took another route back,' I suggested.

But she shook her head. 'There's only the one track.'

I was looking up at the gaunt decayed building. The roof had partly fallen in and there were gaps in the tin walls, the iron framework showing through. She had left the headlights full on and it was still possible to read the faded lettering on the board above the gaping doorway—GOLDEN SOAK MINE: OFFICE. A piece of loose corrugated iron was tap-tap-tapping in the breeze. Otherwise, there wasn't a sound. She had a torch in her hand and she shone it in through the open door—a long bench desk, a high-backed chair lying broken-legged and the walls lined with shelves full of rock specimens, everything covered in a thick layer of red dust. The floor, too, and the dust undisturbed, no footprints.

She got back into the ute and we drove right round the building and out as far as the old shearing shed. But the Land-Rover wasn't there. She started searching for tracks then, found where a vehicle had turned and headed east. 'That must be the Toyota.' She was peering down at the treadmarks.

'So they've left.'

'Looks like it.' She was standing, undecided, with her back against the door of the utility. 'We can't have missed him.'

'What about the mine?' I said. 'Where's the shafthead?'

'Up there.' She nodded towards the shadowed flanks of Coondewanna. 'Halfway up the gully. There's a tunnel driven into the mountain.'

We drove back then, past the mine buildings, picking up the rusted traces of old tramlines half-buried by dust drifts, following them up the gully till we came to a series of shallow trenches or costeans. It was here, where the outcropping quartz had first been mined, that we found the Land-Rover standing empty.

That was when I discovered she had a gun with her. She was scared and she got it out of the back of the ute. It was an old-fashioned repeater with the gleam of silver on it and the sudden click as she worked the breech was disturbingly loud in the hot stillness of the gully. We started to walk then, skirting the open mine pits, still following the old tramlines, and halfway up the quiet was shattered by the sound of somebody hammering on wood.

I don't remember climbing the rest of the way. I only remember that we were suddenly at the entrance to the mine, an arched cave-hole between two outcrops with the tramlines disappearing under a door of rough boards. The bolt with its big padlock had been forced and Ed Garrety was hammering a piece of axed timber across the entrance of the adit. The Alsatian moved towards us, a gliding shadow, her tail waving.

He jerked round, the axe gripped like a weapon. 'Who's that?' Blinded by the torch, he couldn't see us and his voice was sharp and high. The beam of the torch dropped and Janet spoke. 'Oh, it's you,' he said, his voice still strained, but a note of relief in it. And when she asked him what had happened, he said, 'Two of them. They'd forced their way in and the——' He checked himself. 'One of them was just about to lower himself down the shaft.'

'Who were they, do you know?'

But he didn't answer, standing very still, the axe gripped in his hand. 'He had a rope ladder.' His voice shook with anger. 'If the boys hadn't spotted the Toyota, he'd have been able to explore the lower levels without anybody knowing.'

'I thought the lower levels were flooded?' I said.

'Who told you that?'

'I've just been reading your father's Journal.'

'I see.' He was staring at me, and even now, when I know the cause, it's difficult to describe the expression on his face.

62

It was a shut look, the blank stare of a man on the defensive, and there was a strange intensity about him. He stayed like that for a moment, staring, and then he turned abruptly, without a word, and began hammering again with the back of the axe until the timber was wedged firmly across the adit entrance. 'I'll fix it properly in the morning.' He bent down, picked up his rifle, then turned to his daughter. 'Why did you come? I told you I didn't need any help.'

'I was worried. We walked down to the paddock gate to meet you. We waited there about half an hour and when you didn't come . . .'

'Quite unnecessary.' He slung the rifle over his shoulder and then, with a quick jerk of his head in her direction, he turned and led the way back down the tramlines to the vehicles. When he reached the Land-Rover he held the door open for me. 'You'll ride with me. Janet, you follow us in the ute.'

We were out of the shadowed confines of the gully now, starlight pale on the rocks and Janet standing there like a rebellious child, her mouth sulky and those rather prominent eyes brilliant with anger. But she didn't say anything, just turned abruptly, calling to the dog and getting into the ute. The slam of the door was loud in the stillness.

Ed Garrety backed the Land-Rover, turned and drove down to the mine buildings, swinging left and climbing to the rock outcrop and the track leading back to Jarra Jarra. He didn't speak, driving furiously and in silence. I couldn't make up my mind whether it was the mine he was worrying about or his daughter. 'You were a long time,' I said.

'We had a bit of an argument, that's all. And then they had to break camp and load up.'

'You knew them, did you?'

He didn't answer, the silence stretching uncomfortably between us. Suddenly he said, 'What are your plans?'

'How do you mean?'

'You're a mining consultant. Golden Soak's finished. It's not only worked out, it's dangerous.' He glanced at me quickly, 'There's nothing for you here.'

'In the present climate of Australia there's always the possibility of some mining company taking a gamble on it.'

'No.' His voice, hard and flat, had an undercurrent of violence.

'I could at least give you an opinion.'

'No,' he said again, his voice trembling. 'I'm not having anyone risk his life down that mine.' And he added, 'Jan should never have invited you. She knew very well how I felt about it.' He looked at me again. 'I think it would be best if you left in the morning. Jan's got work to do, and so have I.'

So it was his daughter he was worrying about. 'As you wish,' I said.

He nodded and I could see he was relieved. 'I'm sorry, but with this drought and the cattle . . . we're in no state to entertain visitors.'

He relapsed into silence then, his driving erratic and a barrier of tension between us. He didn't speak again until he nearly turned the Land-Rover over avoiding a kangaroo caught in the beam of the headlights. 'Silly buggers,' he muttered, adding, 'That's why we have roo guards on our vehicles. You get a damaged radiator in this country. . . .'

'What do they find to live on?'

'The roos? They don't need much to keep them alive. Another month without rain, when the heat really hits, and you won't see them at all. They'll be lying up in rock holes, preserving their body moisture. And when it's over they'll start to breed again.' He was more relaxed now and driving slower. 'You can have a young joey running beside its mother, still suckling, while she's got a youngster in the pouch and another embryo forming in the uterus. What's more, that embryo can go into a state of suspended growth, so that a female doesn't necessarily need to mate in order to continue the reproductive process.'

It was extraordinary, this ability he had of distracting his mind with talk. It was as though by talking he could exorcize whatever devil it was that had been tearing at his mind up there at the entrance to the mine. '*The wren goes to't, and the small gilded fly does lecher in my sight. Let copulation thrive . . .*' He smiled thinly. 'A strange play, Lear. And I can tell you this, copulation needs to thrive in this wretched land. That's if the animals are going to have any chance of survival.'

I stared at him, wondering at his fascination with Lear. Had he cast himself in the role of that sad, tragic figure? His face, limned in the glow of the headlights, seemed less tense, and there was a note of almost boyish enthusiasm in his voice as he added, 'It's a bloody marvel, the kangaroo.' He shook his head, actually smiling now. 'You'd think God had created the creature just for the sort of conditions we've got here in the Pilbara right now.'

I asked him how he knew so much about the kangaroo, and he said, 'A professor from Sydney. Zoology. He's dead now, but he was an authority on marsupials and monotremes, and a lot of his field work was done here at Jarra Jarra. That was before the war, when I was young and full of wild extravagant plans.'

One of his plans had been to fence off a big slice of land and run it as a sort of nature reserve. He gave a weary, rather cynical laugh. 'What my father never told me was that Golden Soak was bleeding the station to death.'

'Surely you must have known?'

'Mebbe I did,' he answered vaguely. 'But I was a youngster then, riding all day, fencing, putting down bores, drinking and having fun. The old man dealt with all the financial side, y'see —wouldn't even allow me into the mine office. I thought things would go on like that for ever and that one day I'd be able to put my plans into operation.' Again that tired, cynical laugh. 'It didn't work out like that, of course. My whole world suddenly fell apart—and then the war.' Reliving it in his mind, his face became clouded and his voice suddenly sad. 'Afterwards—when I got back . . . well, I was grown up then and Jarra Jarra no longer the place for dreams. We'd lost so much.'

The rattle of the wheels on the cattle grid was a reminder to both of us that we were almost back at the homestead. 'Jan can run you in to Mt Newman first thing in the morning,' he said. 'If that's all right with you.'

I didn't say anything for a moment. It was Nullagine I wanted to get to, but he couldn't be expected to know that. 'How far is it to the Highway?' I asked.

'Forty-three miles. That's to Lynn Peak. But you'd much better go to Mt Newman. You can get a plane from there. Or you could hire a car. The road's reasonable from there to Perth or Kalgoorlie, whichever you want.'

'I'll go to Lynn Peak,' I said. 'I can hitch a ride on from there.'

He drew up beside the petrol pump, and when he had switched off the engine, he turned and looked at me. 'You going to Nullagine then?'

'Probably.'

'I see.' He sat there for a moment, not saying anything. And then he nodded. 'As you wish.' He got out and stretched himself, the two of us standing there in the dust by the pump, waiting for Janet. And when she arrived he told her, curtly and without any explanation, to take me in to Lynn Peak in the morning. He turned back to me. 'I may see you before you leave, I may not.' He was staring at me, or rather, he was staring through me at something that was in his mind, and there was a bleak look in his eyes. 'Sorry we missed seeing the New Year in together.' And then he turned abruptly, a shadow moving round the side of the house, his footsteps hollow on the bare boards of the verandah.

Was this what I really wanted—this sudden dismissal? And Janet standing there, saying, 'So that's that. You're going, and you've hardly even arrived.' I could just see her eyes, the whites brilliant and the stars shining pale behind the loose halo of her hair. In that moment she looked almost beautiful. Abruptly, she turned and went into the cool house, sitting herself down at the table and staring straight in front of her. 'Can I have a cigarette please?'

I offered her the crumpled packet from my pocket. She grabbed one quickly, and as I lit it for her I saw she was on the verge of tears, the cigarette trembling in her mouth. 'You've no idea what it's meant to me—having you here.' She paused, looking away and blinking her eyes. 'For months now I seem to have had the whole place on my back. The times I've wished Henry were alive.'

And then she was looking up at me, the tears ignored: 'I suppose you thought I was tough. Well, I am. I've had to be. Just as my grandmother had to be. But underneath . . .' She shook her head, the sadness showing through, all her self-

66

confidence ebbed away. 'The fact is, I can't cope—not any longer.' She suddenly put her head down and started to sob uncontrollably.

I touched her shoulder, but that was all. 'We'd better leave about dawn,' I said.

She nodded. 'Hell of a way to start the New Year.' She smiled at me through her tears, and then suddenly she was her normal practical self again as she got quickly to her feet, her voice firmly under control. 'We'll have to take the Landy. Daddy told me our track's all right, but on the Highway the bulldust's bad all the way to Lynn Peak. Driving through bulldust's like riding on water; you need a four-wheel drive.'

I didn't see her father again that night. He'd shut himself away in his den and it was she who filled the tank of the Land-Rover and got the spare wheel for me to strap on to the bonnet. The night was very clear, the sky full of stars, and somewhere above us one the Windbreaks a dingo howled. We were standing together on the patio then, a breath of air before going to bed, and she said, 'I enjoyed that trip to England. It was a change and I met a lot of people. But this is where I belong.' And then, so quietly it was like a sigh: 'I hate the thought that we might have to leave.'

'Where would you go?' I asked her.

She shook her head. 'I don't know. I couldn't live in a city. Not after this. All my life I've had this glorious sense of freedom. I don't think I'd feel at home anywhere else. It's part of me, this place.'

The whisper of her words was still with me when I went to bed, her voice, it seemed, the voice of all the countless women who had led solitary, difficult, uncomfortable lives, pioneering the outback of Australia. And lying in her brother's bed, lumpy now with disuse, I couldn't help wondering what he had been like, whether he would have managed any better. Would he have succeeded in holding the place together if he had still been alive?

We were up at five, tea and boiled eggs, and with the dawn we drove out across the cattle grid and took the track that skirted the paddock fencing, heading north-east. It was almost cool and in the flat beyond the northern shoulder of the Windbreaks we saw camels grazing. Ahead, more hills stood black against the newly risen sun. Soon we were crawling through the dry gully courses that feed Weedi Wolli Creek, and by the damp earth of a dried-up spring, Janet seized my arm—'Look!' She was pointing. 'Did you see it? A dingo.' But I hadn't seen it and she said, breathless, 'Just a flash of cinnamon. Beaut!'

She was like a child on that drive, excited by something one minute, relapsing into moodiness the next. Mostly she drove in silence, radiating an atmosphere of constraint—not hostile, but not friendly either. And then, when the gullies ran out into open country again and the going was easier, she turned to me suddenly: 'Why are you leaving—like this?' Her voice was tense, and when I didn't reply she said, 'Is it because you thought I was throwing myself at you last night?'

I didn't know what to say and she went on awkwardly, 'You're afraid I'll do it again, is that it?'

I looked at her then and she was grinning at me. 'I might at that.' And she added, still with that impish grin on her face, 'If you're worrying about my virginity—then thanks. But I'm quite capable of looking after that myself.'

She put her foot down then and I had to hold on to the bar-grip in front of me as we drove flat out across a plain that was near-desert country, the track running out ahead of us, half-obliterated by windblown dust. Driving fast like that, I felt she also wanted to be shot of me, to end the awkwardness of our close proximity.

The sun was striking her face now, the sweat forming in beads as she fought the bucking of the Land-Rover, holding it through the dust drifts, the freckles showing and her hair limp, her eyes fixed on the track. My God, I thought, she'd make a good wife for some lout of a grazier—earthy, practical, and with the sort of boundless vitality that could stand up to the harshness of this outback country. In that moment she reminded me of the picture of her grandmother, the femininiy of her overlaid by an indomitable strength of character. And remembering the features in that oil painting, I was no longer puzzled by her inconsistencies, the way she could appear mature one minute, naïve the next, the odd mixture of old-fashioned Victorianism and down-to-earth frankness.

I was still thinking about this and the strange effect it had on me when we reached the Highway. It was a red gravel road and it hadn't had a grader over it for a long time so that it was badly ribbed. We hit the bulldust in less than a mile, the Land-Rover sliding and slithering on the fine-ground surface, bucking across the truck ruts like a boat in a lumpy sea.

It was like that most of the four miles to Lynn Peak, the turn-off to the homestead marked by a sign that read:

SHORT OF PETROL?
THIRSTY? HUNGRY?
The Andersons welcome you to Lynn Peak Homestead
⟶ ONLY 400 YARDS ⟶

It was just after seven, and as we drove down the track she said, 'Andie's a bit of a mystery. They say he jumped ship at Fremantle, but it's just a story—nobody knows really. His wife's from Port Hedland. She's half Italian. They've a couple of kids now, and when she isn't looking after them, she's dishing out pasta to the drivers who pull in here for a break. It's a funny thing . . .' She was talking quickly as though to cover our parting. 'Ten years ago you wouldn't have got any self-respecting Aussie eating pasta. Steak 'n chips and half a dozen stubbies—that was the staple diet for the roustabouts and jackaroos, all the odds and sods who bummed their way through the North West. Now you'd think they were half Italian themselves the way they roll in here. Pasta—they love it!' She suddenly laughed. 'Mebbe it's Maria they love.'

We were swinging into the yard then and she blew the horn as she braked to a stop beside the house. It was a poor place, built almost entirely of tin with a flyscreened verandah and chickens scuffing in the dust beside the petrol pump. A small, energetic man appeared, about forty with a baldish head, and she introduced me. She didn't get out. She just stayed there behind the wheel talking to him till I had got my suitcase out of the back. 'I hope you find whatever it is you're looking for.' She said it brightly, a quick smile and that was all. She didn't stop to say goodbye; just waved her hand, her face set in that bright artificial smile as she turned the Land-Rover and went roaring off in a cloud of dust.

I stood and watched the dust settle behind her, sorry to see her go. I felt suddenly alone, knowing I'd lost the only person who cared a damn what happened to me.

'So you're wanting a ride up to Nullagine?'

I turned to find Andie staring at me curiously, his eyes crinkled against the sun's glare.

'What are the chances?' I asked him.

'Och, somebody'll be through. In time. It's early yet.' He turned towards the house. 'Janet said to feed you, so come on in and we can breakfast together.'

THREE

Golden Soak

I

I WAS LUCKY. The first vehicle into Lynn Peak that morning
was a Holden driven by a lone prospector from Leonora. He
had driven through the night, heading for the Comet Mine at
Marble Bar, and he was only too glad to give me a lift provided
I took the wheel and let him get some sleep. He was a lean,
taciturn man, dressed in khaki trousers and a white shirt
turned ochre by the dust, his eyes red-rimmed below the
peaked cap and his thin face grey with stubble. He was fast
asleep before I had driven half a dozen miles.

We were heading north, the sun behind us and flat-topped
hills of red rock moving in from the right. Even if he'd been
awake conversation would have been impossible The car was
an old one and the noise of its rattling, the machine-gun clatter
of wheelspun gravel, was incessant. It isolated me, and once I
got the feel of riding the dirt at speed, I began to think over
what Andie had told me about the two men in the Toyota.
Both of them were from Nullagine. Phil Westrop was a new-
comer who'd been driving a bulldozer at the Grafton Downs
Tin Mine for a couple of months. The other was a black by the
name of Wolli. And he had spelt it out for me in that thick
Glaswegian accent of his, explaining that the man was supposed to have been born at Jarra Jarra, in the black quarters
there, and named after Weedi Wolli Creek. 'He's a drunk. But
he wasna drunk when they pulled in here for petrol yesterday
morning. The shakes, yes, but he was just plain scared in my
opeenion.'

Was this the black man Kadek had referred to in his letter
as Wally? I was wondering about that when I hit a dry creek
bed, my head bumping the roof. And why was Westrop so
interested in Golden Soak? Stopping for petrol at Lynn Peak,
when he could have filled up before leaving Nullagine, was just

an excuse to pump Andie for information about the mine. 'Ah dinna ken much aboot him, just met him a few times over a drink at the Conglomerate. An ex-army sergeant invalided out after being blown up by a Viet-Cong mine.' The harsh voice had gone rambling on as I ploughed my way through a plateful of bacon and eggs for which he had charged me an exorbitant two dollars fifty. Six years in Australia hadn't softened the accent. 'There's some say it was a bomb planted in a brothel in Saigon. but they wouldna say that to his face. He's tough, that laddie.'

I was still thinking about Westrop when I ran into my first stretch of bulldust and almost lost control, no feel to the steering, the back tyres spinning and the car lurching wildly. Ahead, round the red shoulder of a hill, loomed a cloud of dust like an explosion, and in the straight beyond, the dust cloud hung in the sky for more than a mile, a glint of glass reflected at its snout. It was the first of the day's traffic, a big refrigerated container truck throwing gravel at me as it thundered past. And then I was into the red cloud that followed in its wake, a sepia opaqueness of nil visibility with dust pouring into the car, filling my mouth, clogging my nostrils.

'Wind the window up for chrissakes!' And by the time I'd done that he was fast asleep again.

The dust cleared and we were into country that was like a miniature Arizona, all small red buttes and dry as a desert. I was driving fast on gravel again and wondering how Westrop had known about me. According to Andie, he'd not only known my name, but what I did. And he had asked a lot of questions: Why had a mining consultant been called in? Was Golden Soak for sale and had I inspected it yet? Had anybody been down there since the disaster? 'What he was after I have no idea, but he was after something, that's for sure, and I told Ed to watch it when he came in for the stores yesterday. He'd never heard of Westrop. Wolli he'd known all his life, of course.'

And yet, when Janet had asked her father who the men were, he hadn't answered her. I was remembering the look on his face as he'd stood there at the entrance to the adit, the axe gripped in his hands. Another truck thundered by, stones clattering on the windscreen and dust seeping in even though I'd closed the window. Christ! it was hot. I'd left the red butte country now, and after I'd crossed the dry bed of the Shaw River, I was into a world of small hills like tumuli, the road dipping and rising endlessly, the rattle of the Holden on the ridged surface permeating my whole body.

To hell with Ed Garrety, I thought. Jarra Jarra was behind me now and no concern of mine. The road stretching ahead led to Nullagine and the prospect of something that might be more rewarding. But thinking of McIlroy, dreaming of his Monster in the heat, my mind came back inevitably to Golden Soak and what Andie had told me of the disaster that had happened there in 1939. I had been questioning him about the disappearance of Big Bill Garrety's partner, but all he had been able to tell me was what I already knew, that the closing of the bank's doors had coincided with the collapse of a speculative boom in West Australian mining shares and that McIlroy was supposed to have been speculating with money deposited by the bank's customers. It was all hearsay, of course, and the people who really knew about it were the people who'd got their fingers burnt, and they weren't the ones to gossip. But he was sure about the disaster. Big Bill Garrety had hired a bunch of out-of-work miners to drive a cross-cut into a badly faulted area of high grade ore. 'No doot the man was desperate, but it was plain bluidy murder from what they tell me.' Several men had been killed, a lot more injured. 'I dinna ken how many.' And he didn't know whether the mine had been flooded then or later. But he was quite certain that the disaster had happened after the crash. 'Sure it had been closed, but when a man's that desperate for money——' He had shrugged. 'Ed's a fool not to sell. I told him so. That mine's got a jinx on it.'

I was trying to remember what exactly the Journal had said about the cave-in, but the sweat was caking salt on my forehead, the glare blinding and I found it difficult to concentrate, heat exhaustion building up and the rush of air through the open window oven-hot. Everywhere along that road there were anthills so big they looked like primitive adobe dwellings. And the hills throbbing in the heat, my eyes tired. Soon all I could think of was the dryness in my mouth, my need of a cold beer. And then at last we were on tarmac, coming down into Nullagine, and my companion woke.

It wasn't much of a place, a huddle of houses roasting on the slope of a hill and the verandahed hotel at the corner where the road turned to the right. I stopped by the petrol pump. 'Can I offer you a drink?' I asked him as I got stiffly out. But he shook his head, rubbing his eyes and stretching. 'No, I got to get on.' He moved over into the driving seat, watched me till I'd got my case out of the boot, and then, with a nod and a slight lift of the hand, he drove on.

I went into the bar and it was comfortingly dark after the glare outside. I hesitated a moment, accustoming my eyes to the change of light. There were only three men there, two locals and an aborigine. They turned their heads to stare at me, their movements economical of effort and no words spoken. A youngster appeared behind the bar counter that ran the length of the room. He was fair-haired and had an English accent. I ordered a beer and drank it fast, feeling dehydrated, dirty, sweaty. 'Anywhere I can get a wash?' I asked him.

'The wash-house is across the road.'

I turned and saw a small building like a dilapidated public lavatory beyond the sun-glare of the tarmac. I ordered another beer and drank it slowly, brushing away the flies and taking stock of the aborigine. He wore a blue shirt and blue jeans and his wide-nostrilled features were black as jet under the broad-brimmed hat. 'Your name Wolli, by any chance?' I asked him.

He stared at me, the whites of his eyes yellow, the pupils dark brown, his face expressionless.

'Yuh give him a beer, mate, an' he'll talk,' one of the locals said, a small man with a ferrety face and narrow eyes. 'But his name ain't Wolli. It's Macpherson. That right innit?'

'Arrhh.' The big lips spread in a tentative grin.

'You know where Wolli is, Mac?'

The black shook his head vaguely, his eyes on me, hopeful of that beer.

'Yuh want Wolli,' the little man said to me, 'yuh better ask Prophecy. She's in there playing cards.' He nodded to the open hatch at the end of the bar. 'She got nothing to do all day now but play cards an' get drunk.'

74

Through the hatch I could see there was a sort of saloon bar with rickety tables and a dart board. The drivers of the two trucks I'd seen parked at the side of the hotel were sitting there, wolfing down steak and chips, and at another table was a big gipsy-looking woman with greying hair and a hard, tough, lively face lined with wrinkles. She was alone, drinking whisky and playing patience, a cigarette dangling from her lips.

'If a fly craps, Prophecy knows about it. She knows everything goes on here.' The little man leaned towards the hatch. 'Don't yuh, Prophecy?'

'Yuh shut yer bleedin' face, Alfie.' She moved a card, slowly and with deliberation, without looking up. After that there was silence as though the expenditure of that amount of energy was enough for the day.

I finished my beer and went across the road to the wash-house. The men's section had a wash-basin, lavatory and shower. Flies crawled on the bare concrete. But it was quite clean, and though the water from the tank on the roof was almost too hot to stand under, I felt a lot fresher when I returned to the hotel. The woman called Prophecy was still sitting with the cards laid out and the whisky beside her. 'Mind if I join you?' I asked.

'Please yerself.' The beady eyes in the sun-wrinkled face watched me curiously as I pulled up a chair and sat down facing her. 'Fresh out from the Old Country arntyuh?' And when I nodded, she said, 'Thought so. And you're looking for Wolli—yuh a mining man?'

'Yes.'

She turned up a red ten, placed it slowly on the jack of spades and moved across four cards headed by the nine of clubs. 'Yuh brought me luck that time. Yuh reckon you're a lucky man?'

'I hadn't noticed it,' I said.

She looked at me sharply. 'Golden Soak never had no luck—not since I come to live in this dump.' I stared at her and she gave her cackling laugh. 'Yuh like me to tell your fortune?' The cackling ended in a smoker's cough. 'No, yuh wouldn't, would yuh? They don't call me Prophecy for nuthin'. I might be too right, eh?' Her eyes watched me, sharp as a bird's. 'Yuh don't want Wolli. Wolli's a bum. It's that gin sister of his you want. She got second sight where gold's concerned.' And then she was telling me how this aborigine girl had found gold on a claim she'd pegged over towards Bamboo Springs. 'Set me up for life, she did. Better'n a dowser any day. Yuh go and see Little Brighteyes. Yuh won't get any sense out of Wolli.'

Talking to Prophecy was like panning for gold in the muddy water of a creek in spate. Her real name was Felicity Clark. She had been born in Leytonstone, north-east London, and had come out to Australia with her husband in 1946. He had been badly shot up in the battle for the Falaise Gap and doctors advised him to move to a drier climate. 'So we picked on the Bar and Christ that was dry enough. The air was so thin Nobby couldn't hardly breathe in the dry with half his lung shot away.' He had died five years ago leaving her with a Land-Rover and a caravan and not much else. 'A fella don't make his fortune working on the roads, an' all the dust—it's a wonder he lasted as long as he did.'

From Marble Bar they had moved to Nullagine and when he wasn't driving his grader he had spent his time fossicking around old prospects. 'Always reckoned he'd strike it lucky one day. Might've done, too, if he'd lived. Knew a lot Nobby did, and when he kicked the bucket I just sort of carried on, living bush and pegging the odd claim.' She had a small pension and when Wolli had got into trouble, stealing tools from a mining outfit up near Bonnie Creek, she had taken his sister Martha to live with her in the caravan. 'Reck'n it was the best thing I ever done. She knew things about this country I'd never've nutted out for myself—'bout plants an' animals an' how to live bush. Never knew a girl with such sharp eyes, and then by Jesus if she doesn't spot the glitter on a claim of mine. I'd never've seen it meself, not in a million years. But she spotted it. That's when I began calling her Little Brighteyes. Wouldn't take any money, not a penny, but she's got a bangle I bet no other gin's got from Darwin right down to Esperance.'

All this was mixed up with a spate of gossip about local people and their affairs. She forgot about the cards. She even forgot about her drink. I was somebody new to whom she could tell her story all over again. And I was fresh out from

England. I think that was important to her. She wasn't home-sick. She had been out here too long. But there was an under-current of nostalgia. And I sat there and let her words wash over me, remembering what I thought was relevant as I drank another beer and had some food. Then, when I had finished my steak and chips, she said, 'Okay, we'll go and see if Little Brighteyes is home. She's shacked up with a man from Grafton Downs, so weekdays she don't know what to do with herself.' And she added, 'Martha can tell you a thing or two about Golden Soak. But she won't go near the place, not her—not even for Wolli.'

'How did you know I was interested in Golden Soak?' I asked her.

She had got to her feet and she stood looking down at me, a big, tough woman, her eyes bright as beads. 'Emilio was delivering stuff here coupla days back. Wasn't it you that wired Ed Garrety's girl to meet you?' She was smiling, the creases in her dark face deepening. 'There ain't much to talk about here in Nullagine, an' yuh being a mining man—bush telegraph you might say. Well, yuh gonna sit on your arse there all day?' And she turned and strode out into the sunlight, moving with a gipsy swing to her skirt and light on her feet despite her bulk.

Looking back on it, I am reminded of Big Bill Garrety's postscript to the discovery of Golden Soak—*the beginning of all my troubles*. That day was the beginning of my troubles, and it was the gipsy woman Prophecy who was the cause of it. Whether she had the gift of second sight or not I don't know, but she was like a witch, and within twenty-four hours, riding the broomstick of her curiosity, I had become so caught up in the past of Jarra Jarra that nothing else has seemed to matter very much since then.

'Your name's Alec Falls, right?'

I nodded, the sun beating down on my bare head, the dry air breathless.

'Then we'll go to the post office first.' She turned to the left, towards the petrol pump which was backed by a general store. 'There's a telegram for you. Don't reckon it'll have gone out yet.'

The telegram was from Kadek and had been despatched from Kalgoorlie: NEED YOUR ADVICE MINING DEAL. FEE AND EXPENSES BUT ESSENTIAL YOU ARRIVE HERE MONDAY MORNING. CONTACT CHRIS CULPIN PALACE BAR. I stood there for a moment, considering it. 'Well?' Prophecy asked. 'You heading straight for Kalgoorlie, or you wanta see Wolli's sister first?'

It was now Thursday. 'I'll hitch a ride in the morning,' I said. 'But it's Wolli I want to see.'

She nodded and crossed the road to a track that led up behind the wash-house. We found the black woman stretched out on a bed on the verandah of a dilapidated corrugated iron house halfway up the hill. She was small and bony, jet black, with strong hands and very thin wrists, and breasts that sagged under the bright cotton shift that was all she seemed to be wearing. In repose her face was ugly, the nose broad over a wide, big-lipped mouth, the brow so low that she looked as though she had been dropped on her head as a child. She got up from her chair on the verandah, a broad smile of welcome, and with the smile her whole face seemed to light up, the quickness of her movements suggesting extraordinary vitality, her whole body instantly and intensely alive. And those big dark eyes of hers bright with pleasure.

She gave us beer, cold from the icebox, and Prophecy talked to her in her own tongue, which was deep from the throat. Abruptly the happiness vanished from her face and her eyes became wary as she stole furtive glances in my direction. The conversation between the two of them went on for a long time. In the end Prophecy turned to me and said, 'You know she was born at Jarra Jarra? Wolli, too. They were both of them born there and worked on the station. Wolli left, of course, but she stayed on.' She paused—as though that had some special significance. 'Ed's wife had gone by then, see.'

'Gone?'

'Nobody told you?' Her quick brown eyes gleamed. 'No, 'course not. Ed wouldn't want to be reminded of that. He married just after the war began—had to, they say—and then, when he came home on embarkation leave, there was this feller from the Ivanhoe station. He took a stock whip to him and rode him off the place. Should have larruped her instead, if you ask me.'

'When was Janet born then?'

'After the war. After Ed came back. Big Bill Garrety was still alive, see, and she was scared of him by all accounts. But then this fella Harrison turns up again—caught a packet in Normandy 'bout the same time Nobby got his—and now they're living down in Perth and Ed's never been quite the same since.'

So Janet had hardly known her mother and, since Henry's death, she and her father had been on their own. I looked at the black woman, seeing the nervous flicker of her eyes. It wasn't easy to guess her age, but I thought she was still only in her middle thirties. 'What's her brother do for a living?' I asked.

'Nuthin'. I told you, Wolli's a bum.'

'What's he do for money, then?'

'That's a question, that is.' She looked at the black woman. 'Yuh gonner tell Mr Falls what Wolli does for money?'

The eyes rolled in the black face. 'No get'im money now. All finished.'

Prophecy looked at me over her beer. 'Ed pensioned him off. But they're so broke down at Jarra Jarra now that the source has dried up.' She was smiling, enjoying the sight of me working it out. It all added up and I was thinking of the terrible loneliness of a man in the outback with his wife gone, the problem he'd had to face with a young daughter growing up. It never occurred to me that the gipsy woman had got hold of the wrong end of the stick, which was a pity, because if I'd asked the right questions there on that verandah, I might have come at the truth. But probably not. Blackmail isn't something you admit to a stranger and the woman knew enough about the white man's laws to keep her mouth shut. Instead I let it go at that, asking her about her father and whether it was true he'd been with McIlroy on that expedition into the interior.

'Me no remember,' And when I pressed her, she laughed. 'Me liddle small girl, only baby.'

'She wouldn't have been more than four or five then,' Prophecy said.

'But she must have heard if her father was with McIlroy.'

'I thought it was Golden Soak you were interested in.' She was staring at me curiously.

'Well, that too,' I said. 'Does she know anything about the mine—anything I don't know already?'

'Her father worked there.'

'As a miner?'

She nodded.

'Ask her about the cave-in. Does she know when it happened?'

She knew all the details, but not the date. 'Long time now. Me liddle girl.' Five men had lost their lives—three whites and two blacks. Seven others had been injured. It had occurred late in the afternoon, during the wet after heavy rains. They were in a drift at the bad end of the mine, men still clearing fallen rock from the morning's blasting and a team drilling into the face, which was badly faulted and running with water. Suddenly the flow of water had increased. Rock had begun to fall from the roof, and then the whole face had crumbled, water pouring out in a great flood and the miners running before it down the drift to the main gallery and the shaft. Her father had been one of the first up the ladders.

All this Prophecy got out of her in her own tongue. The mine had been closed again after that and it had remained closed ever since. 'And what happened to her father?'

'He was given a job on the station.'

'And the other miners—were they given jobs, too?'

But the woman either didn't know or wouldn't say.

'Ask her when it was her father joined up with McIlroy.' That nervous flicker of her eyes again. She shook her head. 'He was with McIlroy, wasn't he?' But she shied away from that, offering us more beer, turning quickly to the big fridge standing pale in the cavern of the bedroom. 'When did he die? He is dead, isn't he?'

'Yes, he's dead,' Prophecy said. 'Died about two years after Nobby and I came here. But he never talked, not about McIlroy.'

The black woman had come back and I turned and faced her. 'Your brother was at the mine last night. What was he looking for?'

She shook her head, her whole body suddenly very tense as though poised for flight.

'Was he looking for gold?'

Again that slight shake of the head. 'Him no find. Not stop there find'im gold.'

'Are you sure it was gold they were looking for?'

God! I was so near to it then, her eyes rolling and that deep husky voice of her saying. 'Wolli not know nuthin'. You talk'im Phil. Mebbe Phil tell'im. Not Wolli.'

Prophecy cackled. 'Yuh want me to translate for yuh? Wot she's saying is Wolli'd beat the hell out of her if she gave you info for free. Yuh go an' see Wolli. Cross his palm with a few dollars an' mebbe yuh find out whatever it is yuh're after.'

But I was looking at the black woman. 'Who's Phil?' I asked her.

She shook her head, the eyes wide and scared-looking.

'It's a white man, isn't it—name of Westrop?' The eyes told me I was right and I turned to Prophecy. 'Do you know Phil Westrop?'

She nodded.

'Where will I find him?'

'Grafton Downs.'

'How far's that?'

''Bout twenty miles.' And she added, 'Odds are he'll be in the bar tonight. The Grafton Downs boys are in for a beer most nights. Why?'

'He and Wolli were down at the mine last night.' I hesitated, looking at the black woman. But she had turned back to the fridge. I looked across at Prophecy. 'You know everything that goes on here. Where was Wolli's father when McIlroy died? Was he with him out there in the desert?'

'I don't know. Nobody knows.' She was frowning. 'Yuh're not interested in Golden Soak, are yuh? It's McIlroy's Monster that's brought yuh here.' There was a harder note in her voice. 'Well, why didn't you say so in the first place? Ed's a good bloke. As good as they come, even if he is a bit of a solitary. And that girl of his, Janet, she's had a poor go of it one way and another. I thought you was having a dekko at that mine of his with a view to finding him a buyer.' She heaved her bulk out of the canvas chair. 'For that I was going to try and persuade Little Brighteyes to go along with yuh. But the Monster——' She shook her head. 'That's a load of horseshit. If yuh believe that. . . . Well, I got other things to do.' And she stepped down into the dust, calling to Brighteyes her thanks for the beer as she headed back to the Conglomerate.

The black woman had come out of the bedroom, a can of beer in her hand. We were alone together on the verandah. 'Where's your brother?' I asked her.

She stared at me, her eyes wide so that I thought for a moment she hadn't understood. Then her thick lips moved. 'Wolli?'

'Yes. Where is he?'

She didn't answer, but her eyes moved, evasive, uneasy. I pushed past her into the bedroom. He was sprawled on the big double bed, a thin spider of a man in ragged khaki shorts, his big horny feet with their splayed toes bare. He didn't move, only his eyes, wide in the heavy black face, staring at me. 'I've come a long way to see you,' I said.

He didn't say anything.

'You speak English?'

'Liddle bit.' His voice was thick and slow. There was a can of beer beside him, but he wasn't drunk. His eyes were alert, the whites showing in the shaded gloom of the room. The brow ridges were very marked, the face heavier and coarser than his sister's, only the faintest similarity in the features.

'You were at the Golden Soak mine last night—why?'

He shook his head, but it was an evasion of the directness of my gaze rather than a denial.

'What reason had you for breaking into the mine?' I spoke slowly and distinctly, his sister hovering in the background.

'Go longa Phil.'

'Why?'

Again the evasive shake of the head, the face impassive, the eyes shifty and his big hands hitching nervously at his shorts. 'You speak'im Phil.'

'All right, I will. But I'm speaking to you now. You told a prospector from Kalgoorlie your father was with McIlroy when he died.'

He grunted and swung his legs off the bed, coming to his feet in one easy controlled movement. 'Who you?' And when I told him I was a mining consultant from England, he repeated, 'You speak'im Phil.'

And that's all I could get out of him. He admitted his father had been with McIlroy at the end, but where they had been, what they had found or what McIlroy had told him before he died—to all these questions he just shook his head. It wasn't that he was stupid or that he didn't understand. He understood all right. At one point he turned to his sister and the two of them went at it so fast they were speaking on the intake of their breathing as well as the exhalation, both of them talking together, a guttural rolling sound. And when finally he turned to me and said, 'Bad spirits all longa that mine,' I thought he was referring to the miners who had been trapped there in the cave-in.

He was scared, but whether it was really the ghosts of dead miners he was scared of or something else I couldn't be sure. I didn't know enough about the aborigine mind, and when he repeated yet again—'You speak'im Phil,' I thought it was more likely Westrop he was scared of. I was wrong there, of course. Westrop was tough, but he was a decent enough man at heart —just an ordinary, hard-drinking, hard-driving, mind-your-own-bloody-business Australian.

He came into the bar that night in a singlet and shorts, a pair of flip-flop sandals on his feet, limping slightly, but with a swagger, his lean body very erect and reminding me vaguely of something, some picture perhaps. He was a very striking man, handsome even in a hard-bitten way. Prophecy wasn't there. It was the English boy behind the bar who tipped me the wink when the truck drove up, half a dozen of the Grafton Downs men piling out of it and moving in on the bar with the determination of men for whom beer is the one solace in a world of torrid heat and dust.

I was having a drink with the Shire Clerk and the man who now drove the grader on the Nullagine section of the Highway. The Clerk, a baldish man in a clean blue shirt who had come originally from Wittenoom, had given me a whole list of contacts, older men who might have known McIlroy back in '38.

Most of them were on outback stations and quite inaccessible to me without my own transport. 'Why don't you go down to Port Hedland then and see the Administrator?' But Port Hedland was almost 200 miles away.

I waited till Westrop had downed his first beer, watching him and trying to work out in my mind how I was going to handle it. He looked as tough as Andie had suggested, lean and fit, with a dour face and sandy hair bleached pale by the sun. I saw the English boy lean across the bar to speak to him and then he was looking directly at me, his eyes narrowed, his mouth a hard line below the beaked nose. One of his mates flipped a coin and he did the same, laughing without humour when he found himself odd man out. He went to the hatch to order another round, his left leg almost stiff as though the knee joint was locked. The Clerk's hand was on my arm, some story about a station owner who'd corralled a bunch of pogies belonging to a man called Stansted. It was a long, involved story and I had to bend close to hear what he was saying. There was a good deal of noise in the room, about twenty people there, some of them women, their faces sweating in the harsh glare of the naked light bulbs. 'What are pogies?' I asked.

'Calves that haven't been branded.' His voice was high against the hubbub. 'Yuh keep'em starved of water for a few days an' when yuh do give 'em a drink they're so bloody grateful they stay put. Well, this fellow Stansted, he doesn't bother with his own bunch, just goes in an' rustles twice as many——'

'Yuh Alec Falls?'

I looked round to find Westrop standing at my elbow.

'Kid behind the bar there says yuh want to speak to me.'

'Yes,' I said, and we moved away, each of us trying to size the other up. 'You were at Golden Soak last night.'

'What's that to do with yuh?'

'I was staying with the Garretys at Jarra Jarra.'

He didn't say anything, standing there with his beer in his hand, the sandy stubble on his chin glistening with sweat.

'That mine's been closed for years.'

'Okay, it's been closed for years. So what's it to do with yuh?'

'I saw Wolli this afternoon.'

His eyes narrowed. 'What did Wolli tell yuh?'

'Nothing. Only that I'd better speak with you.'

'About what?'

'Your reason for going there.'

'Did Ed Garrety send you?'

'Not exactly. I'm naturally interested——'

'So you think I know something about that mine Garrety
don't?' He gave a quick laugh, and with that laugh I was
conscious of tension in him. 'Well, mebbe I do, but I'm not
telling a goddammed Pommie.' He took a gulp at his beer and
wiped his mouth with the back of his hand. 'Yuh go back to
Jarra Jarra and tell the old bugger next time I come I'll be
armed, an' if he pulls a gun on me again. . . . Christ! I wasn't
ten years in the Army for nothing. Yuh tell him that.'

'He owns the mine,' I said. 'You were trespassing and he'd
every right . . .'

'Okay, he owns it. But it won't be long now and I can wait.'

'What do you mean?'

'They're broke, aren't they? That's what they tell me here,
that it won't be long before the mine, the station, the whole lot
will be up for sale.' His eyes narrowed. 'Is that why yuh're here
—to value the mine for them?' He leaned forward and gripped
my arm. 'Yuh bin down there?'

I shook my head and he seemed relieved. 'I'm not interested
in gold,' I said.

'Then what are you interested in?'

'Copper.'

He looked at me as though he'd never heard of the stuff.
'There's no copper at Golden Soak.' He said it quietly, a thin
smile and his eyes cold. 'What the hell are yuh after?'

And when I told him it was the location of McIlroy's
Monster that had brought me to Nullagine, he burst out
laughing. 'Yuh must be joking.' He turned to his mates. 'Here,
fellers. Here's a chap says he's come all the way out from the
Old Country to find McIlroy's Monster.' They crowded round
me, laughing, joking, asking questions, too happy in their
drink to play it any way but the way he wanted it. 'Yuh believe
that one, yuh'll believe anything.'

'That's Wolli's story. . . . Yep, trots it out pat soon as he's short of the ready . . .' And then an older man with no teeth and the face of a dried-up mummy: 'Funny thing though, finding his truck like that, the rad empty, with no body, not even his skeleton.'

'Well, wot d'yuh expect, out there between the Great Sandy and the Gibson?'

'That's right—it'd be covered by sand in no time.'

'It's gibber country.'

'No, it ain't. It's sand—like it is all the way to the Alice.'

'It's gibber, I tell yuh. All red gravel.'

'How d'yuh know? Yuh ain't never been there.'

'It's wot they say.'

'Who says—Wolli I s'pose?'

'No, his father.'

'Yuh weren't around here when Wolli's father was alive.'

'It's wot I heard,' the fellow added lamely and they all laughed.

'Funny thing,' the little mummy-faced man said again, 'but Wolli's father never talked about it—never mentioned the Monster once as far as I know.'

'Why should he, Lenny? I tell yuh, it's just a load of crap dreamed up by that black bastard to get himself a few beers.'

But the little man shook his head. 'Oh no, it weren't. I was in Kalgoorlie at the time an' it was all in *The Miner*, 'bout how McIlroy heard of this mountain of copper from some abo who'd walked into the bank at Port Hedland asking for a loan in return for the location. McIlroy was a gambler, everybody knows that. Now wot was the feller's name?' He scratched his bullet head. 'Buggered if I can remember it now. But he got his loan and when the bank went bust on the de Bernales shares . . . I remember now. Warrampi. That was the abo's name. Well, then Pat McIlroy took off into the blue—his last big gamble—an' that didn't come off either. I remember the pitchers in the papers, too—one of him leaving Port Hedland. Another as he drove through Marble Bar an' him standing in the back of his truck making speeches. Yuh'd've thought they'd've stoned him for losing their money like that. Instead, they lined the streets and cheered him.'

'Yuh're joking,' a voice said, and Lenny laughed and shook his head. 'I ain't, yuh know. I can see the pitchers now. He was a small man, neatly dressed, and he stood there in the back of the truck an' he didn't call it a mountain of copper—he called it his Monster. That's wot got him the headlines—McIlroy's Monster.'

'He must've had the gift of the gab.'

'Sure he did. He was Irish.'

Somebody had bought another round and I found myself with a full glass in my hand again. 'Did you ever meet McIlroy?' I asked. 'I was told he came from Kalgoorlie.'

But Lenny shook his head. 'I was just a kid at the time. My father knew him 'cos he worked at the Great Boulder. I remember him saying he always reckoned McIlroy would come to a sticky end—either that or he'd finish up a millionaire. A clerk, I think, he said, but a boss's man with a tongue that could turn iron pyrites into gold. Come to think of it, I did see him once—it was up at the mine and my Dad pointed him out to me getting into a flash English car. There's a man, he said, makes more money in a day playing the market than I make working my guts out underground in a whole year. But it was the car I was interested in—an M.G. sports it was, all white with a long bonnet and big headlights. Bloody silly, a car like that in Kal, but no doubt it served its purpose. He was a show-off and clever as a monkey'.

I had a picture now of the sort of man McIlroy was, but nothing about the copper deposit that had sent him to his death. All Lenny could tell me was what he'd read in the *Kalgoorlie Miner*, and that was pretty vague, for he was only twelve years old at the time. 'It was the abos found the truck. They'd been walkabout—some corroboree—and by the time the police got wind of it the tracks were all obliterated. Nothing to show where he'd been or whether he'd found his Monster.'

I asked him if there'd been anything in the papers about McIlroy having an aborigine with him on the expedition, but he didn't know. 'All I remember for sure is that the truck's back axle was broken, and that's only because I was getting interested in cars then. I don't recall anything about an abo.'

'Then what's Wolli talking about?'

'Look,' he said, 'yuh're new out here, ain't yuh, same as Phil. Well, put yourself in Wolli's place, half Australia fossicking around for minerals and this old story every bit as good as Lasseter's Reef. It's worth a few beers every time a stranger comes into the bar here and that's all he cares. He's short of money and he likes his booze, see. Nothing else to it. That's what I keep telling Phil—but there you are——' He shrugged and downed the rest of his beer.

I looked round for Westrop, but he was no longer beside me, and when I went to the hatch to order another round, I saw him in the main bar with Wolli.

Drinking there with the Grafton Downs boys, I was able to confirm what Andie had told me, that Westrop had only been at the tin mine a matter of two months and he'd come down from Darwin, straight out of hospital after his discharge, looking for a job. He knew nothing about mining, but he'd been a sapper and he could drive bulldozers. 'It's open cast mining, see.'

A soldier, straight out of Vietnam with no knowledge of mining; it seemed odd that he should be so interested in Wolli. And that night visit to Golden Soak. 'Are you sure he wasn't a prospector before he joined the Army?'

'I tell yer, he don't know a dam' thing about mining.'

'But he's got books. He's learning.'

'Yuh don't learn about mining from books.'

'But you can learn how to recognize a mountain of copper when you see one,' I said.

'McIlroy's Monster!'

They were all laughing, their faces glistening in the lights. Somebody thrust another can of beer into my hand.

'When did he become interested in McIlroy?' I asked.

They didn't know. It was just a joke to them. And then Lenny said quietly, 'Funny thing, yuh asking that. He was interested in McIlroy right from the word go. Come to think of it, he knew about Wolli, too.'

'And he came here immediately he was discharged?'

'Yep.' The brown eyes in the mummified face were suddenly full of curiosity. 'Straight out of hospital.'

88

'Where's he from originally, d'you know?'

'Sydney, so he says. Got his family there.'

'He's married then?'

'Wife an' two kids.' The brown eyes staring at me and both of us thinking the same thing. 'Says he's come to work here so as he can grab himself enough to buy a house and a small business.' But I could see Lenny didn't believe that, any more than I did. 'He's a rum'un, Phil is.'

'D'you believe this story of Wolli's?' I asked him.

"Bout his father being with McIlroy?' He shook his head. 'I dunno. Makes sense to take an abo along if you're headed out beyond Disappointment. It's all desert there, or as near as makes no odds.'

'And what about Golden Soak?' I asked. 'Did you know he and Wolli broke into the mine last night?'

'He was off sick yesterday. How would he get down to the Garrety place?'

'He was driving a Toyota.'

'The only person owns a Toyota around here is Prophecy.' He glanced quickly round the room, then shook his head. 'Bloody fool!' he muttered. 'That mine's dangerous.'

'What was he after?'

He gave me a toothless grin. 'What's any bloke after having a look at a derelict mine?'

'Has he got enough money to buy it?'

"Course not. All he's got is his pension and whatever they give 'im for his leg when he got his discharge. Even a dud mine like Golden Soak's worth more'n that these days.'

'Then what was he doing there?'

A hand gripped me by the shoulder and I spun round to find Westrop there, the sweat damp on his face and his eyes blazing. 'Yuh want to ask questions about me, ask them to my face. Got it?' He'd had a lot of beer by then. So had I. We all had.

'All right,' I said. 'What was it you were looking for last night?'

'Yuh really wanter know?' His voice was loud and truculent. 'I was looking for McIlroy.' He laughed and the others laughed with him. But facing him as I was, I knew he wasn't being funny. He was deadly serious. 'Yuh go back to your pal Garrety—tell 'im wot I said. He'll laugh.' His face was close to mine, his eyes reflecting an emotion I didn't understand and his body trembling so that I could feel it through the hand still gripping my shoulder. 'He'll laugh himself sick.' The pressure of his hand increased and suddenly he was shaking me. 'Yuh go back there and tell'im. See wot he says.' And then he was shouting at me, 'Yuh Pommies—yuh've got a nerve, yuh bastards have. Yuh don't give a bugger for this country, but soon as we start striking it rich, then yuh're out here like a swarm of locusts.' His fist was bunched, the sweat on his face shining, and I stood there, waiting, feeling isolated. And then suddenly his mood changed and he let go of me. 'Yuh mind your business, I'll mind mine.' He was relaxed now, smiling and clapping me on the shoulder, and then he turned and ordered another round.

They left shortly afterwards, and I went with them, glad of the chance of a lift to Lynn Peak. They were going there for a meal. At least that's what they said, and I was sucker enough to believe them, anxious now to be on my way to Kalgoorlie.

2

There were no trees where they dumped me, just the dark out-line of low hills and stars brilliant in the still, arid air. There was a big anthill close by—magnetic ants, the pointed side facing north. I sat down with my back against it, still hearing their drunken laughter as they dropped me over the side on to the edge of the Highway and Westrop saying, 'Just keep going south an' you'll arrive at Kalgoorlie an' don't let me set eyes on yuh again.' Somebody—Lenny, I think—had had the decency to dump my suitcase on the gravel beside me, and then the Chev roared off up the side track to Grafton Downs, the red tail lights and their laughter fading in the distance until they were lost behind the dark shoulder of a hill and I was alone with only the silence of the night for company.

I closed my eyes, a little sobered now, but still feeling sore at being made to look such a fool, cursing all Australians for their crude sense of humour. And thinking about it there in the stillness, remembering the violence in Westrop's voice, the trembling of his hand on my shoulder, I wasn't at all sure he had meant it as a joke. More like a warning, it seemed.

I was still thinking about that, my back against the hard-baked surface of the anthill, when the lights of a vehicle appeared over a rise, coming from the direction of Nullagine. It was already slowing down, the headlights catching me in their glare as I stood waiting beside the road. It was a Toyota and when it stopped Prophecy put her head out of the window. 'I came into the bar just as you were driving off with those jokers. Thought I'd better come and pick you up.' She was grinning as though she, too, saw the humour of it.

'Thanks,' I said and retrieved my suitcase. Then, as I got in beside her, she said, 'I got a full tank.' She was watching me, her eyes gleaming black in the dashboard light. 'Yuh ever been down Golden Soak?'

I shook my head.

'Well, now's your chance to have a dekko before Phil Westrop. After all the questions you bin asking, he'll be down there at the weekend for sure and Ed'll have a fight on his hands if he tries to run him off the property again.'

I didn't know whether it was the thought that Ed Garrety might get hurt or whether it was simply that Prophecy infected me with her own curiosity, but I said okay and we started driving south. 'How do you think I'm going to get down the shaft?' I asked. But she had rope, torches, a miner's helmet, everything we'd need in the back. She always carried them, she said. And then we were talking about Westrop and what it was he was after. But it seemed she knew no more than I did. 'Looking for McIlroy,' she said. 'That's a bloody odd thing for him to say.' But she'd no idea why he'd said it and the noise and the heat of the truck made talking very tiring. With all the beer I'd drunk, my head began to nod and soon I was asleep. Even the jolts as we crossed the creek beds didn't waken me.

It was almost two when we reached the turn-off to Jarra Jarra and at Prophecy's suggestion I took over the driving. I had to concentrate then, for in places the track was difficult to follow and in the hill country there were the gullies to watch for. It was still dark when we came to the paddock fence and I felt like a thief in the night coming back to Jarra Jarra uninvited in a borrowed truck with a woman like Prophecy lolling in a whisky-loaded daze in the seat beside me. I saw the outline of The Governor humped against the stars, and then I had crossed the Mt Newman track and was on to the back trail that led down to Golden Soak.

The first pale light of dawn was seeping into the sky behind us as I turned the red outcrop and saw the chimney thin as a pencil above the rusted mine buildings. I was driving without lights then, feeling my way, with Prophecy awake and sitting bolt upright. I stopped by the mine office, switched the engine off and got out. There was no wind, everything still and very quiet. The dawn was brightening, a thin line to the east, and I stood there on the threshold of the day, listening. Prophecy joined me, a hag in the pallid light, her eyes gummed and her blown hair dry as furze. No jingle of a bit, no exhaust-blown whisper of an engine—no sound except the soundless promise of heat to come. 'Yuh expecting somebody?' Prophecy asked.

'No.' The gully closed around us. Dark now, no sign of the dawn and the place eerie in the headlights, a gaping mouth with quartz like ivory molars showing through the earth's red gums. I reached the old mineworkings, and where they'd once loaded the tip trucks, I was able to back and turn so that the Toyota faced downhill. I switched off the engine and sat there for a moment, listening.

'Wot's s'matter—scared?'

Her face was a dark blur, her voice a little sharper.

'Perhaps,' I said, thinking of Ed Garrety and his father and the dead miners. *Bad spirits all longa that mine.* A cold shiver ran through me, though it was hot as an oven here with the day's heat trapped by the rocks. Hard gnarled fingers touched my bare arms. 'Yuh goin' down?'

'That was the idea.'

I saw the dark shape of her head nod. 'Just be careful, that's all.' The fingers were stroking my arm, a caressing touch. 'Ed's never been down. He told me that once. Nobody's been down since it was closed.'

She took her hand away and reached into the back, passing

me the miner's helmet with its lamp and the battery attached to a belt. She had a geological hammer, too, and a haversack for rock samples. We also took a coil of nylon rope with us and a powerful hand torch. Then, as we started up, picking our way round the black gaping holes of the early workings, she gave me the lay-out of the mine as near as she could remember it from listening to old-timers in the bar. There were four levels at approximately one hundred feet intervals, the lowest, at four hundred feet, being the one that had been flooded following the cave-in. The reef itself more or less followed the fault line that had formed the gully. It was between four and eight feet wide and went down at a fairly steep angle, about 40° she thought. At the eastern end it petered out. At the western end it was badly faulted, and it was at this end that the cave-in had occurred.

'And nobody's been down since then?'

'Not as far's I know.' She was short of breath now, her voice wheezing.

'Too dangerous, is that it?'

She turned her head and looked at me. 'Want to go back?'

'What about the ladders? There are ladders in the main shaft, aren't there?'

'That's how the survivors got out.'

'But that was thirty years ago. They'll all be rotten by now.'

'Wood don't rot so easy in this climate.'

We reached the rock outcrops and the beam of the torch picked out the heavy boarding of the door, new screws gleaming bright against the rusted metal of the bolt. The piece of timber Garrety had jammed across the entrance the previous night lay discarded on the ground. Some time during the day he had been back and secured the door. But with a screwdriver from the truck's tool kit it was a simple job to release the bolt, and then we were inside the mountain, walking along the adit tunnel, which was just wide enough to take the tip trucks. The walls were rock, a brownish red colour and soft enough to show the marks of the miners' picks. Red dust covered the tramlines scuffed by the feet of last night's intruders, the air warm and slightly humid, a musty smell.

I counted 217 paces before the adit opened out into a man-made cavern with a gaping hole in the floor and timber supports for the hoist. A bucket hung there on rusted wires that ran over a pulley and down to the drum of a coal-burning steam engine with its chimney running up into the roof. It was all very primitive and entirely derelict.

Prophecy shone the torch down into the shaft, the two of us hanging on to the baulks of timber and peering into the depths. The shaft went straight down, a rope ladder falling to the staging of the first level, then wooden ladders continuing on down to what looked like the gleam of water at the bottom. Nothing seemed to have changed since the mine had been abandoned, except for that rope ladder secured to one of the timbers of the hoist. The other ladders seemed all right. It was only this first section that had gone and I wondered about that as Prophecy began to pull the rope ladder up. 'Seems sound enough,' she said. 'Home-made, by the look of it.'

The ladder was formed of two lengths of rope, knotted at intervals to support the slats of wood that formed the rungs. The rope was old, but it was good thick manilla and it wasn't frayed or rotted. The slats, too, were sound, though they were of several types of wood. It looked as though it had been made on the station and I was thinking of Ed Garrety going down alone as I lowered it back into the shaft.

'Yuh'd better tie the nylon round you just in case.'

I could feel the tension growing in me as I put on the helmet and buckled the belt around my waist, easing the lead from the battery up to the back of my neck and switching it on to test. The light from the reflector on my helmet was bright on the rock walls. 'Battery all right?' I asked.

She nodded. 'One thing Nobby taught me. I always keep it charged.' She handed me the end of the nylon rope and I tied it round my chest under the armpits. She had already passed the coil round one of the wooden timbers. She knew what she had to do and I slipped the haversack on and tucked the geological hammer into my belt. 'I'll be two or three hours at least,' I said. 'But I'll call to you up the shaft. If a whole hour goes by without my calling, then you'd better go for help.'

She nodded, and I ducked under the timbering and lowered myself into the blackness of the hole, feeling with my feet

94

until I had found the first of the slats. I saw the ropes take the strain as my full weight came on the ladder, then I was moving cautiously down it, my face close to the rock and Prophecy paying out the nylon safety rope from above. The ladder hung close against the rock wall of the shaft and I had to kick it out at each step to get a foothold on the slats. The staging at the first level was still sound and I swung myself into the cavity, slipping out of the nylon rope and using the end of it to secure the ladder to the wooden frame. Then I started along the narrow tunnel.

It was a cross-cut and quite short. In a moment I was in the main gallery and had turned east along the line of the stoping. At this level the technique was crude, large pillars of gold-bearing quartz having been left to support the overlying rock. It was safe and with proper shoring the pillars could have been mined. After about two hundred yards the pillars became shorter, the reef gradually narrowing to the point where it was no longer workable. I went back then, past the cross-cut to the shaft, the going gradually becoming more difficult as I encountered roof falls. The rock at this western end was badly fractured with areas of definite instability, and the reef came to an abrupt end at a point of major faulting.

I went back to the shaft, called up it that I was okay, and then I took a chance and went scrambling down the stoping itself. Beyond the second level the roof pillars became fewer, the overburden supported by hand-built walls of red rock. The air had got to it, of course. It was quite humid at this depth, with moisture glistening on the walls, and this had helped the process of oxidization.

Those two levels were enough to convince me that the mine was valueless. Prophecy's information was largely correct. The reef had had a width of between four and eight feet, inclining down at an angle of roughly 40°. At the eastern end it virtually petered out and at the western end it ran into very heavy faulting. There was granite here, but in the main the overlay was a mixture of iron and silica with some shale, and it was this the miners had used to shore up the roof. Even supposing the reef continued at depth, the place was about as safe as a derelict coal mine with all the pit props rotted. Start drilling and shot firing anywhere underground and the whole thing would collapse.

I was at the third level then, the ground under my feet no longer dust, but packed firm, and damp in places. Tramlines showed intermittently, twin lines of rusted iron, and suddenly in the light from my lamp I saw the outline of a heel, hard and clear. A little farther on, where the floor was almost mud, the imprint of rubber-soled shoes showed for about five yards. The pattern of the soles was quite distinct. It gave me an uncanny feeling, alone down there in the bowels of that abandoned mine and knowing that somebody else had been down there recently, might still be down there. No, that was ridiculous—pure imagination. But there was no doubt. Those footprints were quite fresh.

I had passed the cross-cut to the shaft and was nearing the westward end of the reef where it would finish at the fault. A drift opened up to my left, the floor slippery with damp and more footprints. They pointed both ways. He had gone into the drift and come out again. How long ago?

I squatted, peering at them closely. The mud was soft, the edge of the prints blurred. Water was seeping from a nearby crack in the rocks. Water in a land so dry! It couldn't have been long ago that he'd been here. Ed Garrety probably when he was fixing the bolt on the entrance door. Or had Westrop already been down when Garrety found him? Or was it somebody else, somebody I didn't know about—somebody who was still down here? I swung my head, directing the beam of the lamp along the gallery. Nothing, just the arched rock with a view of the stoping beyond, and on the floor, not two yards away, another footprint, very clear.

I took my helmet off, straightening up and swinging round to flash the lamp back down the way I had come. But there was nothing, of course, and I stepped into the drift. It turned out to be nothing more than a probe. About forty feet in it suddenly ceased. No quartz. No gleam of gold. Just iron-dark rock rusted in streaks by the moisture. What had decided the miners to give up at that precise point?

I went back down the drift, towards the heading where it entered the main gallery, my helmet still in my hand. I didn't care that my head was bare to any falling rock. With the lamp in my hand I could flash it quickly left and right as I stepped out into the gallery. It may seem silly—my nervousness. But an abandoned mine is a strange place. It has its own sort of atmosphere. I've been down quite a few in my time, but never anything as remote and unstable as Golden Soak, and never before or since with that strange sense of somebody watching me, a sort of presence. It wasn't just those footprints. I'm certain of that. Those were physical. This was something quite insubstantial and rather queer. And it was only here on the third level—I hadn't noticed it on the first two.

I don't believe in ghosts. I never have. Certainly not the ghosts of dead miners. If I believed in that sort of nonsense I wouldn't have gone into mining. There aren't many mines that haven't suffered some loss of life and in one or two of the old Cornish mines I'd been down . . . Good God! If you believed in ghosts you'd be meeting the dead round every turn and twist of the narrow workings. But that doesn't mean I'm insensitive to the feel of a place. Old mines, like old houses, have their own atmosphere—a feel, an aura compounded of many things, but chiefly of the way men have handled the problems of working underground. It's there in the construction of the galleries, the cross-cuts, drifts and winzes, the way they have stoped and handled the ore. But here, on the third level of Golden Soak, it was something different, as though the rock itself had absorbed such a radiation of human fear that it could still infect the atmosphere of the place.

All this flashed through my mind as I moved slowly towards the western end of the reef, an attempt to rationalize the growing sense of unease. Another drift probing to the left and ending, like the first, at a bare rock face. I was into the faulted area then. No more stoping and the miners searching desperately for the new line of the reef. A third drift, to the right this time, and then my lamp was shining on the end of the main gallery, the roof so low it was no more than a hole, and to the left a final probe, damp seeping and a mêlée of footprints all made by the same person.

It was here in this final drift that I found what he had been looking for. It was a very narrow passageway, barely wide enough to swing a pick in, the roof all faulted, lumps of rock littering the floor. It reminded me of Balavedra—the older workings. I put my helmet on, the lamp showing rubble ahead, water dripping from the roof. It wasn't level like the others, but descended steeply, an angle of about 20°. It was more like a winze, and it was a deeper probe. I didn't like it. The roof was unstable and there was water in pools among the fallen rocks. About seventy yards in I was clambering over rubble, my head bent so that I could see where I was treading. And then suddenly I stopped. The rubble under me was no longer composed only of that dull red iron ore streaked with rust. Mixed with it were small jagged pieces of rock so white and coarsely crystalline that it looked like Parian marble. I picked up a piece and caught the gleam of gold in the lamplight.

It was quartz.

They had found the reef again. That was my first thought. Then I raised my head, the lamplight showing piled-up rubble half blocking the passage and the roof above it still the same red rock.

I stood there for a moment, puzzling over it. And then I was crawling on my hands and knees over the rubble, peering ahead down the drift to see the reef quartz showing white in the dark recess of it. Quartz in fragments was mixed with the piled-up granite of the fall, a shovel lying on the debris, and in the cleared space, between the jagged rock face and the rubble pile on which I crouched, a pick was propped against the wall.

I didn't go any farther. I didn't need to. The pick and that shovel told their story. They belonged with the footprints I had been following. Garrety? Westrop? Somebody had discovered that the reef continued. Or was it an entirely new reef? I picked up a piece of quartz and examined it more closely. The glitter of the gold was clear to the naked eye. There were specks of black, too, and the white of the quartz was smudged with grey. Gold in antimony?

I looked again at the gaping hole torn out of the roof of the gallery by the rock fall, probing with my lamp. The reef showed as a narrow band of jagged quartz. No way of telling what its width was or how far it extended into the rock. And this wasn't a recent fall. Damp had discoloured the exposed surfaces of the iron formation above and the rubble under my feet showed the rusty discoloration of water seepage from the porous iron ore. Whoever had been working down here recently certainly hadn't caused it. The fall had happened a long time ago.

And then, of course, it came to me—this was the 1939 cave-in. This was where the rock and water had poured in upon the miners Ed Garrety's father had employed in a last desperate attempt to find the reef again. And they had found it. But they hadn't known that as they ran for their lives. The only one who knew was the man whose footprints I had seen.

The atmosphere of the place seemed stronger then and I hastily filled the haversack with samples of quartz and scrambled back over the heaped-up pile of rubble, conscious of the irony of it. To find the reef again and not to know, and all so pointless, the mine uneconomic anyway.

Beyond the rock pile the footprints showed again in the beam of my lamp, and I stared at them as I moved on down the narrow tunnel of the drift, wondering about the man who had made them, why he had opened up the drift so laboriously, working alone down here with nothing more than a pick and shovel. As Kadek had said, if the mine was uneconomic thirty years ago it would be doubly so now. So what was the point, unless the ore content. . . . I stopped then. I was almost back at the main gallery and I stood there, one of the samples in my hand, looking at it closely. The grey smudges. . . . It wasn't the content that had changed, it was the price. The price of antimony.

Gold *and* antimony. I stared at the smudged white glitter of the sample in my hand, excited now, seeing suddenly the solution to my own problems as well as those of Jarra Jarra. But I would need to get it chemically tested, the gold assayed, also the antimony content, if it was antimony. And then we'd have to test drill. A lot of time, a lot of money. I dropped the fragment back into the haversack and stood for a moment staring down at a damp patch that showed the imprint of the man who had discovered it clear and sharp, the whole foot. It was the right foot and I put my own alongside it. A little longer, a little broader; a big man then, and Westrop hadn't been big. Whoever it was, he wasn't here now and I went back down the main gallery, found the cross-cut to the shaft, and then I was leaning out from the staging, the lamplight shining on water and the ladder running straight down into it. The shaft was like a well. Water here in abundance and cattle dying on the surface. It didn't make sense, this crazy, empty, burned-up country. I called up to Prophecy, and when she answered, her voice echoing and swelling down the shaft, I swung myself out on to the ladder and started slowly up it. The wooden rungs were still solid, but the iron fastenings that held it to the rock were loose in places, and though I kept my body pressed close against it, that ladder scared me, so that I was relieved to find the one leading up to the first level more secure. But it was still good to switch to the rope ladder and the security of the nylon safety rope.

'Yuh bin a long time on that third level.' She was leaning down towards me. 'Find anything?' I was almost level with the top of the shaft, and looking up at her, the beam of my lamp showed her eyes bright as beads. I heaved myself out, glad to be on firm ground again. 'Well, what did yuh find?' She had seen the bulging haversack and her voice had a grasping urgency.

I handed her a piece of the quartz and she picked up her torch, bending over it, examining it eagerly. Her hands trembled, the glitter of the gold exciting her. 'Where did yuh find this—on the third level?' She looked up at me, her thin dry hair in wisps across her face and her eyes gleaming. 'Is this from the reef?'

I knew then that I wasn't going to tell her what else I'd found, the footprints, the evidence of work in that gallery. 'Yes. There's a section of the reef exposed. But it's quite unworkable.' And I explained about the state of the mine.

It took a little time to convince her. Gold still has a powerful attraction, and having made money out of one claim, she was eager to peg another, insisting that we try our luck higher up the gully. Even when I told her what the grey smudges in the quartz could mean, I don't think she really believed me—she didn't want to. 'Yuh get it analysed,' she said finally. 'Then we'll see.'

This was obviously the next step, and when I asked her where the nearest laboratory was she said, 'Kalgoorlie.'

We collected our gear then and went back down the adit to the mine entrance. The sun was already well up and the heat hit us as we went out into the red glare of the gully. I closed the door and screwed the bolt back into place. It was just after eight as we drove down the tramline track to the mine buildings. 'If wot yuh say is true and it is antimony in that quartz then it explains why they never made any money out of the mine.'

'Yes.'

She had obviously been thinking it over.

'And I bet that sample runs out at near on six ounces to the ton.'

She was a woman who didn't give up easily and she was talking about it all the way to the cut-off by the paddock fencing. I didn't say much, for I was driving and wondering what I'd tell Ed Garrety if I met him coming down the track from Jarra Jarra. But we didn't meet a soul and shortly after nine-thirty we pulled into Lynn Peak, a mobile drilling rig the only vehicle there. We were both of us very tired by then and I was glad Andie was out seeing to one of his wind bores. His wife cooked us breakfast and while we were waiting for it I picked up a copy of the *West Australian* somebody had left and turned to the financial page. It gave the London price of antimony—£1,130 per ton. Only a few months ago it had been £340.

The bacon and eggs came and we ate it with the children on the floor at our feet and the four drillers at the next table. They were 'dust' drillers and their rig was a rotary percussion drill, a Mayhew 1000 that relied on compressed air instead of mud to bring the rock chips to the surface. They were on their way from Mt Goldsworthy to a temporary job at Mt Newman. Georges Duhamel, the owner of the rig, had been born in the French island of New Caledonia and all through breakfast he was telling me how important it was for Britain to retain her Pacific colonies. 'Some day Australia will need those islands as bases against the pressures of Asiatic populations—the Chinese, the Japanese, mebbe the Philippines, too. You give everything away. Why? Do you no longer believe in the future? Perhaps you think there is no future, hnn?' He was a wiry, dynamic little man with wild penetrating eyes under a thick dark thatch of hair, and a quick, explosive way of speaking. Listening to him, I felt that being an Englishman in Australia had its disadvantages; I seemed to be a target for everybody who had a gripe against the Old Country. But at least he could tell me something about the cost of drilling in this part of the country. It worked out at around $6·50 a foot dust drilling and went up to about $16·50 if he used a diamond drill.

Later, two drivers came in. They had a refrigerator truck loaded with fish from the coast and were headed for Perth by way of Meekatharra and Mt Magnet. From Meekatharra Prophecy said I should have no difficulty in getting a lift to Kalgoorlie, and shortly after eleven I left her sitting there in the Andersons' diner clutching the samples I'd given her, a dreamy look on her face. I had asked her to say nothing to anybody until I had had the analysis done, but as we started out on the long haul south, three of us crammed into the stifling heat of the truck's driving cabin, I thought it was too much to expect that she'd be able to keep her mouth shut.

FOUR

Ora Banda

I

THERE HAS NEVER BEEN anything quite like it in Australia, probably never will be again. Gold rushes, yes. But the nickel boom is something different. Poseidon, its symbol, was rocketed from 7s. 6d. to £112 on the London market, and gamblers in faraway Britain caught nickel fever, calling it the Windarra Wonder and rushing to buy the shares of any company with a hole in the ground and the faintest whiff of ultrabasics. So many claims have been pegged recently that mining registrars have been unable to cope and rumour has it that the Perth Government's Minister of Mines is considering a ban on further pegging until the backlog has been cleared. The Windarra Range is not much more than a hundred miles north of Kalgoorlie, and with Western Mining's Kambalda nickel mine already in production twenty miles to the south, this old gold town became the focal centre of the boom. When I arrived there late on the Saturday afternoon the place was seething with scouts and newspaper men, stockbrokers, business executives, survey parties, crooks, drillers, gamblers, anybody with money enough and a place to lay his head.

The hub of all this feverish activity was the Palace bar. In quieter days it was no doubt adequate enough, but now it overflowed on to the pavement, a mob of men in every conceivable garb, talking, arguing, drinking in the slanting sunlight. The survey truck in which I had travelled the last stretch from Leonora had dropped me at the corner of Hannan and Maritana, and as I crossed the broad intersection the roar of voices almost drowned the traffic. It was the same across the street outside the dark cavern of a bar where a florid Edwardian design in frosted glass proclaimed it *Church's Exchange Hotel— The Young Jacksons of Kalgoorlie*. It was a town of white-wood buildings with verandahed sidewalks, and Hannan Street, with its brothels at one end and the Mt Charlotte gold mine at the other, was wide enough for camel trains to turn in. The whole place was a municipal monument to Hannan's discovery of 1893 and the Golden Mile.

The Palace was half wood, half brick, and extended through several buildings of different vintage. The main entrance was in Hannan Street, in the wooden section, the door to the bar on the left and Reception a dark cubby-hole of a room below the staircase with its balustrade ending in a poor digger's version of the Statue of Liberty. A tired girl stood at the phone, fanning herself against the overpowering stuffiness, and when at last I managed to catch her eye she shrugged her shoulders helplessly at my request for a bed. The hotel was full. They had men sleeping two and three to a room and it was the same all over town. I left my suitcase with her and fought my way into the bar. Ceiling fans stirred the turgid air without cooling it.

I was tired and hot and dusty. But at least the beer when I got it was cold. I drank it watching the hot animated faces reflected in the mirrors behind the bar. 'The London price closed at 106½.' Two men talking about Poseidon close beside me, one of them a youngster in a starched white shirt, the other in bush khaki. Between the mirrors were faded prints of old-timers and wagons and camel trains, a pictorial record of the first rush, when it had been gold, not nickel. 'Newmetals is a better bet—or Tasminex. What about Tasminex?' The beer had disappeared into me like water into parched earth. I ordered another and asked the barmaid if she knew Chris Culpin. Her tired eyes ranged the smoke-filled bar as she filled my glass again. 'Chris is over there talking to Smithie.' She indicated a heavily-built man in a faded shirt with a sweat-grimed hat thrust on the back of his head.

They were at the far end of the bar and when I reached them they were in the middle of an argument. 'They've no business fossicking around the Blackridge.' Culpin's voice sounded belligerent. 'Who told them?'

'You don't have to tell those blokes.' The other was a thin man with a long leathery face and very pale blue eyes. He was swaying slightly, his voice slurred, his long face glistening with sweat. 'Christ! It was all round the bar here last night.'

'That bloody Swede—I'll murder him.'

'It ain't Petersen's fault, Chris. You send samples to the lab for analysis . . .' He stopped there and Culpin turned, both of them suddenly aware of my presence.

'You want something?' Small eyes stared at me out of a brick red face, his belly sagging over the broad leather belt that supported his trousers. He hadn't shaved and the collar of his shirt showed an unwashed line of red dust.

I told him who I was and he nodded. 'So you made it.' There was no welcome in the way he said it.

'Where's Kadek?' I asked.

'Ferdie's in Perth.'

The thin man leaned towards me, the pale eyes staring. 'You from the Old Country?'

I nodded.

'Geologist?'

'Mining consultant.'

'Consultant, eh?' He was suddenly angry. 'You Brits. You're all over us, and we got Swedes, Wops, Kiwis, even Yugos. Wot the hell they teaching them at the School of Mines? Don't reckon there's a real Aussie geologist between here and Dampier.

'You must be joking, Smithie. There's my boy Kennie for one. He's out with a survey party——'

'Pegging for himself, I'll bet. Claim crazy that's wot they are, the whole lot of 'em. I seen 'em come into my office registering claims before they even passed out of the School.

'Kennie's not like that.'

'No?' The long sweaty face leaned down, the pale eyes peering under Culpin's hat. 'Think you know your own son, eh? I betyer, when he gets back, he'll throw up his job and be off up there again inside of a week pegging his own claims.' The thin lips opened, a cackling laugh. 'Wot d'you expect when he sees his old man flogging a bloody mine that's bin dead for years——'

Culpin grabbed his arm. 'You shut your mouth, Smithie—or by Christ I'll shut it for you.'

The other man stood there swaying slightly as the threat sank into his fuddled brain. 'Mum's the word, eh?' He smiled thinly. 'Okay Chris. But wotchit, feller.' He leaned forward, a confidential whisper, 'There's talk already, an' if those boys find . . .'

'Shut your bloody mouth, I said.' Culpin turned abruptly, jerked his head at me and moved into the crowd, heading for the street. 'Silly bastard,' he said as we reached the doorway. 'He's drunk, an' when he's drunk he's 'sfull of gossip as an ol' woman.' Outside, the reflection of sun on the white wood buildings was blinding.'

'Where are we going?' I asked.

'My place. You won't get a bed anywhere else.' His voice was sullen, a brooding anger in him. I got my suitcase and followed him across the wide expanse of Hannan Street. He had a battered ute parked in Maritana, and as we drove off, he said, 'First time I met Smithie he was a mining registrar up north of here. Know how much he's worth now? Half a million at least. That's what Poseidon's done for him. Bought 'em for under a dollar and now he's hardly ever sober. Spends most of his time in the bar there.'

We were headed towards Boulder with the tall stacks and workings of the Golden Mile on our left. 'You don't want to take any notice of that stupid bastard,' he went on. 'Anyway, it wasn't me who sent those samples in for analysis. It was Rip Pender, one of Pete's boys, acting for Lone Minerals.' He gave me a quick sidelong glance. 'Ferdie says you got a degree.'

'Yes.'

'Okay. But you try and muscle in on this deal . . .' He was silent for a moment. Then he said, 'I ain't got no degree, but I know a lot you don't—I was born out here, see. At Coolgardie.' He nodded at the wasteland to our left. 'That's what killed Coolgardie—they all decamped to the Golden Mile. But my Dad, he stayed on, the bloody old fool. You'd think living in a ghost town would have taught me to keep clear of prospecting. But I got it in the blood, see.' Again that sideways glance. 'You known Ferdie long?'

'I met him four years ago in Spain.'

'We was kids together.'

He was silent after that. But as we ran into the sprawling town of Boulder he said, 'I used to stay with an aunt of mine here. There was nine of us and my mother died. That's how I come to be at the same school as Ferdie. Undersized little runt, but clever as a dingo. He did the thinking, I did the fighting. In the end he ran his own gang and we found an adit leading into the old abandoned workings of the Perseverance, going down rickety ladders and crawling through winzes you wouldn't think a grown miner could cut ore outa. That's how Ferdie got his first break.' And he went on to tell me how they'd found a rich pocket of ore, half concealed by the wooden shoring of a stope. They hadn't dared knock the timbers away, but Kadek had gone down on his own night after night and cleared the pocket out with his father's mining tools, humping the pay dirt up through the mine in sacks and selling it to the government stamping mill at Ora Banda. 'The dirty crooked little bastard!' It was said without rancour, almost affectionately. 'Never let on to us. Just took off for Sydney and I didn't hear of him again till he came to Kal 'bout a year ago looking for nickel prospects for some piddling little company he'd formed.' He eased his clutch, then leaned forward and squashed a fly on the windscreen with his thumb. 'So you got a degree.' It seemed to rankle. 'Well, you just remember this, Alec—but for me there wouldn't be any Black-ridge prospect.' The small eyes stared at me from under the battered hat. 'I found it, see.'

We were into the centre of Boulder now and he turned left, following the Kambalda signs. 'What about that mine you were inquiring about—Golden Soak? A washout, eh?' I didn't say anything and he laughed. 'Gold. I'm not interested in gold. Nor's Ferdie. But copper now . . .' He braked sharply, turning into a side road on the outskirts that was sparsely flanked with corrugated iron houses, some of them little bigger than shacks.

'Did you get up to Nullagine?' he asked.

'I was there for a few hours, yes.'

'What did the abo say?'

'Nothing.'

I don't know whether he believed me or not. The tarmac had ceased and we were on a black grit track that ran across a flat wasteland to the long rampart walls of the gold tailings.

'Okay, we'll talk about it later—when we've settled this Blackridge deal.'

The tailing walls were golden in the slanting sun. They were enormous, like Egyptian tombs. A pony all alone eyed us doubtfully as we swung south, the wheels ploughing through grit so fine and black it looked like coal dust, and ahead was a solitary house standing in the shade of two gaunt gum trees. The ugly tin fencing was rusty, and where it wasn't supported by old iron bed-ends, it had fallen in. We stopped in a whirl of dust beside a pair of rusting traction engine wheels that served to mark the entrance. 'Well, this is it,' he said, and climbed out.

I got my suitcase out of the back and followed him through a scattering of hens to the verandah entrance. Like the other houses I had seen, the verandah had a delicately curved tin roof, but it was dilapidated, the holes showing ragged. The smell of pigs hung heavy in the hot stillness. He nodded to a corrugated iron shack. 'The bog's over there when you want it.' He climbed the verandah steps and pushed open the fly-screen. 'Edith!'

'That you, Chris?' a woman's voice answered, thin and high, with an edge of nerves in it.

'I got Ferdie's pal with me.'

'Coming.'

I put my suitcase down and he took me into the parlour. It was cool and dark, the windows shuttered, and the furniture Victorian with lace curtains, even antimacassars, a period piece and spotlessly clean. A small dried-up little woman appeared in the doorway, standing hesitant, brushing a wisp of hair. 'You didn't say anything about company tonight, Chris.'

'Didn't know, so how could I?' He told her my name and she came forward to greet me, wiping her hands on her apron. Her handshake was surprisingly firm, the skin dry and hard. 'I expect you're hungry.' She smiled at me, her eyes almost green in a shaft of sunlight. 'It's all ready. I only got to lay another place.'

We ate in the kitchen at a plain scrubbed table, cold ham and pickles with fried potatoes and thick sweet Indian tea.

Edith Culpin hardly spoke, picking daintily at her food, with the big china teapot in front of her. I was hungry and very tired after the long ride south, but I thought it time I found out exactly what Kadek wanted of me. Culpin didn't seem to know. 'He'll tell you when he gets back from Perth. I've wired him the results of the analysis and he'll have the boss of Lone Minerals with him.' He took a gulp of tea, sucking it in noisily, his mouth full. 'All I know is he's expecting you to give Les Freeman the lowdown on the geology of the area. He's got it all worked out. You're the expert, see.'

'When do you expect him?' I asked.

'Monday. He's going to ring me.'

It didn't give me much time and I soon discovered he knew next to nothing about the geological structure of the country. He could give me the results of geochemical and geomagnetic surveys carried out on various claims, but he couldn't explain the gossans and anomalies usually associated with sulphide minerals or even talk sensibly about the theory of ultrabasics. 'You'd better go and see Petersen first thing Monday morning. Either Pete or somebody at Western Mining. And there's Smithie. He knows the nickel belt as well as anybody.'

'What about the School of Mines?' I asked. 'D'you know anybody there?'

'No.'

'Kennie does,' his wife said. 'If Kennie were here——'

'Well, he isn't.' He swallowed the last of his tea and got to his feet. 'I gotter go now.'

'I baked an apple pie for you.'

Her voice sounded aggrieved.

He shook his head. 'Red's just in from the mulga country up beyond Warburton and I wanta get hold of that abo he had with him.'

'Dick Gnarlbine?' Her voice was frozen. 'It's not right, you drinking with a black.'

'Who said anything about drinking?' He laughed. 'All right. I'm going to pour some liquor into the bastard before any of my pals get at him.' He turned to me. 'Red's been filming up north of the Gunbarrel, over towards the Clutterbucks, says they ran into a bunch of natives been walkabout east from

Disappointment.' He reached for his hat. 'A few beers and Dick'll tell me anything he knows.'

'It's not right,' she repeated wearily.

'To hell with whether it's right or not. If he's learned something that'll make our fortunes, then I don't reckon you'd come it so bloody high and mighty about my feeding a few beers to an abo.' He clapped his hat on his head. 'See you in the morning,' he told me and went out. A moment later we heard the door of the ute slam, the whine of the starter.

'You mustn't mind Chris,' she said as the sound of the engine faded up the track. 'He's had a hard life.' She gave a little sigh. 'We both have.' And she went over to the oven and got out the pie, fussing over me as she served it. 'You were asking a lot of geological questions. I hope you won't do that again. It upsets him. He's not a geologist.'

'No, I realize that.'

'He's not even a prospector, not really.'

The pie was good and I told her so.

She smiled and I caught a glimpse of the girl she had once been, before the dry air and the hard life had shrivelled her. 'Would you like some more tea?'

I let her refill my cup, sensing her loneliness, her need to talk. But the world she lived in was a limited one, her husband out most of the time and the nearest house a fifteen-minute walk across the empty wasteland. 'It's the summers I can't stand. I'm from the South West, from Yeagarup, and I miss the trees. I grew up with great forests of karri all round me and the sea not more'n twenty miles away.' She gave a little shrug. 'There's worse places than Kalgoorlie, I know that. But January, and next month too—the heat and the flies, and the dust from the tailings, it drives you crazy.'

Her family had been small farmers owning a few paddocks and about fifty acres of forest. That was how she'd met her husband. He was just back from the war, working in the timber mills at Pemberton, and at weekends he was felling for a neighbouring farmer. 'Chris has tried almost everything in the twenty-four years we been married. He ran a sheep station for a time, a big place out on the edge of the Nullarbor. He was a butcher, then a dogger. I think he liked dogging best.

He was all through the Pilbara, living bush and on his own. And I had the child. I wasn't too lonely. But Kennie's grown up now and finally we came here. It was the nickel boom brought Chris back. He went to Kambalda as a driller. Then up Laverton way. Now he's on his own and calls himself a prospector, and all he thinks about is striking it rich.' Her thin lips stretched themselves into a sad little smile. 'If he ever did, I don't think we'd know what to do with it, not now.'

I asked her about the mine, then, but she couldn't tell me much, only that it was near Ora Banda and she didn't think there'd be much in it for them. 'Even a place like Blackridge costs money these days. Chris is only the agent. It was Mr Kadek bought it.'

I think she'd have gone on talking for the rest of the evening, but I wanted to stretch my legs before it got dark. She took me across the hall and showed me into a small room with a single bed and home-made shelves littered with rock samples, all carefully labelled. There was a desk with a battered typewriter on it, and above it, another shelf stacked with books on geology, physics, metallurgy—Mason's *Principles of Geochemistry*, *Elements of Mineralogy*, *Elements of Geology for Australian Students*, Bragg's *Atomic Structure of Minerals;* I hadn't seen that since I was a student.

'It's Kennie's room really.'

'Yes, I guessed that.'

'He's twenty-three now, a real bright boy. Solid, too—not restless like his father.' She was smiling. 'I've got a photograph of him in the parlour if you'd care to see it.' She went and got it and I found myself looking at the picture of a tall, slightly-built lad with his mother's features showing through a wisp of beard, an unruly mop of fair hair falling over his face. 'That was taken the day he passed out from the School of Mines. He did very well there.' She said it with a mother's fondness, adding, 'He should be back any day now.'

I asked her where his survey party was operating, but she didn't know. 'Somewhere up north of Leonora.' She was staring down at the photograph. 'He and Chris——' she hesitated, twining her fingers nervously around the frame. 'I don't know what it is, but the young don't seem to look on money the way we older people do. But he's happy, that's the main thing. Seems interested in minerals for their own sake.' Again that hesitation, as though she wanted to tell me something else. But then she said brightly, 'Well, I'll leave you now. I've got to clear up and there's the pigs to feed. I'll have sandwiches and coffee for you when you get back.'

I thanked her and she stood there hovering for a moment, her eyes darting about the room. Finally she left, closing the door quietly behind her. The room was stuffy and I pushed open the shutters, looking out on to a litter of rusting iron with the walls of the tailing dumps red in the sunset beyond the ragged tin of the fencing. Beside the desk there was a washstand with basin and ewer of blue china. The water was lukewarm, but at least it got the dust of travel out of my skin. Then I left the house, heading across the wasteland towards the tailings.

The walls, when I reached them, were about thirty feet high, the sloping sides runnelled by occasional rain storms and reflecting the lurid red of the sunset sky. A wind had sprung up, and as the light died and darkness closed in, I came out through a defile between two of the dumps to a view of what looked like water with a sea mist hanging white and the line of a harbour wall running a dark finger into the gloaming. The mist was white dust blowing, fine as talcum powder, the sea a plain stretching off into infinity, the harbour wall yet another of those monstrous dumps.

I stood there for a while, feeling the strangeness of this land to which I had committed myself. And not just the land, the people, too. The way they behaved, the way they talked, their whole outlook. Above all, the remoteness of it. I felt a million miles away from anything I had known before and standing there, looking out across that misted sea that wasn't a sea but a dust-filled plain, I was conscious of the need of something with which I could identify myself—a sheet anchor for my loneliness. And as night fell and I retraced my steps, walking slowly back through the tomb-like adobe walls, back across that black grit wasteland to the desolate isolation of the Culpin home, I was thinking of Janet and the rock samples I had taken from Golden Soak, wondering what the analysis would show.

It was dark when I got back to the house with the stars a pale glimmer that outlined the gums and the shack that was their latrine. The shack had a flyscreen as well as a door. Inside it was pitch black, no light and the smell of disinfectant. And when I came out I had a sudden feeling that I was being watched. I stopped, conscious of the smell of pigs, the stillness all about me, no wind and the soft glow of an oil lamp in the house. And then I saw it, a figure standing motionless, so still, so black, it might have been the stump of a tree.

I stood there for a moment, rooted to the spot, sensing something primitive. And then the figure moved and the black low-browed face of an aborigine emerged from the shadows as he moved to my side without a sound.

'What do you want?'

His hand reached out and gripped my arm, the thick lips moving below the broad nose; all I got was the name Chris.

'He's not here,' I told him.

'Where? Where I find'im?'

'He's gone into Kalgoorlie.' I hesitated. 'Are you Dick Gnarlbine?'

'Arrr.' A deep chesty sound, an affirmative.

'He's looking for you.'

'No find'im.' And he added, 'Me film-im walkabout longa Red. Me come back, whitefella talk bad something. You tell'im, Chris. Whitefella talk bad something. You got'im beer?'

I shook my head, uneasy at the hard-skinned touch of his hand.

'You tell'im Chris. Kambalda man speak'im no good.'

'What are they saying?' I asked.

But he wouldn't tell me any more. He just said, 'You tell'im Chris.' Then he was gone.

I went into the house and Edith Culpin was waiting for me, coffee and sandwiches in the kitchen and her voice thin and complainful. I didn't tell her about the aborigine, and as soon as I decently could I took myself off to bed.

I must have been very tired indeed for I didn't wake until Edith Culpin brought my breakfast in on a tray. 'Thought you'd like a nice lie-in seeing it's Sunday.' The time was almost ten-thirty and her husband had already left. I didn't see him at all that day. Most of it I spent in Kennie's room, examining his samples, and reading everything I could find that related to the geology of Australia. It was not quite so hot here as it had been in the Pilbara and in the evening I walked the whole length of the Golden Mile. I needed to be alone with time to think; also the exercise got some of the soreness of the long truck ride out of my muscles.

I went to bed early that night and woke with the sun. It was Monday now, the Culpins already up, and by the time I was dressed the house was full of the smell of bacon frying. The kitchen was hot, a blaze of light from the flyscreened window, and we ate our breakfast in silence. Culpin had the *Kalgoorlie Miner* propped up in front of him, his wife was reading a letter. 'Kennie says they're almost through with that survey.' She looked at the date. 'That's Wednesday. He wishes us both a happy New Year.'

Her husband grunted, but made no comment, his eyes bleary. There was the sound of a car and she lifted her head, her thin dry hair a golden halo. The car stopped and she rose to her feet as the verandah door opened and a woman's voice called to her. 'That's Muriel,' she said. 'Mebbe he's phoned her.'

While she was out of the room I told Culpin about his visitor of two nights before, and when I repeated what the aborigine had said, he stopped eating and leaned forward, his bloodshot eyes staring. 'What do you mean—bad something?'

'I don't know what he meant. But he wanted to see you.'

'Stupid bastard!' he muttered. 'I was all over town looking for him.' He glanced over his shoulder. The door was open, the murmur of women's voices. 'What did he want to see me about?' There was tension in his voice, his eyes searching my face.

I shrugged. 'I told you what he said. Some white man had obviously been getting at him.'

'Who? Did he say who?'

'No. He just said to tell you. And he asked for a beer.'

'Been drinking, had he?'

But I couldn't answer that. I didn't know whether he'd been drinking or not.

The verandah door slammed and Edith Culpin came back into the kitchen. 'Muriel just had a call from Mr Kadek,' she said. 'He wants you to ring him back right away.'

Culpin had twisted round in his chair, the sunlight full on his face. A globule of dried blood showed by his left ear and his skin had a bad colour. For a moment he seemed to have difficulty in switching his mind. 'What's Ferdie want?' He was frowning, his voice slow and heavy.

'She didn't say. Just to ring him, and it was urgent.'

He turned back to his breakfast, staring down at the remains of the bacon. Then he pushed his plate away, folded the newspaper and poured himself another cup of tea.

'We ought to have the phone here,' his wife said.

'You say that every time I get a call,' he snarled. Then added, 'Mebbe we will, when this deal's gone through.' He drank his tea in quick gulps, then lumbered to his feet. 'You coming?'

I nodded and went to get the rock samples, which were still in my suitcase. I stuffed four of them into my trouser pockets and went out to join him in the ute.

We stopped at the second house on the dirt street leading to the Kambalda road and he was gone about ten minutes. 'Mickey Mouse have put on a special flight. That's MMA, the local airline. Ferdie wants us to meet them at the airport.' And he added, 'Beer and sandwiches at Ora Banda and you're to get yourself clued up so's you can answer all the questions this feller Freeman's likely to ask.'

I reminded him that I hadn't even seen the mine yet, but he only glared at me. 'What the hell's that matter? The mine's my pigeon. All Ferdie wants from you is geological know-how.' And he added, 'They'll be here about noon. That gives you three hours.'

Clear of Boulder, we took the dirt road that parallels the Golden Mile, the sun blazing hot and the mineworkings looking as though an army had fought a desert campaign across the scarred wasteland. 'I'll drop you in Macdonald Street. There's Western Mining on one side, the School of Mines on the other. And Smithie's usually at the Palace bar around eleven. I'll pick you up there at eleven forty-five. Right?'

It wasn't much more than a couple of miles out to the airport, but it seemed a lot longer with Culpin sitting morose and tense at the wheel, not saying a word. And I was thinking of my interview with Petersen, wondering whether to ask questions or keep my mouth shut.

When Culpin had dropped me in Macdonald Street, I hadn't gone into Western Mining or the School of Mines, but had made straight for Petersen Geophysics, which was in Maritana, close by the railway bridge. Petersen was in, and when I showed him the samples, he agreed with me that it looked like antimony. He was a big man with a long sun-tanned face and hair the colour of bleached straw. He put one of the samples under a microscope and nodded. 'The gold looks goot, at least fife ounces.' His accent was strong, his manner non-committal. 'The antimony——' he shrugged. 'That is for the laboratory to say. You want I do you an analysis?'

I nodded and asked him how soon he could do it. 'Ve are snowed under, if you can say that in this goddammed country.' Big teeth showed in a grin. 'Also, this is a different kind of yob. Most of our lab tests are for nickel. We never before haf been asked for antimony tests.' However, he agreed in the end to do it as a rush job, I think because he was intrigued. And once that was settled I asked him about Blackridge.

'Blackridge? You ask about Blackridge—why?' His slate grey eyes looked up at me over the top of the microscope. And when I told him I would be going out to look over the mine that afternoon, he said, 'Blackridge is not like this.' He held up the samples. 'This is reef quartz, no? But Blackridge is surface dust. Half the work of my laboratory is concerning itself with dust picked up on the surface. This is an old country geologically and because a handful of dust picked up on the surface can indicate the rock structure below ground, men are easily fooled. You know Chris Culpin?'

I nodded and he stared at me a moment. Then he seemed to make up his mind. 'Okay. You ask Chris where that dust come from. I ask him—last night in the Pal. I say is that yob you give me on the level? Ja, I tell him, there is nickel there. But there is also some rumours. You know what he say to me?' The big teeth opened, a grin so wide that he looked like a horse about to laugh. 'Pete, he say, you mind your own bloddy business or I'll ram those tombstones of yours so far down your throat they'll bite you in the arse.' The horse's mouth gaped wider, a gusty roar of laughter. 'So I t'ink that is a yob I don't want any more of. Nickel—pah!' He had risen to his feet and he patted me on the back, still roaring with laughter, his fist like a pile driver. 'I tell you because you are new here and I like your country. England is goot with green grass and trees like Sweden, eh? So be careful. This is better.' He was looking with interest again at the sample in his big hand. 'I tell my feller you want the results tomorrow. Mebbe you get it, mebbe no. Ve do our best, eh?'

The plane was late, the parking lot already thick with cars as we drew in. Culpin switched off, then turned to me. 'I dunno what Ferdie has in mind, but this deal's important, see.' He stared at me a moment, his hands gripping the wheel. Then he got out and I followed him into the wood-verandahed passenger terminal.

The special flight was northbound after Kalgoorlie and the building was crowded with men headed for the bush or back up to the iron ore company towns. They were in shorts or khaki longs, with wide-brimmed hats, some with packs. There were a few women and children, and others like ourselves meeting people off the plane, but the place still had a frontier atmosphere. The interior was dark after the blinding heat outside. Culpin started talking to a station manager bound for Wittenoom and I went back on to the verandah where it was cooler, the ghost of a breeze raising dust on the airfield.

Soon I could hear the drone of a plane coming in from behind the terminal. In a few minutes Kadek would be stepping out of it, expecting me to help him sell a dud mine. Oh yes, I'm not going to pretend it was sprung on me so that I didn't know what I was doing. I hadn't wasted the few hours I had had on my own that morning.

The plane when I saw it was low on the horizon. I lit a cigarette and leaned on the balustrade, watching it as it started the wide circuit of the airfield. One of the Cessnas parked on the apron in front roared into life. It had loaded a survey party and now it was off, scuttling for the runway end. My gaze switched back to the incoming plane, a glint of silver in the sun. I watched it turn on to the flight path for landing, and my mind was still undecided. I was thinking of what the English geologist I had seen at Western Mining had said. Carter had given me the better part of an hour, I think because he had heard of Trevis, Parkes & Pierce, and I had used the name of my old firm as an introduction. 'It's unique,' he had said. 'Most of Australia is unique, the flora, the fauna—and the geophysical nature of the country. It's flat and it's dry. Erosion occurs *in situ*, from wind and violent changes in the temperature. There's no surface movement of the soil, no draining away in river beds.' He had digressed for a moment, talking about the gold finds that had been made earlier in the century. They had been made over an area of about a million square miles, mainly in the mafic and ultra-mafic rocks of the greenstone belt. The same rocks that could produce nickel. These were Archaean rocks of the pre-Cambrian Shield which covered almost half Australia, outcropping in the Yilgarn Block, an area in the south-west that was about the size of Britain, and also in the smaller Pilbara Block, and continuing right through to the Centre, where the Shield was overlaid by sand and gravel. And then he was repeating what Petersen had said—'You can walk the Yilgarn and the Pilbara in the certain knowledge that what you find on the surface is a fair indication of the rock formation below ground.'

He talked about the stock market and the hangers-on in the Palace bar, but he saw it in perspective as an inevitable side-product of the boom, and the morals of it didn't worry him. The fact that the mass of Australians had gone gambling mad and would get their fingers burned didn't make any difference to what was happening on the ground, except that a lot of barren areas were being proved to be just that.

The plane was landing now, its wheels hitting the runway with a puff of smoke from the sun-hot tyres. Kadek belonged to the world of money that thrived on rumours, on leaked information and the dubious reports of scouts. Yet his world and Carter's were all part of the same turmoil of excitement that had begun with Kambalda and a man called Cowcill searching the rock specimens in his garage more than a decade ago when uranium was what everyone was looking for,

I stubbed out my cigarette as the high-winged Fokker Friendship turned at the runway end, a bright blaze of metal in the sun. I was thinking of Petersen again, the way he had looked at me when I had asked him about Blackridge. I wished I had never mentioned it to that ugly Swede. It only complicated the issue. And now the plane was here, the roar of its engines drowning all sound as it swung into its parking position. The noise died to a whisper, the props stopped turning, then the fuselage gaped as the gangway was thrust against it and the passengers began to emerge. Kadek was one of the first, his dark face shaded by a panama hat and wearing a light blue suit.

He saw me, nodded and came across, nursing a slim briefcase under his arm. 'Glad to see you again. You got my telegram? Good. Chris told me you had arrived.' He gripped my hand, his eyes on mine, cold and calculating. And then he was introducing his companion, a quietly dressed man with a round friendly face. 'This is Les Freeman. He's chairman and managing director oi Lone Minerals, a small but very go-ahead Sydney-based company.' He glanced back at me, something in his eyes—a question mark, a challenge? 'Les, I'd like you to meet Alec Falls of Trevis, Parkes & Pierce. He's out here for one of the big London mining houses. Blackridge is one of the prospects he's been asked to look over.'

I should have denied it straight away, but I was so stunned by the barefaced lie that I just stood there, saying nothing.

He was watching me closely, the thin line of his mouth just as I remembered it, like a steel trap. And he had remembered the name of the firm I had been working for when we had last met. 'Have you been out to Blackridge yet?' I heard myself say No, and he nodded. I could see the wheels turning in his mind, the way he was going to handle it. And I just stood there, silent, wondering what sort of a man I was. Later, of course, I told myself that it was Freeman's fault for being so dumb. But that doesn't give you absolution, and Freeman was a nice enough bloke, even if he was an accountant.

'Where's Chris?' Kadek peered inside the terminal, saw him and gave a sharp, imperative jerk of his head that brought Culpin out in a hurry. 'Did you book us in at the Palace?'

Culpin nodded. 'I was lucky, a cancellation. But it's just the one room. You'll have to share.'

Kadek glanced at Freeman, who nodded. 'Good, then let's go.' As we moved out to the ute, he dropped back beside me, speaking quietly. 'Les knows nothing about mining. But his company badly needs a prospect, something he can feed the market with.' He gripped my arm, squeezing it. 'Don't push it too hard. And keep it scientific. Your observations a little beyond his grasp. But not too far. Understand?'

I nodded. I understood all right. 'We'll talk about it later,' I said. 'After I've seen the mine. And I'll want samples of my own analysed.'

He stopped then. 'Why? What d'you mean?' He was looking at me, his features hard and tense. But then he smiled, a conscious effort. 'Nothing for you to worry about,' he murmured, patting my arm. 'The analysis is correct. And it was made by an independent firm.'

'I know. I've seen Petersen.'

'Then what's your worry?' His voice grated.

'Surface dirt,' I said.

'And you want to dig down—do your own checking, eh?' His face was still arranged in a smile, but I could feel his anger. 'Well, let me tell you, I've done some checking myself. You start being awkward and I'll be on to the Commonwealth Immigration Department right away. I don't play for this sort of money with the gloves on.' And then abruptly he offered me $2,000—to help me find my feet out here. He smiled. It was a straight bribe and we both knew it, our eyes locked, each assessing the other, calculating. 'Nothing for you to worry about,' he repeated. 'Petersen Geophysics has a good reputation.' He glanced ahead to where his partner and Freeman had stopped by the ute. 'And if anybody takes the can, it's Chris.'

It was said cold-bloodedly, with no suggestion of regret.

'You mean, in the event of trouble, you'd——'

'I don't mean anything,' he snapped. 'I'm just telling you. Freeman can get any geologist he likes. The surface dirt he picks up will confirm Petersen's nickel percentages, and you're in the clear whatever happens. Now, d'you want the money or don't you?'

I hesitated. I'd less than twenty dollars left and that analysis to pay for. It was manna from heaven and I heard myself say, 'Have you got it on you—cash?'

He nodded, still watching me closely as we moved on to join the others. 'Alec's coming out to the mine with us,' he called out to Freeman. 'Unless you've any objections? He hasn't seen it yet, only the assay figures. He was out at the Geophysics lab checking with Petersen this morning.'

It was a thirty-mile drive out to Ora Banda and I was in the back with the sun blazing down. At Broad Arrow we turned off the Leonora highway on to a dirt road, the dust streaming behind us and the truck rattling over the ribbed surface. It was a hot, uncomfortable ride. I was alone in the back, my shoulders braced against the burning metal of the cab, my eyes half-closed against the glare, watching the gums streaming by on either side, the sweat drying on my body as I thought of what could do with that two thousand, and Golden Soak another Balavedra. It was the prospect of a fresh start that had sustained me through the long shipboard hours coming down across the world, and now the chance was there. I had always thought of myself as lucky, the man who could reach for the stars and grab hold where others were too scared, a loner to whom success was the essential life force. Maybe that's why I had chosen mining. The pot of gold at the rainbow's end.

If my younger brother had lived it might have been different. But he was stillborn, and after that my mother couldn't have any more children. So I was the only one and had to make up for all the others. At least I think it was that, the need to live up to my mother's expectations. And so, whenever I didn't succeed I talked myself into believing that I had. My mother again, for my father was a local government official, a surveyor in the planning department, and she cast me in the role of buccaneer, somebody who could live on his wits and go right to the top. She was ambitious, and living always a little beyond our means, money had been tight. So money became important, particularly after I'd acquired Rosa.

Rosa! It wasn't love. I realized that now. She was just the most beautiful thing I'd ever seen. And because other men wanted her, I had to have her for myself. I closed my eyes. God! How I longed for her, that slim beautiful body, the perfect breasts and the way she'd sit, quite naturally, but her legs unconsciously arranging themselves in open invitation. It seemed incongruous to be thinking of Rosa on that bumpy, dusty ride, but I hadn't had a woman now for over two months and in this hot country I was feeling the need. I wanted a drink, too. And then I was thinking of the rock samples I had left with Petersen, and that girl—gold and antimony and the snub nose, all those freckles like specks of gold. The heat blazed and my blood throbbed, but it wasn't the same—no vision there to meet my need.

I was still dreaming of Rosa when the gums fell back and I saw the pockmarks of old mineworkings in the red soil either side of us. The truck slowed. A car passed us and through a haze of dust I saw the wood façade of an hotel, empty and desolate. We were in a wide dirt street then, flanked by empty buildings; an old concert hall, and opposite it, on the other side, more empty buildings—a meat factory and the words *Ora Banda Dining Rooms* on a faded noticeboard. Two or three homesteads, and that was it. A ghost town, the buildings all of wood, tin-roofed and surrounded by a rusty litter of discarded household equipment and old abandoned vehicles.

Up a slight rise we passed the State Battery with its crusher and a small tailings dump. It looked as though it were still in use. Shortly afterwards we turned off the dirt road on to a track that wound haphazardly through the bush, the red gravel overlaid with black drifts like the scatterings of a coal cart, and everywhere mounds of earth marking the shallow shafts of departed gold diggers, the rusted debris of their camps. We swung round the end of a trenched line of diggings and stopped beside two abandoned tip trucks that lay on their sides flaking in the sun. The track on which they had run was rusted, half buried under a thin layer of wind-blown sand. We were in a grove of bronze-barked gums.

Culpin climbed out, looked up at me, his eyes squinting against the glare. 'Hot enough for you?' He grinned at me.

'Do with a drink, eh?' He reached into the cab and tossed me up a can of beer. I opened it and took a long swig, then climbed out and joined the others. They were standing in the shade drinking beer and eating sandwiches, looking across a flat area cratered with old workings to a timbered shaft head standing above a gaping hole, and Culpin was saying, 'I remember it before the war, when the Three-Eight was opened up. It had a cricket team and a football team then, and that hotel was fair humming with life.' He was talking about Ora Banda. 'Wouldn't take much to start it humming again—just a nickel strike, instead of gold.'

Kadek didn't say anything. Nor did Freeman. They were looking towards the mine with its poppet head and the rusty drag-wires coiled above the tailings dump. Flies crawled and it was furnace hot, the beer too warm and sweet. There was black grit under my feet and small pieces of quartz glistening white in the sun. I bent down and picked up a handful of tiny pebbles, dull black with a metallic look and smooth like well-sucked lozenges. I had seen specimens very like them only that morning in the glass cases at the School of Mines museum. 'Australites?' I asked, holding them out to Culpin.

But he didn't know. 'Meteorites, they say—debris from outer space. Ground's thick with them all round here.' He looked at Freeman. 'You want to have a look at the mine first? Then I'll show you where Petersen's man picked up the dirt that showed traces of nickel.' We left our beer cans winking in the sun and walked to the mine in a cloud of flies. But for the flies and the sun, and the rusty litter, it would have been an idyllic spot, the gum leaves flickering to a breeze and the boles silver through to bronze.

Freeman might not know very much about mining, but he had a shrewd business mind and he asked the right questions. Kadek played it very cool and quiet, as though he didn't much care what the outcome was, deferring all the time to me and leaving Freeman with the impression that bigger fish than his little company were after the bait.

The mine itself had been abandoned in 1959, and though the shoring timbers around the top of the shaft were still sound, it had collapsed in on itself about thirty feet down. The area that had yielded nickel-bearing samples was about five hundred yards north-east of the mine shaft. It looked no different from all the rest of that country, except it was slightly higher, on a ridge that ended at the mine. 'It's all part of the property,' Culpin said. 'They called it Blackridge because of the Black Range, which is all the higher ground north of here.' It was the australites, of course, that had given it its name. They lay very thick, black drifts that emphasized every surface undulation.

Kadek, standing beside me, mopped his brow. 'Remember I wrote you about my Newsletter? It's launched now and all I need is a first-rate geologist. You interested?' He gave me a quick sidelong glance. 'You'd make a lot of money backing the shares we tip.' He smiled, a conspiratorial smile as though we were already in it together. Then he turned to Freeman. 'Just telling Alec about my Newsletter. Maybe I'll do something on Lone Minerals in a month or two.'

The bait was so obvious I couldn't believe Freeman would rise to it. But that sort of talk interested him a lot more than the geological theory of ultrabasics. He'd seen the assay figures, read Petersen's guarded letter, but the ground on which we stood was much the same as the ridge, red gravel interspersed with quartz and drifted with the black of australites. 'What's your opinion?' he asked me.

I shrugged. 'I've told you what I can about the geology of the area. Beyond that I don't know any more than you do.'

'But you'll be sending a report in to your firm.' He seemed to take my silence for confirmation. 'Anything else you want me to see while I'm here?' he asked Kadek.

'No. Don't forget this isn't a claim. Whoever buys Blackridge owns the land, everything—a total of over a square mile. It's a point to bear in mind.' Kadek smiled. 'Look well in your next report.' And he nodded to Culpin and they started back towards the ute.

That left me alone with Freeman. 'You're looking over a number of prospects, I take it?' I didn't answer and he added, 'In fact, Blackridge isn't of any great importance to you.'

'I can't answer that,' I said. 'Not until we've run either a geochemical or an IP survey. Then any anomaly we struck would have to be proved by drilling.'

'Of course.' He was silent for a moment. And then he said, 'I'd like to put a proposition to you.'

The others were out of earshot and I still can't make up my mind whether Kadek put him up to it or whether it was his own idea. What he offered me was an option on 5,000 Lone Minerals shares at their present price of 29 cents if I'd sign an independent report setting out in geological terms the prospects for his acquisition of Blackridge. In short, he was suggesting that I act as a mining consultant for his company. 'In a private capacity, of course.' And he added, 'Ferdie's Newsletter already has an influential following. If the prospect looks good on paper and he tips it, the shares will move up sharply the way the market is right now.' Those were his exact words, the offer made quite openly as though it were the most natural thing in the world. 'Well, what do you say?'

What could I say? There was no point in refusing when I was already in deeper than he knew. 'Where do the shares come from?' I asked.

'From my own holding. I'll give you a letter, of course.'

I must have been out of my mind. If I hadn't accepted his offer. . . . But what the hell! It put money in my pocket when I needed it, and you can't have it both ways. 'Okay,' I said, and he nodded as though it hadn't occurred to him that I might have moral scruples.

We got back to Kalgoorlie just after four and I wrote my report in the stuffy little room that had been booked for them at the Palace. It was at the end of a rambling corridor that ran the whole length of the building and the single window looked out on to a yard and the sound of pigeons drowsing on the rooftops. Kadek came up and read it through, then he had me change one or two phrases, add a paragraph or two. 'That should clinch it,' and he peeled off the cash he'd promised me from a wad of notes he had in his briefcase. 'You invest that in the shares I tell you and you'll have no difficulty in maintaining yourself out here.' He wanted me to move into the Palace Hotel as soon as possible and mail him a weekly report on the information I picked up. 'Got anything on that copper deposit rumour? No? Well, I'll let you know from time-to-time the prospects I want you to take a closer look at.'

I suppose I should hate the man. But I don't. It's difficult to hate a man who has the drive and energy, the sheer guts to try and build a financial empire on nothing more substantial than his wits. Clever, selfish, cold-bloodedly ruthless—he was all that. And the mess I am now in was of his engineering. Yet I don't blame him. He was part of the rawness of that part of Australia.

He had the report typed on hotel notepaper by the girl in Reception. This guaranteed that it would be all over the Palace bar within the hour, which was probably why he went back up to his room to make a phone call. The Sydney and Melbourne exchanges would still be open owing to the time difference.

While he was gone I had a couple of drinks with Freeman and he wrote me a note covering the option. 'That was a good report,' he said. 'Just what I needed—especially that bit about Blackridge being in an area of singular promise with a built-in infrastructure.' This had been suggested by Kadek, a whole paragraph elaborating on the cost advantages of its proximity to Kalgoorlie with an experienced labour force, water, highways, the railway, every facility, in fact, for bringing a mine into production without the enormous expenditure involved in equivalent prospects deep in the outback. 'I think you'll find the option I've given you will more than repay you for any trouble you may have with your firm.'

I should have been warned by that, but he was already asking me what other prospects I had been instructed to examine, and I was thinking of Golden Soak. 'You find something good, then let me know. Lone Minerals is a new flotation. We've got the cash and you won't be the loser. Okay?' And he gave me his card with the Company's address in Sydney.

Kadek rejoined us, smiling and ordering drinks. 'Well, Les, here's to Blackridge being a bonanza.' And he raised his glass. He knew the deal was as good as settled. 'And I meant it about doing a piece on Lone Minerals.'

We had more drinks, then he told Culpin to leave Freeman and himself to sort the details out. 'Come back about eight. We should be through by then.' He looked at me, 'See you in the morning maybe. We'll be catching the seven-fifty flight back to Perth.' Then he turned to Freeman and suggested they had some food, dismissing both of us from his mind.

Culpin drove me back to his home in silence. All down the Golden Mile he never said a word and it wasn't until we were through Boulder that I realized what was on his mind. 'Ferdie said you'd be moving into the Pal. Gonna act as his scout, eh?'

'Something like that,' I murmured.

'An' what about me? Where do I come in?' He was glowering at me. 'Two thousand he gave you, right? Jesus! I don't make much more'n that out of the deal and it was me wot found Blackridge for him.' He was working himself up into a rage, afraid I was muscling in on the partnership. 'Well, I'm warning you. Ferdie's a ruthless, bloody bastard. And I'm not being edged out just because you've got a better education, see. You'll get your ruddy neck broken one dark night if you try that sort of thing out here.'

'You don't have to worry,' I told him. But I don't think he believed me. He was a mean bugger and nursing a grievance was like a drug: it deadened the pain of failure.

'Now if you'd got a line on that fellow McIlroy.' He was eyeing me shiftily, an ingratiating smile on his coarse face. 'You told me you were in Nullagine an' you saw that abo.'

'Yes.'

'And he told you nothing?'

'Nothing that meant anything. The man you want is Phil Westrop and you won't get anything out of him.'

'A prospector, eh?' He peered at me, then slammed the gear lever into second as we turned on to the loose grit track. He didn't say anything more, nursing his grievance in silence. That sense of grievance would have been difficult to stomach all evening if his son had not been home. He was sitting on the verandah steps and he looked up as we drove in, the face a little thinner than in the photograph, and peeling from the sun, the hair longer, but still the likeness to his mother clearly stamped.

'You just got in?' his father asked.

''Bout an hour ago.'

That was their greeting, and neither in their faces nor in the tone of their voices was there any sign of affection. 'You'll have to bed down on the sofa. Alec here's got your room.'

The boy nodded, staring at me very directly out of pale greenish eyes. 'So I gathered.' He smiled and held out his hand. 'I'm Kennie.' The smile stretched the scab of a sore at the corner of his mouth, his eyes crinkling, a depth of interest in them that was very personal.

'Have you had your tucker yet?'

'No. Mum said to wait for our guest.'

Culpin grunted and pushed open the flyscreen, calling to his wife. Then he turned back to his son. 'See anything interesting up there? Any likely prospects?'

'We were doing an aerial magnetic. You don't see prospects from a whirly bird, not when you're watching the instruments all the time.' His mouth twisted in an impish little grin. 'Saw a lot of roos though. Reds mainly.'

'Chrissakes! You bin having a dekko at the nickel country north of Leonora and all you can talk about . . .' Culpin checked himself, eyeing his son suspiciously. 'Well, when you weren't observing the wild life,' he said sarcastically, 'mebbe you found time to have a drink with some of the Poseidon boys.'

'Sure.' The boy nodded, standing there, not volunteering anything.

'Well, what did they tell you?'

'Nothing. They were drillers, that's all.'

The hostility between them was obvious, and it wasn't a generation gap—this was a conflict of personalities. Culpin hitched at his trousers. His back was towards me, the dark leathery skin of his neck a network of creases ingrained with red dust. The anger that had been building up in him all the way from the Palace would have broken out then if his wife hadn't appeared at the flyscreen door to say that supper was ready.

'What happened today?' she asked. 'Did that man Mr Kadek brought with him buy Blackridge?'

Culpin nodded. 'They're sorting out the details now.'

'Well, that's something,' she said tartly, and I glimpsed how tight things had become in this dilapidated house.

We went into the kitchen then and all through the meal Culpin hardly spoke a word. It was Kennie who did the talking, his mother listening, the two of them obviously very close. It had been his first aerial survey and he was very full of it. After the meal, when his father had gone back to the Palace, he came out and sat with me on the verandah in the fading light and for a while he talked about his survey, not as he'd talked about it over the meal, but as one geologist to another. They had been searching for nickel and copper over a lease area of nearly 300 square miles, and when I asked him whether they had found anything, he shrugged:

'One area that's possibly anomalous, that's all. But we won't be pegging. Not yet. There's a strong rumour the government intends to clamp down on all new claims. If that happens the Company will have more time to complete the survey. They'll be starting geochemical work as soon as the magnetometer results we got on this trip have been analysed.'

He picked up a stick and began drawing an emu in the black grit. He wanted to get a job up in the North West next. He'd heard a lot about it from his father and now geologists were saying it would be the next area to attract the attention of prospectors. 'You've just come down from there, haven't you?' And because he was the sort of boy he was, bubbling over with theory that he now desperately wanted to put into practice, I told him a little about the Garrety's and how Golden Soak had been discovered.

'That's the mine my father was making inquiries about.' He looked up from his drawing. 'You trying to buy it? Is that why you were up there?' And when I asked him why he thought it was for sale, he said, 'Just something I heard last night. We were at the Hotel in Leonora, celebrating the end of our survey, and this bloke I was talking to—he was from Marble Bar, some sort of property dealer, I think—he was talking about it. I don't remember all he said, I'd had a lot to drink by then, you see, but it's antimony, isn't it?'

I suppose I should have realized that people up in the Pilbara would know all about the mine, but it still came as a shock to hear him refer to the antimony content so casually. He knew about the price of antimony, too, even knew the reason for the sharp rise in the mineral's value: 'The main source is China and they've cut off supplies to the West, stockpiling against the possibility of war with Russia.' And then he asked me again whether the people I was acting for were going to buy it.

'I'm not acting for anybody,' I said. 'And anyway it isn't for sale.'

He began tracing the outline of a kangaroo, his head bent in concentration. 'You'll be going up there again.'

I didn't answer for a moment, thinking of Jarra Jarra and what it could mean to them. 'That depends on the analysis.'

He looked up, a quick movement of the head that tossed his fair hair back. 'You've got samples then?' His voice was eager, his eyes shining with genuine interest. In the end I took him into his room and showed him a piece of the Golden Soak reef quartz. He had a cheap students' microscope and he took it out on to the verandah, where the reflector could catch the last rays of the setting sun. His excitement when the specks of gold showed as minute chunks of metal embedded in the quartz crystals was infectious. But even under the microscope the grey smudges of the antimony still showed only as smudges. 'If the analysis is good and you do go up there again, can I come with you?'

I laughed. 'I can't afford an assistant.'

But he didn't want to be paid. He just wanted to learn. 'It wouldn't cost you anything and I could organize things for you. There's a friend of mine got an old Land-Rover he'd let me hire, and if you're camping out . . .' He gave a self-conscious little laugh, knowing he had let his enthusiasm run away with him. 'I've never done a practical survey under the direction of somebody with your sort of experience.'

'We'll see how the analysis works out,' I said. And after that we talked of mining generally. He'd worked on an IP survey at St Ives—'That's the other side of the causeway that crosses the salt lake called Lefroy, south of Kambalda.' He had done a geomagnetic on a prospect near Mt Yindarlgooda to the east of Kalgoorlie, another in the Laverton area. He talked of microprobe analyses and how they indicated the cobalt content of pentlandite and the nickel content of pyrrhotite. This was laboratory stuff, all very technical, and soon we were deep in the nature and origins of sulphides and ultrabasics. There was a little breeze out there on the verandah and we stayed there talking until his mother called us in for coffee and home-made cakes.

I went to bed almost immediately afterwards, but the room seemed airless and I didn't get to sleep for a long time. I was woken about midnight by the slam of the flyscreen door, the murmur of voices. They rose and fell, half inaudible; then suddenly Culpin's voice loud and slurred with drink: 'You say that again, boy . . .'

Silence and the hot breeze rattling at the pale square of the window. Then the hoarse voice started again, wheedling at first, then rising quickly in anger: 'I work my guts out, risking my neck to give you things I never had, and you throw it in my face. You silly little fool, you don't know what life's about. Now, come on——' There was the sound of a scuffle, followed by a blow and the crash of something falling.

I was out of bed then, but though I moved fast, Edith Culpin was ahead of me, the parlour door open and her figure framed in the light of a torch. Beyond her, I could see the tumbled bedclothes on the couch and Culpin standing over his son, his big hands gripping his shoulders, shaking him. A small table lay on its side, a china vase in pieces on the floor. And Kennie, his lip cut and blood oozing, speaking in a whisper.

Edith Culpin screamed at her husband, and he turned and stared at her, his bull of a head thrust forward. 'Go back to bed, woman.' His voice, still heavy and slurred, had a hard core of authority in it, and when she flew at him, he flung her back. She fell on to the couch, a breast flopping white above the pink nightdress, hair dishevelled, hate flaring in her eyes.

And then he saw me. 'Thought to keep it to yourself, did you?' He was swaying, his big face glistening with sweat, the small eyes greedy. He'd had a lot to drink. 'Think I don't know the price of antimony?' He let go of Kennie and took a step towards me, his lips pursed in a little smile. 'You come between me and my son, an' I'll break your neck for you.' His eyes were mean now, anger feeding on the alcohol in him. He was suddenly dangerous. I stood there in the doorway bracing myself to meet him.

Kennie was looking at me, the cut lip swelling and his eyes scared. 'I'm s-sorry,' he mumbled.

I started to say something and then I turned away and went back to my room. I knew it was no good. He was afraid of his father and there was nothing I could do to stop him talking. No point now, anyway.

I heard Edith Culpin go back to bed, the sound of her crying audible through the partition. Shortly afterwards her husband's footsteps passed my door. No words between them, only the sound of his movements as he undressed and got into bed beside her. Then silence, the house gripped in stillness. Even the breeze outside seemed to have died.

The sun was up when I woke, shining hot on my face, and the kettle whistled in the kitchen, footsteps padding in the passage outside my door. Culpin was halfway through his breakfast when I went into the kitchen. Small and bloodshot, his eyes glanced at me quickly, then back to his bacon and eggs. He ate with concentration, and his wife at the stove didn't look at me, didn't speak. She was clammed up tight as though desperately trying to keep a hold on her emotions. There was no sign of Kennie.

The smell of coffee, and the bacon frying, were the only good things about the kitchen that morning and I ate in a silence that was tense with unspoken words. Edith Culpin was in her dressing gown, a shapeless cotton print, and sitting there, drinking her coffee, her large greenish eyes fixed on her husband, she suddenly banged her cup down. 'Kennie's gone.' Her voice trembled.

He finished his coffee and wiped his mouth with the back of his hand. 'Time that boy grew up.' And then he looked at her. 'If you hadn't dropped your second, you wouldn't have spoilt him the way you have.'

They stared at each other a moment, hostile and without understanding. Then Edith Culpin began to cry, the tears dripping from her tired eyes, soundless.

We left for the Palace almost immediately, Culpin driving in silence. After he had parked the ute, he didn't get out, but turned to me and said, 'I bin thinking, about this Golden Soak. You gonna mention it to Ferdie?'

'No point till I know what the analysis is.'

'But if it's good and the mine comes up for sale——' There

was a crafty, eager look in his bloodshot eyes. 'I remember the old Comet. That was a de Bernalese mine, one of the few good ones he ever had. Up the track from Marble Bar, just beyond Chinaman's Pool. I was a youngster at the time. Went up there to make my fortune and ended up serving behind the bar at the Ironclad.' He was smiling to himself, the eagerness still there so that for a moment he looked a younger man. 'That's how I know about de Bernales and his Commonwealth Finance.' He gripped my arm, suddenly urgent. 'My cut of the Blackridge deal will be through in a week or two, and this Golden Soak mine's unsafe, Kennie says. I always wanted to go back to the Pilbara an' if we could get it cheap——' He left it at that, apparently content that he'd made his position clear. 'You think about it, eh?' And he climbed out and went into the hotel.

Ten minutes later we were all four of us at the airfield. And the last thing Kadek said to me before he boarded the plane was, 'You put half of that two thousand in Lone Minerals. But don't wait. Do it today.' He was relaxed, almost jaunty. 'I'll tell you when to sell. And keep in touch.' He handed me a card. 'There's my phone number. Ring me in Perth if there's anything urgent. Otherwise a weekly report by letter.'

We drove back by a different route, past a big caravan park, washing listless on the line and the heat already heavy. 'I'll be in the Pal midday,' Culpin said as he dropped me off at Petersen Geophysics. 'We can talk about it then over a beer.' The hide of the man was almost unbelievable.

Petersen was already in his office. 'Is all right, your analysis.' He gave me a toothy grin and a heavy slap on the back. 'Gold $5\frac{3}{4}$ ounces average. Is about what I t'ink. The antimony is not so good, more variable—$2 \cdot 1$ per cent, $3 \cdot 4$, and on the third sample $0 \cdot 2$ per cent. Okay?' He handed me the analyst's typed report, together with my samples, and I paid him his fee from the wad of notes Kadek had given me. 'Now you go t'ink about what you do next, eh?' He seemed genuinely pleased that the results were good. 'Also, I haf a letter for you—is delivered by Chris's son Kennie this morning.'

I read it as I walked towards the centre of the town. It was a long, unhappy explanation of his relations with his father, and it finished up: *I realize what you told me was in confidence, but he's capable of anything when he's got a load on. I must get away from here now, so if you're going north again, please let me come with you.* He gave the address of the friend he was staying with and I wondered whether it was the same friend who had the old Land-Rover for hire.

The local stockbroker's office was a travel and insurance agency in the brick section of the Palace building. I arranged for the purchase of 3,000 Lone Minerals as soon as the market opened in Perth and then I went across to the *Kalgoorlie Miner* in Hannan Street. It was an odd place, a shop selling stationery, books and postcards, the newspaper produced from poky little offices in the rear. A girl eventually produced the file copies for 1939, and when I told her I wanted to look up their report of McIlroy's disappearance, she found it for me immediately. 'Funny thing, you're the second person to ask me for it. There was a man in here about a week ago.' She even remembered his name—Kadek. 'I never heard a name like that before.' She was a big girl, about twenty-five, and she hovered over me while I read the accounts, which covered about three weeks. 'All the time I've been here, nobody's asked me for the 1939 file, and now two of you inside a week.'

I turned the pages, reading quickly. It gave the name of the aborigine who had found the empty abandoned vehicle and I wrote it down, also the name of the constable who had examined the truck and organized the search for McIlroy's body. He had had a well-known native tracker with him on the job, but he had found nothing. The empty truck had been discovered on June 2 and McIlroy had last been seen alive at Nullagine five months before, on January 5. He had then announced that he would be heading out into the blue on an outback track that branched off the line of the telegraph at Ethel Creek, but the people at the Ethel Creek homestead said he had not called there and they had not seen his vehicle or any sign of tracks. And then this paragraph:

Inevitably the mystery surrounding his disappearance has given birth to a number of rumours. The most persistent of these is that, instead of heading east from Ethel Creek, he went first to the Jarra Jarra homestead of his partner, Big Bill Garrety, and that it was from there that he finally set out on his ill-fated attempt to locate his fabulous monster. There is no evidence to support this and in view of the relationship between the two men following upon Pat McIlroy's misuse of the bank's money this seems most unlikely. Indeed, the police have a statement from Mr Garrety categorically denying it.

'I've got some notes, if you'd like to see them.' I could feel the warmth of her body leaning over me. 'I read up on everything we'd printed on McIlroy the other day. It's such an odd story I thought maybe I could sell it to a magazine.'

Her notes were typewritten and very comprehensive. Not only had she included details of his association with Bill Garrety and his investment of the bank's deposits, but his background as well. And it was there, in the information about his private life before he'd come to Kalgoorlie, that I was brought up with a jolt, the name Westrop staring at me from the typescript.

McIlroy had been born in the King's Cross district of Sydney in 1901, the eldest of seven children. Both his parents had been Irish and his father had been a bookie's tout. He had grown up on racecourses. In 1926 he had become a stockbroker's clerk and the following year he had married Elspeth Julia Westrop, daughter of a wool buyer for an English company. They had had two children, both boys, and it was after the birth of the second that he had left Sydney and gone to make his fortune in Kalgoorlie.

'What happened to the family?' I asked.

She shrugged. 'They never came out to West Australia. The two sons died in the war, the wife in 1954.'

'Do you know anything about the wife's family? Had she any brothers, for instance?'

But she didn't know. 'There's only one person here who was at all close to Pat McIlroy—I would guess she was probably his mistress for a time. She is a bit of a hag and too fond of the bottle, but she might be able to tell you.'

She gave me the woman's address and I got a taxi and went there right away. It was a small, rusty-coloured shack at the bend of a dirt road with a view across the workings of the old Iron Duke. She was frail and none too clean, her head wobbling as she spoke, words slipping out in little gasps. Yes, she remem-

bered Pat McIlroy, but she sounded unsure of herself and I
guessed he had only been one of many. His wife? She shook
her head. 'Pat didn't like her. Nor her family. Called them a
lot of bleedin' sheep stealers.' She fixed me with a thirsty,
calculating eye. 'You pop round to the 'otel, dearie, and ask
them for a bottle of Gladdy's usual. Mebbe I'll remember some
more then.'

But I didn't think she knew much more and I was just on the
point of leaving when she wobbled her head at me and said,
'Her brother come here once raising hell. I remember that
now. He was a tall, mean man and I was young then.' She
smiled, nodding. 'More ways of fixing a man . . .' The smile
became a snigger. 'I got a dose of clap at the time, see.'

Had she given it to McIlroy, too? Or perhaps it was the
other way round. I couldn't bring myself to ask her that. It's
a nasty business, trying to glimpse the nature of a man who's
been dead more than thirty years through the eyes of an aged
tart. But walking back into the centre of Boulder I couldn't
help thinking that venereal disease might account for the
recklessness he had shown at the end in gambling with his own
life.

I got a taxi, still feeling unclean, as though I had been in
contact with the woman myself, and drove to the Culpin home
to pick up my suitcase. Edith Culpin looked as though she had
been crying again, her face very pale and the eyes red-rimmed.
'If you see Kennie, tell him to come home. It'll be all right.'
And she added, 'He's all I got really.' The sadness in her voice
was the sadness of loneliness.

Driving back into Kalgoorlie I tried to concentrate on
Golden Soak and what I would say to Ed Garrety when I
reached Jarra Jarra. But the memory of those two women
seemed to dominate my thoughts—so different, yet both of
them facing lives that were empty, a dead end. And Westrop.
If he was really McIlroy's nephew, then his presence in
Nullagine only made sense if he knew something nobody else
seemed to know.

It was almost midday and I stopped off at the broker's to
find he had had to pay 32 cents a share. 'You're lucky,' he said.
'They're quoted at 34 on the Sydney Exchange.' He gave me a

contract and I paid him cash, and I arranged for him to wire me the money when I instructed him to sell.

That contract, a little piece of paper—it's difficult to explain what it meant to me. But I walked out of there a new man. Twenty-four hours ago I had been just about broke. Now I had cash in my pocket and a stake in the country. I was part of the Australian mineral boom, sharing the excitement of other market gamblers. It gave me a feeling of extraordinary confidence as I got back into the taxi and was driven to the address Kennie had given me. It was at the corner of Cassidy and Cheetham, a green-painted verandahed house overlooking the recreation ground, and there was a dusty, battered-looking Land-Rover standing outside.

Looking back on it now, I cannot blame Kennie for deciding to come north with me. He wasn't hard-hearted or any more inconsiderate than other young men of his age. And he was deeply attached to his mother. But he had his own life to live and he refused absolutely to go back and face his father again. 'It wouldn't work. It never has, it never will.' His lips were trembling as he said that and his eyes looked scared. 'I got to get away. Please . . .' He looked so like his mother I couldn't help thinking that the two of them, so close all those years, had been a factor in Culpin's desperate urge to strike it rich, the need to prove himself.

The young man he was staying with had been a fellow student at the School of Mines. His father was Jim Norris, a lapidary with a shop in Hannan Street where he sold semi-precious jewellery he made himself. The business was now established so that other enthusiasts were bringing the stones to him. He and his son no longer had to go out and fossick for them, hence the availability of the Land-Rover. That and Kennie's enthusiasm decided me.

The rest of the day passed quickly as we checked the vehicle and shopped around for the stores and equipment we needed. Mrs Norris gave us an early meal, and as the sunset flared to a lurid purple, I drove out of Kalgoorlie, taking the road north to Leonora, Kennie sitting beside me, tight-lipped and silent.

FIVE

Ed Garrety

I

WE DROVE THROUGH THE NIGHT, tarmac at first, a single
track with verges of red gravel, then dirt. And the country, in
the clear cloudless dawn, flat as a pan. We were into the
northern part of the Yilgarn Block, metamorphosed rock, all
gibber, the gravel eroded *in situ*, hardly any watercourses, but
a great salt lake before we ran into Wiluna. Kennie was driving
then and I was dozing, my eyeballs pricking with tiredness,
the heat already building. I had nearly hit a kangaroo in the
grey hour before the dawn, but there weren't many of them
here on the edge of the Gibson.

We were through the rabbit fencing, heading west for
Meekatharra, the sun behind us, everything very sharp in the
clarity of the early light, the dirt of the road running like a
red ribbon through an infinity of spinifex and bare sun-
scorched rocks. 'What about a brew-up?' Kennie's thin little
beard was thick with dust, his long hair blowing in the wind
from the open window. His teeth were even and very white
as he smiled at me through the dust. 'I could use a good brew
right now, eh?'

I nodded and he drew into the shade of the next patch of
mulga. It was a kind of acacia, but thin stuff, half dead and full
of ants, the air breathless. The flies came at us in a cloud as
soon as we had stopped.

Without Kennie it would have taken me three days to get
back to the Pilbara. It wasn't only the shared driving, it was
the fact that he knew how to live bush—something at least
he owed his father. Within minutes he had a fire going, the
billy on and bacon sizzling in the pan. Except for the flies, it
was the finest breakfast I had had in Australia—the quiet and
the huge sense of space, the close feeling of companionship. I
was relaxed then, thinking how lucky I was, what a wonderful

world. We didn't talk much after we had fed, just sat there smoking and drinking thick Indian tea. *It's old—old geologically.* That was what Petersen and Carter had said. *It's unique.* And now I was out there, looking at it, remembering their words, the country as old as time and my mind involuntarily going back to Genesis and ancient, primitive gods. 'Do you know much about the aborigine?' I asked him.

But he shook his head. 'Only what a Native Affairs officer told us in a lecture he gave at the School. He made them seem a remarkable people, every day in their lives filled by the excitement of survival. Christ, look at it! I'd get a great kick if I could survive out here on my own, no tinned food, no cans of petrol, no gun, nothing but what I'd found and made. Reck'n that fellow was one of the really good ones, for he talked about living for a period with a family in the Gibson. To survive, like that——' He shook his dusty head, an almost dreamy look in those greenish eyes, now sun-crinkled at the corners. 'And living like that, from hand-to-mouth—subsisting, no more— and yet the Dreamtime, all their myths, the complicated sacred side of their lives. After I'd heard that man speak, I found myself looking at all the poor bastards in Kalgoorlie in a different light. They're a very strange people—but I respect them now. Imagine it—out there . . .' He jerked his head towards the east. 'Nothing but your wits, the knowledge handed down to you by your elders, and your bare hands. I wouldn't survive twenty-four hours.'

Later I was to remember that conversation, but at the time, replete and plagued with ants, the flies thick, I was too hot and tired to care a damn about the aborigines, accepting his words as part of the companionship developing between us, nothing more. A small wind rose, drifting red dust like a river across the road, and at Meekatharra we stopped for petrol and a long cold drink of beer. And then we were heading north, the tarmac running out into the dirt after about fifty miles and the sun dimmed by a brown cloud of wind-blown sand that coated the Land-Rover and ourselves. It was a hell of a drive, until shortly after noon the wind suddenly dropped, the air clear again and the sun burning. Cheese and tomatoes, a long siesta among the ghost gums of a dry watercourse, then on again with the sun setting into the Gibson, the dark shape of hills standing like islands in a red-brown sea. Somewhere near Mundiwindi we lit a fire, cooked ourselves a meal. 'What happens when we get to Jarra Jarra?'

'I don't know.' I was too tired, too battered with the jolting to think about that. Janet I knew would be glad about the analysis, but I wasn't so sure about her father. We had our swags unrolled on the hard ground, and lying there, gazing up at the stars, I wished I knew him better.

'This man Garrety, what's he like?'

'All right.'

'Yes, but those samples—he don't know about them. That's right, isn't it? You said last night——'

'Aren't you tired?'

'Yes, of course I'm tired.'

'Then go to sleep.'

'I can't. I'm too excited.' His cigarette glowed in the darkness. 'Everybody I talked to—the old-timers, I mean—they seemed to know all about the Garretys and this station of theirs, the mine. It's part of the history of the North West.' But I had closed my eyes and in a moment the murmur of his young voice was lost in sleep.

He shook me awake shortly after three, the billy boiling and the stars still bright, and half an hour later we were on the road again. Dawn was breaking and Mt Whaleback a solid hump against the paling sky as I took the cut-off by the old airfield where I had waited for Janet to pick me up. Kennie stirred and stretched his legs. 'How much further?'

'About sixty miles—two hours if we don't break a spring in the gullies.'

'Christ! It's back of beyond.' His voice was sleepy. 'What's this girl like—tough?'

'She rides a camel when they're mustering.'

'Sounds like dampers for breakfast and I could do with a good big steak.'

He went to sleep again and I drove all the rest of the way to Jarra Jarra. It was just after eight when we crossed the cattle grid into the paddock. We topped the rise and there was the homestead just as I had seen it that first time, like a deserted settlement in the blazing sun with the galahs a flock of grey shot through with pink, bursting out of the trees at the rattle of our approach.

We stopped in the shade, the homestead silent, no dog barking, no camel crouched there by the further bole, only the galahs wheeling. 'Reck'n they start at first light.' Kennie pushed open the door and got stiffly out. 'Most of these out back stations start early this time of the year.' He was thinking only of the breakfast he had been hoping for. He followed me between the outbuildings, across the patio and into the dim cool of the wire-netted room. It was empty, the house silent I called Janet's name, but there was no answer, the stillness heavy with the heat.

'There must be somebody around.' I went through into the passageway, to the door of Ed Garrety's den. I thought perhaps he might be listening on the radio. I couldn't remember when the morning sked was. But the door was locked, no answer to my call. I tried the kitchen then. A pot of tea and cups on the scrubbed wood table, the paraffin stove cold and nothing on it but a kettle, the water in it lukewarm. A current of hot air behind me and I turned to glimpse dark eyes watching out of a black face. The eyes were huge. 'Sarah?' A flash of teeth, a nervous giggle and the face of the black servant girl was gone. 'Sarah!' But by the time I reached the door she was running across an open compound towards some huts, running like startled deer.

There was nothing for it but to cook our own breakfast, and when we had finished it, we sat dozing in the cane chairs in the cool house. We were both of us very tired and I was dead asleep when the sound of a vehicle woke me. I expected it to be Ed Garrety. Instead, it was Westrop who came in through the beaded flyscreen from the patio. He stopped at the sight of me. I had got to my feet and for a moment we stood there facing each other, both of us too surprised to say anything.

'What do you want?' I asked him.

'Garrety. Where is he—still down the mine?'

'I've no idea. We've only just arrived.'

'And the girl?' He moved towards the passage.

'There's nobody here,' I said.

He paused then, looking at me doubtfully. 'Yuh sure?' And when I didn't say anything, he turned and went outside, and I heard him talking to somebody. He was back almost immediately, coming in with that odd swaggering gait, and suddenly I knew what he reminded me of—the digger of Australian legend, the battle-scarred veteran of the wars they had fought across the world. It wasn't only that he had a wide-brimmed hat on his head and his khaki longs tucked into high boots, it was the long hard face, the steady eyes creased by the sun. His appearance, his whole bearing reminded me of Anzac Day and those pictures of floods of khaki wading ashore at Suvla Bay from old coal-burning troopships. 'Yuh could help me,' he said, standing hesitant. 'No hard feelings, eh?' He smiled, the dour look gone and a flash of warmth.

'No, of course not.'

He nodded. 'Sit down then. I'd like to talk to yuh.' He dropped into a chair, running his hand over the stubble of his pointed chin and staring at me as I resumed my seat. 'You're probably the only man, apart from Garrety, who's been down Golden Soak in years. Did you get into all the levels?'

'Who told you I'd been down there?'

'Prophecy. Yuh didn't expect her to keep it to herself, did yuh? Yuh were down there getting ore samples the night we dumped yuh on the Highway.' That flicker of a smile again. 'Something I didn't expect. But you've been down there, that's the point.' He leaned forward, his elbows on the cane arms of his chair. 'Did yuh see anything that struck yuh as unusual, anything odd?'

'How do you mean?'

'Hell!' he said. 'Yuh must have seen something. Yuh were pretty shaken, Prophecy said—and yuh didn't seem to want to talk about it.'

'You'd be shaken if you'd been down there,' I told him. 'I was on my own and another cave-in could occur at any time.' But I think he knew it wasn't that, for he was staring at me very intently, waiting, and I was remembering the footprints, the strange atmosphere in that third level. 'What are you getting at?' I asked, suddenly certain he knew something I didn't.

'Garrety,' he said. 'I want to know what he's up to down there.'

'Didn't Prophecy tell you?'

'Oh, sure. He's found the reef. There were a couple of prospectors and some truckers in the night Prophecy passed your quartz samples round the bar. By now just about everybody in WA must know he's found the reef again. So what's the point of him going on working down there on his own?'

'You'd better ask him.'

'I'm asking yuh. The samples yuh took came from a side gallery, Prophecy said. Beyond a rock fall, that right?'

I nodded, wondering what he was getting at, seeing the white of the quartz again, remembering the feeling of near-panic that had come over me.

'What caused the fall?' And when I told him the rock was badly faulted, the fall almost certainly the site of the 1939 cave-in, he said, 'Look. We were down there last night and his Land-Rover was parked up the gully. When we reached the mine entrance we were faced with that Alsatian of his, barking its head off. Then he came out, all covered in dust and looking like a bloody Cyclops with his miner's lamp blazing in the darkness. I didn't see the gun at first, but I know the sound of a bolt slamming a round into the breech, too right I do. What's he so scared about?'

'Prospectors—people like you.' But he shook his head and I sat there staring at him, a ghastly thought in my mind, for there was a curious tension in him, an undercurrent of excitement. 'He owns the mine, so you can't claim.' Silence and the thought growing in my mind. 'You're McIlroy's nephew, aren't you?' He was suddenly very still, his mouth clamped shut. 'And you're from Sydney.'

'Wot if I am?' The crinkles at the corners of his eyes deepened, his voice hard and flat.

'You must be all of forty and you've never been in the Pilbara in your life before, never shown the slightest interest in your uncle's death. Why now?'

'That's my business.'

'And you came here from Darwin, straight out of hospital. So it's something you learned in hospital—either there or in

Vietnam.' I was guessing and the expression in his eyes told me I was right. 'What is it? What was it made you come down here and get a job as near to Jarra Jarra as you could?'

He got up then, coming towards me, and now the tension showed in his eyes. I didn't move and he stood there, staring down at me. 'S'pose McIlroy never went into the Gibson?' He leaned down, his face close to mine. 'S'pose he died right here?'

It was out now, the thought in my mind put into words, and Westrop staring at me, trembling slightly like a hound on the scent. 'No,' I said firmly. 'You know where his truck was found. He died somewhere to the east of Lake Disappointment.'

He nodded. 'That's the story.'

'You don't believe it.'

'No.' He was still standing over me, but more relaxed as he said slowly, 'Yuh see, when he left Nullagine, he didn't go into the Gibson. He came here.'

'How do you know?'

He hesitated. 'Okay, I'll tell yuh. It was a man called Gray. Tommy Gray. He was in the hospital bed next to mine and all one night he was rambling on about his childhood here. His father was the doctor in this shire, so what he said was dinkum, and one of the things he was on about was Pat McIlroy's death.'

'And McIlroy came here?'

'That's what Tommy said.'

'Why?'

'I don't know why. He just did, that's all.'

'Gray's dead, is he?'

'Yes. Died the following night, a Cong knife wound in the guts that had turned septic.'

'In other words he was delirious.'

'Of course he was delirious. Otherwise, he'd never have talked the way he did. Oh to hell with it!' he added angrily. 'Yuh wouldn't understand. We didn't have any of yuh Pommies in that war. Yuh don't know what it was like, and if I told yuh he was screaming like an injured rabbit part of the time . . .' He took a step towards me, leaning his face close again and gripping my arm. 'Wot's Garrety doing down that mine? Now come on, be fair. Either he's mad, like his father, or he's trying to cover something up. They never found McIlroy's body, did they?'

'You don't really care what happened to him.' I said it harshly. It was the Monster, of course. It was McIlroy's Monster that had brought him here, the will o' the wisp lure of a mountain of copper. It had to be. And Westrop looking at me with a little smile and saying, 'No, I guess you're right. I don't give a damn. But that doesn't mean . . .' He was interrupted by the rattle of the beaded flyscreen and he turned, his body blocking my view. 'Did yuh find him?' he asked. And another voice answered, 'Sure I did. But getting it out of him wasn't so easy. Like Wolli said, he's a bit gone in the head.'

Westrop moved then and I saw it was Lenny, the wrinkled, mummified face cracking in a grin as he looked across at me. 'So you're back, eh? I told Phil you would be.'

Beyond the beaded curtain I could see Wolli hovering, a black shadow in the sun. 'What's this all about?' I asked, getting to my feet.

Kennie had moved in closer, the two of us facing them. Westrop hesitated. And Lenny said, 'It was Wolli put us on to him. An old black, bin living here ever since he got his skull cracked in that cave-in. They call him Half-Bake. Wolli thought there was another way into the mine.' He looked at Westrop and nodded. 'He was right, too.'

He wouldn't say where the entrance was, but he admitted it hadn't been used for maybe forty years. 'You must be mad,' I told him. 'That mine's a death trap. And to go into it by a disused entrance . . .'

'No business of yours,' Westrop said, and I saw his mind was made up and nothing I could do would dissuade him. And then, as he was following Lenny out to the patio, he turned. 'If we don't meet up with Garrety down the mine, tell him I'll be back. And I'll know the truth by then. Yuh tell him that. And don't try to follow us, see.' He nodded and ducked out through the flyscreen, leaving us standing there.

Shortly afterwards we heard the sound of their truck driving off. It was only then I started for the Land-Rover. But when we reached it the back tyres were almost flat, the air still hissing out. 'Nice friends you have.' Kennie's voice shook as he bent to examine the knife slits plainly visible.

There was no other vehicle available, the ute not there and the aged Land-Rover in the workshop by the petrol pump with the battery flat and the fuel line broken. We started out to search the rest of the buildings for the old miner, but we didn't find him. We found where he had been, in a half-derelict hut on the far side of the compound across which the aborigine girl had run so swiftly. The hut was surrounded by the debris of human life, plastic bottles and rusting cans with the flies swarming; inside it was a slum with nobody there. We searched all the buildings, but there wasn't an aborigine on the place, and though we called his name, and that of the girl, there was no answer, the whole settlement utterly deserted.

We went to work on the Land-Rover then, cursing the flies as we sweated at tyre levers hot as branding irons. We were in the process of getting the covers back on when Janet's voice brought me round on my heels. She was shouting at me, her face white with tiredness, her eyes blazing. She seemed to be accusing me of something, but in the exhaustion of working in the heat after a sleepless night my mind was slow to grasp what it was about. I just sat back on my heels and let her tongue lash over me, until at last it dawned on me that the old abo must have gone running to her and she thought we were responsible for scaring him out of what wits he had.

When I told her it was two miners from Nullagine, she didn't argue. She didn't apologize either. She just seemed to accept it, and though she calmed down, she was still breathing heavily as though she had run a marathon in the heat, her nostrils quivering and the skin below the eyes and around the mouth very white. I got to my feet then. I thought she was going to pass out. She put her hand up to her forehead, wiped ineffectually at the caked dust, and then abruptly sat down on the ground. 'I was on Cleo,' she murmured. 'All the way to the mine. Then back. And Sarah met me.'

The old man was the girl's uncle. I hadn't realized that. 'She said two white men, and when I saw you here . . .' She closed her eyes. 'Why? What were they after?'

'Another way into the mine.' Her eyes were fixed on me, very

146

large, as I explained how they had tried to get into Golden Soak the previous night.

She nodded wearily. 'I knew something had happened. I went to bed about eleven and he still hadn't come back. He's been down there every day since you left. And this morning, the house silent and his room empty, the bed not slept in.' She leaned her head in her hands. 'What is it?' It was a question aimed at herself more than me. 'It's not money. He's never given a damn about money. I've had to look after that. What is it?' She was staring up at me again, her lips trembling. 'He's been so strange.' And then she said, 'I was out all day yesterday with the boys—another bunch they'd found, up by the Deadman Hill. I was beat.' She leaned forward. 'Miners, you said—what do they want?' And then suddenly urgent—'Were they the ones who were here before?'

I didn't answer that. I didn't want her to know what Westrop was after. 'We'll finish getting these covers on, then we'll go down there.'

She nodded. 'I've just been into the shaft myself. Daddy was on the third level. I could hear him picking at the rock, beyond a fall in one of the smaller galleries. He was furious when he found I was there.' Her lips were trembling again, the sweat breaking out in beads on her forehead. 'What's happened? What's he doing down there? He won't tell me anything.' And suddenly tears welled in her eyes and she got quickly to her feet. 'I'll make some coffee.' She turned and hurried towards the house.

'What's up with her? Everybody seems crazy around here.' Kennie was staring at me, a bewildered look on his face.

I was back at the Land-Rover then. 'Come on,' I said. 'Let's get the spare on for a start. Then we'll have our coffee and go on down there and find out.'

By the time we'd got the last cover on and the wheel bolts tightened she had the coffee ready. She'd washed and put some lipstick on, but she still looked desperately tired, her face drained of colour. I asked her about the abo they had called Half-Bake. 'They said he was working at Golden Soak when the cave-in took place.'

She nodded, but absently, her mind elsewhere.

'And he's been here ever since?'

'Yes.'

'Does he remember things?'

'How do you mean—what things?'

'About what happened here afterwards,' I said. 'The cave-in occurred in 1939. Your grandfather's Journal doesn't help. But this man might know. I'd like to have a word with him.'

But she wouldn't agree to that. 'I don't think he'd know the difference between you and the men who were asking him questions. Reminding him, like that—it was cruel.'

I drank the rest of my coffee, knowing it was no good, and she didn't know anything about another entrance. 'All right,' I said. 'We'll get going now.'

She wanted to come with us, of course, but I told her No. I didn't know what I was going to find and I didn't want her along. She was too tired, anyway. She came out with us to the Land-Rover. 'He may not hear you calling to him down the shaft.' And she began to tell me how to reach that drift on the third level.

'I know where it is,' I told her.

She nodded. 'Yes, of course. I forgot.'

The significance of her words passed me by, for by then I was behind the wheel and had started the engine. 'Don't worry,' I said. 'I'll find him and I'll bring him back with me.'

'Yes, but what about those men?'

'An entrance that hasn't been used for at least thirty years isn't going to let them just walk into the third level. They'll need to work at it, and that'll take time.' She stared uncertainly, wanting to believe me. 'We'll be about three hours,' I said.

She nodded, her eyes red-rimmed in the sun, her pale hair blowing in the hot breeze. I turned the Land-Rover and headed down the track to the paddock, leaving her standing there, a still, small figure motionless in my driving mirror. It was just after eleven, barely an hour since Westrop had left. By now he would be at Golden Soak, and if he hadn't run into Ed Garrety on the way, he might at this moment be working his way into the mine by the alternative entrance. I was trying to visualize where it might be as I crossed the cattle grid and put my foot hard down. Previously, driving this track, we had taken the switchbacks and the dry stone watercourses at a leisurely speed. Now I was in a hurry, and I just hoped the springs would stand it and that our tyre patches would hold up to the blistering intensity of the sun and the heat of gravel friction.

'There all night, she said.' Kennie had to shout to make me hear above the roar of the engine, the rattle of the aged chassis. 'Must be pretty tired by now.'

I nodded. 'Maybe we'll meet him coming back.' He had told Janet he wouldn't be long. I hoped we would meet him.

'What is it he's looking for if he's already found the reef?' But I didn't answer. I was tired and though I was driving as fast as I could on that lousy track, the nearer I got the less I seemed to want to arrive. It wasn't premonition. It was just that driving was in itself sufficient activity for my depleted reserves. In the end, I drove in silence, and as we left Mt Robinson behind us, I found myself dreading the moment when I saw the mine buildings again with that thin, solitary chimney towering black against the blinding white of the sky. A sound of thunder rumbled in the distance. But no sign of rain, the whole oven vault above empty of the smallest cloud.

It was eleven minutes to twelve when the mine buildings came abruptly into view round that red outcrop of rock. But everything was obscured, the iron chimney a blurred pencil-line, half lost in a haze of dust. It hung over the gully and the plain below, a red miasma that had both of us choking with our handkerchiefs across our faces as we drove into it. 'Dust storm,' Kennie yelled.

But I knew it wasn't a dust storm. 'No wind.'

'Mebbe wind out there.' He nodded east towards the Gibson. But if this was Gibson sand, driven and suspended over miles of bush, we would have felt the weight of the wind and we'd have been in sand all the way. Whatever it was, it was entirely local, and with my heart suddenly pounding I drove past the tin-tattered buildings wrapped in dust and swung the Land-Rover up the track towards the dark shadow mouth of the gully. I was on headlights then, everything choked with a fine red dust, and where the old workings began it was pouring out of the ground, red boiling smoke billowing up and a great pit just in front of us. If I'd been going downhill I wouldn't have had a hope, but because of the gradient I was able to stop the Land-Rover dead. Even so the front wheels were on the very edge of that enormous boiling unbelievable cavity. An eruption? A crater?

'What the hell's happened?' Kennie was staring.

But I think he knew. I think we both knew as the dust smoke veered and the ragged nature of the pit showed in the headlights.

'Christ! It's a cave-in.'

We got out, handkerchiefs pressed tight over our mouths. It wasn't just one pit. It was a series of pits. All the old workings opened up into gaping holes that vented dust. The whole mine must have collapsed internally. I was thinking of Ed Garrety then as we climbed towards the entrance, wishing to God we'd met him on the track. Down there he hadn't a hope. Even if he were still alive, I didn't think there was a chance of a rescue team reaching him.

The entrance, when we reached it, was still there, the rock mouth gaping and billowing dust, no sign of the wooden door. It was impossible, so soon after the cave-in, to reach the shaft, and I just stood there, gazing about me, too appalled to do anything but wonder how I was going to break the news to Janet.

'That the door you spoke about?'

We had started back and he was pointing to a heavy rectangle of wood lying on the far side of the gully. It had been blown there by the force of the air rushing out of the mine. I was thinking of the two lower levels, the dangerous stoping: the whole thing must have come down like a pack of cards.

The dust-boil had lessened by the time we got back to the site of the old costeans, the headlights of the Land-Rover dimmed by the strange fluorescence of sunlight on dust, a glow that hurt the eyes after the darkness of the gully. We climbed in, not saying a word, and I backed and turned and drove into the brightness, the mine buildings growing ghostly in the iridescent light. 'That noise,' Kennie said. 'Remember? Like thunder. It must have been a hell of a collapse.'

'Yes.' I was out of the gully now, following the tramlines down.

'Couldn't be anyone alive down there, not after that. We must have been two miles away when we heard it. And it was his own fault really. He must have known it would collapse at any moment.' Kennie's face was white below the dust film, his eyes scared.

I said: 'I'm going back to the homestead now. Janet has to be told. And then she can get the authorities on the radio. We'll come back when the dust has settled and see if the shaft is still intact.'

He nodded, but reluctantly, his long-fingered hands clasped tightly about his knees.

'Then there's Westrop. If we can find out where the other entrance . . .' A figure appeared out of the red haze at the corner of the crusher shed. I had reached the bottom of the tramlines then and had just turned left past the mine office. I didn't recognize him at first. He jerked to a stop as though shocked into immobility at the sight of us. The iron grey hair, the stooped, slightly rounded shoulders—I hardly dared believe it. But as I slowed to a stop the Alsatian joined him and I knew it really was Ed Garrety.

'What're you doing here?' His voice shook, his eyes seeming half afraid, his body literally shaking with nervous exhaustion. He looked on the point of collapse. 'Were you here when——' His adam's apple worked as though the dust he'd absorbed had clogged his throat.

'No—about two miles away,' I said. 'Thank God you weren't in the mine.'

He nodded vaguely. 'Two miles away. You heard it?'

'Like thunder,' Kennie cried excitedly. 'And then all the dust. We thought you were a goner for sure.'

He nodded slowly, relaxing a little. 'You saw Janet?'

'Yes.'

'She's back home then.' He seemed relieved. But when I told him about Westrop and how he'd learned of another entrance to the mine he went still as death.

'You say—they're down there now?' He seemed to have difficulty getting the words out.

'I hope not, but I don't know.'

He shook his head as though unwilling to accept responsibility for others getting themselves involved. His face was grey beneath the stubble, his breath short, his eyes desperately weary.

'Do you know where the other entrance is?'

He didn't answer. He seemed completely dazed.

'Do you know where it is?' I repeated. 'Can you show us?'

He nodded slowly. 'That explains it.' He was speaking to himself, the words coming in a whisper.

'Explains what?'

'The other vehicle. An old Chev. I'd only just seen it, down by the shearing shed!' And then he seemed to pull himself together as if he had suddenly reached a decision. 'You follow me.' He called to the Alsatian and walked slowly past the mine office, his head bowed and moving slackly, uncertainly, a man near the end of his tether living a nightmare. He disappeared behind the building that housed the crushing plant and a moment later the ute appeared. He drew up beside me, the Alsatian leaning her head out of the window, her tongue lolling. 'Have you got helmets?'

'Yes.'

'Good.' He nodded, and I followed in his dust stream, round the corner of the building, out on to a track that skirted the scrub-grown mounds of the tailings dump, running out into the flat land beyond. We stopped beside the Chev. It had Grafton Downs Tin Mine painted on the side, and, beyond it, the tattered tin of the old shearing shed stood blistering in the sun, gaps torn in the roof and the door hanging drunkenly on broken hinges. Ed Garrety led the way inside and it was like an oven, the wheels and belt drives for the clippers dim in the darkness above the shearing platform. The big wooden clip bailer had been pushed over on to its side revealing a hole in the ground with rough-hewn steps. 'No dust in here, so we'll probably find the gallery blocked by a fall.' Ed Garrety's voice was bleak. 'Three of them you said, didn't you?'

'That's right. Westrop, a Kalgoorlie miner named Lenny, and the native who used to work for you—Wolli. You saw them last night.'

He nodded, staring down at the dark hole and the steps going down.

'Did Westrop tell you he was McIlroy's nephew?'

'He didn't need to. I knew it already.' And he added, 'The damned fool! Why couldn't he let it rest, instead of digging up old rumours, believing anything Wolli told him?'

I, too, was staring at the steps, wondering what we'd find in that long-disused gallery, thinking of those men deep underground, locked in by a fall most likely, or dead of suffocation. 'He's convinced McIlroy came here before disappearing into the Gibson.'

'That's right. He did.' Ed Garrety turned his head, staring at me, the blue of his eyes accentuated by the red dust that filmed his face. He stood there, very still for a moment, as though bracing himself for more questions. Then he nodded and turned away. 'Well, better see what's down there.' And he donned his helmet. We did the same, switching on our lamps, and taking up the pick and shovel we had brought with us from the Land-Rover, we followed him down into the black hole of that underground gallery.

2

The news that the three men were missing did not go out on the Jarra Jarra radio until after five that afternoon. The search had taken us over three hours, for the way into the mine from the old shearing shed was no more than a pilot gallery barely four feet high. It had been driven from the second level in 1934, when the eastward end of the reef had become so narrow it was no longer workable, and there were innumerable offshoots where the miners had probed in the hope of striking a widening of the quartz band. All these had to be explored crawling on our hands and knees. That was after we had reached the second level and had found the gallery blocked by a new fall at the point where they had ceased mining the reef.

After he had sent the call out, Ed Garrety went straight to his room to have a bath. He looked grey and ill, and he didn't want to talk about it. He was over fifty and had been in a Jap P.O.W. camp for two years during the war. Now he had been at full stretch for over thirty-six hours with no sleep and very little food. But he wouldn't eat. Janet took him a cup of tea which was all he seemed to want. 'He's very tired.' She looked very tired herself, the eyes overbright and her face pinched. 'If he could get some sleep. . . . I put some whisky in it. Do you think he'll drink it? He doesn't usually touch liquor.' Her voice was flat with exhaustion, but it was more mental than physical—with uneasiness in it, too. 'Would you like some?'

She gave us both a stiff whisky, pouring it from the bottle into tumblers, her hand trembling. We drank it neat while she cooked us a steak. And then we took the Land-Rover and went back to the mine. But it was a waste of time. We got as far as the shaft and that was all, the wooden head of it collapsed, the ladders gone and the open well of it blocked with debris about 140 feet down. There was dust and rubble everywhere, and remembering the poor stoping, the softness of the pillars, I didn't reckon it was even worth trying to get in by the shaft. Any attempt to reach the men would have to be made from the other entrance, and it would be slow work in the cramped space of that pilot gallery.

There was nothing we could do, so we went back to the homestead. Janet met us with the news that the Shire Clerk would be arriving from Nullagine around midnight with a team from Grafton Downs. Also, a mining engineer from Mt Newman was waiting to see me. He was Italian, a thickset hairy man who talked with an accent that sounded distinctly Welsh. He had been sent up to assess the situation and Ed Garrety was with him. He listened to what I had to say about conditions underground and the present state of the shaft, then said, 'Tell me now, d'you think there is any chance whatever that they are still alive?'

'Frankly—no,' I said. 'I don't think there's a hope.'

'And you, Mr Garrety, what do you think?'

But Ed Garrety didn't answer. His head was bowed as though in prayer, the heavy-lidded eyes closed. His face shaved now, had a grey, sick look, the eye sockets dark hollows, the skin like parchment stretched over the skull.

'Okay.' The Italian got to his feet. 'I go now. But don't expect too much from us. Mount Whaleback is opencast, you understand.'

He left just as Andie drove in from Lynn Park. Other station owners drifted in during the evening until there were five of them there drinking beer and talking it over in their slow careful way. I left them to it and went to bed. Henry's room had been made over to me again. It was hot and airless and, before turning in, I went out on to the verandah and stood there for a while, smoking a cigarette, with the dark outline of the Windbreaks shouldering the stars. I was just turning back into the room when Janet's voice said, 'Is that you, Alec?' Her shadow emerged out of the darkness. 'Can I have a word with you?'

'Of course.'

She was hugging a thin cotton dressing gown to her, her hair hanging loose across her face. 'Not out here.' She moved into my room, turning to face me as I followed her. 'I hope you don't mind. I saw you smoking out there and . . .' She hesitated. 'Can you spare one please? It's about—what happened—down there at the mine this morning.' Her voice was nervous, not quite under control.

I gave her a cigarette and lit it for her and she said a little wildly, 'I don't know what to do. I must tell somebody, but . . .' She stood there silent for a moment, and then suddenly she blurted out, 'It was an accident, wasn't it?' Her eyes, momentarily lit by the glow of her cigarette, stared at me anxiously.

'What else?'

'You've been down the mine, haven't you? The night after you left here. Andie drove over two days ago to tell us it was all over Nullagine—that you'd been down Golden Soak with that woman Prophecy.'

'She drove me over, yes.' I started to explain what had happened, but she was more concerned with the effect the news had had on her father. 'He's always had this thing about Golden Soak and when he heard you'd been down there . . .' She subsided on to the end of the bed, staring at me, her eyes luminous. 'What did you find there?' Her voice was urgent. 'Please. I must know.'

I told her briefly, and she sat there, very still, listening to me, the cigarette trembling in her hand. 'I see.' There was a long pause, and then she said, 'Ever since Andie was here, he's hardly left the mine, except——' She hesitated. 'Except yesterday morning. He was here for several hours yesterday.'

'Doing what?'

But she didn't answer, just sat there, quite still, as though she'd been suddenly struck dumb.

'What are you trying to tell me?'

'I don't know,' she murmured, her lips compressed, an unhappy look in her eyes. 'He was here, you know, when those miners lost their lives. He would have been in his early twenties then and it made a deep impression on him. And afterwards, when he came back from the war, he wouldn't go down there himself and he wouldn't let anybody else go down. I think he was afraid of it—afraid it would claim more lives. I tried to get him to sell. But he wouldn't. He wouldn't even consider it.'

'Why?'

'I don't know. Well, yes I do in a way. I think at the back of his mind he always believed that ultimately Golden Soak would be our salvation. As long as we owned it he could at least hope.' Her voice trailed off. 'Do you understand?'

'Yes, I think so. But now . . . what happens now?'

She shook her head. 'God knows,' she breathed. 'He'll have to give evidence, I suppose. He knew it was unsafe, that faulted area particularly.' She paused, staring at me very directly. And then suddenly she leaned forward, a note of urgency in her voice. 'You knew it, too. You were down there —you said yourself it was unsafe.'

'Yes, the pillars supporting the overburden were rotten with oxidization.'

'So it collapsed, just like that?' She was staring at me. 'There'll be an inquest and you'll be called to give evidence. You realize that?'

I hadn't thought about it, but this was basically an English country, the same legal procedures. 'I suppose so.'

'Then you'll tell the Coroner. You'll testify it was dangerous and that was why Daddy wouldn't let anybody down there?'

156

She was living the scene in her imagination, her voice low. 'It was an accident.' I didn't say anything and she stubbed out her cigarette and got to her feet. 'I'd forgotten for a moment that you were a mining consultant. That makes a difference.'

'Does it?'

'Well, naturally. It's an expert opinion and they'll accept that.'

She was moving past me then, out on to the verandah, but I caught hold of her shoulders. 'Janet. What was it you came to tell me?'

'Nothing.' I could feel her trembling.

'You said you had to tell somebody.'

'Did I?' Her voice was blank. 'Well, if I did, I've forgotten what it was. I think I just wanted to talk to you.'

She was lying. I knew that. But I couldn't force it out of her and I let her go. I was too physically exhausted to care very much. But back in that narrow bed, with the lumps of the mattress all in the wrong place, I was nagged by the things Westrop had said, her father's behaviour, and the thought that he might have seen them going into the old shearing shed. But clarity of thought was beyond me and, with my mind still groping for a reasonable explanation, I drifted off to sleep.

Andie woke me a little after one. The Grafton Downs men had arrived. Ed Garrety had given them an account of what had happened, but they wanted a briefing from me. There were seven of them, only three of them miners, and I had to tell them I didn't think there was a hope in hell of their getting any further into the mine than we had, let alone find Westrop or the other two alive. 'My guess is it's a total collapse from the second level down.'

'At least we must try and recover the bodies,' the Clerk said.

'But not at the risk of any more lives,' I told him.

The big Dutch foreman looked across at Ed Garrety, sitting bewildered and uneasy, the Alsatian at his feet. 'You agree with that?'

'Yes, of course. You mustn't take any chances.'

'No, vat I mean is, do you agree with your friend's assessment of the situation?'

He hesitated, then nodded reluctantly. 'Yes, I suppose so.'

'Okay. Then ve go.'

They finished their beers and got to their feet. Ed Garrety remained where he was. He seemed dazed and I wondered how he must feel with half the world attempting to break into his mine.

'Anything we can do?' one of the station owners asked.

The Dutchman shook his head. 'From vat I hear there vill be only room for one or two of us to work at a time. And it vill be very slow.'

He was right there. Kennie and I went down shortly after midday. They had shifted about ten tons of rubble, working on their hands and knees, and they were rapidly losing heart, even though Mt Newman had sent half a dozen volunteers. They had all of them been up the gully. They had seen how the old workings had become gaping pits. They had looked down the shaft, too, and they knew it was hopeless. The only thing that kept them going was the thought that Westrop and his companions might have been caught before they had gone any distance into the second level gallery.

We took our turn, but it was a gesture only. We had no hope of achieving anything. It was back-breaking work, the air thick with dust and no room to move. As soon as we had finished our stint we went back up into the open air. Hot though it was, it still seemed wonderfully fresh after that narrow tunnel.

By the time we got back to the homestead it was already dark and the local constable had arrived. He was with Ed Garrety, taking a statement. He took one from me, too, writing it all out laboriously in longhand, and when he finished, he went into Ed Garrety's den to make his report on the radio. He was back a few minutes later with the news that the aborigine, Wolli, was alive. He had been found wandering in a state of exhaustion in the Mindy Mindy Creek area some 40 miles to the north-east. I remember the look on Ed Garrety's face as the constable told us—a sort of shocked disbelief.

Janet saw it, too. She was staring at him, her mouth open, her eyes suddenly very wide. 'If Wolli's alive, then perhaps the others are, too.'

But there was no gleam of hope in her father's eyes.

'Hal Benton found him,' the constable said. 'He's taking him into Nullagine now. He should be there in about an hour.'

We had some food and shortly after nine the constable went back to the radio. He was gone about ten minutes and when he returned his sun-crinkled face was grave. Benton had questioned Wolli on the drive to Nullagine and as a result he was able to confirm that Phil Westrop and Lenny Fisher had entered the tunnel by the old shearing shed entrance at least half an hour before the mine collapsed. They had left Wolli above ground, telling him to stay with their vehicle, which he had done until the noise of the disaster scared him and he had taken to the bush in a panic.

There was no longer any doubt in our minds—both the men had had time to penetrate so deep into the mine that they would have been buried instantly. 'No good risking our necks for nothing.' Nobody said anything. We were all of us too shocked. Ed Garrety's eyes were closed, his face grey and beaded with sweat. I thought for a moment he was going to pass out, he looked so bad. But then the heavy lids flicked back, the blue eyes staring. 'Yes,' he murmured, 'there mustn't be any more deaths.'

The constable nodded, standing there waiting. I think he was expecting Ed Garrety to go with him. But when nobody moved, he nodded again and ducked quickly through the flyscreen, disappearing into the night. A moment later we heard the engine of his Land-Rover.

A silence settled on the room, broken by Janet saying in a deliberately practical voice, 'Well, there's Cleo and the horses to see to, and the chickens—would somebody care to give me a hand?' Kennie was on his feet in an instant. I watched them as they went out together and when I turned back to Ed Garrety, only the Alsatian was still there. His chair was empty.

I leaned back, closing my eyes and thinking of Westrop and the rumours surrounding his uncle's disappearance. I must have dozed off, for the next thing I knew Janet was standing there saying her father would like a word with me. 'You'll find him in his den.' And she added as I got to my feet, 'It's upset him and he's—not quite himself, see.'

I found him sitting at his desk with a glass in his hand and an old plan of the underground workings spread out in front of him. He looked up as I opened the door, his face flushed, his eyes too bright. 'Come in, Alec. Come in.' I could smell the whisky before I had even seen the half-empty bottle. 'Like a drink?' He didn't wait for me to reply, but reached into a drawer for another glass, the neck of the bottle rattling against it as he poured. 'Now sit you down. Time we had a talk—just the two of us, eh?' He spoke slowly and with care. He wasn't drunk, but he had already had enough to make him choose his words with deliberation. 'I'm told you went down on your own and brought up samples. Right?'

I nodded, sitting there drinking his whisky and wondering what was coming, why he should choose this of all moments to talk about the reef he had found.

'And then you hitched a ride to Kalgoorlie. Did you get those samples analysed?'

'Yes.' And I told him the result.

He emptied his glass and poured himself more whisky. 'I don't usually drink. But tonight . . .' He sat there, savouring the taste of it, staring into space. 'It helps. Sometimes.' There was a long pause, and then he was looking down at the plan again. 'It's the future I have to think about now.' He tapped the plan with his finger. 'That's where I came across the reef. At the third level, 149 yards north of the main gallery. Five men died there and seven were injured and my father closed the mine, not knowing they'd found the reef.'

'How did you know then?'

'That old abo, Half-Bake. He always said he'd seen the quartz as the roof collapsed on him. But I didn't believe him. Or perhaps I was afraid to go down there. I told you, didn't I? That mine's got a curse on it. And now there's two more dead.'

'Did you know they were in the mine?'

He looked at me, frowning. 'No, of course I didn't. What made you say that?'

'Golden Soak didn't collapse of its own accord.' The words came out before I had really thought about them. Maybe it was the whisky, or just that I was too tired to think what I was saying.

He stared at me, the room suddenly deathly silent. There were beads of sweat on his forehead, gleaming in the light. Far away I could hear the hum of the generator. He was staring at me a long time without saying a word. Finally he nodded. 'No, you're right. It didn't collapse of its own accord.' Another long silence, and then he said, 'But you saw it, the edge of the reef just showing. How else was I to discover there was any depth to it? I took a chance.'

And he'd killed two men. No wonder he was drinking now. He pushed his hand up over his eyes, the fingers slowly clenching, the fist coming down and hitting the desk. 'I was desperate.' He said it softly, tight-lipped, his eyes with that blank stare.

'Then why didn't you let me do a proper survey for you?'

He looked at me slowly. 'Why should I? Why should I trust you? You may be a mining consultant, but you didn't come to Australia because of the nickel boom. You came here to escape.'

I didn't deny it. The man was saying what he thought, and he was right. 'How did you guess?'

'Australia's always been a bolt-hole for men like you. You've no money, y'see. Hitching rides, clutching at straws. . . .' He nodded, his bright blue eyes staring at me, not accusingly, more in sympathy. 'I won't ask you what you're escaping from. But we understand each other. Right?'

Was that a threat? I wondered.

Then he said, 'I have to think of Jan now.' A sudden smile illumined his face. 'Don't worry, my boy. I like you. We don't see many people here. I liked you the moment I saw you sitting there reading that old Shakespeare. Reminded me of Henry. Something of the same temperament, too.' He looked down at the plan of the mine again, then folded it carefully and put it away in a drawer. 'Well, that's that. That's the end of Golden Soak. All these years and now it's finished.' He saw my empty glass and without a word poured me another drink and then refilled his own, the silence dragging. Finally he said, 'How did you know Westrop was McIlroy's nephew?'

'The *Kalgoorlie Miner*. His wife's maiden name was given as Westrop.'

161

'You read the reports. I see.' He leaned back, sipping at his whisky, looking me straight in the face as he said, 'He was crooked as a rattle-snake, but my father admired him. Don't you think that's strange? He actually admired him. Said he had guts, coming here, brazening it out, and then going off into the desert like that, convinced he'd make a fortune. A cocky little bastard. That's what my father called him. He wasn't a great talker himself. But Pat McIlroy . . .' He paused, staring past me at the wall, at an old sepia photograph of a man with drooping moustaches and a battered hat standing posed beside a team of horses hitched to a wagon. 'Well, not much difference between a mountebank and a remittance man —talkers, actors both. I didn't see much of McIlroy and I was only a kid at the time, but I can remember his voice, the extraordinary magnetism of the man. He liked people, y'see. A flash, brash, cocky, bouncy little bastard, but he rode the outback here with a golden tongue and a rainbow in his eyes and within a year that bank of Father's was bursting at the seams with money.'

'What happened to him in the end?' I asked.

He stared at me blankly. 'In the end? I thought you said you'd read the newspaper reports.'

'They never found his body.'

'The Gibson's a big desert.'

'The police had native trackers.'

'God in heaven!' he breathed. 'After thirty years, still the same rumours.' He put his head down, his hands to his face. 'After all this time it's like a dream. Trouble is, sometimes I don't seem to know what's real and what isn't. I was down at Meekatharra that day y'see. Drove back through the night and when I got here he was gone. Nobody'd seen him. It was dark when he arrived and still dark when he left. And he was drunk, my father said. Drunk on whisky and visions of a great copper mine that would feed Britain's industry in the war that was coming—a fortune waiting for him in the desert. That golden tongue of his . . .' He sipped at his drink, and then his mind switched to Golden Soak and he asked me what the chances were of the reef extending along the line of the gully up towards the gap.

'A possibility, no more.' His guess was as good as mine. 'If you'd let me do a proper survey——'

'And have you kill yourself when I didn't even believe the poor half-wit had seen the reef. I can remember my father recruiting those out-of-work miners, driving them to blast their way into the faulted area, knowing he was taking a hell of a risk. The day it happened I was riding the fences up beyond the Robinson Gap and I came down past Golden Soak at sunset just as the first bodies were being brought up.' He lifted his glass, his hand shaking, staring at nothing. And I could see what he was seeing, remembering that drift offshooting north from the main gallery and the atmosphere that had clung to the third level. 'Father never went down the mine again, and when I came back after the war I'd seen too many men die to try and reopen it.'

'You were telling me about McIlroy,' I reminded him. I didn't like the glazed look in his eyes, the way his hands trembled. The death of two more men seemed to be affecting him the way the death of those miners had affected his father.

He nodded slowly. 'A pity my father didn't go with him instead of pinning his faith to Golden Soak.' He pushed his hand up over his eyes again. 'McIlroy's Monster.' He laughed a little unsteadily. 'Pat McIlroy died and my father went mad. Two sides of the same coin, and a whole era went when the Garrety empire crashed.' He looked at me then, his head lifted, pride mixed with sadness as he said quietly, 'It was an empire, y'know, by Australian standards. Father was the North West —the biggest man of a tough hard bunch. A piece of history you might almost say, like the Duracks further north.' He smiled, sadly and with pity. 'But nobody was sorry for him. He wasn't that sort of man. It was McIlroy they were sorry for. Something about him, and the mystery of his death—going out like that into the desert, chasing a dream.' He turned his head to the picture on his desk, a full-length photograph of Big Bill Garrety in knickerbockers and a stiff collar. 'So who won in the end?' His voice was soft and slightly slurred. 'My father slowly dying, a drunk, and that Irishman going out with a flourish that had everybody in the Pilbara talking about him, endless speculation.'

'And nobody knows what happened to him?' I asked.

He looked at me, a quick twist of the head, smiling a little crookedly. 'Can I trust you? I can't be sure, can I?'

'No.' By God we were being frank, and the whisky deadening tiredness, making it easy for us.

He nodded. 'Well, it doesn't matter now.' He picked up his drink again. 'McIlroy was a sick man. He had syphilis, y'know —suffered from blackouts, hallucinations. He should never have attempted an expedition like that. He knew it, and my father knew it. But he wouldn't go with him. He wasn't a gambler and anyway his mind was set on Golden Soak, not some mythical copper deposit. But when McIlroy left here he had with him the best of our native boys. I know that because, when I wanted Weepy Weeli to ride with me to check the fences beyond Yandicoogina, Father told me he'd gone walk-about. That was nonsense. Weepy—we called him that because he had an eye infection—would never have gone walkabout. He'd been on the station ever since I could remember.'

And then he was telling me how, about two weeks before the cave-in, Weepy had walked in to Jarra Jarra alone. The man had been little more than skin and bone, so weak he could hardly stand. 'I found him out there by the old forge and then——' He hesitated, his hand gripped tight on his glass as though to prevent it shaking. 'Then my father took him straight off to the sacred place of his people—Father knew all the ritual, he was blood brother to one of the elders of Weepy's tribe. What happened there I don't know, but afterwards Weepy wouldn't even admit he was with McIlroy in the Gibson.'

'He told his son,' I said.

'Yes, he told Wolli—when he was dying.'

'So Wolli knows what happened.'

He shook his head. 'No. No, I don't think so.' He sounded a little vague. 'Old Weepy knew the sort of man his son was. He told him just enough to ensure the bastard would keep his job here in Jarra Jarra.' And then so softly I could barely hear him: 'The sins of the father,' he breathed. 'All my hopes, my plans, all my dreams for this place. . . .' He took a quick gulp at his drink, spilling some of it down his chin, wiping the

164

liquor clear with his hand. 'I was a kid then. Just a kid.' He said it as though it cleared him of all responsibility. 'There was a war coming, thank God, and after that I was in the army.' His eyes stared at me with an appalling blankness. 'I was in the army within a month and I didn't see this place or my father again for six years.' He picked up the bottle, holding it to the light, then shared out the rest of it between us. 'Well, what are the chances?' he asked abruptly. 'I have to think of Jan now, and you're a mining man.'

'A possibility, that's all,' I said. His mind had switched and I thought it best to take advantage of it. McIlroy's death was none of my business. That's what I thought then, sitting there in that hot little room full of rock samples and old photographs. 'Are you willing to let me do a survey up the top of the gully?'

'Was that why you came back with this young student fellow?'

'Yes. I was hoping to persuade you to let me do a geophysical, then perhaps drill. And no cost to you. I have some money now, a job I did for a mining company down in Kalgoorlie. The same people might be interested in the development of Golden Soak, provided, of course, my survey results——'

'Not the mine,' he said. 'You keep clear of the mine. I don't want anybody else——' His voice trailed off and for a moment he sat there hunched over the desk, lost in thought, his eyes blinking so that I thought for a moment he was going to burst into tears. But then he seemed to pull himself together. 'The rock samples here—they're all labelled. Go through them if you like. But they're most of them from the flat land to the east. I never took samples from above the entrance. The faulting—it didn't seem right, and the depth so much greater.'

'The faulting doesn't matter,' I said. 'With modern techniques——'

'Yes, of course. I'm only an amateur, y'see.' He leaned back in his chair, pushing his hand wearily up through his hair. 'Well, that's settled then.' His voice sounded very tired.

'I can go ahead?'

'That's what you wanted, isn't it? And if the reef continues

. . . then maybe Jarra Jarra will be safe for another generation. Jan loves the place, y'know. She didn't like Perth. She was down there for a while, at school. But she wouldn't be happy . . .' He was staring down at his glass. 'Nor would I,' he murmured. Then he drained the rest of his drink and got carefully to his feet. 'Good luck!' He held out his hand as though saying goodbye to me for good, and he had to brace himself against the desk.

That was all the agreement we ever had—a handshake. And he was so full of whisky I wondered if he knew what he was doing. There were other things, too. But I only worried about them later, when the men from Grafton Downs and Mt Newman had given up and gone, and Kennie and I were collecting samples from the steep slope of Coondewanna.

The sides of the gully were bare outcrops of red rock—part of what Kennie called a banded iron formation. The sides rose to a rim, and beyond the rim Mt Coondewanna leaned a shoulder gently down towards the Gap. No outcrops here, the surface of the ground coarse-grained silica with a sparse covering of spinifex, occasional patches of mallee. This shoulder was roughly on the line of the faulting I had seen below ground and it was from here that we collected the most promising samples. The flies were bad and it was very hot. We camped at the head of the gully where the air was cooler, a slight breeze funnelling through the Gap, and as the sun set the land to the west took on the colour of dried blood.

That night we slept under the stars, the sky burnt to a diamond clarity and not a sound anywhere until a dingo started calling from the gully below us. I was tired, but sleep did not come easily, my mind on Golden Soak, and the lost, lonely cry of that dingo reminding me of the lives it had cost. I was thinking of Westrop, his body buried now under tons of rock, wondering about McIlroy. Had Westrop been right? Was McIlroy's body down there, too? Was that why Ed Garrety had fired that charge? *I was desperate*, he had said. Desperate for money, or because Golden Soak held a secret that must be kept at all costs?

It was the heat. The night was very hot and my mind in a

half-world of fantasy and reality. God knows, Big Bill Garrety had had reason enough to kill the man. But to tell his doctor and not his son. . . . Whatever the truth of it, Ed Garrety must have known. I was thinking of Drym then, the reek of that room and the candle flame burning—the picture in that newspaper, the blackened beams a skeletal cap to the gutted house. We all have our secrets. . . .

'You awake, Alec?' Kennie rolled over on his swag, his eyes open. 'I thought I heard something—a cry.'

'A dingo,' I said.

He lifted his head, listening. 'Yes—of course. This place gives me the creeps.' He gave a nervous laugh. 'D'you believe in Quinkans?'

'Quinkans?'

'Mythical abo beings. Ghosts, if you like—Quinkans is the Queensland name. I read a book about them, by an Ansett pilot. I don't know the name for them here, but they'll be the same breed. They come out at night, and if they're bad, they're killers. All abos believe that.' He was silent for a moment. Then he said, 'What time do you reckon we ought to leave tomorrow?'

I didn't answer, thinking of the inquest fixed for the day after and the evidence Ed Garrety would have to give.

'Port Hedland's a long way.'

'We'll decide in the morning.' It would be an all night drive and at the end of it I would have to lie—unless Ed Garrety decided to tell them the truth. I was staring up at the stars, thinking of the Gibson and McIlroy and that abo walking out alive, trying to picture what had really happened, my thoughts ranging and the truth elusive. I lay there a long time, dozing on the edge of sleep, my mind groping for the solution to that thirty-year-old mystery and the sound of that dingo gradually fading until the next thing I knew the sun was up over the shoulder's rim, a red-hot poker boring at my eyeballs.

Kennie was already up, a smell of wood smoke and the bacon sizzling. His body, crouched there, was a dark silhouette against the flaring sunrise. 'Thought we'd better make an early start.' He gave a little laugh. 'Last night—that dingo startled me. I was only half awake.'

'If we'd got a rig here,' I murmured sleepily, 'I think I'd take a chance and drill in that hollow over there.'

He nodded. 'The best samples we got. But you haven't got a rig and even if you had——'

'We might be able to hire one,' I said, remembering that Frenchman from New Caledonia.

We ate our breakfast, took final samples from the one part of the hollow we had not yet covered, and then we left. It was shortly after nine and we met Tom on the track to Jarra Jarra. He had a note from Janet to say they had started at first light and that she was relying on me to make the Coroner understand the dangerous state of the mine.

The inquest was held at 10 a.m. on the Tuesday and lasted all day. There should have been a jury of three since it was a mine accident, but the Coroner had dispensed with this on the grounds of possible prejudice—in any case there seems to be a natural reluctance on the part of West Australians to have anything to do with courts of law. But that did not inhibit them from crowding into the little courtroom. The heat was stifling, and after lunch most of the men were so full of beer they were half asleep. The verdict at the end of it was 'death by misadventure'. That should have settled it, but the evidence had taken a long time, a lot of witnesses had been called, and the Coroner, a conscientious lawyer, had asked questions that undoubtedly jogged the memories of many of those present.

Who started the rumour I have no idea. Probably no one in particular. Prophecy, when we saw her after breakfasting at the Conglomerate next morning, told me it was suddenly all round the bar that same night. And Andie, when we called at Lynn peak for petrol, said he had actually heard it the day before the inquest, from an engineer taking equipment into Port Hedland for servicing. Personally, I think it was one of those rumours that just well up out of the ground, based on half-truths and hearsay and fed by the envy and malice that exist in every isolated community. And though nobody could accuse Ed Garrety of being evasive, his evidence, and the impression he had made on the Court, was certainly a contributory factor.

I don't think he had been drinking, but his face was flushed, his voice barely audible as he told the Court what had happened the day the mine had collapsed. Several times the Coroner had to ask him to speak up or repeat what he had said, and all the time he stood with his hands gripping the wood of the witness box, leaning a little forward so that the stoop, the slight rounding of his shoulders, made him look older.

'You say you knew what you were doing because you had been down the mine as a young man and had watched the reef ore being blasted out?' The Coroner was a big, friendly man, but he liked to get his facts straight. 'Surely they drilled shot holes even then to take their charges?'

'Not always. Not if there were crevices.'

'And you used a crevice.' The Coroner glanced at his notes and nodded. 'The rock was faulted, in fact.'

'It was only a small charge.'

'Yes, you said that before. But what I am getting at is this—' The Coroner leaned forward, his glasses in his hand, his face blandly inquiring. 'You were in a gallery of the mine that had caved in.' The glasses went on again as he peered at his notes. 'That happened in 1939. On April 4, 1939, to be exact. The gallery caved in with the loss of five lives. Right?' He looked up, noted Ed Garrety's nod and said, 'So you knew just how dangerous it was.'

I saw his hands tighten their grip on the edge of the box. 'I took a chance, that's all.'

'Because you were short of money?'

'Yes.'

'But you knew it was dangerous.'

'I told you, I took a chance.'

'You have heard the witnesses, their description of what your small charge did to the mine.' The Coroner paused. 'Did it never occur to you that you ought to make certain there was nobody in the mine or in its vicinity who might get hurt?' I could not hear Ed Garrety's reply, but the Coroner did and he said sharply, 'Never mind whether they had a right to enter the mine. That's not the point. What this Court must be concerned about is that you were very well aware these two tin mining men were wanting to get into the mine. Alec Falls's evidence shows that you knew about the concealed entrance in the old shearing shed. And we have heard from Weeli Wolli how you stopped them at the main entrance the previous night. In fact, you pointed a loaded gun at them. Why didn't you check that there was no vehicle around the mine before detonating your charge?'

Ed Garrety shook his head, the sweat glistening on his forehead. 'It just never occurred to me,' he breathed.

And then came the question I had asked myself—'Can you tell us why Westrop was so anxious to gain access to the mine?'

Again that shake of the head, the stoop of the shoulders more pronounced.

'Was it anything to do with his uncle's disappearance?'

'I don't know. It may have been.' His voice was barely audible.

'You spoke to him twice—the first time when he and the aborigine were camped by the old shearing shed, and then again the night before he died. Didn't he refer to his uncle's disappearance?'

'No.' The slight hesitation was noticeable.

'He didn't mention the name Pat McIlroy at all?'

'Only to say he was related to him.'

'Go on.' The Coroner waited, finally asking him in what context the relationship had been stated. There was a long pause, and then Ed Garrety said, 'It's not easy to remember his exact words, but he seemed to think his relationship gave him some sort of claim on the mine.'

'And did it?'

Ed Garrety's head came up. 'No, of course not.' And then in a voice that was hard and high and trembled slightly: 'You know what happened to my father, to everything he'd worked for all his life. McIlroy destroyed him utterly. After that, how could he, or any relative of his, have the slightest claim?'

There was a long silence. Finally the Coroner nodded, and after glancing down again at his notes, he told Ed Garrety to stand down.

We were near the end then, but before giving his verdict, the Coroner asked Wolli to come forward again. The tall, gangling aborigine had a scared look on his face as he slowly took up his position on the witness stand. He, too, was sweating, beads of moisture glistening on his black face, the whites of his eyes showing yellow in a shaft of sunlight. The Coroner spoke very slowly, very distinctly. Had Phil Westrop ever said why he wanted to get into the mine? Wolli's eyes shifted from the Coroner to Ed Garrety. Then he shook his head. 'No.'

'Your father was with Pat McIlroy when he died. That right?'

'Yah. Thas wot he tella me.'

'And did he tell you how the white man died?'

Wolli shook his head. 'He don'tella me that.'

'Did he say anything about Golden Soak?'

'Yah. He tell me plenty bad spirits longa that mine.'

'So you were afraid to go down there.' Wolli nodded dumbly. 'Did your father ever say anything to you about McIlroy's Monster? Did he tell you whether they found it before he started walking out of the Gibson on his own?'

'He not sayin.'

And then the final, inevitable question. 'Why didn't he report the white man's death to the police?'

Wolli glanced round the courtroom, no other black there and the whites all watching him. His gaze settled on Ed Garrety, and though his face remained impassive, no flicker of an expression, I sensed hostility. But whether for Garrety, or for white men in general, I could not be certain. And then he was answering the Coroner in that slow uncertain voice. "Fraid'im speak. Boss whitefella don'want'im speak.'

The Coroner leaned back, blowing out his cheeks, dismissing the witness with an irritable wave of his hand, while the murmur of voices filled the room, a buzz like flies as the older men recalled the whispers of the past. And though the verdict exonerated Ed Garrety officially, it did not stop the men who had been in that courtoom talking.

In sparsely populated country rumour travels fast. We made Kalgoorlie in just over thirty-six hours, which was good going, but the rumour was there ahead of us, and it had grown with distance. Chris Culpin gave me the Kalgoorlie version in the Palace bar.

That was after I had taken the samples in to Petersen Geophysics for analysis. I was in a state of wild excitement then, for while waiting for the girl to list them, I had picked up a copy of the *West Australian*. I wanted to see how Lone Minerals were doing, not only because I owned shares, but also because, if the analysis was at all promising, I intended wiring Freeman in Sydney. I thought it might make a difference if his shares were a firm market. I got a shock when I found the quotation. The price was listed at 79, up 12 cents on the day.

Petersen came in just before I left. 'So, you are back again. What you got for me this time?' And when I told him, he said, 'Golden Soak, is it? Always Golden Soak. But you are lucky man you do not also lose your life, eh?' He had read all about it in the *Miner* and the *West Australian*. 'And Blackridge. They have a drill working there now and there is talk they make a strike. So everything you touch . . .' He grinned his horsey grin, slapped me on the back and added, 'You want I should do this analysis fast like before, eh?'

I nodded. 'If you can. I have to get backing.'

'Ja. Everybody haf to get backing. But you are English. I like Englishmen, and very much when they are lucky. I haf two rush yobs first. Very important. Per'aps tomorrow evening. Okay?'

From there I had gone to the broker's office in the Palace building and his wife had directed me to the bar next door where he was drinking with a client. I had a quick beer with him and he told me Kadek's Newsletter tipping the shares had come out that morning. Lone Minerals were now 84 and he was convinced they would go higher. I arranged with him to sell at a dollar, which would give me just enough to take up the whole of the option Freeman had given me, and I left him with that heightened sense of living that comes with the excitement of gambling, like a man who has put his shirt on an outsider and sees it coming up on the rails to challenge the favourite.

I was pushing my way through the crowded bar, feeling in tune with all the hubbub of speculation around me, my mind leaping to the prospect of making enough to get an IP survey carried out, perhaps start a drilling programme, when my arm was seized and I turned to find Culpin beside me. He was unshaven, his hat pushed back on his head and his heavy features beaded with sweat. 'Where's Kennie?'

He had gone to see his mother, but I didn't tell him that. 'I've no idea,' I said.

'But he's here with you?' He didn't wait for me to answer that. 'You packed it in, eh? I don't blame you. Nasty business. It's murder—near as dammit from what I hear.'

'What the hell are you talking about?' I asked him.

'Golden Soak—an' that man Garrety. I don't want Kennie mixed up in it, see.'

The man was full of liquor and I started to move away from him. But his grip on my arm tightened. 'Two men killed. That right, innit? An' one of them McIlroy's nephew. Blew the whole mine down on top of them.'

'It was an accident.'

'Oh, sure.' His voice was heavy with sarcasm. 'But a bloody convenient one, eh?'

'What do you know about it?'

He grinned at me slyly. 'Not as much as you, I bet. But Christ! It's obvious, innit? Westrop trying to get into that mine and McIlroy's body never found.'

I was shocked. It was as though my own thoughts had been projected all the hundreds of miles from Coondewanna to this bar. 'Is that what they're saying now?'

'What else? They always was a law to themselves, the Garretys. Don't forget I was up there as a kid. There was talk then.' He reached to the bar for his drink, swallowed it at a gulp and banged the glass down on the counter. 'I don't give a bugger what happened to Westrop, or McIlroy for that matter. All I care about is what they were after, same as you. Think I don't know you were checking at the *Miner* offices last time you were here?' He leaned close to me, his voice a whisper, the smell of whisky strong on his breath and his eyes red-rimmed. 'Well, where is it?' he demanded urgently. 'You've found out, haven't you? You wouldn't be here otherwise.' And then on a wheedling note, 'Come on, Alec. Be a pal. I let you in on Blackridge.'

I jerked my arm free, anger mounting as I thought of Janet's father. 'I don't know what you're talking about.'

173

'Sure you do.' He was grinning again. 'I'm talking about a mountain of copper somewhere out in the Gibson beyond Disappointment. That's what it's all about, innit—Pat McIlroy and his Monster.'

The sins of the father! I could remember the blank look in Ed Garrety's eyes as he had said that.

'Now come on, Alec.' The wheedling note was stronger now. 'You're new out here. You'd never get through on your own. And all Kennie knows about living bush is what he learned from me. I've been a dogger all through that country, see?'

'When did you first hear this rumour?' I asked him. 'Who told you?'

'I don't know.' I watched him searching back in his fuddled mind, his forehead creased in a frown. 'It was straight after the *Miner* had reported the inquest. They were all talking about it here in the bar. And then somebody—I don't remember who it was—some Company man, he said it'd be worth hiring one of the Trans-West Cessnas an' having a dekko. But nobody ever found anything just flying over the country, 'cept that fellow Hancock. Iron ore's different though, an' if it could be seen from the air somebody would've found it by now with all them survey parties skittering around. No. You've got to hoof it into the desert, and that means an abo or somebody like me who knows how to live bush in that sort of country.' He stared at me. 'You think it over. You know where to find me. An' tell Kennie . . .' He hesitated. 'Tell him to come home. Edith misses him.' His hand was on my arm again and suddenly there were tears in his eyes. 'Tell him that, will you?'

But Kennie was still with me when I started north again two days later. If his mother had been on her own he would have stayed, but not with his father there. 'Mebbe I lack guts,' he said. 'But I'm scared of him. An' he's a b-bastard—a real bastard.' This was after I had passed on Chris Culpin's message, alone in the room we were sharing in the Norrises' house on Cheetham. Now, as we headed up towards Leonora, with the late afternoon sun straight in our eyes, I glanced at his quiet, serious face and realized he wasn't a boy any more. He had grown up a lot in the week we had been together.

Perhaps in saying that I am trying to evade responsibility and so lessen the sense of guilt I had before the end. Driving north that day all I knew was that I was glad he was still with me. We had grown accustomed to each other. And in my case, I think it was more than that. I had grown fond of him. He was the only real friend I had in Australia. No, not just in Australia—anywhere, in fact. I had no friends, no wife, no relations, nobody—only Kennie sitting there beside me, the young face set beneath the silky beard as he watched the tarmac reel out ahead of us, a dark ribbon between the red gravel verges. But the guilt remains with me, the feeling that I should have refused to take him. But even then I am not sure he would have gone back to his family. Anyway, he was old enough to make up his own mind. And once we had started north I had other things to think about.

The analysis had turned out much as we had expected, the rock samples blank, but some of the dirt containing a percentage of quartz granules with just a trace of gold and antimony. Enough at any rate to foster the belief that far back in geological time, millions of years ago, the reef quartz had banded the slope of Coondewanna above the gully. But the slope was still the same iron formation, and though the rainfall was minimal, it was still sufficient to have washed the reef traces down from higher up on the mountain's shoulder. Only the hollow offered a reasonable chance of the surface indications being repeated at depth.

My problem was really a financial one. I had been lucky. The broker had held off selling my Lone Minerals for another day, and by then the price had risen to 106. After taking up my option, I reckoned I had enough cash in my pocket to hire a rig and drill one hole, at most two. The alternative was an IP survey to give me readings that would register an anomaly if any existed. But I would still have to drill into that anomaly to prove that it was a continuation of the reef. So it was a question of either playing safe and proceeding step by step, or of cutting the corners and putting down a drill.

I had wired Freeman with enough information to whet his appetite. But to get a bid out of him, or even an agreement by which Lone Minerals would finance a proper development programme, I had to have reef samples that Petersen could report on favourably after laboratory tests. Allowing for one drill hole only, I would be pitting my geological wits against odds that time had made very long indeed. It was something that occupied my mind throughout that drive.

We lay up in the heat of the day and at dawn after the second night drive we left the Highway on the cut-off to Mt Newman, a black mare standing poised for flight beside a salmon gum, her neck arched above her foal. The stallion crossed the dirt road ahead of us, his tail so long it brushed the ground. 'Brumbies,' Kennie said. 'Plenty up here. Gone wild like the camels.' The stallion had halted beside the mare, his head up and facing us, his nostrils quivering, the three of them jet black and looking like thoroughbreds. I turned in my seat to see him shoulder the mare and her foal into the shelter of some eucs, thinking of Jarra Jarra and the stock there dying for lack of water, while here horses that had reverted to the wild looked as though they had never known a drought.

The sun came up and by then I was dozing, not waking again until the wheels were humming on tarmac and we were almost into the Mt Newman township. Kennie had been there before, but to me it was a revelation—neat rows of houses, like the married quarters of a garrison town, the lawns sprouting green with sprinklers going. It was the absolute antithesis of old Kalgoorlie with its period clapboard houses and camel train wide streets, all the ordered neatness of it set against a wild background of iron ore hills red-brown in the sun. We turned down by the administration buildings and drew up at the Walkabout, a very modern motel of Moorish design with cabin rooms built around a swimming pool, great lumps of polished rock by the glass entrance doors to the restaurant and bar. Inside it was cool with pretty waitresses in freshly-laundered mini-skirts.

Even now I can remember the mini-skirts, the girls' long legs and the enormous breakfast we ate. The coolness of it, the sense of being in some sheikh's palace, an oasis of comfort set in the middle of nowhere; what a difference it made to have money in my pocket! And afterwards, shaved and refreshed and full of food, we drove to Whaleback, where 120-ton

Haulpaks thundered down the mountain loaded with ore for the crusher, the whole world a dustbowl, the sun hazed in sepia red.

The mine manager's office was air-conditioned, staffed by girls as well as men; we might have been in a city office, except for the faint background hum of giant machinery and the movement in and out of men in dust-brown overalls and yellow safety helmets. A young Australian, fresh out from his home town of Broken Hill across the other side of the continent, pinpointed the position of Duhamel's drilling rig for me and we drove on up the mountain, giving way to the loaded Haulpaks coming down, their wheels higher than the Land-Rover.

The rig was on exploratory work, drilling a test hole high up on Mt Whaleback. Across from where it was spudded in the view was of a mountainside being gnawed to destruction by blasting and giant shovels. And beyond the huge stepped gashes of industrial erosion stretched the ever-endless wastes of the Australian outback, iron hills rising red out of the prevailing flatness and the heat throbbing through a miasma of ore dust so fine it hung like a haze that half-obscured the sun.

They were adding a fresh rod when we arrived, Duhamel and his off-sider working in unison, both of them stripped to the waist and red with the grime of ore dust. As soon as the drill started up again, he came across to me, his teeth white in a grin against the dustiness of his bearded face. 'You looking for a job or just come to see how we earn our tucker here?'

'I want to hire your rig,' I said. I had to shout to make myself heard against the throaty throb of the diesel and the higher sound of compressed air forcing the dust from the tungsten bit to the surface.

His eyes widened a little in surprise and then he walked me along the ridge to a crumbling cliff edge where we could hear ourselves speak. Below us, on the flat platforms of the mining benches giant shovels were loading Haulpaks, a strange ballet of mechanized Jurassic monsters. Beyond them, through the haze, the twin lines of steel ran ruler straight along the valley floor.

'One hole, eh? What depth?'

I told him seven hundred feet, at most eight, and he nodded.
'Above the water table?'

'Down to it,' I told him.

'But not into it?'

'No.'

'And the rock?'

'Softish till we hit the quartz—if we do.'

'Okay. I talk to my mate. We finish our contract here end of
this week. Maybe the boys want to go to Port Hedland, maybe
not. We'll see.'

Kennie and I waited there while he talked it over with his
off-sider, the two yellow helmets huddled close against the
noise of the rig. Then Duhamel came back nodding his head.
He'd have to check with his other team, but he thought they'd
do it provided there was plenty of beer and somebody to do
the cooking. 'Josh'll bring his guitar and we make a party of it,
see.' He was smiling. 'And if we strike the reef first go we get
double. Right?'

I didn't argue about that, or about his price. 'When can I
expect you?' I asked.

'We pull rods here five-thirty Monday. If there is no
problems then we hitch-up and go. You meet us outside the
mine manager's office six o'clock. Okay?'

I nodded, but his eyes were on the bench down below. He
glanced at his watch. 'Better you wait now,' he said. 'They'll
be blasting in a few minutes and until then everything's
frozen.' He walked us back along the ridge, to the crumbling
cliff edge with its view of the gashed mountainside, and there
we waited as a stillness, a sort of paralysis, crept over the whole
scene. Benches and haul roads had suddenly become deserted.
The shovels had stopped their prehistoric dance, and on the
bench below us half a dozen Haulpaks had backed up against
one of the expensive monsters, their empty truck bodies at
maximum lift to shield it from the blast. A lone man moved
quickly, checking white cable lines on an empty mining bench
away to the right, then ran to his car and drove furiously up
the haul road, the only vehicle in the whole of that mechanized
operation that wasn't frozen into stillness.

Two minutes later the mountainside below the shot cables heaved in a series of convulsions. The noise and the air blast hit together, the ground shock thudding at the soles of our shoes as two hundred thousand tons of ore collapsed on to the next bench down in a great billowing cloud of dust. 'Okay, mon ami.' Duhamel clapped me on the back. 'You can go now. But don't forget—see we got plenty of beer an' the tucker's good. An' see you got the right place for us to spud in, hnn?'

We shook hands on it and then Kennie and I started back down the mountain, back to the Walkabout where we sat drinking ice-cold beer in the bar until it was time for lunch. We had brandy afterwards and then more beer, so that we were both of us in a happy frame of mind when we finally drove out across the tracks and took the cut-off to Jarra Jarra. It was blazing hot, the scrub shimmering and the leaves of the gums hanging limp, no breath of air. But I didn't care. Even the flies didn't bother me. I had the use of a drilling rig for four days and all I was thinking about was how to make the best use of it. I had two days in which to make up my mind the exact position we'd spud it in. And if we hit the reef spot on. . . .

I was still thinking about that as we climbed to the gap in the Ophthalmia Range, Parmelia Hill to our right and Mt Robinson a vague blur on the horizon. A piddling little opera-tion compared with the huge ore complex I had just seen, but my own, with no outsider, no consortium of financial houses involved; I was singing softly to myself, thinking of Janet—how excited she would be.

We reached the boundary fence of Jarra Jarra shortly after six and a few minutes later I drove into the homestead, blaring the horn as I stopped under the big Mexican poinciana trees, my spirits still buoyed up by all the beer we had drunk. And when Janet came out to see what all the racket was about, I shouted to her that it was fixed—we had a rig and we were going to drill. 'With luck you'll have a new mine for Easter.' And I picked her up and swung her round. 'We'll call it Coondewanna.' I would have kissed her then, but she was stiff and wooden, no answering spark to my own excitement, and when I let her go I saw her eyes were sullen, her face flushed. 'Can't you understand what I've been telling you?' I demanded.

'You're drunk,' she said, and she looked as though she were on the verge of tears.

'What the hell's the matter? Where's your father?' At least he'd appreciate what I had achieved.

'He's had to go to Port Hedland again.'

'Port Hedland?' I felt suddenly deflated, the beer and the excitement drained out of me, everything flat. 'Why?'

'About the Watersnake. They've found our cattle there and they're insisting we clear them off the Pukara at once.'

'So what? Can't you understand? If we strike the reef, the cattle don't matter.'

'But they do matter,' she snapped. And she added with slow emphasis, 'This is a cattle station and if we have to move them they'll die.'

'Then you get some more. If that's what you want. We strike that reef at the head of the gully . . .'

'You stupid, insensitive bastard—can't you understand?' Her voice was shrill, her eyes flashing. 'We sweated our guts out to save those animals. They've got water now. They're alive.'

'I'm sorry,' I said. I hadn't thought of it that way. 'It was just that I couldn't think of anything . . .'

'And there's something else.' The sullen, angry look was back in her eyes. 'Rosalind's here.'

It didn't register for a moment. 'Rosalind?' I stared at her. 'You mean she's here—come all this way . . .'

She nodded dumbly.

'But why?'

'To see you, I imagine.'

So that was it. It wasn't the cattle, but Rosa's arrival that had upset her. 'How did she get here?'

'By plane. She came up from Perth yesterday and one of the Mount Newman men drove her over last night.'

The world seemed suddenly a much more complicated place. 'Where is she now?'

'Gone for a walk, I think.' And she added with a trace of bitterness, 'While I cook some sort of a dinner.'

'Does she know I'm here?'

'No. How could she?'

'In Australia, I mean.'

'Of course.'

'You told her?'

She stared at me, those prominent eyes of hers very wide. 'I said you'd gone to Kalgoorlie. Why? What did you expect me to say when your wife turns up out of the blue asking for you?'

So Rosa had guessed it was phoney—that I hadn't died in that fire. But to come all this way. . . . There didn't seem any point. Or couldn't she bear the thought of one man escaping her? 'What's she want?' I demanded.

But Janet didn't answer. She just stared at me for a moment, her eyes brimming with tears, and then she turned abruptly and walked back into the house, leaving me standing there.

'What's the trouble?' Kennie asked.

'Nothing,' I muttered. 'My wife's turned up, that's all.' I got my gear out of the Land-Rover and went to my room, feeling dazed and suddenly tired. What the hell did she want? I lit a cigarette and sat on the bed trying to work it out. Rosa! Here. My body was suddenly trembling. I felt hot, conscious of the stale smell of sweat and my shirt sticking to my back. To come all this way on the off-chance. . . . But why? I lay back on the bed and closed my eyes.

I was on my third cigarette and still unwashed when Kennie put his head round the door to tell me supper was ready. 'You all right?'

'Yes, of course I'm all right.' He looked so bloody clean, a fresh shirt and his hair slicked down with water. 'Why?'

'Well, I don't know.' He was staring at me uncertainly. 'When a man's wife turns up . . .'

'Where is she now?'

'Waiting for you—in the cook house. Janet, too. I'll tell them you're coming, shall I?'

I nodded and swung my legs off the bed. 'Yes.' It would be awkward in front of Janet, but the moment had to be faced. 'I won't be a minute.' I had a quick wash and changed my shirt, and then I went down the passage into candlelight and an atmosphere of tension that reminded me of Drym. Rosalind was reclining in one of the cane chairs smoking a cigarette. She didn't move as I came in, only her eyes, those large dark luminous eyes. She looked cool in a neat, close-fitting linen frock, cut low to emphasize her breasts. Her breasts were just as I remembered them, small and firm, and the dark sheen of her hair falling about her face. The long slim legs were carefully arranged. By God, I thought, she did it well. And Janet, the silly little idiot, wearing a flouncy dress that was much too fussy instead of the practical simplicity of her hardworn jeans.

I stood there for a moment staring at my wife, our eyes locked and the other two waiting. What did they expect—a conventional greeting? 'I thought you said you'd never go to Australia?'

'I changed my mind.' She was smiling.

'So I see. Who paid for the flight—not your father surely?'

'No. The insurance.'

So she'd got the insurance, and now that she knew I was alive . . . 'So you changed your mind. Why?'

The dark eyes gleamed. Was it amusement, or something else? What the hell did she want? 'I was curious, that's all.' That husky, almost throaty voice, so suited to the dark glow of a cocktail bar. Here it seemed strangely out of place. And yet . . . My legs felt weak, an ache growing deep inside me. Damn her! Damn her to hell! She always knew when I wanted her. I pulled myself together and went over and kissed her on the cheek. The same perfume and her hand on mine, a touch that was a promise of more intimate caresses. 'You haven't changed,' she said. 'And you're still very much alive, aren't you?' The gleam in her eyes was sheer devilry. And then she looked across at Janet and in a cool voice said, 'If we can't have a drink, shall we feed? Now that we're all here.'

The girl's cheeks flamed. 'If you like.' She looked across at me, her eyes pleading. 'There's no beer, you see—they drank it all that night.'

'I've a bottle of Scotch in the Land-Rover,' I said.

She looked relieved and without waiting to be asked Kennie went and got it. The Scotch helped, but it was an uncomfortable meal. I couldn't help thinking of the last dinner party we had held at Drym, the furniture all good pieces and gleaming in the candlelight, silver on the table and Château Beychevel '57 to go with the Diane. Right to the end we had done things in style, keeping up appearances. Here there was no style, everything run down and the old homestead haunted by memories and the reek of better days. Yet Drym was gone, Balavedra bankrupt, while here, in spite of everything, the house continued, a piece of Australian history that might yet come to life again if the Golden Soak reef continued.

I looked at Rosa, wondering what she was thinking as she sat there talking to Kennie and drinking Janet's instant coffee. She was so cool and composed, so very elegant—and that low-cut dress catching Kennie's wandering eye. Was she, too, comparing this with Drym? The candles, almost burned out now, were beginning to gutter. In the uneven light I caught her eye and she smiled. But there was no warmth in it, just amusement. And I wondered again what the hell had brought her all this way.

Janet rose and snuffed out one of the candles. Moonlight filtered through the gaps in the hessian. 'So romantic,' Rosa murmured in her huskiest voice. 'If you had pot plants here we might be in a rather primitive conservatory.' Her words conjured visions of English country houses.

'I'm afraid there's nothing romantic about Jarra Jarra,' Janet said in a small tight voice that sounded distinctly girlish. 'And I have to be up early so I'm going to bed.' She gave us candles and then she left us, a Cinderella-like exit—one minute she was there, the next she was gone.

'What an extraordinary child,' Rosa murmured, and I could have slapped her.

'She just about runs the station,' I said.

'I'm sure she does.' She smiled at me sweetly. 'But not very well from what I've been told. Their cattle herded on to somebody else's property and not enough fuel to run their lighting plant. And their future apparently in your hands.'

'Who told you that?'

'The boy who drove me here. The word seems to have got around that you're a mining consultant. With your old firm, too.' Her eyes reflected the guttering of the last candle so that

I couldn't see their expression. 'It seems they're very simple people out here.'

I got to my feet. 'We'll be starting early, too.'

She sighed and got out of her chair. 'Do I go with you?'

'You'd find it very hot and dusty.'

'I see.'

'You don't see at all,' I said angrily. 'We have to clear a track up a gully on the slopes of Mount Coondewanna.'

She smiled, and it was still that cool smile of amusement. 'I gather we're in separate rooms, so goodnight then.'

But it wasn't goodnight. Stripped to my pants, I was sitting on my bed, smoking a cigarette and wondering what to do about her, when a shadow moved against the stars and I heard her voice, a whisper in the night: 'Alec. Are you there?' Something leapt inside of me, my blood pounding as I got to my feet and went to the verandah where she stood, quite still, just a shadow in the moonlight.

'What is it? What do you want?' But I knew. It had been like that from the moment we had first met, at a country club near her home in Hampshire. The chemistry of our bodies was something we had never been able to control. She didn't answer, simply stepped past me into the deeper darkness of the room and then stood waiting. I followed her, knowing what would happen, the ache overwhelming, the sense of incompleteness. 'I couldn't talk to you out there,' she breathed.

'Do we have to talk?'

She came closer, not touching me, but I could smell her scent and her hair loose over her face, the flimsy garment falling apart, the pale breasts exposed. 'Not if you don't want to, darling.' The voice so soft, so inviting. Damn her! She was like a bitch on heat. She had always been like that when it came to the moment. And my need, all these weeks. . . . I reached for her, grabbed hold of her, the softness of her yielding, coming against me, her lips on mine and her hands straying. And then we were on that narrow bed and she had the lumps as I took her in a fury of urgency. It wasn't love. But it was something we both needed.

Released at last, we lay close, the sweat on our bodies cooling. 'I wonder what they'd say if they could see you now?'

The whisper of her words and her hands like silk. 'So very much alive!'

'Are you glad?'

'Haven't I shown it?'

If she had kept her mouth shut we could have lain close like that all night. But her words had reminded me of the insurance money and I reached for a cigarette. If she could guess the truth, then others might reach a similar conclusion. The flare of the match showed our naked bodies and the spartan simplicity of the room. Even if she didn't talk, her mere presence threatened everything I had achieved, the desperate attempt to rebuild my life.

'I could do with a cigarette, too.'

I gave her one, lighting it from my own, and the glow of it as she inhaled showed the relaxed beauty of her features. 'What are you planning to do?' I asked.

'I'll wait,' she said.

'What for?'

'To see whether you make it. A new mine—by Easter.' The tip of her cigarette glowed and I saw her eyes laughing up at me. 'I was there, between two of those cowsheds, wool sheds, whatever they are.' She raised herself on her elbow. 'You think I'll let a chit of a girl like that take over my husband when he's struck it rich?' She laughed. 'I've got you, Alec, haven't I? Still talking big and reaching for the sky. But here, in this mineral-crazy land, you might just prove as big as your words.'

So that was it. She was going to hold that over me, and if I succeeded, we'd be back where we were before I'd lit that bloody candle and burned Drym to the ground. She'd be round my neck for ever then. And if I didn't succeed, then I could rot for all she cared. 'You can't wait here,' I said, keeping a tight hold on myself.

'Of course not. Too damned uncomfortable.'

'Where then?'

'Perth. Or there's an island called Rottnest. I met somebody on the plane who invited me there.'

'A man?'

She gave a soft laugh. 'I'm a perfectly normal woman. You should know that by now.'

185

My hands clenched, a cold fury sweeping over me. I could have taken her by the throat then. But suddenly the anger was gone, leaving only a feeling of disgust that she could still do this to me. And after that I didn't say anything, the two of us lying there in silence until finally she leaned over me and stubbed out her cigarette. 'I'll leave you now. I'm sleepy and this bed is too small.' She climbed over me and put on her dressing gown. 'Goodnight, Alec.'

I watched her shadow disappear into the night, and long after she had gone I could feel the touch of her body as she had leaned over me.

In the morning, when I woke, it all seemed like a dream. But I knew it wasn't, and there to remind me was the stubbed-out butt of her cigarette, red with lipstick. I got up, dressing slowly, wondering how I was going to face Janet. But at least I was spared that. Kennie was waiting for me, a pot of tea on the table. 'Janet went about an hour ago. She left this note.' He handed it to me: *Sorry, but you'll have to fend for yourselves. Back this evening.* He poured me a cup of tea. 'She was riding that camel of hers and she had Tom and one of the boys with her.'

The tea was lukewarm and I drank it quickly. 'Well, let's go,' I said. 'We've work to do.' A hell of a lot, in fact, if that rig was going to be able to reach the drill site. 'We'll breakfast up the top of the gully.'

He nodded and got to his feet. 'What about your wife?'

But that was a problem I didn't want to face at this hour of the morning and I was hoping to God she was still asleep as I went out into the arid, blinding sunlight. A moment later we were in the Land-Rover and heading down the track towards Golden Soak.

3

We began drilling at dawn on Wednesday, January 21, in the hollow on the north-eastward running spur of Mt Coondewanna. My choice of site had been limited by the terrain, the projected line of the reef cutting diagonally across the sloping shoulder of the mountain and the rig only able to operate on reasonably flat ground. Drilling on the back of the spur had one advantage. Here erosion had probably occurred *in situ*, so that there was every chance that the surface samples I had taken from the hollow were a true indication of the rock formation below. But it was all Archaean country of great antiquity and I had no means of knowing how Mt Coondewanna had been formed or what changes in its formation had occurred over the millennia. In the circumstances, the odds against a single drill hole proving successful were very long indeed.

I reckoned that if we did intersect the reef it would be at a depth of about 700 feet. Ed Garrety had found it at the Golden Soak third level, 300 feet below the surface, and where we were now was a good 400 feet above the mine entrance. When we started we were drilling into the weathered mantle, so that progress was rapid, a new 10-foot length of pipe being added almost every hour.

From that hollow we could just see the top of Coondewanna above an outcropping ridge of rock that gradually changed from the black of shadow to the red of full sunlight. It was hot, but there was a slight breeze and the flies were not too bad, particularly when Kennie got a fire going. By lunchtime we were already down over 60 feet and Duhamel and his second team runner, Josh Meyer, ate one at a time, the diesel thundering and the rods turning steadily as the drill ground its way down into the bowels of the earth.

Anybody who has ever watched a drilling operation will understand the fascination. But to see this single rig operating in the immense loneliness of the Pilbara, the twin mountains of Coondewanna and Padtherung blocking our view to the west, and all to the east the country stretching out into infinity, not a sign of life, a flat emptiness of antediluvian antiquity blistered with heat, arid as a desert—what hope had we, flying thus in the face of nature? But the drillers did not see it that way. To them it was just another job, accustomed as they were to the country and the climate. Watching the drill go down foot by foot, I could barely face the huge steak Kennie grilled for me. At this rate we'd be down to 700 feet with the prospect of the dust sample piles showing the glitter of gold in quartz inside of three days, and if we did strike the reef, then I could get a good price out of Freeman or anybody else, or we could lease on a royalty basis that would give the Garretys a stake in the mine. I could even form a company, operate it myself.

Strange how you dream in the heat. Or was it nervous exhaustion? I had finished my steak. I had had two beers, but I didn't feel sleepy. The tension in me was too great and at that moment I wasn't thinking of anybody else, how they might react, or the pitfalls that lay ahead. Even Rosalind's presence meant nothing to me any more. I had picked her up the day before on my way into Mt Newman to meet Duhamel, and having seen her on to the MMA plane to Perth, had wiped her right out of my mind. All I could think about now was the success of the operation, and I sat there, my eyes on the drill.

Then Kennie's voice: 'Alec. Somebody coming.' I turned to find him buttoning up his flies as he emerged from a patch of mallee. 'Down in the gully. A ute by the look of it.'

It never occurred to me it would be anybody but Ed Garrety. He still hadn't returned from Port Hedland when I had picked Rosalind up at Jarra Jarra and I had asked Janet to tell him what I was doing so that he could come up and see for himself as soon as he did get back. We watched as the ute appeared on the back of the spur, bumping its way slowly along the track we had cleared. It stopped on the rim of the hollow and Chris Culpin got out. His face was brick red in the sun, the same hat pushed back on his bullet head, his stomach bulging over the broad leather belt as he came towards us.

'Thought I'd come and see how you were getting on.' He was smiling.

'Who told you where to come?'

'Girl at the homestead. That'd be Garrety's daughter, eh?' His eyes shifted to the rig. 'Looking for my son, see, so she told me where he was.' He didn't even glance at Kennie, his eyes all the time on the rig.

'There's nothing for you here,' I said.

'Not yet perhaps. You're still drilling.'

'Nothing at all,' I repeated.

He was standing close to me now. 'Have you told Ferdie what you're up to?'

'It's nothing to do with him.'

'Suits me. But it may not suit him.' He leaned closer, the stubble on his chin dark against the sun-reddened skin. 'An' he's got you, pal. Got you cold if ever they rumble the Blackridge deal.'

'What the hell are you talking about?'

'You can think that out for yourself. Meantime, I'll hang around for a bit, see how you're making out. Mebbe collect a few samples for myself.' And when I told him to get the hell out, he was on private property, he just laughed. 'This isn't the Old Country. This is Crown land and I got a prospector's licence, see.'

'Golden Soak belongs to Ed Garrety,' I said.

'That's right.' He nodded. 'He owns the mine and all the flat land below it. But not up here. Not according to Smithie. This is leasehold, and leaseholders don't own mineral rights. You got to claim.' His small eyes narrowed. 'You registered a claim? I don't see no claim pegs.' He stood there, staring at me, waiting for me to say something. 'You ain't even got a prospector's licence.'

'I don't need one,' I answered angrily. 'Not here.'

'We'll see about that. I'll be in Nullagine this evening and I'll check just what Garrety does own. An' if Smithie's right, then I'll go on to Marble Bar and have a look at the Mining Register. I don't reckon Garrety's put in a claim, 'cause if he had he'd be required to spend money on development.' And at that moment Duhamel appeared at my elbow.

'We're through the soft stuff. It's hard rock now.'

I thought of Balavedra, all those weeks hoping against hope, the luck gone sour on me. And now here. Only a few minutes ago I had been dreaming of a strike in two days' time. I watched Culpin go back to his ute. He drove it under the shade of a mulga and set about preparing his lunch. Nothing I could do about him. Nothing I could do about the hard rock country the drill had entered. And Rosalind in Perth, waiting. I went over to the Land-Rover, tugged the ring seal off another can of beer and stood there drinking it, watching the percussion drill, its progress imperceptible now, and Kennie clearing up on his own, white-faced and unhappy. His father hadn't said a word to him, not a single word. He had behaved as though the boy didn't exist.

I finished my beer, went over to the shelter we'd built with branches of gum brought up from the gully and lay down. Nothing to do now but wait—and hope. The noise of the drill was like the drone of a huge insect, a solid roaring hum in the heat, and I dozed off. When I woke Culpin had gone and Kennie was sitting beside me, smoking a cigarette.

'Where's your father?' I asked.

He shrugged.

'Gone to Nullagine, has he?'

'He was down at the rig talking to Georges, then he loaded up and drove off. He didn't tell me where he was going.'

And from Nullagine he'd go on to Marble Bar. I knew damn well Ed Garrety hadn't pegged the area. I got to my feet, watching the drillers busy about the rig, sweating in the afternoon sun as they added another rod. 'How far are they down?'

'Seventy—seventy-five maybe.'

At that rate he had all the time in the world. 'He'll be back,' I said.

'Oh, sure. He'll be back. Pa wouldn't miss a chance like this.' Kennie looked at me. 'What are you going to do? You can't stop him coming here, and if he thinks you're on to something . . .' He hesitated, and then, his voice barely audible: 'You want to watch it, Alec. He's a real bastard when he smells money, and he doesn't give a damn about people. That's the trouble with Australia—men like my father, and that man Kadek, they don't care who they hurt, what they destroy, s'long as they get what they want. I tried to tell him—that night. But it's like I was speaking a different language. It's a free country, they say. Christ! I'd rather it was Communist.'

'Then you'd have bureaucracy. And that's just as soulless.'

'So what's the answer?'

'Same as it's always been,' I said. 'You fight. To survive in this world you've got to be a fighter.'

'And you think I'm not?' He was staring at me very directly.

'I didn't say that.'

'No, but you implied it.' His gaze wandered to Coon-dewanna, the escarpment of red rock like a battlement. 'And you're right. I've never stood up to him. Not really. I'm not a fighter. I'm a bit of a coward, I suppose.' And he added, softly, 'Mum, now—she's a fighter. All her life she's struggled to make a go of it. And the strange thing is she still loves him.'

I walked out into the sunshine then. The boy was very near to tears. 'You stay and look after the drillers,' I said. 'I'm going to Jarra Jarra. If Ed Garrety's back I want a word with him.' And I left him and went over to the Land-Rover. 'Anything you want out of the back?'

'No, I got it all here.'

I had to use my handkerchief to open the door, the metal of it was so hot, and inside it was like a furnace. I started up and drove along the spur and down into the shade of the gully, thinking of that boy . . . an only child, his problems similar to my own. Yet not entirely, for my father had been a very different man to Chris Culpin. Then I was thinking of Ed Garrety. He'd been an only child, too. But he had worshipped his father.

I was still thinking of Garrety when the sunlight hit me at the bottom of the gully, the mine buildings blazing red and a streamer of dust coming down the track from the outcrop. It was the station ute and coming fast, and when it was near, it slithered to a halt and Janet got out, coming towards me quickly in the heat. 'It's you, Alec. Thank God!' She spoke in a rush, her face sweaty and covered in dust. 'I was coming up to get you. Daddy's back and I don't know what to do. He's got Tom loading the Land-Rover, petrol, water, a new set of tyres we've been hoarding, and he's sitting there alone in his den going through his papers, writing letters. He won't say what he's up to, won't tell me anything. All I know is that they're going to start repairing their fence in a few weeks. They've given us to the end of February; any of our cattle left on the Watersnake after that they'll regard as scrubbers. They'll just add them to their own stock. They're going to run a cattle station of their own to supply their township.' She paused, breathless, her eyes wide, the whites brilliant in the hard light. 'I'm scared,' she breathed. 'Scared of what he'll do.'

'When did he get back?'

''Bout three hours ago. And he's driven non-stop from Port

Hedland. He's dead tired But he won't rest. He's wound up so tight I don't think he knows what he's doing. And he looks bad. He's told Tom to load the Land-Rover, food and water for a fortnight, and just about all the fuel we have in the pump.'

'To get the stock back on to your own land?'

'No. He knows they'd die. It's something—something else. But he won't say. He won't tell me anything. He's so dead tired I can't get any sense out of him. And now he's locked himself in. Please. You must come and talk to him.'

She was trembling, half out of her mind with worry. 'If you can't get him to tell you——'

'He'll talk to you,' she said quickly. 'I'm sure he will. I'm just a girl. Oh God! If only Henry were alive. He says you remind him of Henry. Please, Alec. Come back and try. I'm sure he will. I'm sure he'll talk to you.' She was staring at me, her eyes pleading.

'All right,' I said. 'I wanted to see him anyway.'

She clutched my arm. 'Oh, thank you. I knew I could rely on you.' And she added, 'If only I understood what was in his mind. When he drove in, I'll never forget—he looked . . . he looked quite crazy, his eyes staring, and so white, so short of breath. It wasn't just tiredness. It was something else. But I don't know what. I just don't know. He won't tell me.' Her grip on my arm was tight and there were tears in her eyes.

'Okay, you lead the way,' I said. 'I'll follow.'

She nodded slowly. Then she turned abruptly and ran back to the ute.

The sun was dropping behind the Windbreaks by the time we reached Jarra Jarra. No dogs and the Land-Rover standing under one of the poincianas, Tom squatting beside it, his wide-brimmed hat tipped over his broad nose, his back against the rear wheel. 'Is he still there?' Janet asked him.

'Yes, Jan. Alla time in den.'

We went through into the cool house and along the dim passage. The door to the den was shut, and not a sound. 'Daddy, are you there?' There was no answer. She tried the handle, but the door was locked. 'Alec's here. He wants to see you.'

There was a moment's silence, then his voice, hesitant and weary: 'What about? What's he want?'

Janet glanced at me, her eyes just visible in the dimness. 'Can he come in?'

'It's about the land above the gully. I've got a drill up there . . .'

'All right, I suppose so.' His voice sounded reluctant as though he were too tired to talk to anybody. A long silence, then the scrape of a chair, the sound of the key turning in the lock. 'Come in, then.'

He was standing in the middle of the room staring at the desk, which was littered with papers. 'Sorry to disturb you,' I said, 'but it's important.' The Alsatian had her head lifted beside the desk, her ears pricked, her tail just moving.

He nodded absently. I don't think anything to do with Golden Soak was important to him at that moment. His mind was on something else. But I wasn't to know that. Not then. He turned, his eyes lack-lustre. 'Hot,' he said vaguely. 'Very hot.' And then he added as an afterthought, 'Some tea?'

The tired blue eyes shifted to Janet as though seeing her for the first time. 'Daughter, you get us some tea, eh? The big tin pot—full.'

She nodded, relieved. 'Yes, of course.'

The door closed and we were alone. 'Sit down.' He waved me to a chair stacked with papers. 'Push that lot on to the floor. Never realized there was so much. Should have dealt with it years ago.' He sat down, with me facing him across the desk, and I was glad to see an empty plate there. At least he had had something to eat. 'Jan told you, did she? About what was decided.'

'The cattle, you mean?'

He nodded. 'Can't blame them. The lease is theirs now.' He leaned back, his hand brushing across his eyes, smoothing the unruly bushiness of his eyebrows. 'Glad you came. Something I wanted you to sign.' He searched the litter on his desk and produced a foolscap sheet, handwritten. 'Do you mind witnessing my signature on it?'

'No, of course not.'

He signed his name and pushed it across to me. It was his will and I hesitated, looking across at him, seeing the lines of his face, the tiredness of his eyes. 'Why now?'

He looked out of the window at the dying sun flaring the sky, the gums all gold. 'Suddenly I realized I hadn't done anything about it since Henry's death.' His voice sounded vague. 'Not that it'll do Jan much good. They've given us till the end of February. But with no rain . . .' The words trailed away, his tiredness engulfing them. 'Still, if anything happened to me, then she'd get something out of selling Jarra Jarra.' The words were muffled, almost a whisper.

'I've got a drill operating up on Coondewanna.'

'Yes, Jan told me.'

But when I asked him about the mineral rights, he shook his head. It was Crown land and he hadn't registered a claim. 'Nobody wants gold and the price of antimony won't last.' Prophetic words, but I was in no mood to listen to them. My own future was at stake. I witnessed his signature and pushed the paper back to him, telling him about Freeman, how if we struck the reef I could pull off a deal that would give Jarra Jarra a new lease of life. But he didn't seem able to take it in. 'You do what you like.' He said it vaguely, his mind on something else. 'I'm fifty-four and I had two years on the Burma railway. Seemed like a lifetime, and nothing to do but think about Jarra Jarra, remembering what it was like when I was a kid here. That was about all that kept me alive, the thought of coming back. And when I did . . .' He was staring out of the window again, his eyes narrowed against the reddening blaze of the sunset. '*Soft! I did but dream.*' He sighed, remembering the words and smiling sadly to himself. '*Give me another horse! bind up my wounds.* But there wasn't another horse, only Jarra Jarra, jaded and sick, the land gone sour, a desert in the drought, and those damned sheep dying in hundreds. *Have mercy, Jesu! I did but dream.* Two years I lived on that dream and when I did get back . . .' The door opened and Janet came in with the tray of tea, a large tin pot and slabs of ginger cake. He nodded absently as she put it down, waiting for her to go.

She hesitated, her eyes switching from her father to me, and then she was gone and the door closed. 'Milk?' His hand shook slightly as he poured. There were just the two cups and he took up where he had left off—'That's what Golden Soak did to this place. A war is always good for Australia. Wool for uniforms, y'see. The quality don't matter then, provided it's a northern war. The last good war we had was Korea. Vietnam . . .' He shook his head, remembering his son's untimely death. 'When I got back in '45 Jarra Jarra was lousy with sheep and nothing left for them to feed on. All I could do was watch them die, the old man half insane and the debts mounting.' He stared at me, his blue eyes bluer than ever, staring at me very wide. 'You do what you like. Get yourself a prospector's licence, peg a claim, sell it if you can. That vein of glittering quartz has never brought anything but sorrow to my family.' He gulped at his tea, his hand still trembling. 'Sometimes I think it was cursed long ago, by the elders of the tribe my father took it from. That soak was important to them, y'see. Not just the water that vanished into the bottom of the mine as they dug down for the gold; it was a ritual place. If you climb the sides of the gully you'll find all manner of rock drawings—strange animals that represented their Dreamtime ancestors, concentric circles and other ritual patterns, and drawings of men and women—the men with enlarged genitals, the women with marks that represent menstruation. You look next time you're there.' He looked down at his empty cup. 'Mapantjara—witches . . . *adder's fork, and blind worm's sting, lizard's leg, and howlet's wing* . . .' He shook his head slowly. 'Mebbe the luck will change for you. But for me—never.' He leaned back, his eyes closed. The sunset glow was on his face, but the skin had an unhealthy pallor, his forehead damp with sweat.

'You all right?' I asked.

He nodded. 'Tired, that's all. Very tired. Think I'll get some sleep.' His eyes opened, staring at the cluttered desk. 'I'll clear this up—tomorrow, before I leave. I didn't realize there was so much.'

I asked him where he was going, but he didn't seem to hear, his eyes closed again and his breathing quick and shallow. I called Janet then and she came immediately as though waiting upon my call. It was more than tiredness, and when we had got him to bed, she said, 'I don't know what to do. He's exhausted. He can't take any more. And these filthy, vicious rumours. Do you know what they're saying?—that he deliberately killed those men, that he destroyed the mine to safeguard . . .' She stopped then, staring at me, her large eyes wide. 'How can people do that to a man when he's down? How can they?'

'I think you'd better get a doctor,' I said.

But she shook her head. 'I daren't. He'd never forgive me, calling the Flying Doctor Service, the chance of others listening, tongues wagging. They'd say it was true, that he'd packed it in. No, I can't. And anyway, it's no use. I know what the doctor would say—keep him in bed, sedatives, give him a chance to recover his energies. What else? He's worn himself out—mentally as well as physically.'

She was right, of course. The cure was rest and peace of mind. I stayed the night and in the morning he was running a temperature. I saw him briefly and he told me once again that as far as Golden Soak was concerned I had a free hand to do what I thought best. And he thanked me, his face flushed and a dullness in his eyes as though he'd given up hope.

I left shortly afterwards. The Land-Rover, still fully loaded, had been parked in the big shed that served as a garage. Tom and the boys were mooching around, doing odd jobs without any sense of purpose, the two dogs wandering aimlessly in the heat. Even Janet seemed affected the same way. She came out to see me off, her face strained and her eyes reflecting the same hopelessness. She thanked me for coming, but she didn't refer to what I was doing or wish me luck. She just stood there, brushing at the flies, her mind on her own problems. 'Did he tell you why he had Tom load the Land-Rover?' Her voice was barely audible above the sound of the engine.

'No. He didn't mention it and I didn't ask him.'

She nodded, and I knew she was thinking what I was thinking—that it had been done without purpose, a form of escapism. The man was on the edge of a nervous breakdown.

I backed and turned, thinking it over. Then I called to her. 'I suggest you tell Tom to unload the Land-Rover and to come to you before carrying out any order given him by your father.'

She nodded. 'Yes, I'll do that.' And she raised her hand, a

tired gesture of farewell—or perhaps she was just brushing at the flies. I drove down the dusty track between the buildings, out into the sered brown of the paddock, thinking how forlorn she looked, standing there alone, the world she loved in ruins about her. By Christ! I thought, it was up to me now—that single drill hole just had to intersect the reef. Nothing else could save the place, or Ed Garrety from going the way his father had gone.

I drove hard, thinking of what I would find on the spur of Coondewanna, hoping to God we were through the hard rock now, drilling down to the point where the dust piles would show quartz, willing with a gambler's concentration that we'd strike the reef and strike it rich.

It was almost eleven-thirty when I turned up into the gully, driving round the collapsed costeans, the dust of the cave-in lying in smooth long slopes descending to the black shadow of moisture, and above me great boulders and outcrops of rock. I was remembering the rock drawings he'd talked about, wondering whether it was true that the aborigines had put a curse on the mine. In the shadow there, with the smooth outlines of giant rock shapes hanging over me, anything seemed possible.

Then I was out in the sunshine again and the blinding heat of the mountain's shoulder made nonsense of such superstitious fears. Ten minutes later I drove into camp and stopped on the edge of the hollow, Kennie coming towards me, moving slowly so that even before I saw his face I knew he had nothing good to report. The rig shimmered in the heat, the only sound in the hot oven of that hollow, and Kennie walking as though every step were an effort. 'Well?' I called as he came within earshot. 'What's the news?'

He didn't answer, and when he reached me he simply climbed in and told me to drive on. 'Something I got to show you,' he said and his sun-cracked lips were tight behind the beard. He directed me along the rim of the hollow to an area of wattle dominated by a skeletal mulga deformed by heat and wind. And then we got out and walked a few yards to where a brand new stake had been set upright in the ground. It was about four feet high, the wood of it gleaming brightly yellow in the sun, and from the base two trenches had been dug forming a right-angle.

'What is it?' I asked, bending to examine a piece of paper in a plastic envelope nailed to the post.

'Pa must have come back and done it during the night. He's pegged the usual rectangle—four corner posts covering three hundred acres. This one's the datum post.'

So that was it, and he hadn't heard a thing. 'Couldn't be expected to with the noise of the drill going all night.' And he added, 'I'd have gone after him, but you'd got the Landy—I'd no means of catching up with him.'

'It wouldn't have done any good,' I said. It wasn't his fault. It was mine for not realizing that this was Crown land and that Chris Culpin had come prepared to stake a claim. 'What happens now?'

Kennie shrugged. 'The usual routine. That's a copy of his Form 22. He'll take the original to the Mining Registrar at Marble Bar and he'll make formal application for registration of the claim on Form 24, pay the necessary fee and then advertise details of the claim in the local paper. After that it's up to the Registrar. If you can show he's jumped a claim then the case goes before a Warden's Court, but when, Christ only knows. Did Ed Garrety ever register a claim?'

'No.'

'And it's Crown land.'

The paper nailed to the post gave his name, *C. Culpin*, and his address in Great Boulder, the hour he had marked off the land, *6 o'clock a.m.*, and the date, *January 22, 1970*. He described it as a *Mineral claim for gold, antimony, silver, nickel, iron, lead, zinc, chromium and copper*, and the dimensions of the ground as *60 chains × 50 chains*. The boundaries of the claim were also given in chains from the datum peg, which was described as: *1·8 miles 28° North of Golden Soak Mine buildings*. And right at the bottom of it he gave the number of his Miner's right.

'That's his prospector's licence, I suppose.'

Kennie nodded. 'Pa's been making claims now for more than six years, but none of them came to anything, only Blackridge.' He took me round the other three posts so that I could see for myself that the claim covered the whole area of the hollow, and the only encouragement he could give me was that there was a backlog of thousands of claims. 'But they'll get around to it in time.'

I was blazing with anger then, the drill still in hardish rock, down only 170 feet, and now this. 'Do they know your father's pegged the area?' I nodded towards the rig.

''Fraid so. We bin using that patch of wattle as a latrine and it was Georges who found the datum peg. Just after breakfast.'

So we couldn't uproot the pegs, and with Garrety ill there wasn't a hope of registering a claim ahead of Culpin. I stood there, staring at the rig, the blazing heat oppressive now. That bloody drill burning up my hard-earned cash, and for what? I was drilling another man's claim. I began to laugh then, a little wildly, suddenly hating the place. A curse, Ed Garrety had said, and by God he was right. 'Go down and tell Duhamel to pack it in.' I saw the boy hesitate and I screamed at him, 'Stop that bloody rig, I tell you.'

4

It wasn't as easy as that, of course. Duhamel didn't have any work for his rig until January 26, when he was due back at Mt Goldsworthy. He was a decent enough sort, but he had wages to pay and he insisted on completing the programme we had originally agreed. I was stuck up on that spur another three days and the joke of it was we did strike the reef. They broke through into softer rock that Friday evening and at dawn on the Sunday Josh Meyer called me to examine the first dust sample to show the white of quartz crystals. They were then just on 700 feet and the gold in the quartz was visible to the naked eye. But in less than five minutes the compressed air was bringing up granitic dust samples. We had struck the reef, but only through a drill hole length of about three inches. And less than an hour later the dust samples ceased and the drill slowed. We were down to the water table and it would need a diamond bit and the lubrication of wet mud to drill further. Whether it was the edge of the reef we had struck or whether it dwindled here to a mere three inches in width there was no means of knowing without drilling another hole alongside. It would have been exciting, a cause for celebration, if that bastard Culpin hadn't got in ahead of me. And all Duhamel could do was pat me on the shoulder and say, 'You'll catch on, mon brave. You're in Australia now and they don't use the word crook for nothing. Everything's crook here—the climate, the country, the people.' He was grinning, his wild bright eyes laughing at me. 'You put it down to experience, hnn? And next time you make dam' sure you got a claim registered before you start drilling.' But he had the decency not to insist on double rates for striking the reef first go.

We started packing up then, and by sundown we were off the ridge and camped at the foot of the gully in sight of the mine buildings. After the evening meal I took a torch and climbed with Kennie the sides of the gully. The rock drawings Ed Garrety had talked about were everywhere. Some of them were painted, some just scratchings on the surface of the outcrops, the best of them in what looked like waterworn caverns. It was a strange, haunting place—the ghostly presence of long-dead people substantiated by their primitive ritual drawings. And below us the embers of the cook fire glowing through the ghost-white boles of the gum trees, the faint sound of Josh's guitar and the mine buildings pale in the starlight.

We slept stretched out beside the Land-Rover and I was woken in the middle of the night by a black man on a horse. It was one of the two Jarra Jarra boys. He sat his horse in the darkness calling my name in a way I barely recognized, and when I stood up, he said, 'Come, you come quick. Jan say you come.' The others were awake by then and to my surprise Duhamel knew something of the language—one of the few people I met in Australia who ever bothered. 'It's not a dialect I know, but as far as I can gather the Boss has disappeared and the girl's gone to Lynn Peak to look for him. She told this feller to come down here and get you.'

Put like that I could visualize her panic, the native boy riding through the night and Janet heading for the Andersons' place, driving the ute flat out in the hope of catching up with her father. We got going straight away. We were sleeping in our clothes and all we had to do was roll up our swags and toss them in the back, say goodbye to Georges Duhamel and his drillers and hit the track.

I was thinking then of the rock drawings, of the Soak as it had been before the white men came, a source of water for ritual gatherings, of life in time of drought, and remembering all that had happened there since Big Bill Garrety started blasting that quartz for gold, I knew that if I were Ed Garrety I'd leave the mine alone. I knew exactly what I'd do, and as I drove through the night up that track I was determined to turn the homestead inside out in search of the missing pages of that Journal.

Oh yes, I knew they were missing. Whatever Janet might say, you don't end your life story like that—not when you've been keeping a record as long as he had. He might conceal the truth about McIlroy's death from his son, but I couldn't believe he hadn't confided it to his Journal. And Ed Garrety, reading it after his death, had done the only thing he could; but whether he had destroyed those pages, or merely hidden them away—that was something I couldn't be sure about. Janet said she had searched the house, but she would hardly have searched her father's den, not without his permission, and she certainly wouldn't have gone through his private papers. If he hadn't burned them, that's where the missing papers would be, in that room amongst the litter of papers that had strewn his desk, the chairs, even the floor, when I had last seen him.

I was thinking of the Gibson then, clear of the dry water-courses and driving flat out, the dirt track faintly red in the headlights. Why else would he want me to witness a new will? And the Land-Rover loaded for a two-week journey, the faithful Tom waiting beside it. I knew nothing about the Gibson, only that my tourist map showed it blank, apart from the Canning Stock Route, and the end of summer not a good time to drive into the red wastes of one of Australia's worst deserts. Was he bent on suicide? Or did he really believe in the Monster? Pushed to the point of desperation, did all Australians clutch at straws?

'Ever been in desert country?' I asked Kennie.

'The edge of the Nullarbor, that's all.'

'Not the Gibson?'

'Jesus! No.'

'What about your father? He ever been in the Gibson?'

'Part of the Canning yes. But no dogger goes into the desert and no white man strays from the Woomera Range tracks if he can help it.'

We crossed the grid into the paddock, the Windbreaks a familiar outline against the stars. There was nobody about as we drew up by the poinciana trees, no sound when I cut the engine, the outbuildings silent shadows. The house was open, her bed not slept in, no sign of life and the door of her father's den locked, but nobody there. Back in the cool house Kennie had lit a candle and was staring at the table still laid for two. 'Doesn't look as though they had any supper.'

I went into the kitchen. Two steaks uncooked beside the paraffin stove, potatoes in a pan and onions already sliced. She had obviously waited supper for him, hoping against hope that he'd return, and then about eleven, or a little after, had finally decided he wasn't coming back. It would have taken the boy about an hour and a half to ride to the mine and he had woken me shortly after one.

'Well, what do we do now?' Kennie asked.

'Wait till she gets back,' I said. There was nothing else we could do, and I told him to see if he could work the petrol pump. 'If you can, then fill the Land-Rover's tank, the jerricans, too, and we'll need spare cans for water. Then get some sleep.'

'And you?'

I told him what I was going to do. 'And if I find what I'm looking for, and Janet doesn't bring him back, then we'll have a lot of driving ahead of us, so get some sleep.'

I went outside then, round the house to the window of his den. There was no glass, only the flyscreen, and that was easily dealt with by slipping the blade of my knife up the edge of it to release the catch. I had brought candles with me and, once inside, I lit one, the soft glow showing the room much as it had been when I was last there, an untidy litter of files and papers. The only difference was that the desk top had been cleared except for a sealed envelope marked *Will* and beside it a brief note written in a rather shaky hand:

202

My darling Jan,

This may be goodbye—in which case do not grieve. It will be a merciful release. I am going on a long journey now and I have little hope that it will prove successful. If it does, then maybe we can find some happiness. But I am very tired now, too tired to face any longer the hopeless struggle to keep Jarra Jarra.

And you, though you love the place as I do, must be tired of the struggle too. Little of happiness I have been able to give you and to say that it was not all my fault is no answer.

God bless you, my child, and do not fret. Tom will see me to the end, and after that I pray you will make a new and better life for yourself.

Your loving father,

He had signed it simply 'Ed', and standing there in the candlelight, reading it through again, I felt a lump in my throat. It was such a desperate, sad letter. I put it back on the desk beside the will, wondering whether Janet had read it before she left.

I moved the candle from the desk and began going through the piles of papers, the silence of the house reminding me of Drym, a waiting stillness. And as the candle burned lower and the past, with its deeds, its birth and death and marriage certificates, its accounts and correspondence, filled the silence with the hopes and fears of those that had peopled the house for more than half a century, a feeling of depression settled over me, my eyes growing tired with peering at dusty papers faded with age. And reading what I had no right to read, I began to realize how hard a struggle Ed Garrety had had, the debts he had paid, the effort he had made to restore the land, the constant battle to rebuild from nothing. Above all, the loneliness of the man, and all the time the sense of hopelessness growing.

In the end I sat down at the desk exhausted. No sign of the missing pages of the Journal. I added a fresh candle to the old, not caring any more. Somewhere to the east of Lake Disappointment, deep in the Gibson Desert. . . . If Janet didn't find him, then that's where I would have to look. But should I? What was the point of bringing him back? He had fought his battle and now he was finished. To bring him back would be like resuscitating somebody who had deliberately thrown himself into a river. I must have fallen asleep there at his desk for the next thing I knew the candle was guttering with the draught from the open door and Janet was standing there, the pale first light of dawn showing through the empty window, her face white with exhaustion. 'You didn't find him.'

'No. The Andersons hadn't seen him.' She came a few steps into the room, her eyes on the letter. 'You've read it?'

'Yes. I shouldn't have, but I did.'

'It doesn't matter.' She was surprisingly calm. In the long drive to Lynn Peak and back she seemed to have come to terms with the situation. But accepting it had meant putting her emotions in cold storage, so that there was an almost frozen quality about her calmness. She had guessed where he was headed. 'I thought he'd take the track east from Ethel Creek. That's twenty miles south from where our backtrack joins the Highway. But they hadn't seen him either and there wasn't a sign of any tyre marks. Anyway, I had Yla with me and I think she'd have known.'

'Could he make it across country?' I asked.

But she didn't think so. 'In the Gibson, maybe, but between the Highway and the desert it's hilly country and I'm sure he'd go for one of the tracks.'

I turned to the world aeronautical chart on the wall. It was the Hamersley Range chart, No. 3229, and though the Highway was almost on the edge of it, it did indicate the start of another track running east from Mundiwindi. But that was nearly a hundred miles south of Ethel; a hundred miles of ribbed gravel, dried-up creek beds and bulldust. It would have taken her half a day at least.

She came and stood beside me as I tried to project it on to the big tourist map. It certainly looked the most direct route to Lake Disappointment, through Mt Newman, then south from the Sylvania homestead and east from Mundiwindi. But when I pointed it out to her, she shook her head. 'That track only goes as far as the old rabbit fence. That's what I've been told anyway. It stops at Savory Creek. After that it's just desert.' She pointed to a second track running almost east from

Sylvania. 'I think he'd more likely take that. It isn't shown on this map, but it continues across the Highway to the Murramunda homestead and on to Jiggalong Mission, again on the line of the rabbit fence. Daddy knows it. He's been to the Mission. And there's another track goes from Murramunda up to Walgun. He might have taken either.'

I asked her when he had left, but she didn't know. She had been over beyond the Windbreaks with one of the boys most of the day.

I went back to the desk and flopped into the chair again. He already had at least half a day's start. Not much hope of catching up with him and none of finding him once he was into the Gibson. 'I was looking for the rest of the Journal,' I said.

'Yes, I guessed that's what you were doing.'

'If we had that, we might know the location he's headed for.' I leaned back, rubbing the sleep out of my eyes, staring round the room. 'You got any ideas?'

'You've been through all the papers?'

I nodded. 'Most of them.'

She sighed. 'Well, I'll go and make some tea. I need something to wake me up.'

Dawn broke as we sat there drinking it in that untidy office, both of us certain he was heading for the Gibson, but neither of us knowing quite why or what to do about it. 'Janet.' I was staring down at my empty cup, feeling unsure of myself and not at all happy about what I was going to say. 'Your father was right, wasn't he, when he said McIlroy disappeared in the desert?'

'You've heard then.' Her voice was a whisper, barely audible. 'What they're saying—this rumour. That's what you mean, isn't it?'

I looked at her, her face frozen and pale. 'Yes. Are you quite sure in your own mind that McIlroy didn't die here at Jarra Jarra?'

'You're suggesting my grandfather killed him?'

'No. No, I'm not suggesting anything. I wouldn't know. But you, living here, growing up here. . . . I just want to know what you think really happened.'

She looked away towards the window, the colours flushing

205

with the dawn. 'I don't know,' she said after a while. 'I've thought about it a lot these last few days, ever since the inquest.' The tears suddenly started to her eyes. 'Oh God!' she breathed. 'It's horrible—horrible. All these years. Why can't they let it rest?' And she bowed her head slowly, her hair all limp and dusty and falling across her face. 'If they'd only forget it. That wretched man still haunts the place.' Her hands clenched. 'I hope he's rotting in hell, the bastard!'

I put my hand out to touch hers and her fingers gripped hold of mine. 'Perhaps,' I said, 'that's what your father is trying to do—lay McIlroy's ghost.'

She nodded, holding my hand hard. And then she suddenly lifted her head, staring at me a little wildly, 'But how would he know where to look?'

'The Journal,' I said. 'Those missing pages.'

'Maybe.' But there was doubt in her voice and her eyes were troubled. And then she said a strange thing. She said, 'I've had this hanging over me all my life. The rumours, I mean. Daddy wouldn't talk about it—ever. Not even when I was grown up. If I mentioned it, he'd close up like a clam and a sort of terrible blank look would come over his face. I thought when I typed out that Journal—I thought somehow I'd be able to read between the lines. But there was nothing. And when I began turning the house upside down for the missing pages, he got very angry, said I was wasting my time, that I already had all that Grandpa had ever written.'

Silence then and her eyes staring. 'You believe these rumours.' She said it accusingly. 'Well, don't you? Why not be honest, you believe what they're saying—that Big Bill Garrety killed him and buried his body in the mine.'

I didn't say anything. What could I say? It fitted, and the Pilbara was a tough world in those days with not much chance of the law catching up on him. I pushed back the chair and got to my feet. 'You'll radio a report on the morning sked, will you?'

She hesitated, half shaking her head. 'Not yet,' she said. 'Not yet, Alec. If I do that. . . . No, I can't.' And then she was standing, very close, her hand on my arm. 'Alec. I'm sorry, I shouldn't be relying on you like this.' She hesitated, staring up

206

at me, all her loneliness laid bare as she added, 'But I can't help it.'

I put my hand on her shoulder. 'I've nobody either.' I said it lightly, squeezing her shoulder. 'Don't worry. We'll catch up with him.' I don't think she was convinced any more than I was, and of course she wanted to come with us. But I told her it was essential she stayed with the radio. 'If you don't hear from me after a week, then do your best to get an air search organized. We'll be going to Mt Newman for petrol and stores first. Then the Sylvania homestead. After that we'll head for this other homestead you mentioned.'

'Murramunda?'

'Yes.' I left her then and went to wake Kennie.

While he was getting dressed I checked the Land-Rover, now heavily laden with jerricans of petrol and others marked 'water'. The guns were there, the shovels and the sand mats, food containers, bucket, axe, saw, petrol funnel. I went across to the workshop, gathering into an old sack all the Land-Rover spares I could see. Janet came to see if she could help and I sent her off to look for more containers, anything that would hold water and petrol.

I was checking that the compass we had used on our geophysical was still in the dashboard locker when I remembered we would need the map from Ed Garrety's den. At least it would take us as far as the Highway. I went back to the little room littered with papers and ripped it off the wall. That was how I discovered the Gibson desert map. It was another aeronautical chart—Oakover River No. 3230 and the same size as the Hamersley Range chart so that it had been completely covered by it, the two of them Sellotaped to the wall together.

I stood there for a moment, staring at it, vaguely wondering why he hadn't taken it with him. Had he forgotten it was there? Kennie called to me he was ready and I took the charts out and spread them on the bonnet of the Land-Rover. The Oakover River chart showed the track eastward from Sylvania crossing the Highway and then splitting in two at the Murramunda homestead. Both tracks led to the Walgun homestead, the left-hand one direct, the other via the Jiggalong Mission and turning sharply north to make two sides of a triangle. There was nothing to the east of it, only desert. But from Walgun a track ran through the abandoned rabbit fence to the Talawana homestead and then due east between the Horsetrack and Poisonbush ranges and on through the Wells, Emu and McKay ranges to join the Canning Stock Route north-east of Lake Disappointment at Well 23. The Stock Route ran diagonally right across the chart as far as Well 45. But at Well 24, which was marked Karara Soaks, another track ran eastward into an area that was a topographical blank, and it was here, 40 miles or more beyond the Midway Well that I noticed a faint mark on the paper. It was in the form of a rough circle and looked as though it had been made by the point of a pencil and then rubbed out, the surface of the paper very slightly roughened.

'You found a map then?'

I looked up to find Kennie at my elbow. And then I saw Janet coming out of the house. 'Yes,' I said. 'It'll take us to the Lake anyway.' And I folded the charts and tossed them into the Land-Rover.

She had a Thermos full of coffee and two skin waterbags, the sort you hang on the side of your truck so that the water sweats through the bag and keeps cool. 'Don't forget,' I said as we climbed into the Land-Rover, 'if you haven't heard from me after a week, then you'll know we're in trouble.'

She nodded dumbly, standing there, the Alsatian beside her and one hand absently stroking its head. And as Kennie started the engine, I leaned my head out of the window. 'Better get started on those cattle. You've only got till the end of February.'

'You know there's no water for them this side of Coondewanna.'

'Have a look at Golden Soak then,' I said. 'There was plenty of water at the fourth level and now the mine's collapsed that soak might start working again.' And I nodded to Kennie to get going. Not much of a chance, but anything was better than having her hang around the place with nothing to do but wait.

We took the backtrack to Mt Newman, colour flooding the

landscape as the sun's light grew behind the Ophthalmia Range. And two hours later, in a garage in Newman township, we got news of Ed Garrety. He had brought his Land-Rover in for servicing just before lunch the previous day and had finally set out around five-thirty.

I had talked to enough Aussies, seen enough of their country now, to have no illusions about what lay ahead. The bush was the nearest thing to hell on earth, they said, and bush bashing like trying to drive through barbed wire entrenchments. But surely that depended on the locality. It couldn't all be as bad as that, and the desert wasn't the same as the bush. Surely to God it would be more open. I ordered a set of new tyres and instructed the foreman to give the Land-Rover a thorough overhaul, tipping him a ten-dollar note to get the job done in a hurry. After breakfasting at the Walkabout, we shopped for stores, then went in search of more jerricans, loading them full of fuel into the back of the Land-Rover until there wasn't an inch of space left. It was almost midday before we were finally ready, everything checked, and on our way.

We reached the Sylvania homestead shortly after one, but Ed Garrety had not called there and they had seen no sign of his Land-Rover. We were in flat country then, the hills behind us as we took the eastward track, and an hour later we had crossed the Highway and were at Murramunda. The heat was intense, the place abandoned. The track continuing eastward was fairly good and we were able to make Jiggalong in two-wheel drive. Ed Garrety had not called there, but we found an abo who had seen the dust streamer of a vehicle heading for the Walgun homestead shortly after sundown. We had a cooling drink of water and then drove on, the track running northward now.

The sun was setting as we reached Walgun, and though the place seemed deserted, an abo in a singlet and shorts eventually answered the blare of our horn. No whitefella had stopped there the previous night, but he showed us the fresh tyremarks of a vehicle heading up the track to Balfour Downs.

There were low hills to the north of us now as we drove through the gathering dark and it was night when we passed by the Balfour Downs homestead. We did not stop, driving east-north-eastward to the old abandoned rabbit fence and the source of the Oakover River, still in two-wheel drive. But though the going had been pretty fair, we were utterly exhausted by the time we reached the Talawana homestead. No lights, no sign of life. We camped by Talawana Pool, which was dry in the starlight. A meal and a couple of hours' sleep, then we were on the long drive eastward towards Lake Disappointment, and in about ten miles we were reduced to four-wheel drive, the track invaded by spinifex and saltbush, the going slow.

Dawn found us in the low hills of the Wells and Emu ranges, the sun coming up in a fire-ball blaze of brilliant light and the McKay Range standing black in silhouette like humped up islands in a desert sea. By then we could hardly keep our eyes open, and when we hit the sand I was driving so carelessly I stalled the engine. It took us a good two hours to dig ourselves out and get clear of the soft patch, using the sand mats, and a mile or two further on I drove the Land-Rover into the sparse shade of a small grove of snappy gums. We didn't eat, just drank some of our water that was warm and tasted of metal and then fell into the back and lay there dozing, too tired and listless to sleep properly. I remember looking at my watch, the time ten-thirty. Except for the breaks at Mt Newman and Talawana we had been driving steadily for twenty-four hours. According to the chart we were within 60 miles of the Stock Route with the Lake less than 40 miles to the south-east. Vaguely I wondered how far ahead of us Garrety was now. Even with Tom driving, and used to the country, could he stand it continuously, hour after hour?

I wondered whether I could, and I was fit, the heat exhausting and my mind wandering. And the desert still ahead of us. Did anybody still use the Stock Route? And that other track—would we be able to follow it? I was thinking then of the faint mark of that circle on the Oakover River chart and McIlroy dead these thirty years. Was that where he had died? Or was that the rough position of his copper monster? Was it all a dream, a mirage? Then why the mark? And the chart itself—it was an aeronautical chart. It couldn't have existed in Big Bill Garrety's day. So his son Ed had made that mark, and then thought better of it and rubbed it out. Why? And how had he known?

So many questions, my mind wandering and the heat enclosing me, weighing me down, my skin prickling and my eyes gritty as though clogged with sand. The desert. Soon we would be in the desert. And the wells all dry most likely at this time of the year. It was madness, this driving into the unknown, following a man whose sanity I began to doubt—in search of what? And for what? What the hell was I doing it for? For Janet? For a chit of a girl with a turned-up nose and a freckled face? Or was I, like McIlroy, risking my life for the vague chance of a fortune?

Over and over, around and around, the questions rattled in my throbbing head. Never an answer, only questions, and the heat burning up my sleep, destroying the rest I needed. And then Kennie started talking to himself—some row with his father. Talking in a sort of delirium from which he woke suddenly with a cry, sitting up wild-eyed and staring at me in the hooded glow of the interior. 'Pa—I thought he was here.' He leaned forward, lifting the back flap and peering out at the sand-glare. 'Dreaming, was I?'

'Something like that,' I murmured, the glare red through my closed eyelids. 'Close the flap for God's sake.'

'It's hot in here.'

'Close it.' I snapped irritably.

Silence and a moment's pause, then the red glow was gone from my eyeballs as he let it drop. 'We must be out of our minds,' he mumbled. 'The engine's only got to pack in . . .'

'Why should it?'

'Well, a spring then.'

'I brought a spare.'

It silenced him, but only for a moment. 'You should've hired a plane, searched for him that way. The shade temperature must be all of 120°. We get bogged in sand or lose our way— men die every year trying to walk out of the bush in summer. Twenty-four hours. That's all you got if you start walking. Twenty-four hours without water and you're done, finished. It's crazy.'

I stretched out my hand and gripped his arm. 'You didn't

have to come. Now shut up. Try and get some sleep.' I looked at my watch. Only eleven-fifteen and the worst of the heat still to come. 'We'll brew up at the nice conventional hour of five o'clock and start again at sunset. Okay?' I could feel his body trembling, the skin of his arm hot to my touch and damp with sweat.

He nodded his head. 'I suppose so. At least it isn't September. September is the worst—blows like hell Pa always said.' And he added, 'I wish Pa was here. He knows this country.'

'And I don't. Is that what you mean?' God! How irritability got one by the throat in this heat. But he was right. I'd never been in a desert in my life. And I lay back, wondering whether Ed Garrety had ever been in the Gibson before, remembering that letter of his, the note of hopelessness, thinking that whether he had or not, it didn't matter a damn, for there wouldn't be much help from him. We were on our own, and dozing the slow, burning minutes away I couldn't get the thought of the Gibson out of my head—the knowledge that it was out there waiting for me, stretching endlessly away into the Red Centre of Australia. The hot midday wind began to get up, drifting sand, a rustling hard-grained reminder of endless desert miles to disturb my restless sleep.

That evening, as the sun set and the sky ahead darkened to purple, a velvet mantle with the diamond-hard glitter of stars, we passed through the McKay Range, heading about 100° east with the Harbut hills fading as we neared them in the increasing darkness. The track was difficult to follow in the headlights, at times almost non-existent, only a faint lessening of the vegetation indicating where it had been, and spinifex everywhere, hard and spiky. Little but brumbies, donkeys and camels appeared to have used it in living memory. Indeed, but for the animals I imagine it would have disappeared entirely. We saw their tracks and their droppings everywhere, camels chiefly, and when we paused in sand halfway between the McKays and the Harbuts I found in torchlight the faint marks of a vehicle. But though they looked recent, there was no way of knowing whether it was the Jarra Jarra Land-Rover or some survey party.

The going was slow as we probed for indications of the

track, not daring to drive across country on a compass course. And when the moon came up it was little better. It was an old moon, and though it revealed the dead dry desiccated country through which we were driving in a pale translucence that washed all colour from the scene, it only confused us, dimming the headlights and straining our eyes.

We never saw the junction with the Canning Stock Route. I didn't know it then, but the track marked on the chart as the Stock Route doesn't exist. There never was a track, just a series of wells, the stockmen driving their cattle cross-country from one well to the next. Whoever marked that track on the chart had certainly never been within a thousand miles of Canning's route. I cursed him as we strained our eyes for a sight of the well marked No. 23, finding it more by luck than judgment, a draw wheel on an upended post, leaning drunkenly over a pit boarded with desert oak. The water when we got it up in our billycan was brackish.

From this well to Karara Soaks was only seven miles and the survey track we were now on led straight towards it. The country was hilly—mesa and butte formation sprawled like miniature Table mountains along the skyline. It was on this section that we found the wheelmarks again. They were clear and sharp in the dawn and the same width as our own.

The sun was coming up ahead of us as we reached the Soaks, which was not a soak at all, but another derelict-looking well-head between low hills of red broken rock with a dry creek bed skirting them. The hills had small trees on them and there were trees in the distance beyond the creek bed, and around the wellhead there was saltbush and the sered wispy remains of grass killed by drought and the salt in the wind. The water, when we got it up, proved surprisingly good. It was also refreshingly cool. We topped up our containers, then stripped and washed ourselves down.

Before turning in and lying up for the day's heat, we drove to the base of the hill nearest us and clambered the broken rock to the small trees at the top, taking our personal cloud of flies with us. The sun was already blazingly hot and away to the south-west a salt-white glimmer marked the flat immensity of Lake Disappointment. All to the east now was nothing but desert, speckled with the golden yellow of spinifex, and the sandridges like a flat red swell coming in from the north-north-east. High overhead two wedge-tailed eagles worked the air currents, soaring on great wing spans, intent, searching for anything that still had life in that arid hell of drought-ridden sand.

We drove back to the wellhead, had a brew and a large breakfast and then turned in. The height above sea level was about 1200 feet, but it made no difference, tiredness and heat catching up with us as we lay in the back of the Land-Rover, the flap closed and the sweat drying salt on our bodies, unable to sleep.

Two miles to the north of us the Stock Route was joined by the lone track coming in from the east. The chart showed it coming in at right-angles, and in its whole length of well over 100 miles there was only one feature marked, the Winnecke Rock. And there was only one well, the Midway Well, and that about five miles south of the track. I doubted whether we could find it, and even if we did it would probably be dry. It was midway between our present camp and a track that ran north-south across an area of the chart that was completely blank, not even the lines of the sandridges marked. That track looked fine on the chart, but Kennie didn't think it was any more of a track than the Stock Route, and in such featureless country it was most unlikely that we would ever find it.

I didn't need to look at the chart as I lay there restless and hot and completely naked. It was all in my mind, every detail clearly imprinted. There were so few, and the faint pencil indent of that rubbed-out circle. Before sundown that evening, two miles to the north, we would have to make our decision— continue on the line of the Stock Route where at least we had the chance of water or turn east into the empty featureless desert, banking on that faint circle mark being Ed Garrety's objective. Dizzily I wondered where he was camped now. He couldn't be far ahead of us surely. Perhaps camped at the track junction. Would we have caught up with him if we had driven those two extra miles?

All that blistering day the evening's decision nagged at my mind, the hot wind drifting the sand and the flies crawling.

And that was the measure of my tiredness, for we really had no alternative. The Stock Route was known. If there was, in fact, a big copper deposit, then it had to be in the unknown part of the desert, and so I came back again and again to that pencil mark. To find it we should have to locate Winnecke Rock and then work our way eastward slanting across the sandridges, driving on a compass bearing. I didn't know how high the sandridges were or what the going would be like. I just hoped to God we could follow his tracks. If we could follow his tracks we might catch up with him before he was dangerously deep into the desert. It was the Canning Desert really. The Gibson was more to the south. But the name didn't matter. It was all the same—the Great Sandy, the Canning, the Gibson. All sand and sparse, dried-up vegetation, and once into it we only needed to have one breakdown. . . .

I dozed and woke, dozed and woke, fear of the waterless oven of sand and the days ahead twisting at my mind like a drill. And all for what? For a man who wanted to die. Or was it the Monster? Was I, too, willing to risk my life for a pot of gold under a burning sky? I didn't know. I just didn't know what my motive was. My mind was too confused. Heat and exhaustion, my bare skin covered in salt from the sweat I couldn't feel, the pores of my body prickling and Kennie naked beside me, turning restlessly and mumbling in his sleep. Why the hell didn't we turn back now, while it was safe, while we still could?

But shortly after five I started a fire going, woke Kennie and we brewed tea and had a meal with large ants pestering us and a small goanna playing hide and seek in and out of a clump of spinifex. And then we drove north up the Stock Route until the speedometer showed we had covered a mile and a half, when we slowed, watching for the eastward track. Here and there tyremarks showed faint in the sand. We found the turn-off, the tyremarks clearer as he had swung away to the right. I looked at Kennie. 'Well, we can't be far behind and if he's gone east . . .' I waited, watching him, his face red and blistering with the sun, his greenish eyes wide as he tossed his bleached hair back and gazed into the flat empty land ahead. I saw him swallow jerkily, his adam's apple rippling the silky beard where it ran down across his throat. 'Then we'd better get cracking,' he said quietly. 'The sooner we catch up with him the less desert we'll have to cover.'

So we drove east, following the faint intermittent wheel-tracks, driving slower and slower as the light faded and it became more difficult to pick them out, driving on the edge of a confusion of piled-up dunes, the salt pans of small lakes bordering our route—outriders of the great dead lake now behind us. Soon we were having to stop repeatedly and search for the wheeltracks on foot by torchlight. Sometimes they were concealed in the hard dry vegetation of long-forgotten rains, at others they were lost in a harder surface or on the everlasting damnable spear-pointed spinifex. Going slow like this, we were using a lot of fuel, and it was hard on the vehicle, hard on ourselves. In five hours we had covered no more than twenty miles by the speedometer, the engine overheating, the radiator boiling. And then we bogged down in soft sand. Kennie voiced my own feelings: 'Hell!' he said. 'We can't go on like this.'

We dug ourselves out and got moving again, the tracks still faint, the sandridges rolling shallow in the headlights, but getting higher, the flat sandplains between them wider. And then we came to a broader plain, dead flat but covered in spinifex, and the tracks vanished. We found them again half a mile ahead, over the top of a sandridge, but it was more by luck than judgment and it cost us the better part of an hour. I stopped then. Nothing but a jumble of sandridges now, very confused, the tracks running in a straight line through a flat plain between the ridges, but very faint. The engine was sizzling hot, steam showing from below the radiator. We had some food, sitting there in the sand waiting for the engine to cool, not saying much, only thinking about the miles of desert that lay ahead. The stars were very bright, the ghost of a moon just risen. It was airless and still and hot, so still and silent that the sad featureless landscape surrounding us seemed petrified. In that weird pale light it had the stillness of death. It scared me, and I knew Kennie was right—we couldn't go on like this.

I lit a cigarette, noticing that my hand trembled slightly, and then I got the chart out and sat there with it spread out on my bare knees, staring at it in the light of my torch. 'Only one thing to do,' I said, my voice slow and uncertain. I held the chart for him to see, pointing to the Winnecke Rock. 'It's thirty-six miles. If we drive a compass course just short of it, say thirty-five miles, we should be able to locate it in the dawn.'

He nodded. 'You think he's making for the Rock?'

That was when I showed him the rubbed-out mark of that pencilled circle. 'I think that's where he's heading. If it is, then he can only locate it by a compass bearing from a known position, and the only features shown here are the Rock and the Midway Well.'

'And that track.'

The note of sarcasm in his voice, the little worried laugh— neither of us believing now in its existence.

'When we've found the Rock, we'll cast around for the treadmarks of his Land-Rover.'

'Use a lot of petrol,' he murmured.

'Not as much as stopping and starting and driving slow the way we have been.'

'Okay,' he said. 'Let's go then.' His voice was pitched a little high, nervous and uneasy.

We got to our feet, and while he topped up the radiator, I took a bearing on the tracks running out ahead of us. Converted from magnetic to true they were headed 103°, slanting across the sandplain towards the next ridge. According to the chart, 103° was the correct bearing for the Winnecke Rock. The track bearing, on the other hand, was nearer 110°, so we were almost certainly north of it, heading direct for the Rock. I took the speedometer reading and then we got going.

Steering a compass course required concentration and it was difficult driving because of the spinifex. The clumps were small and widely spaced, but each clump the size of a molehill, hard as concrete, so that, riding them, the jolting was incessant, and Kennie at the wheel twisting and turning to find the easiest route, the strange opaque light making it difficult for him to pick his way. Three miles of this, and then the spinifex thickened, forcing us into four-wheel drive, the going slow and the tracks lost, the needle of the speedometer flickering between nought and five. We found the tracks again on the slope of the next sandhill, deep-scored where he had taken it fast. We made it to the top, but only just, the engine labouring in four-wheel drive, the wheels spinning in the soft sand of the crest. Another sandplain, much wider, full of spinifex and here and there the skeletal remains of wind-uprooted mulga lying prone, their spiked roots like tank traps, like the battle maces of medieval giants.

We had lost his tracks completely now and our course, slanting across the lie of the sandridges, meant that every few miles we had to turn into the face of a petrified sandwave, take it at a rush in four-wheel drive, both of us clinging on for dear life, our heads bumping the roof. Twice we had to stop on the far side of a ridge to let the engine cool. It was a nightmare drive, but at least our course was generally parallel to the line of the seif dunes, and in the sandplains between the ridges the going was less difficult, fairly flat and the spinifex patchy, so that there were moments when we almost reached 15 mph. I am told we were lucky, that the area we were in must have been better than most of the Gibson, but, even so, dawn was paling the eastern sky before we had completed those thirty-five back-breaking, exhausting miles.

We stopped on top of a sandhill that was about 40 feet high, the desert rolling all around us, a long undulating sandswell, the ridges showing like pale red waves above the green-gold sea of spinifex. Lizards scuttled dryly through a patch of scrub, ants moved busily in the sand and we saw our first scorpion. But it was the fantastic surrealistic beauty of the scene that held me spellbound, the breathless cruelty of it, the hardness of the colours in that clear dry air, above all the terrible infinity of it, the sense that it went on for ever. There was no sign of anything that could be described as a rock, only limitless sand and scrub, the waves of the ridges rolling endlessly to the horizon.

We gathered enough material to make a fire, had tea and a short rest, and then, as the sun rose and the contrast of colour and shadow heightened the sense of having become part of some mad artist's canvas, we began our search, driving north across three ridges, east 6 miles along an easy sandplain, then south across the dunes, their backs less steep going in this direction. Oddly enough, it wasn't the Rock we found, but the tracks again. We were 2·4 miles on the southward leg, in a particularly bare sandplain between two ridges, and they were quite clear, still bearing 103°.

The sun was well up by then, all the colour gone out of that terrible landscape and the heat already so violent that every movement was an effort. Even so I wanted to drive straight on, catch up with him and get it over, or at least reach the area of that pencilled circle.

But Kennie, his head bent over the chart, the skin of his nose peeling and his hands trembling, insisted it was madness. 'It's all of fifty miles, nearer sixty.' He looked up at me, his eyes slitted against the glare. 'Driving in daytime, it'll just about finish us. The rad'll boil. The engine'll probably over-heat again, and if we hit soft sand or have a puncture. . . . It could take us all day.' He didn't want to drive on through the heat.

We drank some water and had a meal, talking it over in the shade of the Land-Rover. But I couldn't persuade him. 'What the hell's it matter whether we catch up with him now in daylight or later when it's a little cooler?' Mirages were already forming, the scant, desiccated vegetation swimming on the flat horizon, the dunes bobbing crazily on the skyline. In the end I agreed. What the hell did it matter? We stripped and lay in the back, our bodies burning with the growing heat of the sun, the back of the vehicle glowing like a furnace. And then, when I'd just got off to sleep, a hornet's drone woke me, growing gradually to a roar, ripping like a buzz-saw into the muzzy drowsiness that still engulfed me.

I sat up, pulling back the flap and peering out. The blinding white of the sky hit my eyes and I could see nothing, the sound fading. Kennie slithered naked to the ground, yelled as his bare feet touched the burning sand, and then the noise was back, growing again from the south. And suddenly I saw it— a small twin-engined plane coming in low across the sand-ridges, and as it roared over us, barely 100 feet from the ground, the pilot waggled its wings.

So Janet had got scared and notified the authorities. That was my first thought. I had thrown Kennie his shoes and now we were both of us standing naked in the sun watching the plane. 'One of the new Cessnas,' he murmured. We watched it as it banked to the north of us, circling and then banking again as it picked up the tracks of Ed Garrety's Land-Rover to the east of us and followed them, still flying low. The sound of it dwindled, fading into the immensity of desert space till the plane itself was no bigger than a fly on the horizon. 'Well, that's one thing,' I said. 'They know where we are now.'

'Who?'

'The authorities.'

Kennie smiled at me sourly. 'You're joking. The Administration up here runs on a shoe-string. They don't hire planes to search for fools who go driving around in the desert.'

'Who then? Somebody has.'

He shrugged. 'Prospectors. Maybe it's a survey party.' But he sounded doubtful and his face had a troubled look.

It seemed too much of a coincidence that a survey party doing an aerial magnetic or a mapping job should have happened on our tracks by chance. The same thought seemed to have occurred to him, for he said, 'You're a mining consultant. Not many mining consultants operating on their own like you. And going off into the desert in summer. They'd think you were on to something.' He hesitated. 'It'd be all round Mount Newman, and the Conglomerate in Nullagine. . . . That bar'd be full of talk.'

'What are you getting at?'

He hesitated again, as though unwilling to put his thoughts into words. 'Pa,' he said at length. 'Pa might hire a plane. You're lucky, see. First Blackridge, then Golden Soak. And he knows about the Monster.' He started to climb back into the Land-Rover, but then he stopped, his eyes on the horizon to the east. The plane was still there, a speck circling.

'Do you think he's found something?' My voice sounded strange, a dry croak, my eyes riveted.

He nodded. 'I reck'n.'

I reached for my shirt and shorts and put them on, the plane still circling. He did the same, and we stood in the sun watching it, our eyes screwed up and the minutes passing. Then it was coming back, still a speck and climbing. It was flying high and fast as it passed over us, the sound of it barely audible.

'Must be near 10,000 feet,' Kennie said. It was slightly to the south and took no notice of us. We watched it until it had disappeared, a speck high in the sky to the west.

I got into the driving seat and started the engine. The position over which it had been circling was not more than ten miles away and the tracks led straight towards it. Half an hour, an hour at the most. The engine couldn't overheat in that time, not with the breeze beginning to blow, a hot little wind from the south-east. We got going, following the tracks in four-wheel drive, the breeze increasing until sand was flowing like a tide towards us along the desert floor. This wasn't the normal heat wind. This was more like a gale and in an instant the tracks were gone. One minute they were there, the next they had vanished, overlaid by the wind-blown drift of the sand. Kennie leaned towards me. 'Bedourie,' he yelled. 'Sandstorm. No wonder that pilot was in a hurry.'

Away to the south the horizon was blurred, the white of the sky turning sepia. In moments the sand had lifted from the surface, rustling against the bonnet of the Land-Rover, millions of grains on the move, a drift waist high and the broken twigs of dry shrubs blowing against the windscreen. And then it hit us, the sky darkening, the desert world turned suddenly brown. I stopped then. I couldn't see a thing, only the sand like brown smoke, the howl of the wind, the noise rasping at the aluminium panels like the sound of a train as I cut the engine. Nothing to do now but sit in the tight-closed Land-Rover, handkerchiefs tied round our mouths and nostrils, wrapped in the hot protection of our blankets, the noise indescribably vicious. And nothing visible through the windscreen but the sand pouring like a sea, the occasional wrack of desert vegetation uprooted and whirling by.

We didn't talk. We just sat huddled there, desperately trying to breathe, while the sand got into our noses and ears, into our clothes, and the floorboards were gradually covered inches deep with the brown wash of the storm. The noise. . . . I don't know which was worse, the clogging, insufferable sand or the noise. And it went on and on, the hot wind blistering and abrasive, the minutes dragging into hours. To look at it was to get one's eyeballs seared with grit, and as we sweated, the sand clung to our bodies, a perpetual irritant. It lasted all day, and then died in the evening as quickly as it had started. From nil visibility and daylight drab as a nut-brown night, suddenly there was stillness, the sun showing as a faint pale circle there in the west and the desert taking shape around us. It was like breaking surface after being half-drowned in the brown tide of a swollen river. Another moment and everything was still, not a sound in the world, and the air becoming crystal clear in the slanting sun. Far away to the north anvil tips of cu-nim showed above the horizon.

We shook ourselves out and had some water, the first we had had for over six hours. We were dried up, desiccated, exhausted by the battering. The tepid water cleaned our mouths, but did little to refresh us. We opened a tin of baked beans and wolfed them cold. I would have given anything for a bath. Kennie's skin was coated red with dust and sweat. I was the same and we couldn't even wash our faces. Instead, I lit a cigarette, my nerves crying out for it more than food, even though my nostrils were still clogged with sand.

It was then, as I inhaled the first long drag of that cigarette, staring at the clear, impersonal hostility of the desert, that I saw it. Away to the north-east, just short of the horizon, like a rock awash in a petrified sea. I thought it must be the Winnecke Rock and I called to Kennie, who had started clearing the sand out of the back of the Rover. But then I realized it couldn't be the Winnecke. We were half a dozen miles at least beyond the Winnecke. The sun was slanting, a softer light, the desert golden red, the white heat of the sky paling into an ephemeral blue, and my eyes were tired. 'That's not a rock,' he said. And in that instant I saw it for what it really was, a vehicle hull-down below a ridge of sand, just the rectangle of the canopy showing.

I moved to the driving seat, but he stopped me. 'Better top the rad up first.'

We did that and cleaned some of the sand off the engine. Then I turned the ignition key and for a long minute the starter whined and nothing happened. Sand, I thought. My God! All this way, and then, just when we'd sighted him . . . The engine coughed, lost itself, then coughed again and roared into life. Sweat trickled between my shoulder blades. Kennie swung himself in beside me, grinning with relief. 'Bit of luck that.' We were both of us grinning as I put her into gear and headed north-east across the line of the next ridge.

I had forgotten to put her into four-wheel drive and within minutes we were up to our axle in a fresh sand drift. Heat exhaustion slowed us badly and it took a long time to dig ourselves out and get moving again, everything an appalling effort. Kennie drove the rest of the way, the sun sinking to the horizon, the flaming ball of it reddening the desert to the colour of blood, the cu-nim gone from the horizon ahead and the sky to the east taking on that egg-shell greenish tint of evening. It was a Land-Rover all right, stuck halfway up a dune, its bonnet raised and facing east. A canopy had been rigged against one side of it, and as we neared it, I could see a solitary figure in a broad-rimmed hat collecting vegetation for a fire. No sign of anybody else.

We drew up in the trough below the sandridge on which it had stalled and a figure emerged from the lean-to shelter and staggered to his feet. Tall and stooped, he was instantly recognizable. I got out and went to meet him. 'You, is it?' There was no welcome in his voice, only tiredness, a touch of resentment even. 'What d'you want?' His voice was slower than ever, a little slurred with the effort of speaking.

'I came to look for you.'

'No need. I'm perfectly able to look after myself.'

I glanced at the Land-Rover, nettled by his reaction to our arrival. 'Trouble?' I asked, nodding at the lifted bonnet.

'Sand in the fuel line, that's all. I'll deal with it—later.' The weariness in his voice was very apparent, his body swaying slightly with exhaustion and Tom standing defensively a few yards off, the black face below the wide hat wrinkled in a puzzled frown.

The sun was almost gone now, a red wound gaping along the horizon to the west. I turned to Kennie. 'Better see if you can fix it before the light goes.'

'Did you send that plane out looking for me?' There was a distinct note of hostility in Ed Garrety's voice.

'No.'

'Who did then?'

'I've no idea.'

He nodded slowly, then looked about him and folded his long thin legs, collapsing on to a bare patch of sand. He said something to Tom, who answered, 'Yes, boss,' and set about getting a fire going. 'We'll have a brew-up together, then we'll see,' Ed Garrety murmured. 'Come and sit down.' He patted the sand beside him. 'You look tired. Not used to the desert, eh?'

I sat down beside him, both of us silent for a long time. The sun had gone, the sky a lurid blaze of colour, except in the east where it was already darkening to the velvet purple of dusk. There were questions I wanted to ask, but I didn't know how to begin and so I remained silent, and he said softly, '*You would play upon me—you would pluck out the heart of my mystery.*' He smiled suddenly. 'But you're no Guildenstern come to trick me. You're honest. Or I believe you are.' He peered at me, still with that tired smile, his face warmed by the sunset colours so that the skin below the stubble no longer had that parchment look. 'But I don't know your motive, do I? Why are you here?'

'To get you back home.'

'Think I can't make it on my own?'

'Janet's worried.'

'Ah, yes. Janet.' He paused.

'I read the letter you wrote her.'

'That was a private letter.' The hostility was back in his voice.

I told him how one of the boys had woken me in the night. 'Janet had gone to Lynn Peak looking for you. The house was empty. I read it because I wanted to find out what had happened to you.'

'And you followed me, knowing I wanted to do this on my own.'

'Janet was worried,' I said again.

'And that was all? No other motive?'

'I was curious, of course.'

He nodded. 'Of course. You want to know what happened.'

He was silent then, staring into the desert. The colour was fading now, the washed-out look of dusk creeping over the sand. And then abruptly he said, 'D'you love her?'

I stared at him.

'My daughter—d'you love her?' He was looking at me very intently, his eyes searching my face.

'I'm fond of her,' I muttered, my eyes shifting from the directness of his stare, uncertain of myself and what he expected of me.

'Fond?' He leaned a little forward. 'You've never been in an Australian desert and you risk your life for an old man because you're fond of his daughter?'

'There's Kennie,' I said, nettled by his words. 'He's here, too. Why don't you ask him if he loves her?'

'That boy.' He shook his head, the dulled blue eyes still staring at me out of the drawn, tired face. 'I wonder if you realize how attractive you are to people. It's a quality that's rare. But you have it. That boy, the drillers, Janet—even myself, and I've had a lot of experience of men.' He lowered his head, staring down at the sand. 'And you want to know what happened.'

'Not if you don't wish to tell me,' I said.

I saw him smile. 'That's the trouble. I do. All these years . . .' He didn't finish, but continued staring down at the sand. There was sweat on his forehead and he suddenly looked very old and alone. Then Kennie called to me that the union to the carburettor was threaded. The moment was gone and he murmured, 'Later. We'll talk about it again later.'

'You're a sick man,' I said.

He didn't answer and in the end I got up and went to help Kennie repair the union, while Tom brewed a billy of tea over the fire. We got the engine going in the end and backed the Land-Rover down the ridge, parking it on the flat beside our own.

We fed in the last of the light, and then drove on, following in the wake of Ed Garrety's Land-Rover. Tom was driving it and the bearing varied between 100° and 105°. We were held up only once by sand and that only briefly. Otherwise we made steady progress, all in four-wheel drive with two pauses to let the engines cool. Shortly after midnight we stopped. We were just short of the pencil mark on the chart. Ed Garrety's face appeared at my window, lit faintly by the light from my torch shining on the chart. 'Where did you get that?'

'From the wall of your den.'

'You searched the place then.' His voice was strangely detached, no resentment in it.

'I was looking for the rest of the Journal.'

'You knew, did you—that it was incomplete?'

'I guessed.'

'Does Janet know about that map?'

'No.'

He seemed relieved.

Kennie leaned forward. 'We stopping here, Mr Garrety?'

'Yes. We'll camp here.' His gaze returned to the chart. 'I should have brought that with me.'

'I only found it by chance,' I said. 'It was under the Hamersley Range chart.'

He nodded. 'I forgot all about it.' He leaned his head in at the window, looking down at it. 'The mark's still visible.'

'Yes.'

'So you'd have come straight here.' And he added, smiling, 'Well, perhaps it's for the best. I'm not a mining man myself.'

'This is the position then?'

He gave me a long slow look, then nodded and turned away. 'We'll have a look round in the morning, eh?'

I got out and followed him as he moved slowly back to his own vehicle. 'How did you know?' I asked.

We were alone then, midway between the two Land-Rovers. He stopped, a shadow in the gloom.

'Did McIlroy get as far as this?'

I saw him nod his head, slowly, almost reluctantly.

'How do you know?'

He didn't say anything, his eyes glinting in the starlight, the outline of his body sagging.

'And that chart left there on the wall. You didn't need a map to find your way here.'

'I brought a quarter mill map along.'

'But you didn't need it.'

'No,' he said. 'I knew the way.'

The truth was staring me in the face, but I didn't recognize it. Instead, I thought it was the Journal. 'The missing pages,' I said. 'Your father gave the position in his Journal.'

He stared at me and for a moment I thought he wouldn't answer that. But then he said, 'No, he didn't know that. But everything else. He wrote it all down, everything, just as . . . as it was told to him. He was a great one for keeping records. He should have been a diarist.'

'Where is it then?' I asked. 'Where's the rest of his Journal? Have you got it with you?'

He shook his head. 'I burned it. When the old man died I burned all the last part.'

'Why?'

'Still curious, eh?' He patted me gently on the shoulder. 'All in good time. Don't rush me.' He stood for a moment in complete silence. 'Ever been in a desert before?'

'No.'

'Then you wouldn't understand.' And then so softly I could barely hear him, 'But Christ did. He understood . . . the peace, the solitude, the immense impersonal hostility that cleanses the soul. I was a young man, hot-blooded, and full of the certainty that justice . . .' His voice trailed off. 'Now I'm old before my time, my body worn out by a twist of fate that was equally unjust. In Burma I had a lot of time to think, and death all round me. Since then it's been a long hard struggle, and no time to think. But now . . . now I want to make my peace.' His hand was on my arm again. 'We'll talk again— later. I'm a sick man, as you say. Only one lung left and that's going now. Janet doesn't know. She only suspects. I've never told her.'

'And the copper deposit?' I asked.

'A chance, that's all,' he said. 'Like you drilling at Golden Soak. We're all of us gamblers, y'know.'

'You're not certain then.'

'About what?'

'That it's here.'

'How could I be?'

'So McIlroy never saw it.'

He shook his head slowly. 'All he ever had was the rough position given him by a black feller.' And when I asked him how an abo could possibly have known what copper looked like in the ground, he said the man had been employed at one

227

of the mines near Nullagine. And he went on to repeat the story of how the aborigine had been walkabout in the Gibson and had come into the bank to trade the information for cash. And after that he closed right up on me, wouldn't say another word and went off to give Tom a hand.

That night we had bully beef and damper and thick sweet Indian tea. And afterwards the four of us sat for a while by the glowing ashes of the cook fire, Ed Garrety slumped in a camp chair and Kennie questioning Tom about the desert people and their spirits. But Tom was a Pukara. His parents had lived and died in the Turee Creek area halfway between Jarra Jarra and what is now the iron mining township of Tom Price. He had only met the desert people—the Ngatatjara he called them— when he had been walkabout, crossing the Gibson Desert to the Clutterbucks. He had done this twice as a young man, the second time to attend a corroboree at Ayers Rock. 'Before me talk'im desert people. Forget'im plenty.' And his broad black face cracked in a grin that showed his broken front teeth. But he knew the names for the ghosts of their dead that haunt the desert at night. 'Call'im *mamu*.' He cocked his head on one side, affecting to listen, hugging himself with laughter. 'Plenty *mamu*, but keep'im far going, no trouble us.' And then he was telling a long story about a *mamu* that had taken the shape of a watersnake. It was, I think, a story from the Dreamtime of his own people, but it was complicated and I was too tired to follow his uncertain English. The last of the firelight flickered and died, my head nodding.

The back of our Land-Rover was fusty with the smell of sand and our own sweat. We slept in the open that night, a small breeze blowing hot from the north-west, no flies and the stars shedding a ghostly light on the desert around us. It was very quiet. I had a last cigarette, wondering what we'd find in the morning, and then I fell into a deep sleep. Something woke me shortly after two, but I was too tired to lift my head, glancing at the gold hunter tied to my handkerchief and falling asleep again in the same moment, vaguely conscious of a sound fading. And then the sunrise hit me, heat again and flies crawling on my face, seeking the moisture of eyes and nostrils.

I sat up, bleary-eyed, still half asleep, my limbs cramped by the hardness of the sand. A large centipede was feeling its way over my feet, a reptile slithering sluggishly to the shelter of a brittle bare bush. Nature called and I got up, walking a few yards before relieving myself. Kennie stirred as I came back, stretching himself. 'Christ! It's hot.' He sat up then, his face burned red beneath the beard, his eyes looking wildly about him. 'Where's that Rover gone?'

I thought he was still half asleep, the Land-Rover right in front of us, not a dozen yards away. But then he was on his feet, moving to get a clear view beyond it and suddenly I realized what he meant. There was just our own vehicle there, the other had gone. He pushed his hand up through his tousled hair. 'When did he go? I didn't hear him.'

I stood there for a moment, too surprised to do anything but stare vacantly at the empty desert. 'Something woke me. Just after two.'

'You saw him go?'

'Of course not. Something woke me, that's all. I was dead asleep again before I'd time to think about it.'

We walked to where his Land-Rover had been, the tracks of it clear in the sand heading east.

'What do we do now?'

'Follow him,' I said.

'In this heat? You're joking.' He turned to me his eyes still wild, his voice trembling. 'Playing hide-and-seek in the desert like this. Are you mad?'

I turned then, a sudden premonition sending me stumbling back to our own Land-Rover. The bonnet catches were undone, a sheet of paper lying, white below the steering wheel. I grabbed it. *Sorry, but I didn't ask for your company. You'll have to wait here. Back in two days.*

'What is it? What's he say?'

I handed Kennie the pencilled scrawl and lifted the bonnet. The distributor head was off, trailing its four cables, and the rotor arm was gone.

We had no spare, of course, and I stood there helpless, wondering why the hell he had done it. To immobilize us, yes. But why was he so determined to be on his own? *We are all of us gamblers.* I remembered his voice, slow and tired, but if he found the Monster he must know he couldn't keep it to himself. A copper mine in the desert wasn't something like Golden Soak. To develop it would require big company finance. Kennie was swearing softly to himself. 'Two days,' he muttered. 'Two goddammed blistering days. And not a thing we can do about it.'

'No.' We'd just have to stick it out.

'And how do we know he'll be back?'

'He could hardly leave us to fry here indefinitely.'

'Oh, I don't doubt he intends to come back. But will he be able to find us again?'

'He's got Tom with him. He should be able to backtrack along their own tyremarks.'

'And suppose there's another sandstorm?'

The thought had occurred to me, but it wasn't one I wanted to dwell on. 'We'll just have to keep our fingers crossed,' I said lamely.

'Well, you keep yours crossed. I'm going to see if I can file a piece of metal down and rig a replacement for that rotor arm. And if I succeed, we're getting out. Okay?' And he went to the back of the Land-Rover and began rummaging among the bits and pieces of spares I had picked up in the workshop.

All that day, through the long fly-ridden heat, the rasp of his file sounded as he worked at a piece of brass clamped in a vice on the tailboard, while I lay and dozed in the back. I knew it was no good. Such a small, insignificant thing, but a rotor arm is a machine-made, precision job with the metal contact arm insulated in a barrel of oven-hardened bakelite. But at least it kept him occupied, his mind off the deadly danger of our situation, as the dust devils he called whirlies twisted and twirled in an endless sand dance and the dunes stood on their heads in blinding pools of throbbing heat.

Night came and he sat there, exhausted, the glow of his cigarette lighting his face. 'It won't work. I can't get it accurate enough, and I've nothing to make the barrel outa.'

'We'll just have to wait,' I said. A week I had told Janet. 'If he doesn't come back tomorrow, then we've only two more days before they send out a search party.'

'A fine job they'll have, searching for our tracks

under a fresh layer of sand! But the plane may come back.'

'Perhaps.'

Nothing to do but wait. I thought of the desert war, men frying in tanks, living like nomads and fighting in the heat. I had only just been born then, but Rosa's father had been with the Desert Rats. We had talked about it over the port the few times I had visited him. I had read about it, too. If they could stand it, then so could we. But it's different when you've no organization behind you, nothing to do but wait, and all the time that secret niggling fear that nobody will bother and you'll be left to die of thirst. I checked the water before I turned in, doing it surreptitiously. We had twenty gallons at least. And though it was tepid and tasted of metal, it was enough to see us through if Janet did what I had asked.

That night, as the sun set, the sandhills ceased their heat-throb dance and colour crept back into the landscape, the temperature dropping back towards the hundred and the atmosphere clearing, so that our world of blinding, desiccated emptiness had form again and beauty, a terrible lonely beauty, but still beauty, with its shades of red and gold and the translucent unbelievable green of the eastern sky. But for the heat and isolation, the extreme discomfort of our situation, I could have sat there everlastingly entranced, believing it to be the most breathtakingly beautiful sight I had ever seen. Instead, it was a sort of frozen hell, all that red and gold, and the sun a great disc blazing on the lip of the desert, sinking till its lower rim touched the horizon, melting along it like some great steel mould pouring molten metal. There was a movement away to the east, a drifting of strange shapes. Emus. There must have been a hundred in that flock, flowing northward like a dark tide merging with the lengthening shadows.

'Must be water somewhere,' Kennie muttered.

Night fell and we watched the stars grow brighter, lying sprawled beside the glowing ashes of our fire, plagued by ants and too exhausted to sleep. And in the morning, nothing to do but wait, with the heat building and the sand moving with the midday wind, the dust devils swaying to their twisting sand dance, mirages turning the desert upside down. It was a long day that frayed our nerves. Too tired to talk, we just lay fending off the flies, hating ourselves and the desert, frustrated beyond endurance. And then, as colour flooded back into that deadly waste of petrified sandhills, sound invaded the desert silence. It was a long way away, but we both of us knew what it was, both of us starting to our feet, searching the sky to the west.

Nothing. Nothing but the blaze of the slanting sun—blinding. Kennie seized his shirt and started up the sandhill behind us. I followed him, the sound of the plane growing as I stumbled up the slope, needle-sharp spines of spinifex pricking my bare knees. I reached the top and there it was, to the north of us, a flash of sunlight on its fuselage and Kennie waving his shirt frantically. But it kept going, flying eastward at about 1,000 feet.

We watched it as it dwindled, the sound of it fading. 'He never saw us.' Kennie's body seemed to sag, his arms limp and the shirt dangling. 'Christ all bloody mighty! The bastard wasn't even looking.'

'He was flying a course,' I said.

'But he'll come back. He's got to come back. Quick! A bush signal.' He was suddenly galvanized into action, running back down the slope, back to the Land-Rover.

I stayed there, watching. The sound of it died in the distance, but it was still visible, a speck and dropping to the horizon, and then it was gone. But only for a moment. I saw it again, much lower. It had banked, searching low down along the desert rim. I called to Kennie to take a bearing, but he couldn't see it from where he was. He had one of the jerricans out of the back of the Land-Rover, a rag in his hand. I yelled at him to bring me my compass, my eyes concentrated on the plane. 'The compass,' I screamed at him.

The plane was still there, circling low down, when he thrust it into my hand. The bearing was 112° magnetic, the distance —what? Ten miles? Fifteen? It was difficult to tell. I slipped the compass into my pocket and stood waiting, the old gold hunter in my hand, holding it up so that I could see it and still keep my eyes on the plane. 'Twin-engined, wasn't it?'

'I think so,' he said.

The same plane then. 'What's its speed?'

But he didn't know. 'The small Cessnas do about 140, I reck'n.'

Say 160–180. It would be a question of counting the seconds. Out of the tail of my eye I saw him running back down the slope. He reached the jerrican, was soaking the rag in petrol. And then the speck was turning and heading back and my eyes were on my watch, counting aloud as it grew larger, the sound of it faintly audible again.

Fire blazed in a patch of spinifex, the crackle of flames momentarily distracting me. Thick oily smoke began to billow up. But slowly. Too slowly. And the plane a long way to the south of us, climbing steadily. The fire died and the smoke with it. Four minutes. Five. Six. And twenty-thirty-forty seconds. It was due south of us now, still climbing, the sunlight on its wings, but five miles away at least. Fire crackled again in the spinifex, the black smoke rising in a thick cloud. Six minutes forty-five seconds. Allowing for reduction of speed due to the angle of the climb, that made it just over a dozen miles to the point where it had been circling. Say five hours' walking. If Ed Garrety failed to return by nightfall. . . .

I was almost back at the Land-Rover then, suddenly conscious of Kennie yelling at me, blaming me for the fact that they hadn't seen us. 'You and your damned compass. If you'd left me to get that fire going . . .'

'We know where he is anyway,' I said.

'And what good's that do? Look at it now!' The fire was racing through the whole area of spinifex, the resinous smoke rolling skyward, a thick black streamer. 'They'd have seen us.' He was almost crying with exasperation.

'They couldn't land,' I said wearily. That damned boy! Why couldn't he shut up? 'Be practical.'

'You be practical,' he shouted at me. 'You think you're going to walk it?'

'Maybe.'

'You're crazy then. You'd never find him.'

'Got any better ideas?'

'If you'd left me to get that signal fired . . .'

'Oh, shut up!' I was sick and tired of him. 'You waste your energies fooling around with a bit of metal. Then you expect a plane to land in this stuff.' I could hear the high trembling in my voice, nerves screaming and the exhaustion of heat wearing my patience. 'I'm sorry,' I said, forcing myself to speak slowly, rationally. 'I'm tired, that's all. We're both of us tired.'

'You can say that again.'

'We'll have some food—a brew-up. We'll feel better then.'

'Like hell! We've missed our chance, I tell you.' I could hear his voice cracking.

'Pull yourself together.'

'And what about you? Shut up, you tell me. Well, shut up yourself for Chrissakes. I didn't ask to come on this bloody trip.' And he added, his voice still strained to a high pitch, 'I don't know who's crazier, you or that old man. I want to get out of here. That's all. Out of here, and alive, see.'

I didn't answer him. Better to keep my mouth shut or I'd end up striking the young fool. I began collecting sticks of vegetation, the sun sinking and the desert all on fire with the redness of light and sand. A dozen miles. Five hours in the cool of the night. Then search for him in the dawn light. It ought to be possible. Distance and bearing were both pretty accurate. I got the cook fire going, filled the blackened billy with water and put it on the flames. Midnight. I'd give him till midnight. If he hadn't returned by then, I'd start walking.

In fact, I started before midnight. Twelve miles doesn't sound much, but in the dark, with the sand dotted with spinifex clumps, littered with dry vegetation—it would be like stumbling through a teeming mass of porcupines. And I was scared. I can admit that now. I was scared that in the dawn I'd find nothing. Nothing but that blinding emptiness, with the sand-ridges bobbing dizzily in the heat and no alternative but to retrace my steps. Fear feeds on inaction and the fear in me started the instant darkness clamped down. The headlights of a Land-Rover would be visible for miles then, but though I stood for a long time on the top of the ridge staring into the dark of the desert there wasn't the glimmer of a light anywhere. Only the stars above, and all around me the frozen stillness, the empty silence of the desert.

I began collecting my gear shortly after ten—waterbag, compass, torch, food, matches, cigarettes. And Kennie arguing all the time. It was crazy, he said. I'd lose my way, wander aimlessly till I died of thirst. First he tried to dissuade me, then he wanted to come with me. But how else would I find our Land-Rover again if he wasn't there to light a bush signal to guide me in? He saw the sense of that, but he didn't like it. He was scared, scared of being left on his own, stranded beside a useless vehicle. 'If I don't come back,' I told him angrily, 'then the plane will find you.' But I don't think he was very sure about that, any more than I was. 'Well, what else do you suggest?'

That shut him up because he hadn't anything else to suggest. We couldn't just stay there, waiting and doing nothing. Not when there was a chance Ed Garrety was only a dozen miles away. And then, just as I was leaving, he said a bloody stupid thing to me. He said, 'If you started walking south instead of east, a few hours and you wouldn't be all that far from where Gibson disappeared.'

I rounded on him then. 'I'm not disappearing,' I said. 'I'm going twelve miles, that's all. And if I don't find him, I'll lay up during the day and walk those dozen miles back tomorrow night.' And I told him to fire a patch of spinifex just before sunrise to guide me in.

'Well, I hope to Christ you find him,' he said.

'So do I.'

I left him then and started walking, the satchel with my gear bumping my hip, the compass in one hand the waterbag in the other.

The first hour wasn't so bad. I had changed into a pair of khaki longs and the spinifex wasn't very thick, plenty of sand between the clumps, and I was in a flat plain, walking diagonally across it with the next sandridge a good two miles away. At first I found it difficult to hold a course, the light of my torch blinding me every time I checked the compass. I solved that by lining the bearing up with a star, then I didn't have to use the torch and could concentrate on where I was putting my feet.

If it had all been like that I would have made it in four hours, but over the next sand ridge the going was bad. I was in a narrow trough between two ridges, the spinifex thick, my feet stumbling and spines like darning needles stabbing through my trousers. Ridge succeeded ridge, almost no gap between, the slopes steeper and the sand soft. I was sweating, conscious of the weight of the waterbag and beginning to tire. A gap opened out and I was into a patch of dead mulga scrub, the roots like giant spikes. I had to make a long detour round it and in spinifex again I began to stumble.

I paused then for a breather and checked my watch. One hour twenty-two minutes. I could have sworn it was longer than that. I went on again until I had done two hours, and then I sat down and smoked a cigarette. My knees were trembling and I was very tired. Two hours. Did that mean I had covered four miles? How fast had I been walking? I finished my cigarette and went on for another hour, the going variable with two long detours to the north across the ridges. It was easier after that, patches of open sand and gravel, but the stillness, the loneliness, getting on my nerves. I began to understand why the aborigines believe in their *mamu*. Time and again I could have sworn I saw a movement, shadows flickering in the desert. Kangaroo perhaps, or euros. I think they were really wallaby. But no sound, only the soft scuff of my feet in the sand, the scrape of the spinifex spines against my trousers.

I was stopping every half hour, moistening my mouth with a few drops of water. The temperature was around 100°, and though I knew I was sweating, my skin was dry, only the scum of salt to tell me I was losing body moisture. I walked on, right through the hours of darkness, and as the sky began to lighten with the dawn I collapsed on to the ground at the top of a sandhill, lying there exhausted, watching the desert take shape around me. There were wallaby moving in the flat sand trough below me, grey shapes that shifted their position with slow movements, crouching as they browsed on the dry, desiccated vegetation. And a little kangaroo rat that seemed oblivious of my presence. But no sign of the Land-Rover, nothing to indicate the presence of another human being in all the miles that stretched away to the surrounding rim of the horizon. The night receded, the washed-out grey of early dawn quickly taking on colour as the light strengthened. The dunes were 'braided' here, the stark beauty frightening. I didn't see the wallaby go. They just suddenly weren't there any more. I was alone then, seemingly the only living thing in that great red frying pan of a desert—except the flies in a cloud around my head and the ants in the sand at my feet, and that little marsupial rat.

I had some food and a slow, careful drink of water, and then, as the moment of sunrise neared, I began my search, keeping to the top of the dunes and walking on a bearing of roughly 120°. I couldn't be sure how far I had come during the night; I thought just under the twelve miles, allowing for rests and detours. But while the idea that I could locate that Land-Rover on the basis of course and distance walked had seemed sensible enough at the outset, now that I was in the presumed locality I realized how near-impossible it was in practice. Parked in a trough below a sandhill, I could walk within a few hundred yards of it and never see it.

The sun rose and I turned south, angling across the ridges, pausing on each top to search the valley between. It was my only hope. Even then I wouldn't have seen it but for the fire. The sun had risen an hour ago and I was nearing the point of exhaustion, the heat intense and mirages beginning to haze my vision. My legs were trembling as I stumbled up the next ridge, nerves stretched and panic only just within my power to control. And those words of Kennie's at the back of my mind. Coming out in the ship, I had read about the Warburton, Gosse and Giles expeditions, and how Gibson, going back for fresh horses, had lost his way and disappeared. As Kennie had said, it wasn't all that far to the south, somewhere near the Alfred and Marie Range. But here there were no ranges, not the ghost of a distant blue range-top lipping the horizon to give me hope of shade and water. And then I had staggered to the top of that ridge and was standing there, the sun blazing, sand and vegetation dancing before my eyes, my body sagging and the flies crawling around my eyes.

I knew I must lie up now, find some shade, try to sleep. And then, when night fell, the trek back. I turned towards the sun, thinking of Kennie and the Land-Rover. Company at least. To die alone. . . . I suddenly had a feeling that I was in a void, hopelessly lost, with no hope of finding my way back. I was remembering how I had told Kennie to burn spinifex. But if I was lost, how could I see it? How could I possibly be certain I'd be near enough to him in the dawn—the next dawn?

Panic was very close then. I wanted to run. I wanted to run all the way back, just to be certain. And then I saw it, beyond the next ridge—a wisp of black smoke. And for a moment I was crazy enough to think I had run those twelve miles back. Today—tomorrow . . . time had no meaning. I was too damned tired.

The wisp of smoke was dying, and I was running, running down the slope of the ridge, across the floor of the trough, the smoke receding and the next ridge far away, hardly getting any nearer as my blood pounded and my feet staggered. Birds rose, flights of bright colours—budgerigars I think—and the wisp gone now. Christ! A mirage! That's what kept me staggering at a shambling run, the fear that it was a mirage—a dream, my mind wandering, crazed in panic, dried seed pods rasping at my trousers and everything vivid in the blinding light. It seemed an age before I reached the top of the sand slope and then suddenly the scene had changed, the sandhills gone and in their place rough rock, red-knolled and eroded into little escarpments. And below one of these, far away and shimmering in the distance, my tired eyes glimpsed the blunt box-shape of the Land-Rover.

Sanity came back, all panic gone, and the going easier as I reached the bare rock surface. It was a conglomerate of some sort, rough and hard under my feet with only here and there a sparse covering of dwarf spinifex and grasses. I heard my voice, unrecognizable as I shouted, my mouth furred and my larynx sounding as though I had newly discovered the power of speech. A movement then, a figure coming out from behind the Land-Rover, standing staring and finally moving towards me. A black face and a wide hat, black hands gripping me as I reached for him, stumbling. The blessed certainty that he was real and not some mirage of my imagination. 'Tom.' The black face split, his teeth showing in a grin of recognition. And then I passed out—not exhaustion, not shock, just pure bloody relief.

I was only out for a second. I didn't even fall. Tom had hold of me and in a moment the grogginess was gone, the knowledge that I had found them giving me strength again. They were camped close under one of the little escarpments, a cavity hollowed out by the scouring action of wind and sand, Ed Garrety sitting there propped against the rough conglomerate wall and in the hollow at his feet the sand unbelievably darkened by moisture.

He nodded to me, smiling vaguely. 'You made it, eh? I wondered whether you would.' He didn't seem at all surprised.

'Two days you said.'

'That's right. But when we tried to get going again, we found the jets clogged with sand, and after we'd dismantled the carburettor and cleaned it that threaded union leaked so badly we could only just start the engine. It wouldn't give us any power.' His voice trailed off, very weak, his breathing shallow and his skin paper-white.

'I'll try and fix it,' I said.

He shook his head. 'No good. I've tried. Nothing to fix it with.' He reached into his pocket and tossed me the rotor arm he'd taken from our Land-Rover. 'That's what you came for, isn't it?'

'I suppose so.' I was stretched out now in the shade of the overhang, reaction setting in and a great lassitude creeping through my limbs. Outside, the blinding white of the sunlight fell on a straight, dark-trunked tree with bark like cork and feathery needles, an anthill mounded beneath it and the pests scuttling over the conglomerate, large, long-legged and wiry, busy at some unidentifiable task.

'Bulldog ants,' he said. 'Find a kurkapi—that's a desert oak —and there's always one of their damned nests under it. The shade, y'see. It's the best shade tree in the desert.' His voice was so faint I could hardly hear him. 'Glad you came. I had Tom keep a fire going from first light. To signal you in. But not much spinifex here to make a proper smoke.'

I closed my eyes against the glare, the lassitude deepening, my head nodding.

'Who sent the plane?'

I think he asked me that several times before I dragged

myself back to consciousness enough to give him an answer. 'Don't know,' I said. 'Could be a prospector—that man Culpin perhaps, or Janet may have changed her mind and notified the authorities.'

There was a long silence and I drifted back into the lethargy of half-consciousness, not sleeping, not waking, just lying there in a state of exhausted oblivion. The next thing I knew I was being shaken and a black hand was thrusting a mug of tea at me. It was strong and sweet and very hot, and it did the trick. It woke me up and put a little energy into me.

'Better?'

'Yes.' I took another gulp at the hot strong tea. 'Yes, better, thanks. It was the loneliness. I bloody near panicked.'

He smiled. 'I guessed it was that.'

He was looking at me, a very direct stare, his blue eyes wide. I dropped my own gaze down to the mug, looking down at the tea leaves floating and a dead ant, flies clinging with thread-like legs to the rim, realizing suddenly that I hadn't bothered to conceal my fear. Somehow this sick, worn-out man, with a face so parched of blood it was like a lizard's, had the knack of holding me to the truth. Something in his personality, or perhaps it was the wretchedness of his situation. Or was it the country? Was it the starkness of the red centre of this country that brought a man face-to-face with reality?

I stared at the rotor arm in my hand, the golden gleam of the brass bright in the strong light, the brown of the bakelite. Was that really what I had come for? If I made it back to our own Land-Rover in tomorrow's dawn it meant release from the torture of this red desert. The engine would go again and we could get the hell out. I leaned back against the rough curve of the rock, flicking the flies off, sipping at the hot, sweet contents of the enamel mug. All this way just to turn back. It didn't make sense, though something at the back of my mind screamed at me to go—to go while the going was good, while I still had some reserves of energy left.

But man isn't made like that. Given the faintest spark of energy there's always that need to reach for something, regardless of physical discomfort, regardless even of the fear of death. I closed my eyes, trying to concentrate, conscious all the time of Ed Garrety there beside me. Logic. A sensible decision. But my brain seemed incapable of that, and the man beside me—nothing logical there. A gamble, a last desperate gamble. But if it was that, why had he immobilized our vehicle? A dozen miles and on his own—why? Why, when he had a mining consultant at hand to confirm the nature of the deposit?

I sucked at the last drop of tea, spitting out the leaves and that dead ant, the flies buzzing. My eyes were open now, staring into the sun-glare at the red-scabbed rock, a petrified sediment of tiny fragments welded into a conglomerate and bared by the wind, worn by the blowing sand into a gentle undulation, a low swell frozen with sudden knoll-like outcrops carved in strange shapes. 'There's no copper here,' I said.

'No.'

'A conglomerate—of no value at all.' I looked at him, a thought taking slow shape in my mind. 'Then why in God's name——' But something in his face stopped me. He was slumped there, his eyes closed, the muscle at the corner of his mouth twitching and an expression of extreme agony on his face. Behind his head a complicated pattern of concentric circles had been painted on the rock wall, the pigments faded now, but still showing faintly. White and ochre and some sort of blue—indigo perhaps. It was like an old frescoe, a primitive halo framing his parchment face, the saint-like effect emphasized by the lidded eyes, the suggestion of a death mask.

The lids flicked suddenly open and he was looking at me again with that wide-eyed unblinking stare, and I saw he was deep in some private hell of his own. Christ! I thought. He's over the edge now. He's mad like his father. 'What is this place?' I heard myself ask, my voice a whisper.

'The blacks call it a *rira*. It's a conglomerate, as you say.' His words were slow, like a man talking in his sleep. 'And this soak here—not many in the Gibson. It's called the Kurrajong Soak. See that tree there?' He nodded vaguely towards a brilliantly green tree. 'That's a kurrajong. It's always like that. Not many of them, but even in a drought like this it stays green. The greenest thing in the desert.'

I waited, not saying anything. And then, very quietly, very matter-of-factly, he said, 'The last time I was here this soak had water in it. We only had to dig down about a foot and we got all the water we wanted—good water, too. Not brackish.' And he added, 'There was a lot of game here then. But last night nothing. No emu. No wallaby.' His eyes were closed again so that he was like a man talking in his sleep. 'If I hadn't come on this soak I'd have lost my camels. They'd just about reached the limit. I'd never have got out alive. I was crazed with thirst myself. And like you, on the verge of panic. But with more reason.' He was living something that had happened a long time ago, silent once again. I kept my mouth shut, knowing it would come of its own accord or not at all.

A shadow moved and Tom stooped in under the overhang, took the mug from me and disappeared, back to some separate burrow of his own. And then his voice again, quiet in the silence: 'He'd never have made it this far without Weepy. Weepy Weeli knew all the soaks. This was the second they'd camped at, so you might say he owed his life to my father.'

I don't know whether he was conscious of me or not at that moment. He seemed to be talking to himself rather than me, talking for the sake of talking, perhaps the way people do in a confessional. I think he had to get it off his chest and it was just that I happened to be there. There was more to it, of course, but I only realized that later, when it was too late— after the wind had died.

There was a long silence, and while I was considering the implications of what he had said, I think I dozed off, for the next thing I heard was him saying: 'When I woke I was sitting about where you're sitting now, right here in this hollow in the rock. And what woke me was the sound of a shot. I stumbled out and there he was with a gun in his hand and one of my three camels lying drumming with her legs on the *rira*. I can remember the smoke was still curling from the muzzle of the gun as he raised it to his shoulder again. I shouted at him and he wheeled round, the gun pointing at me. But I just didn't care. The camel was the best I had. I'd broken her myself. I went straight at him and he was in such a state when he fired that he missed. The shot went just over my head. And then I was on him, my hands wrenching at the gun, tearing it out of his grasp. He wasn't a big man and I was young. He hadn't a hope after he'd missed me. And when I got hold of the gun I was in such a rage I shot him. I shot him through his forehead and I can still see the look on his face, the staring, horror-struck eyes as he realized what I was going to do. It's haunted me all my life. For I did it in cold blood. I killed him quite deliberately.' He paused then, his eyes wide, a distant look as he saw every detail of the scene he had lived with all these years. 'He didn't even twitch. He just folded up with a glazed, surprised look, and then lay out there in some thin grass, pitched forward on his face. I put the camel out of her misery, wishing I had been awake in time to stop him. The sun was just setting, everything blood-red, and when I moved that little bastard the wisps of spinifex he'd fallen on were red, too —the blood that had drained out of the hole in the back of his head.'

There was another long silence, his eyes closed, his breathing in quick pants. 'Well, now you know. Funny that I should want to tell you when you're on the run for something yourself. Or perhaps that's why. But I still wanted to be on my own when I got here. You understand?'

I nodded. To make his peace, he had said. I remembered that now. 'Yes,' I said. 'I understand.'

'Well, d'you think I did wrong?' He waited. And then he said, 'All right. I killed a man. But what would you have done? In the circumstances. Jarra Jarra ruined. Everything I'd dreamed of gone. And all the fault of that grasping little crook. And then slaughtering my camel for meat. Would you have stood for it? That camel had carried me for six days. She'd have carried me to her last gasp. She deserved better than that. And McIlroy—did he deserve anything better than I gave him?' Another pause, and then he said slowly, 'No. The camel was just an excuse, the spark that triggered my hate of the man.' He was silent then and I didn't know what to say. What *would* I have done?

'I think,' I said slowly, 'that I might have killed him the moment I came up with him.'

I don't know whether he heard that or not. As I have said, he was living his own private hell and I doubt whether it made any difference what I said. I was merely his confessor, and only because I happened to be there and had problems of my own.

'It was 'bout six in the morning when I went down to the blacks' quarters to get Weeli. I was running a new fenceline and I wanted Weeli and two of the boys. But he wasn't there. Father had come for him 'bout two hours back. I found the old man in his den, a bottle of whisky in front of him and his eyes bleary with drink and lack of sleep.' He paused for breath, licking his lips, his tongue coming out but no moisture there. 'He lied to me,' he went on slowly. 'That's what got my dander up right at the outset. I knew very well Weeli hadn't gone walkabout.' He found some saliva, licked his lips again, speaking fast now: 'It took me the better part of an hour to get the truth out of him and by then I was so darned mad I'd have killed McIlroy with my bare hands—if he'd still been around. It took me six days—six days on a camel to catch up with him. It's a long ride from Jarra Jarra here, the days burning hot, the nights beginning to cool. Autumn, y'see. It was March. All that time to think what I'd do if ever I caught up with him. Lucky for me it rained, the tracks of that old Austin truck of his showing quite clearly wherever the sand was soft.'

He stopped there, staring into space. 'At the end of six days' riding camel the desire to kill the man was overlaid by a lot of other things—the loneliness, the feeling of being lost at times, like travelling in a vacuum. And when it came to the moment . . . when I was standing here, confronting him . . . all I could think of was water. I hadn't had any water for more than twenty-four hours; all the way from the Stock Route I hadn't found a single soak. I was down there in the sand, lapping it up, the camels bellowing. And the blarney of the man, that damned tongue of his pouring out excuses, explanations, encouraging me to believe that it would all turn out for the best. He and I, we'd go on together. No need for the camels now. And we'd return rich. His Monster would solve everything.'

He gave the ghost of a laugh, half amused, half cynical. 'Instead of killing him I went to sleep in the middle of his monologue, too damned tired even to give him the hiding that would have got some of the hate out of my system.'

He paused again there, and then after a moment he said quietly, in a flat, even voice: 'It was still there, y'see—the hate

I mean—all ready to explode inside me the moment that shot woke me.'

'You buried the body?'

He nodded. 'In soft sand at the edge of the *rira* here. A sort of natural grave between two exposed edges of rock. Then Weeli and I started back. I got the Austin almost to Lake Disappointment. But the axle bust. There wasn't much petrol left anyway. I dumped the old bus there and we made it back to Jarra Jarra by camel, travelling at night so nobody would see us. Father dealt with Weeli—made him swear never to tell a soul what had happened. Did it at the sacred place of his ancestors down in the Watersnake country. And then the cave-in—the last hope gone. After that the old man started drinking in earnest. McIlroy had broken him anyway. I got the hell out into the army. There was talk, of course. But nothing more. Four months had passed, the tracks covered by the time the police found that vehicle. And then the war, and we were overseas—boys from the outstations getting killed and captured. McIlroy's death wasn't important any more.' His voice faded, his eyes staring blankly. 'Sometimes I wish I'd killed him the moment I saw him strutting towards me. Other times I try to make-believe I never rode into the desert after him. The first would have been more honest. The second is what I've tried to live. Then Westrop, those rumours . . . after thirty years. I had to come.'

'Why?'

He looked at me with a puzzled frown. 'To see if it was true, of course. I didn't know. After all those years I couldn't be sure I really had killed him. Burma. Hospital. The old man's death. It was in the Journal, of course. It was all there, just as I had told it to him. But once I'd burned those pages . . . And then Janet's mother, the years of trying to rebuild and make something of the station. It faded, y'see. It wasn't real. Just something I'd read.' And then haltingly: 'The old man, y'see —out of his mind. You can't live with a thought like that.' There was perspiration on his brow, his face twitching and the effort of trying to put it all into words too much for him, his whole frame shivering.

'And now?'

'Now I know.' His voice was back to a whisper. 'Now I can't fool myself any more. What I did—it finished him, broke him completely.'

'The body, I mean—you found it?'

'Not the body.' He shook his head. 'Not even the skeleton. He was just carrion as soon as the sand had blown off him, and the wedge-tails and the ants, they picked him clean. All that was left was a heap of bones, but lying exactly where I remembered, and of course it all came back to me then. No room for doubt or self-deception any more.'

Silence and my head dropping on to my chest, my eyes closing; the rustle of sand grains moving, the heat wind stirring the desert. I should have said it didn't matter any more. I should have encouraged him, given him the support he needed. But I was too tired, too bone-weary to care. What the hell did it matter after all these years? I was drifting into sleep, but not yet losing consciousness, the silence nagging. 'And now,' I muttered. 'Now you've found him, what are you going to do?'

He didn't answer, the silence heavy between us so that I was forced back to consciousness, my eyes open. He hadn't moved, his head still framed by that strange motif on the rock wall behind him, his eyes open and staring vacantly, his breathing shallow. He looked like death. It should have warned me. But I hadn't come all this way to worry about a man who had died thirty years ago. I was thinking of Janet and Jarra Jarra and what a real big strike could do to get them out of the mess they were in. I thought, God help me, it was the future, not the past, that mattered, and so I said, 'Well, what about McIlroy's Monster? Does it exist or doesn't it?' I thought it would help to concentrate his mind on something practical.

Silence still and I had to repeat the question before he turned his head and looked at me, his eyes still vacant as though fixed on some far distant horizon. Slowly he shifted his position, groping in the hip pocket of his trousers. 'That's something I shall never know.' And he handed me a worn leather wallet. 'I took that from McIlroy's body.' And then he said something I didn't understand till much later: 'If it exists, and if you find it, pray to God for guidance. This poor country has been raped too often by greedy whites and that—that Monster—belongs to them, to the aborigine of the desert.' And he added softly, 'I would like to think that my boyhood dream could be made a reality. Yes, I would like to think that, very much. I had it all planned—Jarra Jarra a nature reserve, the goodness of the land gradually restored and the blacks free to live their natural, self-sufficient lives.' His breath came in a sigh. 'It was just a dream, and dreams fade y'know—with age and the passage of time. But you're young. You can still make it a reality.' And then, looking at me very directly with those startling blue eyes: 'Any man who uses that for his own ends will suffer a violent death. Or else he'll end up with blood on his hands. I don't know why I know that, but I do.'

I was fully awake then. 'So you think it exists?'

He nodded his head slowly. 'Yes. Yes, I do.' And after that he wouldn't say any more. He seemed exhausted, leaning back, his eyes closed. I didn't examine the contents of the wallet. Not then. I just put it in my pocket, wondering whether he was sane or not, thinking about his words, the strange prophetic sense he had intended them to convey. And shortly afterwards Tom came to tell us there was a storm brewing. He had blankets with him and he wrapped one of them around Ed Garrety, tucking it in carefully as though he were nursing a sick child.

The wind came quickly, sand driving past our shelter, at first a river of small grains close to the surface of the rock, then a brown cloud engulfing everything, uprooted bushes whirling past, the air thickening until it was hardly possible to breathe, the sun-hot desert sand-blasted to hell. I buried my head in the blanket and sank into a mental oblivion, unable to think, scarcely able to breathe, yet not unconscious—not entirely.

The storm lasted right into the night. I was dimly conscious of movement, a body crawling past, but I was wrapped in a cocoon of misery and hardly noticed, lying there thankful for the shelter of the rock which protected my body from the full blast of the wind, the sand flood pouring over me and nothing to do but huddle close within the insufferable heat of the blanket.

It died at last, the howling of the wind subsiding slowly to a moan, the sand-filled air thinning till there was only the whisper of a breeze and the soft abrasive rasp of grains on rock. That was when I first realized I was alone.

It took time for it to sink in, and even when it did, I didn't do anything. I was dazed and too exhausted. It was dark and the wind had gone, everything was still. My voice croaked his name. No answer, and when I reached out there was only the blanket half-buried in sand.

I got up then in a sudden panic. My limbs were cramped, my eyes and mouth all scummed, and as I staggered out a meteor, blazing a snuffed-out trail across the sky, showed me the Land-Rover still there. I stood for a moment, trembling with relief, and then, thinking perhaps he had been caught short and gone for a squat, I walked over to the Land-Rover and got myself a drink of water. I sipped it slowly, flexing my limbs and shaking the sand out of my clothes. The minutes passed and no sign of him. I started calling, but there was no answer. Tom had appeared like a dark shadow out of the ground, and after a while, with no response to our calls, we began searching.

We must have searched for an hour before giving up, and by then I knew it wasn't an accident. He'd walked out into that sandstorm deliberately. Tom knew it, too. 'Him sickfella golonga tingari.' Tingari I guessed correctly were Dreamtime spirits. The old black didn't talk much. He accepted it, may even have expected it, but he was deeply affected. He went off by himself and I didn't see him again till dawn broke. Then we searched the whole of the *rira* and beyond it, out into the sand, until heat exhaustion drove me to seek shelter. Tom was all day searching, but without finding a trace of him. It was as though the storm had lifted him up and spirited him away.

Night fell again and we had a meal. Then we collected the things we needed from the Land-Rover and began walking. There was no point in staying there. No point in continuing the search. The sand had done what perhaps he had intended; it had buried him under a clean new drift. But why? Why had he gone like that, walking out into a sandstorm? I was thinking about it all night, feeling there was something I had missed. And then, as tiredness made me stumble and I began to fall, I developed a strange feeling that he and I had changed places;

one moment I felt that all the problems that had sent him stumbling out into the storm had devolved upon me, the next it was I who was stumbling out into the desert to die.

I wouldn't have made it without Tom. He stayed with me, and sometimes he talked to himself in his own tongue, not bothering with pidgin. In the end, all I could think about was the compass, which I clutched so tightly for fear I lost it in a fall that my fingers eventually had to be prised loose from it, the bone all bruised by the metal case. We kept to the reverse of the bearing I had followed two nights before, but when dawn broke and I flung myself down exhausted on the highest sand-ridge I could find, Tom said he didn't think we had gone far enough yet, not more than nine miles, and so we went on, out into a wide plain between that ridge and the next with the heat increasing and the sky flaring to the moment of sunrise. And he was right. When the sun came up behind us the black of Kennie's smoke signal was no more than a wisp far out on the horizon. It took us almost two hours—two hours before Kennie came stumbling towards us, shouting hysterically.

Another long day waiting out the heat, and then, the sun just dipping below the sand-sea horizon, we started driving, heading straight into the last of the daylight. There were new drifts of sand now, the going bad in places and frequent stops to cool the engine. We had two punctures that night and we only made 42 miles, a lot of it in four-wheel drive.

'You in a more reasonable frame of mind?'

'What do you mean?'

Tom had rigged us a shelter of sorts and Kennie was propped up on one elbow, staring at me, his sun-blistered body chequered with the light beams coming through the furze.

'You were pretty crazed when I found you yesterday morning.'

'You didn't find us. We found you.'

'Have it your own way.'

My hands gripped hard on the mug I was holding. 'All right.' I said, my mouth, my whole throat hurting. 'You lit a fire so we knew where you were.' The mug was hot, the tea too scalding to drink, and I was sweating, a feeling of nausea creeping up from my guts.

'What happened?' he asked. 'All you said was he walked out into that sandstorm.'

'That's right.' My throat was sore and I found it difficult to formulate my words.

'Christ, man. You can't just leave it at that. There must be something more.'

I shook my head and then he was leaning forward, gripping my arm. 'For God's sake, Alec—a man doesn't just walk out— into a sandstorm—for no reason. That's what you said. That he just walked out. While you were huddled in a blanket.'

There was a long silence. Finally he let go of my arm. 'You don't want to talk about it.'

'No.' How the hell could I explain to him the complicated motives of a man who had reached the point of no return. Even if I understood them myself.

He sucked noisily at his tea. 'Okay, I'm your pal and you won't talk to me. So what are you going to tell the police? And there's Janet. What are you going to tell Janet?'

Oh Christ! I thought. Couldn't he leave it alone? Just accept the truth of it. 'God damn you,' I muttered. 'Shut up, can't you.' That strange feeling was there still, the feeling that Ed Garrety and I had changed places, that with his death I had somehow stepped into his shoes. 'It's crazy.' I heard my voice, a hoarse whisper, and he had heard it too.

'Did you find the Monster? Was it there, where he died?' He was staring at me intently.

'No. No, of course it wasn't.'

'Then why did Garrety stop there—a *rira* Tom said. That's a geological formation.'

'There was no copper,' I said. 'Now shut up, can't you.'

'But you know where it is?'

'Shut up for Christ's sake,' I screamed at him.

His hand was on my arm again, shaking me. 'He told you, didn't he? You got it out of him—the location of McIlroy's Monster?'

Something in the way he said it made me hold my breath, staring at him. 'What the hell are you getting at?' In that moment I hated him.

He saw that, for he hesitated, licking his lips. And then he blurted out, 'Only that you got the rotor arm out of him, and I thought . . .'

'You stupid, mean-minded little fool!' He was cringing away from me, scared of my anger and the croaking fury of my voice 'What the hell do you know about a man like Ed Garrety? He didn't go into the desert after the Monster . . .' I stopped there, leaning back, panting. Christ! The boy was right. If Ed Garrety wasn't prospecting, then what the hell was he doing? I was thinking of Janet then, wondering how I could ever face her if I came out of the Gibson saying her father had taken his life because of a murder he had committed thirty years ago.

I drank the rest of my tea slowly, conscious of Kennie watching me all the time. Then I closed my eyes and tried to sleep. God, what a mess! And no way out that I could see.

We got going again shortly after five, and just before sunset a single-engined plane came over. It must have picked up our dust streamer for it came in very low from the north, circled us slowly, then headed back into the fireball haze that was reddening sky and desert.

We made better progress that night, fewer stops and only one puncture. We caught a frozen ice-glint glimpse of the great salt lake in the dawn and by nine we had reached Karara Soaks. The police were waiting for us there, a sergeant and a constable with two Land-Rovers and native trackers. The sergeant had a warrant for my arrest.

Fremantle Gaol,
30th April, 1970.

SIX

Interlude on Remand

WELL, THERE IT IS—the whole truth of how I came to
Australia and what happened to me there. I have been working on it for over two-and-a-half months, sometimes in the
library, sometimes in my cell here. At least I have been honest
with myself, or as honest as I am ever likely to be, and now
that it is finished I shall give it to my lawyer and he will have
to decide how much needs to be revealed in my defence when
the Lone Minerals action comes up for hearing in a fortnight's
time. In any case, it has served some purpose. It has kept me
mentally occupied so that I'm still reasonably sane, even if I
have been living in a kind of vacuum.

The only thing that really worries me is Janet. I would like
to have broken the news of her father's death to her myself.
But the sergeant took me straight to the police station at Mt
Newman. I had pustules on my legs where the spinifex spines
had set up sores that were beginning to turn septic and he
wasn't taking any chances. It was 70 miles to Jarra Jarra and
70 back—another day's driving. 'Anyway,' he said, 'she'll
have heard it by now.' Which was probably true since he had
radioed a report back from the Soaks.

I have written to her, of course. I did that shortly after I
arrived here, a difficult letter because I did not want her to
know how McIlroy had met his death or that her father had
deliberately gone out into that sandstorm. I thought she might
have read between the lines and guessed it was suicide, but
maybe she didn't want to. Maybe she wanted to believe that I
was in some way to blame for his death. At any rate, I have
had no letter from her, not a line all the time I have been here
—81 days to be exact. I don't blame her, and with the station
wrapped round her neck, all the problems of her father's
death magnified by the financial mess he was in, she probably

hasn't had much time. But I am sorry all the same. Somehow a letter from her would have made a difference. And Kennie . . . Kennie might have made an effort to see me.

It was this feeling of being alone in Australia, without one single friend, that started me writing a full account of all that had happened. I finished it yesterday. I suppose the idea originated from that Journal, a record while it was still clear in my mind. As I say, it kept me sane in my solitary, friendless state, cooped up in my cell here with the sunlight swinging across the bare little room, day giving way to night, to dawn again and the glimpse of an endlessly blue sky, my weekly visits to the remand court at Perth the only relief from the monotony of it.

My lawyer had been almost my only visitor, a short, dark man, with eyes that dart restlessly behind heavy-framed glasses. His name is Chick Draper, and though his manner is deliberately abrupt, he is a kind fellow and has taken a great deal of trouble on my behalf, even though he knows he hasn't much hope of a worthwhile fee. It started as a straightforward immigration case—entering the country under a false name and with a false passport. He advised me to plead guilty, since the alternative might be extradition to face criminal charges of arson and fraud in England. This I did and was remanded in custody pending further inquiries. I hadn't enough money for bail, even if they would have granted it, so there was nothing for it but to watch the Australian autumn fading into winter from my cell while ᵗhe immigration people and my lawyer tried to sort the tangle out. And then just when he thought he was getting somewhere, he was faced with the further charge of fraud while on Australian soil.

This was brought against me by Lone Minerals shortly after I was remanded in custody the second time. Their No. 2 drill hole had given core samples showing 0.2 nickel in pentlandite over a band width of 15 feet at a depth of 600 feet. It was this news, confirming the optimism of their annual report, that had caused the shares to rise so dramatically back in January. They had fallen just as fast since, for Freeman had brought in extra equipment and half a dozen holes drilled in quick succession had shown no trace of nickel. Following this announcement the shares hit an all-time low of 12 cents and there was an outcry from both the public and the Sydney and Perth stock exchanges. I was the obvious scapegoat and I suppose I should have realized that proceedings were inevitable once I had agreed to plead guilty to the immigration charges, for if I wasn't Alec Falls then I had no right to pose as a mining consultant.

By pleading guilty my lawyer had hoped for a short sentence and permission to remain in Australia under my second name of Wentworth, which was my mother's family name. But with a criminal charge pending he had agreed I should change my plea to one of not guilty when the immigration charge came up for hearing again. And then Kadek came to see me.

Ever since my arrest, it had puzzled me how the authorities could have known I had entered the country on the passport of a man supposedly dead. There was always, of course, the outside chance that a zealous immigration official had been sent a copy of one of the English papers that had reported the Drym fire. But it was really too much of a coincidence, and at that first court appearance no evidence had been given covering this point. It had to be either Kadek or Rosa—they were the only ones who knew. And after Kadek had visited me here in prison I had no doubt who had tipped them off. Not that he admitted it, but it was there all the same, implicitly understood between us.

The date of Kadek's visit was February 23, just four days after I had been informed of the Lone Minerals action. He was seated when I was brought into the interview room and he got up very abruptly. But he didn't come forward to greet me, nor did he shake hands. I remember feeling at the time there was something almost guilty about the way he started to his feet. 'Sorry about this,' he said with a gesture that seemed to include, not just the room, or even the prison, but the whole system. He had the same slim briefcase with him and he held on to it throughout the interview. 'Treating you all right, I hope?'

I nodded. 'All right.' The same steel-trap mouth, not the flicker of a smile, and his eyes slitted as though he had brought the sun's glare in with him. 'I get bored, that's all.' That was before I started writing.

He sat down again and I took the other chair, facing him across the table. The door shut and we were alone. 'Well?' I asked. He still seemed hesitant, as though he didn't know quite how to begin, and I said, 'Is it about Lone Minerals? Is that why you're here?'

'Yes.' And then quickly, as though he wanted to get it over with: 'You're in a bit of a spot, Alec. You've pleaded guilty, which was sensible in the circumstances, but looking at it from Freeman's point of view, that means your report on Blackridge was fraudulent.'

'It was your idea,' I said. 'You introduced me as representing Trevis, Parkes & Pierce.'

'Which you weren't, of course. But then I'm not going to admit that I knew that.'

'Then you'll be committing perjury.'

'If I'm called—yes.'

'You will be,' I told him.

'But you went along with it. You didn't deny it. And you wrote that letter. Les included it, every word of it, in his annual report. Signed—Alec Falls, Mining Consultant. It was that letter, more than anything else, that was responsible for the rise in the shares; that and the assay figures based on the surface sampling——'

But I wasn't letting him get away with that. 'The surface samples were taken by Petersen's geologist from an area recommended by Culpin. If the dust was planted there it's nothing to do with me.' And I added, 'I think you've forgotten something.'

'What's that?'

'*If anybody takes the can, it's Chris.* Remember? Culpin salted that area with nickel tailings taken from Western Mining by that aborigine, Gnarlbine. You know it, and I know it.'

'I don't know anything of the sort.'

'*Nothing for you to worry about.* That's what you told me.'

I can still see that thin-lipped smile of his, the way he shook his head. 'No, I'm afraid I don't remember.' And then he was leaning towards me across the table. 'Now look, Alec, I'm here to help you. But not if you're going to put words into my mouth. You understand?'

255

I understood, all right. He would lie. Even under oath he would lie. He was crooked as hell, but it would be my word against his. 'No,' I said, 'I didn't think you'd want to be reminded of what you said.'

He nodded, knowing he had made his point. But just to be certain, he added, 'This case will be before a jury. And they'll all be Australians.'

'And you're an Australian and I'm not.'

'Right. You haven't a chance of implicating me, or Chris. In fact, if you try that, I can promise you things will go badly for you, very badly indeed. You had an option, don't forget. And you took it up—5,000 shares.' He was smiling, sure of himself now. 'Your only hope—and this is what I want you to understand—is to persuade Les Freeman to withdraw the case.'

'And how do you suggest I do that?'

'If you were to offer him something in exchange. Information, see. A company like Lone Minerals is dependent entirely on prospects. A really good prospect, something that would put the company on the map—if you could offer him that, then I am sure he would have his lawyers back down.' He was watching me now, his face tight-lipped, his eyes slitted, his whole body tense as though willing me to accept.

The brazenness of it! The sheer thick-skinned audacity. . . . 'You have the bloody nerve to come here——' I stopped, suddenly aware that I was shouting. 'What do you want?' I was still trembling, but I had myself under control now. I knew very well what he wanted.

'Come on,' he said quietly. 'You're not that dense. You were with Garrety when he died. And we all know why he went into the Gibson.' He left it at that, his eyes fixed on mine, waiting. And I let him wait, the silence hanging in the stuffy air of that little room. In the end he sighed. 'Okay. I'll spell it out for you. Garrety knew the location of McIlroy's Monster. That right?'

I didn't say anything, watching fascinated at the sudden gleam that had come into his eyes, the naked greed of the man. I could deny it, of course. But if I denied it, then there had to be some other reason why Garrety had gone into the Gibson, and I wasn't going to admit that. So I kept my mouth shut, the two of us staring at each other in silence. At length he said, 'We're pretty certain he never reached the actual location. His Land-Rover had broken down and that's the reason he stopped where he did. There's no copper there as far as we know.' He leaned a little further forward, his eyes searching my face. 'Or is there? You were with him there when he died. You're the only man, apart from that black, who knows what's there in the ground.' He was staring at me, tense and waiting.

'It was your plane then that came over us?'

He nodded. 'Yes. Chris chartered a Cessna on my instructions. He made two flights. On the second flight he flew very low several times over Garrety's last camp. He could see him working on the Land-Rover's engine, the black standing beside him. And there was rock showing through the sand. He says it was some form of conglomerate, and as far as he could see there were no indications of copper. But then Chris isn't a geologist and he wasn't on the ground. You were.'

For a moment, just for a moment, I thought of telling him it was the location. But then he said, 'You tell me Chris was wrong and we can move petrol up to the Stock Route and have a helicopter and a geologist on the spot inside a week.'

'No,' I said. 'Culpin was right. It's a conglomerate formation.' I didn't want him sending a helicopter in when the real location was only twenty or thirty miles from the Kurrajong Soak. They could so easily fly a radial search.

'Well, where is it then?'

I didn't answer.

'For Christ's sake, don't be a fool, Alec. You can't handle a thing like this on your own. It needs a consortium. And if Les goes ahead with this case, you'll be in prison a long time.'

I still didn't say anything. I was thinking of Ed Garrety and his love of Jarra Jarra, the hopes he'd had, the dreams. Giving me that battered wallet, he had handed on to me a trust—an obligation, a challenge perhaps. It wasn't something I could just give away, even if it did mean my liberty. I wouldn't be able to live with myself if I did that.

'Look,' Kadek said. 'You'll get three years at least. Don't think in those three years nobody'll go looking for the Monster.

They will. And they'll find it. Everybody's talking about it. Prospectors, I mean. A man dying like that, a mining man with him at the time—just because you're out of touch, don't imagine they haven't put two-and-two together. If it's there they'll find it all right, so you might just as well . . .'

'Go to hell!' I said, and I got to my feet. I was angry then, angry at myself for being tempted. Nobody likes the prospect of wasting three of the best years of their life, and I knew he was right. Three years was what my own lawyer had said. 'If there is copper there, then it belongs to Janet Garrety.'

'It doesn't belong to anybody. You know that.' He had followed me slowly to his feet. 'All right,' he said. 'I'll leave you now. But think it over. There's no immediate hurry. Nobody can peg a claim at the moment, and it may be a month or two yet before the ban is lifted. So you've still some time. And your lawyer knows where to contact me.'

I didn't understand what he was talking about. 'What ban?' I asked.

'Didn't you know? The Minister of Mines imposed a ban on pegging so that mining registrars could catch up with the backlog.'

'When?' I asked. 'When was the ban imposed?'

'Initially on January 22, and then on February 3, he announced he was reserving all Crown land. Nobody could peg after that.' He tucked his briefcase under his arm. 'Well, you think about it.' And he added, 'In addition to dropping the charges, I'm sure I could persuade Les to do something for you personally if it turned out as big as the name implies. Mining consultant to the consortium throughout the development period. That would set you up in Australia for the rest of your life.' Again that tight-lipped smile. 'Think about it. And when you've made up your mind, all you have to do is tell your lawyer feller. Okay?'

He left me then, and when I got back to my cell, all I could think about was that Chris Culpin had pegged the hollow on Coondewanna the very day the ban had been imposed. That claim of his had never been registered and couldn't be registered until the ban was lifted. I wrote to Janet that night, and then I started on my manuscript. By then, you see, I knew there was something in me that prevented my ever bartering the possibility of freedom for the knowledge Ed Garrety had passed on to me. It might be nonsense, but that didn't matter. I suddenly found I had principles, and at a time when I could least afford them. A bit of a joke that.

I have described the interview with Kadek in detail in an endeavour to explain my own irrational behaviour. Maybe it was in character. I don't know. Or maybe I've grown up a bit during the days I've spent in prison. Again, I don't know. I'm so cut off, so solitary—but at least I have come to terms with myself. I no longer belong to Kadek's world, or to Rosa's. I'm not the man who set fire to Drym. I'm somebody else now, though my name is still Alec Wentworth Falls and I still inhabit the same body.

But perhaps it isn't the days in prison. Perhaps it was the days in the Gibson Desert that changed me. And Ed Garrety. Particularly Ed Garrety. To go back there. To go back to the place of his crime, if it was a crime, in search of peace, knowing he was dying—and then to end it, quickly, cleanly. How can you betray a man like that? How can you not be influenced by him? A term in prison is nothing to the long years he was imprisoned within himself, and if, by accepting my fate, I can achieve something of the same moral stature . . . God help me, I am not made of the same material, but at least I can try.

Fremantle Gaol,
1st May, 1970.

SEVEN

McIlroy's Monster

I WAS RELEASED FROM PRISON on Monday, May 18, following a brief court hearing at which the authorities dropped their charges of illegal entry. The criminal charges of fraud in connection with the Blackridge prospect had also been withdrawn. Even the possibility of extradition had become remote. As my lawyer explained, for the insurance company to succeed with their charges of obtaining money by false pretences, when it was Rosa who had put in the claim, they would have to prove either complicity or arson. He thought, in the circumstances, I would hear no more from them now that my identity was accepted by the Commonwealth Department of Immigration. 'There's no law against a man leaving his wife, and since we now have evidence that she had been cohabiting with a man on Rottnest Island . . .' He had left it at that with a smile and a broad shrug.

It's a strange feeling to suddenly find yourself free again after being held on remand for so long—a hundred days exactly. And though nobody in their senses would say they have enjoyed being in prison, I cannot say that I regretted it or that I actively disliked it. This may seem strange, but it gave me an opportunity to take stock, something I had not had time to do since I had landed at Fremantle on December 27. In a way it was like being back at school, or in the services, for it enabled me to get to know an extraordinary cross-section of Australians, some good, some bad, but most of them men I should not have come across otherwise. There were other nationalities there, of course, but it was the Australians that interested me, and those hundred days, living in that close, ever-changing community, taught me a great deal about the country and the people. I do not recommend it as essential training for immigrants, but it is certainly one way of attending a crash course on the behaviour pattern of men whose grass roots are very different to those of almost any other nation. And I came out of prison, not in any state of uncertainty or depression, but knowing exactly what I intended to do, my mind wonderfully clarified, my metabolism like a dynamo recharged and my senses sharpened. I celebrated by staying the night at the Parmelia, a luxurious room with a view over the Swan River and a meal I still remember.

The fortnight before my release had been relatively crowded. Three days after I had finished my manuscript Kennie came to see me. He was on his way back from a survey down near Yornup in the South West. He had had a letter from his mother telling him she was still on her own and that his father was at Nullagine trying to organize an expedition into the Gibson. 'That letter was written on the 2nd, so he's probably out there now. There's talk, you see, that the pegging ban will be lifted soon.' And he had added, 'I'd hate to think Pa and that partner of his are going to grab the Monster while you're stuck here awaiting trial.' He had guessed that Kadek had had something to do with my arrest and he felt sorry for me, which somehow annoyed me. And he annoyed me even more when he said he had been to see Janet the day after we had reached Mt Newman. 'She took it badly, you know. The old man's death. Have you heard from her at all?'

'No.'

He gave that irritating little laugh of his. 'Oh well, not surprising really. She'd been so sure you'd bring him back. And then being told of his death like that on the radio. I did my best to make her realize you'd done all you could.'

I wondered about that. If he was in love with her . . . but I didn't ask him. Instead, I found myself asking about the station, what she had done about the cattle, and his face brightened. 'It worked, your suggestion about bringing them into the gully.' Apparently water from the lower levels of the mine had been forced to the surface. Neighbouring station owners had lent her boys and she had spent the week we had been in the Gibson mustering and driving the cattle out of the Pukara to water at channels they had cut in the old costeans. 'But there's precious little feed for them, of course.'

And the drought still on, not a drop of rain all the time I had been in prison.

It was seeing Kennie that started me thinking again about the Monster, and then two days later I was brought into the interview room to find Freeman and another man sitting there. He bounced to his feet and came towards me, his short stocky body radiating vitality, his hand held out and his round, smooth face strangely jubilant. 'Soon as I got the news I took the first plane out of Sydney.' He was smiling as he gripped my hand, but a little uncertainly, the uncertainty reflected in the nervous blinking of his eyes. 'I just wanted to say I was sorry. We're withdrawing the charges, of course, and we'll work out some form of compensation. That's why I've got our lawyer with me.' He introduced the other man—Ian Macclesfield. 'But the first thing was to see you and apologize personally.'

All this in a rush of words that left me feeling slightly dazed. 'What's this all about?' I asked.

He stared at me, and then he suddenly laughed. 'Oh my goodness,' he said. 'I forgot for a moment where I was. With everybody talking about it and the shares over five dollars . . .' And then he told me. As a final resort, before abandoning the Blackridge prospect altogether, they had had Petersen do an IP, and the survey had shown a strong anomalous formation at a depth of just over 1,500 feet, almost underneath the poppet head of the old mine. The first drill hole had been completed three days ago. 'Petersen cabled me the core sample analysis yesterday—4·2 nickel between 1,530 and 1,553 feet. So you were right, you see. I made an immediate press release. That's what put the price of the shares up.'

'And you're withdrawing the charges?'

'Of course. It doesn't matter to me whether you're Alec Falls or Bill Smith. It's not my business how you got into the country. I don't even care whether you're a mining consultant or not. You were right. That's all I'm interested in, and I'm sorry—I wanted you to know that straight away, and I hope you'll accept my apologies.'

'And you flew straight here?'

'Yes, I got the night plane.'

I went over to the table and sat down in the vacant chair,

feeling suddenly a little weak. He'd taken the night plane, come all that way, two thousand miles, to apologize. I wanted to laugh, or cry, anything to express my feeling of relief. I could hardly believe my luck. So many times these last months I had remembered Petersen's words: *So everything you touch . . .* remembering them as a bad joke. And now Freeman was here, telling me Blackridge of all unlikely prospects had come out trumps. I really did believe for a moment that I was born lucky.

'No hard feelings, I hope.' I remembered Westrop, so long ago it was almost unreal, and Freeman hovering there, mis-understanding my silence. I didn't say anything, feeling dazed and thinking of the future. It was ages since I had dared to think of that. And Kadek. . . . I wondered what Kadek would do, the ground cut from under his feet. And suddenly I was laughing, laughing wildly and uncontrollably, and Les Free-man and his lawyer standing there in embarrassed silence.

In the end I told them the whole story of the Blackridge deal. They didn't believe it at first, but when I called the warder and got my manuscript, they believed me then all right. Not that there was much they could do about it, but it served its purpose. It opened Freeman's eyes to Kadek and got me the backing I needed if I did eventually go back into the Gibson.

In the event, it wasn't money that held me up, but the claims ban. Freeman had paid my lawyer's fees and given me a draft on the Company's bank for $10,000. In addition, I still had the 5,000 shares acquired when I exercised my option, and though the market had broken by the time I reached Kalgoorlie, Lone Minerals were still firm at $9·72, so that my total capital at that moment was more than enough to mount a small-scale prospecting expedition.

Culpin was still in the North West and Kennie living with his mother again. But I didn't stay with them. I stayed with Jim and Edwina Norris. They were as kind and hospitable as ever, and it was Jim who put me on to a long-wheelbase Land-Rover that was almost brand new, owned by a survey outfit that was cutting back. The nickel fever was dying down, the Palace bar less crowded. Iron and copper, that was the future of Australia, according to the wise boys, and any day now the pegging ban would be lifted. Rumour had it that there would be changed claim requirements so that all those who had jumped the gun would have to peg again. 'It's going to be like the old gold-rush days,' Kennie said, as I sat with him once more on the battered verandah, the hens pecking in the dust at our feet and his mother singing softly as she got our supper ready. 'Laverton in particular. They'll be lined up, waiting for the off—waiting for the mine wardens to announce the new pegging regulations. But this time there'll be men in helicopters coming down from the skies. Nearly six months' backlog, it'll be like an army on the move.' His voice was excited, his mood one of intense anticipation, and he kept on glancing at me, knowing why I had come, waiting to be asked.

I suppose it was my fault in a way. Chris Culpin was still somewhere in the Pilbara, and though Kennie had heard he was now concentrating on a prospect in the Bamboo Springs area, I had an uneasy feeling that Kadek would have notified him that I was out of prison and told him to keep an eye on me. I should have warned Kennie. I should have made it absolutely clear to him that a confrontation with his father was a distinct possibility if he persisted in accompanying me to the Gibson. But I didn't. He was a trained geologist, and now that he had been in the desert, now that he knew what it was like, just the two of us in the empty desolation of that vast area of sand, I preferred to have him with me rather than somebody I didn't know. And he wanted to come. The moment I had arrived back in Kalgoorlie he had been pestering me to take him.

It wasn't only that he was fascinated, almost obsessed, by the idea of discovering whether the Monster existed or not, I think it was also the challenge that appealed to him. And we were into winter now, the going would be easier, the heat and flies less exhausting.

It was settled that evening after supper, Edith Culpin knew why I was there. She was very quiet during the meal, but she knew her son had got to make his own way, and I think she liked me. 'You're going back into the Gibson, are you?' She was sitting facing me in the Victorian parlour, the best tea

264

service in front of her, the antimacassars white in the lamp-light, the furniture and the bric-a-brac all gleaming.

'Not immediately,' I said. There was no hurry since I was the only person alive who knew the location. And now that I had a prospector's licence there was something I wanted to do first. But I didn't tell her I was going to peg the Coondewanna claim. She was a loyal little woman and I was afraid she might tell her husband.

'And Kennie?' She was looking at her son, not apprehensively, but her face looked sad and the loneliness showed. 'He's going with you, is he? That's why you're here.' And I realized that she had been bottling this up, consciously keeping herself in check all through the meal.

Kennie laughed, that quick nervous laugh I remembered so well. 'Alec hasn't asked me yet, Mum.' His eyes were on me, a pleading look.

'Okay,' I said. 'I'm asking you now. I'd like you with me if you can manage it.' I was watching his mother and I saw the blank look in her eyes.

But she said at once, 'I think you should go, Kennie.' And then she turned to me again. 'But don't take any chances, please. Chris always said the Gibson was about the worst. And you ought to have two vehicles.'

'We will have two,' I said. And I told her about the Land-Rover waiting for us at the Kurrajong Soak, Ed Garrety's old Land-Rover. All it needed was a new fuel line and carburettor union.

'And when will you be in the desert, so's I know?' Her voice was low, the nervousness well under control.

'The middle of June I would think.' The pegging ban was being lifted at noon on June 5. The new regulations would be published in the Government Gazette that day and we might have to start from Marble Bar in order to get the full details from the Mining Registrar's office. Even if they were broadcast over the radio, we would still have to go to Marble Bar to register the Coondewanna claim.

Edith Culpin didn't say much after that. She had accepted that Kennie would go with me, but she still needed time to get used to the idea. And Kennie, now that it was settled, was full of questions, plans, the things we would need. He had the sense not to ask me about the location, but I showed him the battered wallet that had belonged to McIlroy. 'It was in here, was it—the location?' He was turning it over in his hand. And then he opened it and peered inside. There were a few old Australian pounds there, that was all, and he looked at me, his eyes questioning.

'I destroyed it,' I said. 'It's in here now.' And I tapped my head.

He smiled. 'Safest place, I reck'n.' He passed the wallet to his mother, who held it for a moment in her hands, gingerly, as though it were a tiger snake. 'Won't bite you, Mum,' he said, laughing.

She looked at him, and then down at the wallet again. 'So this was Pat McIlroy's—his actual wallet.' She turned it over in her dry, neat hands that were almost as worn as the leather. 'Well I never—all these years. You know, Chris would have given his eyes to have got hold of this. Once those rumours started, he couldn't hardly talk about anything else.'

'You tell him to lay off, Mum. That don't belong to him. That belongs to Janet Garrety now her father's dead.'

She nodded. 'I expect you're right, but Chris wouldn't see it that way and no good my telling your father what he ought to do.' She handed it back to me, carefully, as though it were a museum piece. 'That's two men it's killed,' she said, so quietly that I hardly heard her. 'Don't let you be the third.'

I put it back in my pocket, thinking only of Ed Garrety and his young hopes for Jarra Jarra, and three days later we left for the Pilbara, just the two of us in my new Land-Rover.

Before leaving we had checked that ABC would be broadcasting details of the new pegging requirements, and at noon on June 5 we were back on the shoulder of Mt Coondewanna with our portable radio tuned in to the Kalgoorlie station. We had reached Golden Soak just before seven the previous evening and in the dusk the scene around the old mineworkings in the entrance to the gully had been appalling, the fly-blown carcases of dead cattle everywhere and those that were alive so gaunt, so bone-staringly thin as to resemble nothing less than a horrible cartoon of famine. Water they now had—not much of it, but enough. It welled out of the ground in the hollows of the caved-in costeans. But cattle can't survive on water alone and now all the flat land below the mine buildings was a desert, the arid vegetation eaten out, the mulgas stripped of bark, even the spinifex gnawed to its roots. Many of the beasts were too weak to move, lying thick in the gully so that it was only possible to get the Land-Rover through by the horrible process of terrifying them with shouts and the blaring of our horn so that they were forced to their feet.

This gully had now become the graveyard of Jarra Jarra and all Ed Garrety's hopes. God knows how many head were starving to death there. The sick reek of it hung in the air and one wretched cow, still just alive and lying with its starved udder draped like a pancake over a boulder, blocked our way so completely that I had to get out and shoot it and then drive over it. I had switched on my headlights in the gloom of the gully, and lying sleepless for a long time that night under the stars I could still see its eyes, enormous in the bony skull and crawling with flies, a sad patience in their expression as it waited motionless for the end.

We had seen nobody on the drive down to Golden Soak and when we reached the shoulder of Coondewanna the hollow was deserted, the little piles of dust samples still there around the hole Duhamel's rig had drilled. And now, as we waited for the broadcast with our portable standing on the tailboard of the Land-Rover, I was thankful that Culpin had not returned to re-peg his claim. Presumably the Bamboo Springs prospect had proved more promising. The newscaster's voice, tinny and unnatural in that wild, remote setting, began reading the details from the Government Gazette as they were phoned through from Perth. The new regulations called for corner pegs 5 foot high and 6-foot trenches in addition to the sub-stantial 3-foot corner posts Culpin had erected and the 4-foot angled trenches he had dug. And further pegs or cairns 3 foot high set in 4-foot long trenches were required at 15-chain intervals. The ABC announcer had read slowly enough for us to take it all down, and when he had finished, we read it through and then checked our stock of timber. Even allowing for the use of Culpin's posts, we hadn't enough to fill in along the sides of the claim every 330 yards.

'We could peg at the corners, register the claim and fix the intermediary pegs later,' Kennie suggested. But I shook my head. I wasn't taking any chances this time. 'Okay. Then we need some more timber.' He was looking at me and I knew what he was thinking, what we were both thinking, that there would be fence posts available at the Garrety homestead. 'You going, or shall I?'

'You,' I said. I didn't want to face Janet, not yet—not until I'd got this claim pegged and had been into the Gibson again.

He nodded. 'You start on the trenches then. I'll be back in time to give you a hand with the corner pegs. At least we'll get those in before dark.' He was already offloading the timber, and then, as he started to get in behind the wheel, he paused. 'Any message?'

I shook my head. What the hell message could I send her? And as I stood watching him drive off the shoulder into the gully, I was thinking that it hurt that she hadn't written, hadn't even bothered to answer my letters.

He was back just as I had hammered in the last corner peg and was starting on the intermediary trenches. 'No fence posts,' he said. 'But I got some shed timbers.'

'You saw her, did you?'

He nodded, staring at me rather strangely.

'Is she all right?'

'Yes, she's all right.' But he didn't sound very sure.

'You told her what we were doing?'

'Yes. She said we could do what the hell we liked. It didn't make any difference and she didn't care now.'

'Did you tell her we were pegging it for Jarra Jarra?'

'Sure. But I don't think it registered.' He hesitated, still with that strange look in his eyes. 'Tell you the truth,' he said, 'she seemed sort of dried-up inside.'

'How do you mean?'

He shrugged. 'Oh, I dunno. Scared maybe—about the cattle, the future. But she seemed dazed, half dead if you like—'sthough nothing mattered any more. But she let me take all I needed from one of the old sheds.'

If I hadn't been so anxious to get the claim registered, I'd have driven up to the homestead myself. As it was, we went right on into the dark, working by the Land-Rover's headlights.

We finished pegging just after ten, had some food and started straight away, headed for Marble Bar.

Driving through the night along that ribbed highway, I had plenty of time to think about what Kennie had told me. The hell of it was Coondewanna still had to be proved, and the Monster, even if we found it, would take years to develop. Mining prospects don't bring rain. They don't put green growth back into a drought-ridden land. And all the wealth in the world cannot bring a dead man to life again.

Dried-up inside Kennie had described her, and now that I was in the outback again I could appreciate how she must feel, the loneliness of her solitary life eating into her like a canker, destroying the natural resilience of youth. God knows, I now knew what loneliness was like, but strangely enough, the loneliness of a prison cell is quite different from the loneliness of a vast empty country. There is a curious protectiveness in four walls. Prison shuts you off from the world outside. Here, in this dusty, arid, desert world, the exposure to elemental forces was total and crushing.

I was tired when we finally got into Marble Bar. We both were, for the ribbed dirt road and the speed at which we'd been driving had made it difficult to sleep. Trucks and Land-Rovers were parked both sides of the sloped tarmac of the main street and there was a queue for breakfast at the Ironclad. There was a crowd, too, gathered outside the Mines Department building, waiting for the office to open. We parked just off the tarmac at the bottom of the slope and cooked our breakfast. I didn't notice Culpin until we had joined the queue of prospectors and he came out after registering his claim. He had Smithie with him and he walked straight past us, a quick sideways glance of his eyes the only sign of recognition.

It was almost eleven by the time we were through. The crowd of vehicles had thinned by then, but a Chev ute was backed close up against our roo guard, Culpin leaning against it, waiting for us. 'Claimed above Golden Soak, did you?' And when I didn't say anything, he added, 'Too bad. I missed it by a day. Remember?' He was smiling, trying to be friendly. 'Smithie here reckons you're lucky. The Swede said the same.' He came away from the side of the ute. 'What about the Gibson? You goin' to be lucky there, too?'

'What do you want?' I asked him.

'We could team up,' he said, his eyes squinted against the sun-glare from the tarmac. 'I know that desert country. You don't.' And he added, as though it made a difference, 'I got the use of a helicopter when I want it.' He waited, watching me, his legs straddled and his hands thrust into his belt. A big survey truck roared past us. 'All right,' he said. 'But I'm warning you. You try and go into the Gibson without me and I'll make dam' sure you never get beyond the Soaks. For your own good,' he added, thrusting his head forward.

Out of the tail of my eye I saw Kennie suddenly very tense, his face white with anger. 'You t-try that, Pa, and I'll . . .' He checked himself, and then with more control: 'The Monster doesn't belong to you. It belongs to——'

'Belongs to nobody till a claim's registered. You know that as well as I do.' He had swung round and was facing his son. 'If Alec wants to risk his life, that's his concern. No reason for you to risk yours. You stay here. Understand?'

'That's for him to decide,' I said.

'No, it bloody isn't. I'm his father and he does what I tell him. Right?' He wasn't looking at me. He was watching Kennie and I think he knew this was the moment when the boy would finally rebel, for he went on quickly. 'Now you listen to me, boy. A man's already lost his life out there. Mebbe it wasn't Alec's fault. But he was alone with him at the time, and as I told his daughter, when a fortune's at stake men don't always act the way they should.'

'You told Janet Garrety that?' I should have beaten the daylights out of the bastard there and then, but I was too appalled to do anything.

And then Kennie stepped forward and was standing there between me and his father, his body literally trembling with fury. 'You ch-cheapen everything,' he stammered. 'You and that man Kadek. You t-talk of a f-fortune. You can't think

270

beyond your pocket. You've never understood there are other things in life. That's what's wrong with this country. It was men like you slaughtered the blacks, destroyed the ecology so that most of the land's now desert. First the sheep, and now minerals.' And he went on, the words pouring out of him, his lean body tense. 'You don't b-bloody understand the word ecology. You can't see that it's people like you that'll destroy Australia. Take, take, take . . . you never think of giving. You never have. Well, let me t-tell you this—the reason I'm going with Alec is because if he finds it he'll do what Ed Garrety would have done. He'll use the money to enrich the land, not himself. It'll go to Janet and she'll carry out her father's wishes. You understand?'

Culpin was staring at him open-mouthed. 'You believe that,' he muttered. And then he thrust his head forward, his small eyes glaring. 'So he's pulled the wool over your eyes the way he did Les Freeman. You can't kid me, boy. The Gibson's tough and nobody goes into it unless there's money in it.'

'You honestly think that?' Kennie was looking at him with disbelief. 'There are Native Affairs officers, missionaries—there was an American professor and his wife who spent a whole year there, living with an aborigine family. You think they did it for money?' There was a moment's silence, and then he said, 'You don't understand what I'm talking about, do you?'

'No, I don't,' his father snapped. And Smithie said, 'Come on, Chris, we're pegging my claim now an' I don't want anybody getting in ahead of me.'

Culpin hesitated. He was watching as Kennie turned away and got into the driving seat of our Land-Rover, his heavy forehead wrinkled in a frown. He looked strangely bewildered. 'No,' he muttered to himself. 'I'm buggered if I understand.' And he turned slowly and went to his own vehicle. They drove off, taking the track that followed the course of the Cougan River towards the Comet Mine. We kept to the tarmac, on the road that led to the Highway, and then we headed south, back to Nullagine and Lynn Peak.

We fed that evening with Andie and his family. He had seen Janet only once in the last three months. She had come in to collect the monthly supplies and cancel the order. 'Christ knows what they're living on now at Jarra Jarra. We've had a little rain. No' verra much—just a quick storm. But I'm told they didna have a drop over to the west of here.'

The Lynn Peak bore was still flowing and after our meal we filled up with water and got the petrol we needed. I was alone with him for a moment at the pump and I settled the Jarra Jarra account. I also gave him enough for another month's supplies and he promised to take them over himself. 'Do I tell her who's paying for them?'

'No,' I said. 'Just tell her a friend sent them.'

He looked doubtful. 'I'm no verra sure she'll accept that. She's proud, like her father, and they're not used to receiving charity.'

I hesitated, thinking of the Gibson and the possibility that I might never come out of it alive. 'All right,' I said. 'Tell her it's from me—payment on account for something her father told me. That should do it.'

'And do I tell her where you've gone?' The curiosity he had been bottling up all the time we had been at the homestead showed in his eyes.

'You think you know?'

He nodded his round dark head. 'Aye, the Gibson I reck'n.'

'Well, keep it to yourself.'

'And what if you get stuck out there?'

'Give me to the end of the month,' I said. 'If we're not back by then . . .' I didn't say any more because Kennie joined us. But Andie understood. By the end of three weeks we'd be out of water.

We got as far as Walgun before bivouacking for the night and we started again at first light. With the vehicle we now had and driving in daylight, we made much better time. We were beyond the Soaks and into the desert by sunset. Shortly before noon the following day we actually sighted Winnecke Rock, away to the north of us, and by nightfall we were camped somewhere close to the spot where Ed Garrety had disappeared. Dusk was closing in and we did not start searching for the *rira* until dawn the next day.

It should have been easy to locate, knowing roughly where it was and the whole area of that rock conglomerate extending a dozen acres and more. But nothing was easy in that rolling sand sea, our view obscured by the troughs, and even from the tops nothing visible but the next sandhill and the intervening valley floor. The directions were from the actual soak so that it was essential to find it. We operated a box search, working our way steadily eastward on a six-mile front, and again it wasn't the *rira* we sighted first, but Ed Garrety's abandoned Land-Rover.

We saw it away at the end of a shallow trough. We were on the southward leg then and it was half-hidden by a new drift of sand, only the canopy showing. The broken rock of the *rira* started just beyond it, over a slight rise, the astonishing green of the kurrajong tree visible as soon as we walked to the top of the dune.

I showed Kennie the rock shelter where we had huddled against the fury of the sandstorm, the soak in its rock basin marked with the dark of moisture welling to the surface. It was damper now that winter had cooled the ground, and by scraping out handfuls of sand, we were able to produce something very near to a puddle of water. At least we wouldn't die of thirst and we celebrated with a can of beer each. But we didn't drink it there. The soak and the rock shelter was too unhappy a place for me, the memory of Ed Garrety very strong. I wished to God he was with us now. But it had been his choice, and surely a man has a right to die in his own time.

We had parked our Land-Rover alongside his and we drank our beer standing by the tailboard, small birds darting among the spinifex, flashes of blue, and some delicate little grey birds that looked like finches. It was hot in the sun, but not as hot as I remembered it, the sky clear blue and no vestige of cloud on the horizon. 'Where do we go from here?' Kennie asked. And I knew by the way he said it that this was a question he'd been wanting to ask for a long time.

'It's not going to be easy,' I said, remembering how long it had taken to find the *rira*. 'They're not compass directions. They depend on the sun, some trees, and the distance a man can walk in a day.' I had been over it in my mind so many times, but that didn't make it any less vague, and as I began to repeat it to him it sounded even vaguer, more like the wishful thinking of an aborigine seeking payment for a lie. 'From Kurrajong Soak walk short day into sunrise, find'im three ngalta. Then, facing high sun, walk till him half set. Small gibber hill, all rock him same ngalta.' I looked at him, wondering what he'd make of it. 'That's all, except that McIlroy added a note to say that ngalta was how the black had described the green of the copper deposit.'

'A bit vague, innit?' Kennie's features were creased in a frown. 'Short day into sunrise; that's presumably east—north of east if you take short day to mean it's winter. How long do you reck'n a short day's march—twenty miles?'

'I doubt whether you or I would cover as much as that.' I was remembering the two night treks I had done, the sand and the spinifex and how exhausted I had been. 'But an aborigine might.'

He nodded. 'Call it fifteen then, and take a bearing on tomorrow's sunrise. Shouldn't be far out. But I doubt whether we'll find the ngalta. That's the abo word for the kurrajong tree. Right? It has water bearing roots and the blacks can practically live off the seeds when they're ripe. Those trees will surely have disappeared after all these years.'

'What about the kurrajong here?'

'Could be a new one, a seedling.'

In the end we agreed we would drive fifteen miles on our sunrise bearing, then due north for eight. After that we'd start a box search working steadily eastward and hoping for the best.

By then we had finished our beer, and after a quick meal, we began repairing the fuel line of Ed Garrety's Land-Rover, watched by a goanna and interrupted periodically by flights of small birds coming in to the soak. It took us the rest of the afternoon to get the engine going and clear the sand drift that had built up around the chassis. And that evening after sunset we buried the remains of Ed Garrety's body. Kennie had found it while stalking the goanna with my rifle. It was away to the south, just beyond the edge of the *rira*, the covering of drifted storm sand blown away to expose the whitened bone of the skull and one skeletal hand. It was something I could have done without, and after a restless night, cold and plagued by

274

ants and the presence of several small snakes, we took a compass bearing on the sun as it heaved itself up over the horizon like an erupting orb of red-hot metal.

We had our first puncture that morning, but all Kennie said was, 'Lucky it's a drought an' the spinifex not in seed, otherwise you'd have a clogged rad, the engine running hot—you wouldn't be able to see either, it'd be that high. Wouldn't worry 'bout a little thing like a puncture then.' He was strangely patient, almost subdued as we sweated at the cover, a spinifex wren darting flashes of blue. It took us three hours to cover the fifteen miles. We were into an area of steep sandhills then, the vegetation sparse and all burned up, not a sign of a tree anywhere, only wattles. At noon we headed into the sun, holding on a course due north until we had covered eight miles. The same dead scene, poor scrub and no trees, and the sandhills rolling endlessly, shimmering like liquid in the afternoon heat. After a meal we began our search and by nightfall had completed two boxes, which meant that we had made three north-south runs and moved the search area eastward four miles.

That night I remember we were both of us very tense as we sat huddled in sweaters over a miserable fire. It was surprisingly cold after the day's heat. Kennie was smoking, a thing he seldom did, and he hardly spoke. He seemed shut up inside himself. Quite what the Monster meant to him at that moment I'm not sure. But I know it meant something much more than a geological phenomenon.

We didn't talk much, both of us wrapped in our own thoughts, but we did discuss the next day's search. I think we talked about it twice, and each time his eyes shone with a strange inner light. It wasn't just excitement. It was something more, something deeper. I don't know what put it into my head, but suddenly I found myself remembering lines from a poem I had had to learn as a boy: *Naught in the distance but the evening, naught to point my footsteps further. . . . Burningly it came on me all at once, this was the place!* And then at the end of the poem: *Dauntless the slug-horn to my lips I set, and blew. 'Childe Roland to the Dark Tower came.'*

I leaned forward, pushing a charred and blackened spike of

mulga root into the fire's glow, now almost dead with white ash tendrils, smiling to think that I should remember Browning when Ed Garrety, if he had been here, would have quoted Shakespeare. God help me, I didn't realize how near I had come to understanding. Kennie was no Childe Roland, but he had developed strong moral convictions as a reaction to an unscrupulous father, and like so many young men in the process of growing up, uncertain of his physical courage, he had the need to prove himself.

These are afterthoughts, of course—an endeavour to explain the inevitability of what happened. But I still cannot excuse myself for not being prepared for it. I should have talked to him, there over the dying ashes of that fire. I knew that this second journey out into the desert was a self-imposed ordeal, that he was tensed up and scared. But I thought it was something physical, a weakness to be overcome, a challenge. I never appreciated his real fear. I never understood, till it was too late, that this search for a copper deposit in the Gibson Desert had become for him a sort of purification of the greed he had grown up with.

He was awake at first light, his eyes dark-rimmed with lack of sleep. 'We'll find it today, won't we?' His voice was high and trembling. 'We must find it today.'

'Perhaps,' I said. 'If it's there.' Instinctively I felt the need to damp down his intense eagerness.

We had completed the first box by nine o'clock. The going had been bad, but it was worse on the second leg north, the sandhills steep-faced, requiring a running start flat out in four-wheel drive. I was driving at the time, the sun in my eyes; Kennie was acting as observer. I saw him suddenly lean forward as the wheels churned at the top of a sandhill. I thought he had seen what we were looking for and I slammed on the brakes, the bonnet of the Land-Rover dipping to the sand trough below. 'What is it?' I was looking at him as we sat there motionless, the radiator steaming. He was still leaning forward, staring straight ahead, his eyes wide and his face drained of all colour, almost white.

He didn't answer and I cut the engine to let it cool, shading my eyes and staring into the sun. But the view hadn't changed, the desert a series of giant sand swells rolling away to the horizon, an ocean of red sand patched with vegetation. And then, very faint above the boiling of the rad, I heard the sound of an engine. 'A plane?'

He nodded, pointing, his hands clenched and his body strained forward. The drone of it was moving across our front from left to right and a moment later I caught a glimpse of silver beyond a distant sandhill. It was flying low, literally skimming the surface. We caught another glimpse of it, a flash of sun on metal, to the right of us now and flying south. The sound of it faded. 'Your father?' I asked. It had looked like the same plane.

He held up his hand, sitting listening, his body rigid. The radiator had stopped boiling and in the silence we heard it again, flying north this time. We didn't see it, but both of us knew what the pilot was doing. He was flying a low level search, doing exactly what we were doing, but doing it faster and with much less effort.

The sound came and went for perhaps ten minutes, and then we lost it. We didn't hear it again until at 09.42 it passed to the north of us, a speck high in the sky flying back towards the west. We were both of us out of the Land-Rover then, standing in the hot sun at the very top of the sandhill, and when the sound had gone and we had lost sight of it, Kennie turned to me. 'D-dogging us like that—why didn't we do it by plane?' He was suddenly very tense.

'You think he's found it?'

He shrugged, his eyes still staring at the empty sky to the west.

'If I'd hired a plane and we'd failed to find it, then you'd be telling me we should have done a ground search.'

He looked at me then. 'You can't win, can you?' He said it with a smile, but the tension was still there and his face looked pale.

We didn't say anything after that, but pressed on fast, taking a chance and moving the area of our search forward a few miles. We were then into a patch of old mulga scrub, all dead and their roots half buried in the sand, and we had two punctures in quick succession. Altogether it was a bad day with only two boxes completed from our new starting point. Clouds came up in the late afternoon and the night was very dark. Our position was now 26 miles east of the *rira*, and I remember thinking that the abo who had given McIlroy the directions must have been a hell of a tireless walker. Either that or the Monster didn't exist.

We filled up as usual and checked our petrol before turning in.

The situation was becoming critical. Each box was 13 miles of ground covered and at our present rate of consumption we had just about enough fuel for five or more box runs, unless we decided to rely on finding the *rira* again. We had already taken two cans from the abandoned Land-Rover, but there was still a sufficient reserve there to see us back to the Stock Route. We argued it out for some time, lying wrapped in our swags, but when we started out the next morning we had still reached no definite decision.

We need not have bothered. Our search ended that morning just as we had completed the first run north. I was driving, keeping an eye on the clock and the compass as we began the eastward mile. We were then cutting diagonally across the sandhills and for just over a third of a mile we were on the flat floor of a trough, travelling quite fast for once. Then we came to the slope beyond. I didn't change into four-wheel drive, just kept my foot hard down. It was a mistake. I hit a soft spot near the crest and we slowed, the rear wheels digging in, the chassis slewing and tilting.

It took us half an hour to dig ourselves out and get the Land-Rover to the top. We stopped there for a breather, both of us hot and tired, our tempers frayed. And it was while we were standing there, grateful for the breeze and the clouds that had obscured the sun, that it gradually dawned on us that we were looking across, not at another sandhill, but at an area of gibber eroded from the younger Permian overlay to form a shallow rounded hill, and that the green that showed in patches through the light brown of the gravel was not the green of vegetation.

I don't know which of us realized this first. I think it hit us in a flash almost simultaneously, for both of us suddenly dived for the Land-Rover and the next minute we were roaring down the slope. We hit the bottom hard on rock, our heads bumping the roof. We were lucky not to break a spring, and when we got out, staring upwards now at the rounded, gentle slope of that hill, it looked like the dead carcase of a giant whale, its petrified flesh blotched with gangrenous streaks of malachite.

'Jesus Christ!' Kennie breathed. 'It really does look like a monster.' And he started work there and then collecting and examining samples, moving with feverish haste, literally dancing on his toes with excitement. It was copper. No question of that. The whole red-brown hill was patched with a lighter brown, the surface smooth and rounded and littered with stones and small rocks, and the copper, exposed by the weathering of the calcareous sediments and sandstones that had overlaid it, showed in streaks and blotches that were a greenish bown in colour and merged with the sparse covering of spinifex

Kennie was immediately convinced that it was a discovery of major importance. I was more cautious, fearing he was letting his excitement run away with him. But, growing up with the geology of Australia constantly in mind, he had developed a sort of sixth sense that I respected, and after we had climbed to the top, so that we had a clear view of the whole hill, he argued very convincingly that this was an old leach area, the Permian sediments worn down by the winds and the extremes of temperature over millions of years to expose the trapped ore in the Archaean rock beneath.

The first thing was to surface map the entire area, and it was while we were discussing this, back at the Land-Rover, planning how we would do it, that the silence of that strange place was invaded by a low droning sound. It was high up to the south-west, but growing all the time, and then we saw it like an insect descending towards us. It was lost for a while behind the whaleback hill, the sound of it beating against the sand-hills behind us, and then suddenly it was there to our right hovering over the tail end of the Monster.

We watched as it settled and the blades stopped turning. A man climbed out, glanced quickly in our direction, and then he began unloading an aluminium peg about 6 feet long. The battered hat, the bulky body—no question who it was. And Kennie staring, his body rigid, his face gone white as death. I could literally feel the anger in him as he watched his father start to set up the first corner post. The pilot got out, and another man, and they began attacking the rock with hammer and chisel.

That was when Kennie moved. He gave a sort of grunt, not quite a cry, but a furious expellation of breath that expressed the pent-up fury within him. Then he moved, very fast, and the next thing I knew he was in the Land-Rover, the engine roaring as he slammed it into gear and went bucketing across the rock slope towards the helicopter.

I followed on foot. But I didn't hurry. I didn't think there was any need. I knew he had to get this off his chest, have it out with his father, and there were two other men there if it came to blows. I saw the Land-Rover stop, saw him jump out and go towards his father, who was standing there, leaning on the post, waiting for him. They were arguing there for about a minute. I could hear Kennie's voice, high and strident, but not his father's. Culpin seemed to be reasoning with him quietly.

Then suddenly the whole scene erupted in violence. Culpin dropped the post, caught hold of his son by the collar of his shirt and shook him. The others said later that he was merely trying to shake some sense into him, that there was no reason for him to call his father names like that. But there must have been more to it than that for I heard Kennie scream something at him, and then Culpin hit him.

That was when I started to run. But too late.

Kennie had come up off the ground with an inarticulate cry that seemed to express some inner horror. He was round the back of the Land-Rover in a flash and came out holding my rifle. He took about a dozen steps towards his father, then stopped and raised the gun. Culpin didn't say anything, didn't move; he just stood there, his mouth open and an expression of shock on his face. Kennie's movements were quite deliberate. He took careful aim and fired.

I had stopped by then, of course. But at the sound of that shot I started running again.

Culpin's body took a long time falling, a slow crumpling at the knees. The boy had, in fact, shot him through the heart. But I didn't know that. I yelled to the other two. I wanted them to grab him before he could fire again. The sand drifts tugged at my feet, the rock stony and uneven, and as I raced the last few yards, Kennie standing there dazed, his father dead at his feet and the gun lying where he had dropped it, I saw his legs begin to go. He was in a state of shock, trembling violently and unable to speak, and then he fell forward, his arms flung out, reaching for the rock as though to embrace the entire monstrous body of the ore.

The ten days it took me to get out of the Gibson were the loneliest I have ever spent in my life. The real reaction to what had happened didn't come until after the helicopter had taken off with Kennie and the body of his father. For the rest of that day I just sat there by the Land-Rover, or mooched around, unable to think, or even to feel anything. And all the time the greenish brown of that copper showing through the gibber stones and the redder brown of the whale's back.

And that night, lying sleepless and cold, with nothing there with which to make a fire, I thought back to McIlroy. My God, he'd named it well! McIlroy, Ed Garrety and now Kennie facing a charge of murder—the murder of his own father. And the guilt was mine, or so I felt, alone there in the Gibson with the desert all round me and that hill of copper rising beside me. Edith Culpin's warning words, Kennie and his talk of *mamus*. So like his mother, and I lay there remembering his voice, the way he tossed his head when the long hair fell over his face, that irritating little laugh. I wished to God I could have had that day again, change what had happened.

In the morning I drove the Land-Rover to where there was some wattle and snappy gums, built myself a fire and had coffee and a large breakfast. And after that, I went back and pegged the bloody Monster, using a pick to set the stakes and cut the trenches. It was hard, slow work in the sun, and it took me two days all on my own. And when I had finished setting up the intermediary pegs, I got my camera and photographed the datum post as proof that I had done it.

Then I started back.

I didn't go near the *rira*. I couldn't face that place again on my own. I just headed back west, on a compass course for the Soaks, hoping to God I'd make it on the fuel I had left. And then the rain started. That was the one thing I hadn't expected. Rain.

There was a day of broken cloud, the second I think after I had started back, and then about noon the next day it began. Showers at first, some of them quite heavy, but intermittent, so that I was able to keep going. It was like that all night. And then in the morning the clouds thickened, very low clouds and heavy rain, torrential at times, with lightning and thunder around midday.

The desert was suddenly changed, the sandhill troughs awash with water, the air damp and humid, difficult to breathe, and a cold wind blowing. I lay up all that day, and the next, the Land-Rover parked just below the crest of a sandhill. And then the clouds dispersed, the sky was blue again and the sun blazed down, and the desert took on a sheen of fresh green before my eyes. It was a sudden, extraordinary miracle of re-birth.

I was there altogether four days until the sand had sucked up all the flood water. And after that I was able to drive quite fast in places, the going surprisingly firm, almost like a black-top road in the flats between the ridges.

My fuel carried me all the way to Lynn Peak, but when I got there I was suddenly too tired to go any further. They made up a bed for me and I stayed there two days, sleeping most of the time, too exhausted even to bother about shaving. They knew what had happened, but they had the sense not to talk about it. Kindness is a great healer and they couldn't have been kinder, Maria fussing over me and Andie sitting beside my bed for long stretches during the day, not saying much, just sitting there so that I wouldn't be on my own. And the kids came and went, little Anna Maria, aged five, and Bruce, who was two years younger. They did more than anything to restore my sanity.

The third morning I got up. That was when Andie let me see the papers. Culpin's body had been flown to Kalgoorlie and the inquest had been held there. Smithie and the helicopter pilot had given evidence. But it was Edith Culpin who had told the court what lay behind the tragedy. 'Kennie took after me. He was farming stock. He was always working for the future. He believed in it. My husband lived for the present. The two of them just didn't suit.' And there was a picture of her, dressed in black, neat as always, but stony-faced. It was a sad picture that seemed to say everything.

Sometime soon there would be a trial and I would have to give evidence. I thought a lot about that, and about Edith Culpin—it was what I could say to her that worried me most. And there was Janet, too. Andie told me that when he had driven over to Jarra Jarra with the supplies she had burst into tears. She wants to see you, he said. But that, too, would have to wait.

I left that morning, driving north up the Highway, and with the creek bottoms bad after the floods, it was late afternoon before I reached Marble Bar. I drove straight to the Mines Department office and there I registered the claim to McIlroy's Monster, the first I think that had ever been registered deep in the Gibson Desert. I could have stayed the night at the Ironclad. Instead, I drove up the valley of the Cougan River towards the Comet Mine and camped above Chinaman's Pool, by the Jasper Bar that had given the gold-rush town its name. The river was running fast over the cream and ochre striped marble of the bar and the pool below it was peaceful in the still of the evening, the sand at the edge marked by the feet of countless birds.

I didn't sleep that night. It was just after the shortest day, the moon past the full, and I sat there beside the pool, the sound of the running water, the soothing stillness of the night giving me a sense of peace. I was still there when the moon set and dawn broke, a few kangaroos coming down to drink, a heron and other birds moving very close. And after breakfast I started out for Jarra Jarra, feeling more myself but still surprised to be driving the Land-Rover on my own down that familiar road.

I reached the homestead just before sunset. The paddock was all green with new grass, a mass of cattle grazing, and the ghost gums on the Windbreaks had a fresh sheen that glimmered in the slanting sun. The camel Cleo was crouched under the poinciana trees, just as she had been when I had first come to Jarra Jarra, and the bitch Yla came out barking, then seemed to recognize me, her tail revolving in sudden pleasure as I got stiffly down from behind the wheel. I walked slowly between the outbuildings and was halfway across the quartz-paved patio when Janet emerged from one of the french windows that opened on to the verandah. I stopped then, not knowing what to say or how to greet her, the Alsatian nuzzling at my hand.

She stood there for a moment, absolutely still, her face frozen as though she were seeing a ghost. I remember she was wearing blue jeans tucked into mud-bespattered boots, a dark blue shirt, and her hair looked wild, a bright halo catching the light.

And then she moved, her boots sounding hollow on the bare boards, and suddenly she was running towards me, her face, her eyes, her whole being alight with excitement. 'Alec. The paddock. Have you seen it?' She reached me, grasping me, her head buried against my chest. 'It's all green.' She was laughing and crying all at the same time and holding me very tight. 'It's like a new world. Everything fresh. Oh my God, it's wonderful to see you.'

I felt peace then, real peace—as though I had come home at last. And that spark between us. I felt it again. But it wasn't the same spark. It was there. But it was different now.

It was only later, over the evening meal, just the two of us there and the candles lit, that I began to talk. And when I had told her everything, I gave her the registered claim to Coondewanna.

'That's for you to keep. I don't know whether it's worth anything or not. But if it is . . .'

'You already gave me the one thing I needed,' she said. 'Only I was——' She hesitated. 'I'm sorry. I should have written, come to see you. But I was too shocked by what had happened to Daddy, and there was so much to do here—I couldn't seem to think straight.'

'What did I give you?' I asked.

'Why, Golden Soak. The water from the lower levels. Just as you were driving off—remember? You told me to try Golden Soak for the water we needed. It saved over two thousand head. And now the rain.' She was smiling, her freckled face looking almost beautiful, and her eyes, those blue eyes reminding me suddenly of her father, bright with hope.

That was when I explained to her what we would have to do about the Gibson claim, how Kennie's hopes paralleled the dream her father had once had. But I didn't tell her the other parallel, that Ed Garrety had also killed a man out there in the Gibson. She knows now, of course. But it was too soon to tell her then.

I fear we are still upsetting some of the more conventional folk around here, living together, waiting for my divorce to come through. And there is a child on the way, which makes it look worse, of course. During this period I have worked harder than I have ever worked before—new fences, a deep bore and reservoir down by Golden Soak, and the drilling on Coondewanna. We have proved the reef there, but in the meantime the price of antimony has slumped. So has the price of copper. The bottom has dropped out of the stock market and until there is some sign of recovery nothing can be done about the Monster.

But it has done something for us already. Les Freeman took a lease on the claim, and before the winter of 1970 was out Lone Minerals had completed a geophysical and two exploratory drill holes, confirming it as a major copper strike. As the price of the lease we got $20,000 in cash, which is what we have been living on for the last eighteen months. Most of it has gone now, in improvements and the purchase of stock. I doubt whether I shall ever be able to get the station back to what it was in the days of Janet's grandfather. But at least we have made a start, and the future is bright. The price of antimony is still at rock bottom, but the American dollar crisis has raised the value of gold and I reckon Golden Soak is profitable at anything above $50 an ounce. And if copper recovers, too, then part of the deal with Lone Minerals is that we get a royalty of 5 per cent on the value of all ore extracted from the Monster. That's a long way into the future, but whatever happens about the Monster, Jarra Jarra is now secure, the grass coming back and water in the dry. My son will inherit at least some of his grandfather's dream . . . or if it is a girl, then pray God she grows up with the same qualities as her mother, the same love of this harsh demanding place where I have now put down my roots.

Jarra Jarra,
Nullagine,
Pilbara, W.A.
February, 1972.

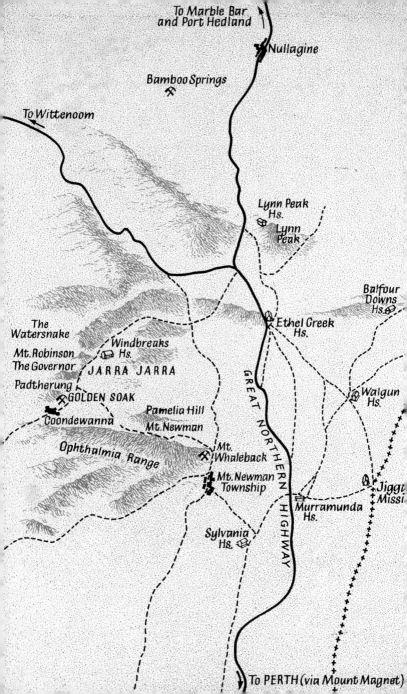